SELECTED SHORT STORIES

THE BOW STREET LIBRARY
EDITED BY HUGH GREENE

W. W. JACOBS

Selected
Short Stories

Edited and
introduced by Hugh Greene

THE BODLEY HEAD
LONDON SYDNEY
TORONTO

ACKNOWLEDGMENT

I should like to express my gratitude to the children of W. W. Jacobs who told me so much about their father.

For the picture which emerges in my Introduction I must take full responsibility.

BIBLIOGRAPHICAL NOTE

'The Rival Beauties' is taken from *Many Cargoes*, first published in 1896; 'A Will and a Way', from *Light Freights* 1901; 'The Monkey's Paw', 'Bill's Paper Chase' and 'A Tiger's Skin' from *The Lady of the Barge* 1902; 'The Money Box', 'Bill's Lapse', 'The Persecution of Bob Pretty', 'Dixon's Return' and 'The Third String' from *Odd Craft* 1904; 'Captains All' from *Captains All* 1905; 'In the Family' and 'The Dreamer' from *Short Cruises* 1907; 'Self Help' and 'Keeping Up Appearances' from *Sailors' Knots* 1909; 'Watch-Dogs' and 'The Bequest' from *Ship's Company* 1911; 'The Unknown' from *Night Watches* 1914; 'Shareholders' from *Deep Waters* 1919; and 'The Interruption' from *Sea Whispers* 1926.

This selection and
Introduction © The Bodley Head 1975
ISBN 0 370 10938 4
Set in Monotype Imprint
by Gloucester Typesetting Co Ltd, Gloucester
Printed and bound in Great Britain for
The Bodley Head Ltd
9 Bow Street, London WC2E 7AL
by Redwood Burn Limited
Trowbridge & Esher
This selection first published 1975

INTRODUCTION

In a writing life of thirty years between 1896 and 1926 W. W. Jacobs produced twelve volumes of short stories, containing in all more than one hundred and fifty stories, one volume with two long short stories and five full-length novels. Then for the remaining seventeen years of his life, although he had been one of the most successful, and loved, writers of his time he fell completely silent: he never took up his pen again. For several years now not one of his books, no selection of his stories, has been in print.

And yet his achievement had been very great. To my mind there is no doubt that, with P. G. Wodehouse and George Birmingham, he was the best humorous writer of our time. He is less immediately funny than Wodehouse, but, perhaps, more subtle and less good-humoured. There was some bitterness mixed with the gaiety, and he was also a minor master of the macabre. Jacobs and Wodehouse met once and got on very well. Jacobs said jokingly to Wodehouse that he regarded him as his 'hated rival'. Wodehouse said many years later that he was a 'young disciple' not a rival.

What is lasting in Jacobs' stories and novels is his creation of a world of cheap sailors' lodging houses in the Port of London, the wharves of Wapping, little coastal steamers, small towns in the Thames estuary full of cosy pubs and retired sea captains and, in a different key, the village of Claybury (based on a Suffolk village he used to visit) where the oldest inhabitant sits in the 'Cauliflower' telling tall stories about Bob Pretty, surely one of the great comic characters of English literature, and other ruffians.

For all his writing life Jacobs drew on the experiences of his youth and when his memories dried up he dried up as a writer, not with resignation but with pain. He had been born in 1863 in Wapping, where his father was manager of the South Devon Wharf and a bit of a Micawber. He had a stepmother whom he hated. In a short autobiographical sketch Jacobs remarks that it was because of the connection with Wapping that 'some tang of the sea and the foreshore of the Thames' insinuated itself into his work. 'That', he adds drily, 'did not happen until some years after I had left the house on the wharf at Wapping. I suppose distance lent enchantment to a view that certainly needed it.'

Jacobs worked for some years as a civil servant in the Savings Bank, a job which he hated. After his stories, which first appeared in magazines like *The Idler* and later *The Strand*, were a success he decided, with relief, that he could live on his writing.

In those early years he used to go for expeditions on coastal steamers and for walks on the Kent coast with his close friend Will Owen, who illustrated most of his books. In this way he stored up the impressions and anecdotes which kept him going as a writer for thirty years. The Night Watchman, the narrator of most of his best stories about the sea and the Port of London, was based on a longshoreman at Deal called Bob Osborne, himself a great storyteller, and the immortal Sam Small, Ginger Dick and Peter Russet were based on three of Bob Osborne's friends. From the same figures Will Owen took the inspiration for his drawings in which he has left as clear an image of the Night Watchman and his friends as Sidney Paget did of Sherlock Holmes and Watson.

Few writers in the whole of English literature have taken such a consistently low view of women. His older women are nagging shrews not above a bit of physical violence when their husbands misbehave themselves. His younger women are artful liars who once they have, like carnivorous plants, got their prey in their clutches proceed to grow like their

6

mothers. One of his last stories, the last in this collection, deals with wife murder.

In this we can probably trace his lasting hatred of his step-mother. His marriage, too, was far from easy, though one does not have the impression that the love he felt for his wife ever turned to hatred in spite of a good deal of provocation.

The Night Watchman, who knew what he was talking about, once remarked, 'If a man marries he wishes he 'adn't, and if he doesn't marry he wishes he 'ad.' Romance plays little part in the matrimonial game. 'She's got a home and money. It don't matter about 'er looks,' says one of his men on the make.

Jacobs was an intensely shy and retiring man, very small of stature. He was always afraid of life. His wife was a passionate suffragette, who was imprisoned for breaking windows with a hammer which she carried hidden in her muff. She was a Socialist, while he was intensely Conservative. Their life was a series of furious quarrels about their children, about holi-days, about education, about politics, about everything.

Shortly before the First World War the Jacobs family (they had two sons and three daughters) moved from their house near Epping Forest to Berkhamsted, where there were good day-schools for boys and girls. Jacobs was afraid of the effect of boarding schools on their morals.

In Berkhamsted the drying-up process proceeded apace. Jacobs did not like the country. 'Too many cows.' One of his few recreations was a walk to the Swan, an ancient inn in the High Street, for half a pint of beer—he was a very abstemious man. He would also spend half an hour at noon every weekday at Smith's bookshop and attended the six o'clock performance at the Court Theatre, the blue-domed cinema in the High Street, every Monday and Thursday without fail, always alone.

Only his last three, rather inferior, books came out in the fourteen or fifteen years he lived in Berkhamsted, and some of the writing for those had been done earlier. I can remember seeing him quite frequently in the High Street, a small

7

grey-faced sad man with something of Buster Keaton about him. Others remember him wandering along the towpath of the Grand Junction canal with a straw in his mouth. They thought he was sucking new stories out of the straw. Alas, he was not.

The strange thing is that if he had not been so shy and withdrawn Jacobs might have found Berkhamsted full of stimulating company. The town, and Berkhamsted School, were packed with writers or future writers. They included the formidable Mrs Humphry Ward (whom at the age of about four I once peremptorily ordered out of a drawing-room chair usually occupied by my mother), the great historian George Macaulay Trevelyan, his wife Janet Penrose, who wrote the life of her mother Mrs Humphry Ward and books about Italy, his daughter, Mary Caroline, who as Mary Moorman was to become the great authority on Wordsworth, Marjorie and C. H. B. Quennell, the authors of the Everyday Life series of history books, and lesser historians in Esmé Wingfield Stratford and F. S. Marvin. At the school were Graham Greene, Claud Cockburn, Peter Quennell, Humphry Trevelyan, author of *Goethe and the Greeks*, Cecil Parrott, the translator of *The Good Soldier Svejk*, and J. Keith Winter, a fairly successful novelist and playwright of the thirties.

I should not be surprised if, in the recesses of some American university, somebody is already at work on a thesis about 'The Influence of Berkhamsted on English Literature and Historiography in the Twentieth Century'.

In London Jacobs had been on quite friendly terms with H. G. Wells (in spite of disliking his morals even more than his politics) and with Jerome K. Jerome, author of *Three Men in a Boat*. But he avoided the Berkhamsted writers, though he had an improbable friendship with a very violent character called J. L. Hardy, who had been an escaper in the First World War in which he served in the Connaught Rangers and wrote one of the classics of escape and who was later, I believe, a Black and Tan. Hardy, perhaps rightly, was always prepared for an attempt on his life and would whip out a revolver if the front door bell rang or a branch tapped on the window.

It is sad to think of this meticulous writer, who had given so much pleasure to so many people, with nothing whatever to do for the last seventeen years of his life (he died in 1943) and very little for fifteen years before that. He had been accustomed to write, very slowly, about one hundred words a day. With much re-writing and polishing one short story would take him about a month.

Evelyn Waugh as a schoolboy used to visit the Jacobs family in Berkhamsted because of his friendship with Jacobs' daughter Barbara, who was engaged to his brother Alec. In his autobiography *A Little Learning* Evelyn Waugh describes W. W. Jacobs as 'a writer who in his middle years developed an exquisite precision of narrative'. Behind the drab façade, he adds, invisible to his boyish eye, 'there lurked a pure artist'.

One hopes that this selection of W. W. Jacobs' stories will help to revive the memory of a writer who does not deserve to be forgotten.

Hugh Greene

CONTENTS

The Rival Beauties

If you hadn't asked me, said the night watchman, I should never have told you; but, seeing as you've put the question point blank, I will tell you my experience of it. You're the first person I've ever opened my lips to upon the subject, for it was so eggstraordinary that all our chaps swore as they'd keep it to theirselves for fear of being disbelieved and jeered at.

It happened in '84, on board the steamer *George Washington*, bound from Liverpool to New York. The first eight days passed without anything unusual happening, but on the ninth I was standing aft with the first mate, hauling in the log, when we hears a yell from aloft, an' a chap what we called Stuttering Sam come down as if he was possessed, and rushed up to the mate with his eyes nearly starting out of his 'ed.

'There's the s-s-s-s-s-s-sis-sis-sip!' ses he.

'The what?' ses the mate.

'The s-s-sea-sea-sssssip!'

'Look here, my lad,' ses the mate, taking out a pocket-hankerchief an' wiping his face, 'you just tarn your 'ed away till you get your breath. It's like opening a bottle o' soda water to stand talking to you. Now, what is it?'

'It's the sssssss-sea-sea-sea-sarpint!' ses Sam, with a bust.

'Rather a long un by your account of it,' ses the mate, with a grin.

'What's the matter?' ses the skipper, who just came up.

'This man has seen the sea-sarpint, sir, that's all,' ses the mate.

'Y-y-yes,' said Sam, with a sort o' sob.

'Well, there ain't much doing just now,' ses the skipper, 'so you'd better get a slice o' bread and feed it.'

13

The mate bust out larfing, an' I could see by the way the skipper smiled he was rather tickled at it himself.

The skipper an' the mate was still larfing very hearty when we heard a dreadful 'owl from the bridge, an' one o' the chaps suddenly leaves the wheel, jumps on to the deck, and bolts below as though he was mad. T'other one follows 'im a'most d'reckly, and the second mate caught hold o' the wheel as he left it, and called out something we couldn't catch to the skipper.

'What the d——'s the matter?' yells the skipper.

The mate pointed to starboard, but as 'is 'and was shaking so that one minute it was pointing to the sky an' the next to the bottom o' the sea, it wasn't much of a guide to us. Even when he got it steady we couldn't see anything, till all of a sudden, about two miles off, something like a telegraph pole stuck up out of the water for a few seconds, and then ducked down again and made straight for the ship.

Sam was the fust to speak, and, without wasting time stuttering or stammering, he said he'd go down and see about that bit o' bread, an' he went afore the skipper or the mate could stop 'im.

In less than 'arf a minute there was only the three officers an' me on deck. The second mate was holding the wheel, the skipper was holding his breath, and the first mate was holding me. It was one o' the most exciting times I ever had.

'Better fire the gun at it,' ses the skipper, in a trembling voice, looking at the little brass cannon we had for signalling.

'Better not give him any cause for offence,' ses the mate, shaking his head.

'I wonder whether it eats men,' ses the skipper. 'Perhaps it'll come for some of us.'

'There ain't many on deck for it to choose from,' ses the mate, looking at 'im significant like.

'That's true,' ses the skipper, very thoughtful; 'I'll go an' send all hands on deck. As captain, it's my duty not to leave the ship till the *last*, if I can anyways help it.'

How he got them on deck has always been a wonder to me,

14

but he did it. He was a brutal sort o' a man at the best o' times, an' he carried on so much that I s'pose they thought even the sarpint couldn't be worse. Anyway, up they came, an' we all stood in a crowd watching the sarpint as it came closer and closer.

We reckoned it to be about a hundred yards long, an' it was about the most awful-looking creetur you could ever imagine. If you took all the ugliest things in the earth and mixed 'em up—gorillas an' the like—you'd only make a hangel compared to what that was. It just hung off our quarter, keeping up with us, and every now and then it would open its mouth and let us see about four yards down its throat.

'It seems peaceable,' whispers the fust mate, arter awhile.

'P'raps it ain't hungry,' ses the skipper. 'We'd better not let it get peckish. Try it with a loaf o' bread.'

The cook went below and fetched up half-a-dozen, an' one o' the chaps, plucking up courage, slung it over the side, an' afore you could say 'Jack Robinson' the sarpint had woffled it up an' was looking for more. It stuck its head up and came close to the side just like the swans in Victoria Park, an' it kept that game up until it had 'ad ten loaves an' a hunk o' pork.

'I'm afraid we're encouraging it,' ses the skipper, looking at it as it swam alongside with an eye as big as a saucer cocked on the ship.

'P'raps it'll go away soon if we don't take no more notice of it,' ses the mate. 'Just pretend it isn't here.'

Well, we did pretend as well as we could; but everybody hugged the port side o' the ship, and was ready to bolt down below at the shortest notice; and at last, when the beast got craning its neck up over the side as though it was looking for something, we gave it some more grub. We thought if we didn't give it he might take it, and take it off the wrong shelf, so to speak. But, as the mate said, it was encouraging it, and long arter it was dark we could hear it snorting and splashing behind us, until at last it 'ad such an effect on us the mate sent one o' the chaps down to rouse the skipper.

'I don't think it'll do no 'arm,' ses the skipper, peering over

15

the side, and speaking as though he knew all about sea-sarpints and their ways.

'S'pose it puts its 'ead over the side and takes one o' the men,' ses the mate.

'Let me know at once,' ses the skipper firmly; an' he went below agin and left us.

Well, I was jolly glad when eight bells struck, an' I went below; an' if ever I hoped anything I hoped that when I go up that ugly brute would have gone, but, instead o' that, when I went on deck it was playing alongside like a kitten a'most, an' one o' the chaps told me as the skipper had been feeding it agin.

'It's a wonderful animal,' ses the skipper, 'an' there's none of you now but has seen the sea-sarpint; but I forbid any man here to say a word about it when we get ashore.'

'Why not, sir?' ses the second mate.

'Becos you wouldn't be believed,' said the skipper sternly. 'You might all go ashore and kiss the Book an' make affidavits an' not a soul 'ud believe you. The comic papers 'ud make fun of it, and the respectable papers 'ud say it was seaweed or gulls.'

'Why not take it to New York with us?' ses the fust mate suddenly.

'What?' ses the skipper.

'Feed it every day,' ses the mate, getting excited, 'and bait a couple of shark hooks and keep 'em ready, together with some wire rope. Git 'im to foller us as far as he will, and then hook him. We might git him in alive and show him at a sovereign a head. Anyway, we can take in his carcase if we manage it properly.'

'By Jove! if we only could,' ses the skipper, getting excited too.

'We can try,' ses the mate. 'Why, we could have noosed it this mornin' if we had liked; and if it breaks the lines we must blow its head to pieces with the gun.'

It seemed a most eggstraordinary thing to try and catch it that way; but the beast was so tame, and stuck so close to us, that it wasn't quite so ridikilous as it seemed at fust.

Arter a couple o' days nobody minded the animal a bit, for

16

it was about the most nervous thing of its size you ever saw. It hadn't got the soul of a mouse; and one day when the second mate, just for a lark, took the line of the foghorn in his hand and tooted it a bit, it flung up its 'ead in a scared sort o' way, and, after backing a bit, turned clean round and bolted.

I thought the skipper 'ud have gone mad. He chucked over loaves o' bread, bits o' beef and pork, an' scores o' biskits, and by-and-by, when the brute plucked up heart an' came arter us again, he fairly beamed with joy. Then he gave orders that nobody was to touch the horn for any reason whatever, not even if there was a fog, or chance of collision, or anything of the kind; an' he also gave orders that the bells wasn't to be struck, but that the bosen was just to shove 'is 'ead in the fo'c's'le and call 'em out instead.

Arter three days had passed, and the thing was still follering us, everybody made certain of taking it to New York, an' I b'leeve if it hadn't been for Joe Cooper the question about the sea-sarpint would ha' been settled long ago. He was a most eggstraordinary ugly chap was Joe. He had a perfic cartoon of a face, an' he was so delikit-minded and sensitive about it that if a chap only stopped in the street and whistled as he passed him, or pointed him out to a friend, he didn't like it. He told me once when I was symperthizing with him, that the only time a woman ever spoke civilly to him was one night down Poplar way in a fog, an' he was so 'appy about it that they both walked into the canal afore he knew where they was.

On the fourth morning, when we was only about three days from Sandy Hook, the skipper got out o' bed wrong side, an' when he went on deck he was ready to snap at anybody, an' as luck would have it, as he walked a bit forrard, he sees Joe a-sticking his phiz over the side looking at the sarpint.

'What the d—— are you doing?' shouts the skipper. 'What do you mean by it?'

'Mean by what, sir?' asks Joe.

'Putting your black ugly face over the side o' the ship an' frightening my sea-sarpint!' bellows the skipper. 'You know how easy it's skeered.'

'Frightening the sea-sarpint?' ses Joe, trembling all over, an' turning very white.

'If I see that face o' yours over the side agin, my lad,' ses the skipper very fierce, 'I'll give it a black eye. Now cut!'

Joe cut, an' the skipper, having worked off some of his ill-temper, went aft again and began to chat with the mate quite pleasant like. I was down below at the time, an' didn't know anything about it for hours arter, and then I heard it from one o' the firemen. He comes up to me very mysterious like, an' ses, 'Bill,' he ses, 'you're a pal o' Joe's; come down here an' see what you can make of 'im.'

Not knowing what he meant, I follered 'im below to the engine-room, an' there was Joe sitting on a bucket staring wildly in front of 'im, and two or three of 'em standing round looking at 'im with their 'eads on one side.

'He's been like that for three hours,' ses the second engineer in a whisper, 'dazed like.'

As he spoke Joe gave a little shudder; 'Frighten the sea-sarpint!' ses he. 'O Lord!'

'It's turned his brain,' ses one o' the firemen, 'he keeps saying nothing but that.'

'If we could only make 'im cry,' ses the second engineer, who had a brother what was a medical student, 'it might save his reason. But how to do it, that's the question.'

'Speak kind to 'im, sir,' ses the fireman. 'I'll have a try if you don't mind.' He cleared his throat first, an' then he walks over to Joe and puts his hand on his shoulder an' ses very soft an' pitiful like,

'Don't take on, Joe, don't take on, there's many a ugly mug 'ides a good 'art.'

Afore he could think o' anything else to say, Joe ups with his fist an' gives 'im one in the ribs as nearly broke 'em. Then he turns away 'is 'ead an' shivers again, an' the old dazed look come back.

'Joe,' I ses, shaking him, 'Joe!'

'Frightened the sea-sarpint!' whispers Joe, staring.

'Joe,' I ses, 'Joe. You know me, I'm your pal, Bill.'

'Ay, ay,' ses Joe, coming round a bit.

'Come away,' I ses, 'come an' git to bed, that's the best place for you.'

I took 'im by the sleeve, and he gets up quiet an' obedient and follers me like a little child. I got 'im straight into 'is bunk, an' arter a time he fell into a soft slumber, an' I thought the worst had passed, but I was mistaken. He got up in three hours' time an' seemed all right, 'cept that he walked about as though he was thinking very hard about something, an' before I could make out what it was he had a fit.

He was in that fit ten minutes, an' he was no sooner out o' that one than he was in another. In twenty-four hours he had six full-sized fits, and I'll allow I was fairly puzzled. What pleasure he could find in tumbling down hard and stiff an' kicking at everybody an' everything I couldn't see. He'd be standing quiet and peaceable like one minute, and the next he'd catch hold o' the nearest thing to him and have a bad fit, and lie on his back and kick us while we was trying to force open his hands to pat 'em.

The other chaps said the skipper's insult had turned his brain, but I wasn't quite so soft, an' one time when he was alone I put it to him.

'Joe, old man,' I ses, 'you an' me's been very good pals.'

'Ay, ay,' ses he, suspicious like.

'Joe,' I whispers, 'what's yer little game?'

'Wodyermean?' ses he, very short.

'I mean the fits,' ses I, looking at 'im very steady. 'It's no good looking hinnercent like that, 'cos I see yer chewing soap with my own eyes.'

'Soap,' ses Joe, in a nasty sneering way, 'you wouldn't reckernise a piece if you saw it.'

Arter that I could see there was nothing to be got out of 'im an' I just kept my eyes open and watched. The skipper didn't worry about his fits, 'cept that he said he wasn't to let the sarpint see his face when he was in 'em for fear of scaring it; an' when the mate wanted to leave him out o' the watch, he ses, 'No, he might as well have fits while at work as well as anywhere else.'

We were about twenty-four hours from port, an' the sarpint was still following us; and at six o'clock in the evening the officers puffected all their arrangements for ketching the creetur at eight o'clock next morning. To make quite sure of it an extra watch was kept on deck all night to chuck it food every half-hour; an' when I turned in at ten o'clock that night it was so close I could have reached it with a clothes-prop.

I think I'd been abed about 'arf-an-hour when I was awoke by the most infernal row I ever heard. The foghorn was going incessantly, an' there was a lot o' shouting and running about on deck. It struck us all as 'ow the sarpint was gitting tired o' bread, and was misbehaving himself, consequently we just shoved our 'eds out o' the fore-scuttle and listened. All the hullaballoo seemed to be on the bridge, an' as we didn't see the sarpint there we plucked up courage and went on deck.

Then we saw what had happened. Joe had 'ad another fit while at the wheel, and, *not knowing what he was doing*, had clutched the line of the foghorn, and was holding on to it like grim death, and kicking right and left. The skipper was in his bedclothes, raving worse than Joe; and just as we got there Joe came round a bit, and, letting go o' the line, asked in a faint voice what the foghorn was blowing for. I thought the skipper 'ud have killed him; but the second mate held him back, an', of course, when things quieted down a bit, an' we went to the side, we found the sea-sarpint had vanished.

We stayed there all that night, but it warn't no use. When day broke there wasn't the slightest trace of it, an' I think the men was as sorry to lose it as the officers. All 'cept Joe, that is, which shows how people should never be rude, even to the humblest; for I'm sartin that if the skipper hadn't hurt his feelings the way he did we should now know as much about the sea-sarpint as we do about our own brothers.

A Will and a Way

The old man sat over the tap-room fire at the 'Cauliflower', his gnarled, swollen hands fondled the warm bowl of his long pipe, and an ancient eye watched with almost youthful impatience the slow warming of a mug of beer on the hob.

He had just given unasked-for statistics to the visitor at the inn who was sitting the other side of the hearth. His head was stored with the births, marriages and deaths of Claybury, and with a view of being entertaining he had already followed, from the cradle to the altar and the altar to the grave, the careers of some of the most uninteresting people that ever breathed.

No, there ain't been a great sight o' single men hereabouts, he said, in answer to a question. Claybury 'as always been a marrying sort o' place—not because the women are more good-looking than others, but because they are sharper.

He reached forward, and, taking up his beer, drank with relish. The generous liquor warmed his blood, and his eye brightened.

I've buried two wives, but I 'ave to be careful myself, old as I am, he said, thoughtfully. There's more than one woman about 'ere as would like to change 'er name for mine. Claybury's got the name for being a marrying place, and they don't like to see even a widow-man.

Now and agin we've 'ad a young feller as said as 'e wouldn't get married. There was Jem Burn, for one, and it ain't a month ago since four of 'is grandchildren carried him to the churchyard; and there was Walter Bree: 'e used to prove as 'ow any man that got married wasn't in 'is right mind, and 'e got three years in prison for wot they call bigamy.

But there used to be one man in these parts as the Claybury women couldn't marry, try as they might. He was a ugly little man with red 'air and a foxy face. They used to call 'im Foxy Green, and 'e kept 'appy and single for years and years.

He wasn't a man as disliked being in the company o' women though, and that's wot used to aggeravate 'em. He'd take 'em out for walks, or give 'em a lift in 'is cart, but none of 'em could get 'old of 'im, not even the widders. He used to say 'e loved 'em all too much to tie hisself up to any one of 'em, and 'e would sit up 'ere of a night at the 'Cauliflower' and send men with large families a'most crazy by calkerlating 'ow many pints o' beer their children wore out every year in the shape o' boots.

Sometimes 'is uncle, old Ebenezer Green, used to sit up 'ere with 'im. He was a strong, 'earty old man, and 'e'd sit and laugh at Foxy till 'is chair shook under 'im. He was a lively sporting sort o' man, and when Foxy talked like that 'e seemed to be keeping some joke to hisself which nearly choked 'im.

'You'll marry when I'm gone, Foxy,' he'd say.

'Not me,' ses Foxy.

Then the old man 'ud laugh agin and talk mysterious about fox-hunts and say 'e wondered who'd get Foxy's brush. He said 'e'd only got to shut 'is eyes and 'e could see the pack in full cry through Claybury village, and Foxy going 'is 'ardest with 'is tongue 'anging out.

Foxy couldn't say anything to 'im, because it was understood that when the old man died 'e was to 'ave 'is farm and 'is money; so 'e used to sit there and smile as if 'e liked it.

When Foxy was about forty-three 'is uncle died. The old man's mind seemed to wander at the last, and 'e said what a good man 'e'd always been, and wot a comfort it was to 'im now that 'e was goin'. And 'e mentioned a lot o' little sums o' money owed 'im in the village which nobody could remember.

'I've made my will, Foxy,' he ses, 'and schoolmaster's takin' care of it; I've left it all to you.'

'All right,' ses Foxy. 'Thankee.'

'He's goin' to read it arter the funeral,' ses 'is uncle, 'which is the proper way to do it. I'd give anything to be there, Foxy, and see your face.'

Those were 'is last words, but 'e laughed once or twice, and for a long time arter 'e'd gone Foxy Green sat there and wondered at 'is last words and wot there was to laugh about.

The old man was buried a few days after, and Foxy stood by the grave 'olding a 'andkerchief to 'is eyes, and behaving as though 'e 'ad lost money instead of coming in for it. Then they went back to the farm, and the first thing the schoolmaster did was to send all the women off before reading the will.

'Wot's that for?' ses Foxy, staring.

'You'll see,' ses the schoolmaster; 'them was my instructions. It's for your sake, Mr Green; to give you a chance—at least, that's wot your uncle said.'

He sat down and took out the will and put on 'is spectacles. Then 'e spread it out on the table and took a glass o' gin and water and began to read.

It was all straightforward enough. The farm and stock, and two cottages, and money in the bank, was all left to Josiah Green, commonly called Foxy Green, on condition——

There was such a noise o' clapping, and patting Foxy on the back, that the schoolmaster 'ad to leave off and wait for quiet.

'On condition,' he ses, in a loud voice, 'that he marries the first Claybury woman, single or widow, that asks 'im to marry her in the presence of three witnesses. If he refuses, the property is to go to 'er instead.'

Foxy turned round like mad then, and asked Henery Walker wot 'e was patting 'im on the back for. Then, in a choking voice, he asked to 'ave it read agin.

'Well, there's one thing about it, Mr Green,' ses Henery Walker; 'with all your property you'll be able to 'ave the pick o' the prettiest gals in Claybury.'

'"Ow's that?' ses Joe Chambers, very sharp; 'he's got to take the first woman that asks 'im, don't matter wot 'er age is.'

He got up suddenly, and, without even saying goodbye to Foxy, rushed out of the 'ouse and off over the fields as 'ard as 'e could go.

'Wot's the matter with 'im?' ses Foxy.

Nobody could give any answer, and they sat there staring at each other, till all of a sudden Henery Walker jumps up and goes off if anything 'arder than wot Joe Chambers had done.

'Anything wrong with the drink?' ses Foxy, puzzled like.

They shook their 'eads agin, and then Peter Gubbins, who'd been staring 'ard with 'is mouth open, got up and gave the table a bang with 'is fist.

'Joe Chambers 'as gone arter 'is sister,' he ses, 'and Henery Walker arter 'is wife's sister, as 'e's been keeping for this last six months. That's wot they've gone for.'

Everybody saw it then, and in two minutes Foxy and the schoolmaster was left alone looking at each other and the empty table.

'Well, I'm in for a nice thing,' ses Foxy. 'Fancy being proposed to by Henery Walker's sister-in-law! Ugh!'

'It'll be the oldest ones that'll be the most determined,' said the schoolmaster, shaking 'is 'ead. 'Wot are you going to do?'

'I don't know,' ses Foxy, 'it's so sudden. But they've got to 'ave three witnesses, that's one comfort. I'd like to tell Joe Chambers wot I think of 'im and 'is precious sister.'

It was very curious the way the women took it. One an' all of 'em pretended as it was an insult to the sex, and they said if Foxy Green waited till 'e was asked to marry he'd wait long enough. Little chits o' gals o' fourteen and fifteen was walking about tossing their 'eads up and as good as saying they might 'ave Green's farm for the asking, but they wouldn't ask. Old women of seventy and over said that if Foxy wanted to marry them he'd 'ave to ask, and ask a good many times too.

Of course, this was all very well in its way, but at the same time three Claybury gals that was away in service was took ill and 'ad to come 'ome, and several other women that was away took their holidays before their relations knew anything

24

about it. Almost every 'ouse in Claybury 'ad got some female relation staying in it, and they was always explaining to everybody why it was they 'ad come 'ome. None of 'em so much as mentioned Foxy Green.

Women are artful creatures and think a lot of appearances. There wasn't one of 'em as would ha' minded wot other folks said if they'd caught Foxy, but they'd ha' gone half crazy with shame if they'd tried and not managed it. And they couldn't do things on the quiet because of the three witnesses. That was the 'ardship of it.

It was the only thing talked about in Claybury, and Foxy Green soon showed as he was very wide-awake. First thing 'e did was to send the gal that used to do the dairy-work and the 'ouse-work off. Then 'e bought a couple o' large, fierce dogs and chained 'em up, one near the front door and one near the back. They was very good dogs, and they bit Foxy hisself two or three times so as to let 'im see that they knew wot they was there for.

He took George Smith, a young feller that used to work on the farm, into the 'ouse, and for the fust week or two 'e rather enjoyed the excitement. But when 'e found that 'e couldn't go into the village, or even walk about 'is own farm in safety, he turned into a reg'lar woman-hater.

The artful tricks those women 'ad wouldn't be believed. One day when Foxy was eating 'is dinner William Hall drove up to the gate in a cart, and when George came out to know wot 'e wanted, 'e said that he 'ad just bought some pigs at Rensham and would Foxy like to make fust offer for 'em.

George went in, and when 'e came out agin he said William Hall was to go inside. He 'eld the dog while William went by, and as soon as Foxy 'eard wot 'e wanted 'e asked 'im to wait till 'e'd finished 'is dinner, and then he'd go out and 'ave a look at 'em.

'I was wantin' some pigs bad,' he ses, 'and the worst of it is I can't get out to buy any as things are.'

'That's wot I thought,' ses William Hall; 'that's why I brought 'em to you.'

'You deserve to get on, William,' ses Foxy. 'George,' he ses, turning to 'im.

'Yes,' ses George.

'Do you know much about pigs?'

'I know a pig when I see one,' ses George.

'That's all I want,' ses Foxy; 'go and 'ave a look at 'em.'

William Hall gave a start as George walked out, and a minute afterwards both of 'em 'eard an awful noise, and George came back rubbing 'is 'ead and saying that when 'e lifted up the cloth one o' the pigs was William Hall's sister and the others was 'er nephews. William said it was a joke, but Foxy said he didn't like jokes, and if William thought that 'e or George was going to walk with 'im past the dog 'e was mistook.

Two days arter that, Foxy, 'appening to look out of 'is bed-room window, saw one o' the Claybury boys racing 'is cows all up and down the meadow. He came down quietly and took up a stick, and then 'e set out to race that boy up and down. He'd always been a good runner, and the boy was 'alf-blown like. 'E gave a yell as 'e saw Foxy coming arter 'im, and left the cow 'e was chasin' and ran straight for the 'edge, with Foxy close behind 'im.

Foxy was within two yards of 'im when 'e suddenly caught sight of a blue bonnet waiting behind the 'edge, and 'e turned round and went back to the 'ouse as fast as 'e could go and locked 'imself in. And 'e 'ad to sit there, half-busting, all the morning, and watch that boy chase 'is best cows up and down the meadow without daring to go out and stop 'im.

He sent George down to tell the boy's father that night, and the father sent back word that if Foxy 'ad got anything to say agin 'is boy why didn't 'e come down like a man and say it hisself?

Arter about three weeks o' this sort o' thing Foxy Green began to see that 'e would 'ave to get married whether he liked it or not, and 'e told George so. George's idea was for 'im to get the oldest woman in Claybury to ask 'im in marriage, because then he'd soon be single agin. It was a good idea, on'y Foxy didn't seem to fancy it.

'Who do you think is the prettiest gal in Claybury, George?' he ses.

'Flora Pottle,' ses George, at once.

'That's exactly my idea,' ses Foxy; 'if I've got to marry, I'll marry 'er. However, I'll sleep on it a night and see 'ow I feel in the morning.'

'I'll marry Flora Pottle,' he ses, when 'e got up. 'You can go round this arternoon, George, and break the good news to 'er.'

George tidied hisself up arter dinner and went. Flora Pottle was a very fine-looking gal, and she was very much surprised when George walked in, but she was more surprised when 'e told 'er that if she was to go over and ask Foxy to be 'er 'usband he wouldn't say 'No'.

Mrs Pottle jumped out of 'er skin for joy a'most. She'd 'ad a 'ard time of it with Flora and five young children since 'er 'usband died, and she could 'ardly believe 'er ears when Flora said she wouldn't.

''E's old enough to be my father,' she ses.

'Old men make the best 'usbands,' ses George, coaxing 'er; 'and, besides, think o' the farm.'

'That's wot you've got to think of,' ses her mother. 'Don't think o' Foxy Green at all; think o' the farm.'

Flora stood and leaned herself up agin a chest o' drawers and twisted 'er hands, and at last she sent back word to say that she wanted time to think it over.

Foxy Green was very much astonished when George took back that answer. He'd thought that any gal would ha' jumped at 'im without the farm, and arter going upstairs and looking at hisself in the glass 'e was more astonished than ever.

When George Smith went up to the Pottles agin the next day Flora made a face at 'im, and 'e felt as orkard as if 'e'd been courting 'er hisself a'most. At first she wouldn't 'ave anything to say to 'im at all, but went on sweeping out the room, and nearly choking 'im. Then George Smith, wot was a likely young feller, put 'is arm round 'er waist, and, taking the broom away from 'er, made 'er sit down beside 'im while 'e gave 'er Foxy's message.

He did Foxy's courting for 'im for an hour, although it on'y seemed about five minutes to both of 'em. Then Mrs Pottle came in, and arter a lot of talk Flora was got to say that George Smith might come agin for five minutes next day.

Foxy went on dreadful when 'e 'eard that Flora 'adn't given an answer, but George Smith, who liked the job much better than farming or making beds, told 'im she was coming round, and that it was on'y natural a young gal should like to be courted a bit afore givin' in.

'Yes,' ses Foxy, biting 'is lip, 'but 'ow's it to be done?'

'You leave it to me,' ses George Smith, 'and it'll be all right. I sit there and talk about the farm as well as wot you could.'

'And about me too, I s'pose?' ses Foxy, catching 'im up.

'Yes,' ses George; 'I tell 'er all sorts o' lies about you.'

Foxy looked at 'im a moment, and then 'e went off grumbling. He was like a good many more men, and because Flora Pottle didn't seem to want 'im 'e on'y fancied 'er the more. Next day 'e sent George Smith up with an old brooch as a present, and when George came back 'e said 'e thought that if it 'ad been a new one it would 'ave done wot was wanted.

You can't keep secrets in Claybury, and it soon got round wot Foxy Green was arter. That made the other women more determined than ever, and at last Foxy sent up word that if Flora wouldn't ask 'im to let 'im know, as 'e was tired o' being a prisoner, and old Mrs Ball 'ad nearly 'ad 'im the day afore.

It took George Smith two hours' 'ard courtin' afore he could get Flora Pottle to say 'Yes', but at last she did, and then Mrs Pottle came in, and she shook 'ands with George, and gave 'im a glass o' beer. Mrs Pottle wanted to take 'er up to Green's farm there and then, but Flora said no. She said they'd go up at eight o'clock in the evenin', and the sacrifice should be made then.

Foxy didn't like the word 'sacrifice' at all, but if 'e'd got to be married 'e'd sooner marry Flora than anybody, and 'e 'ad to put up with it.

'There'll be you for one witness,' he ses to George, 'and Mrs Pottle is two; wot about the third?'

'I should 'ave 'alf a dozen, so as to make sure,' ses George.

Foxy thought it was a good idea, and without letting 'em know wot it was for, 'e asked Henery Walker and Joe Chambers, and three or four more 'e 'ad a grudge against for trying to marry 'im to their relations, to come up and see that 'e'd been able to pick and choose.

They came at ha'-past seven, and at eight o'clock there was a knock at the door, and George, arter carefully looking round, let in Mrs Pottle and Flora. She was a fine-looking gal, and as she stood there looking at all them astonished men, 'er face all blushes and 'er eyes large and shining, Foxy thought getting married wasn't such a bad thing arter all. He gave 'er a chair to sit on, and then 'e coughed and waited.

'It's a fine night,' he ses, at last.

'Beautiful,' ses Mrs Pottle.

Flora didn't say anything. She sat there shuffling 'er feet on the carpet, and Foxy Green kept on looking at 'er and waiting for 'er to speak, and 'oping that she wouldn't grow up like 'er mother.

'Go on, Flora,' ses Mrs Pottle, nudging 'er.

'Go on, Flora,' ses Henery Walker, mimicking 'er. 'I s'pose you've come to ask Foxy a question by the look of it?'

'Yes,' ses Flora, looking up. 'Are you quite well, Mr Green?'

'Yes, yes,' ses Foxy; 'but you didn't come up 'ere to ask me that.'

'It's all I could do to get 'er 'ere at all, Mr Green,' says Mrs Pottle; 'she's that shy you can't think. She'd rather ha' 'ad you ask 'er yourself.'

'That can't be done,' ses Foxy, shaking 'is 'ead. 'Leastways, I'm not going to risk it.'

'Now, Flora,' ses 'er mother, nudging 'er agin.

'Come on, Flora Pottle,' ses Bob Hunt; 'we're all a-waitin'.'

'Shut your eyes and open your mouth, as if Foxy was a powder,' ses Henery Walker.

29

'I can't,' ses Flora, turning to her mother. 'I can't and I won't.'

'Flora Pottle,' ses 'er mother, firing up.

'I won't,' ses Flora, firing up too; 'you've been bothering me all day long for ever so long, and I won't. I 'ate the sight of 'im. He's the ugliest man in Claybury.'

Mrs Pottle began to cry and say that she'd disgraced 'er; but Foxy Green looked at 'er and 'e ses, 'Very well, Flora Pottle, then we'll say no more about it. Good evening.'

'Good evening,' ses Mrs Pottle, getting up and giving Flora a shake. 'Come along, you tantalising mawther, do. You'll die an old maid, that's what you'll do.'

'That's all you know,' ses Flora, smiling over at George Smith; 'but if you're so fond o' Mr Green why don't you ask 'im yourself? He can't say "No".'

For half a minute the room was as quiet as a grave, and the on'y thing that moved was Foxy Green's eyes as he looked fust at the door at the other end of the room and then at the window.

'Lor' bless my soul!' ses Mrs Pottle, in a surprised voice. 'I never thought of it.'

She sat down agin and smiled at Foxy as if she could eat 'im.

'I can't think why I didn't think of it,' she ses, looking round. 'I was going out like a lamb. Mr Green——'

'One moment,' ses Foxy, 'olding up 'is 'and. 'I should be a terrible, bad, cruel, unkind husband to anybody I didn't like. Don't say words you'll be sorry for arterwards, Mrs Pottle.'

'I'm not going to,' ses Mrs Pottle; 'the words I'm going to say will be good for both of us; I'm far more suitable for you than a young gal—Mr Green, will you marry me?'

Foxy Green looked at 'er for a moment, and then 'e looked round at all them grinning men wot he'd brought there by mistake to see 'im made a fool of. Then in a low, 'usky voice he ses, 'I will'.

The Monkey's Paw

I

Without, the night was cold and wet, but in the small parlour of Laburnum Villa the blinds were drawn and the fire burned brightly. Father and son were at chess; the former, who possessed ideas about the game involving radical changes, putting his king into such sharp and unnecessary perils that it even provoked comment from the white-haired old lady knitting placidly by the fire.

'Hark at the wind,' said Mr White, who, having seen a fatal mistake after it was too late, was amiably desirous of preventing his son from seeing it.

'I'm listening,' said the latter, grimly surveying the board as he stretched out his hand. 'Check.'

'I should hardly think that he'd come tonight,' said his father, with his hand poised over the board.

'Mate,' replied the son.

'That's the worst of living so far out,' bawled Mr White, with sudden and unlooked-for violence; 'of all the beastly, slushy, out-of-the-way places to live in, this is the worst. Pathway's a bog, and the road's a torrent. I don't know what people are thinking about. I suppose because only two houses in the road are let, they think it doesn't matter.'

'Never mind, dear,' said his wife soothingly; 'perhaps you'll win the next one.'

Mr White looked up sharply, just in time to intercept a knowing glance between mother and son. The words died away on his lips, and he hid a guilty grin in his thin grey beard.

'There he is,' said Herbert White, as the gate banged to loudly and heavy footsteps came toward the door.

The old man rose with hospitable haste, and opening the door, was heard condoling with the new arrival. The new arrival also condoled with himself, so that Mrs White said, 'Tut, tut!' and coughed gently as her husband entered the room, followed by a tall, burly man, beady of eye and rubicund of visage.

'Sergeant-Major Morris,' he said, introducing him.

The sergeant-major shook hands, and taking the proffered seat by the fire, watched contentedly while his host got out whisky and tumblers and stood a small copper kettle on the fire.

At the third glass his eyes got brighter, and he began to talk, the little family circle regarding with eager interest this visitor from distant parts, as he squared his broad shoulders in the chair and spoke of wild scenes and doughty deeds; of wars and plagues and strange peoples.

'Twenty-one years of it,' said Mr White, nodding at his wife and son. 'When he went away he was a slip of a youth in the warehouse. Now look at him.'

'He don't look to have taken much harm,' said Mrs White politely.

'I'd like to go to India myself,' said the old man, 'just to look round a bit, you know.'

'Better where you are,' said the sergeant-major, shaking his head. He put down the empty glass, and sighing softly, shook it again.

'I should like to see those old temples and fakirs and jugglers,' said the old man. 'What was that you started telling me the other day about a monkey's paw or something, Morris?'

'Nothing,' said the soldier hastily. 'Leastways nothing worth hearing.'

'Monkey's paw?' said Mrs White curiously.

'Well, it's just a bit of what you might call magic, perhaps,' said the sergeant-major off-handedly.

His three listeners leaned forward eagerly. The visitor absent-mindedly put his empty glass to his lips and then set it down again. His host filled it for him.

'To look at,' said the sergeant-major, fumbling in his

pocket, 'it's just an ordinary little paw, dried to a mummy.'

He took something out of his pocket and proffered it. Mrs White drew back with a grimace, but her son, taking it, examined it curiously.

'And what is there special about it?' inquired Mr White as he took it from his son, and having examined it, placed it upon the table.

'It had a spell put on it by an old fakir,' said the sergeant-major, 'a very holy man. He wanted to show that fate ruled people's lives, and that those who interfered with it did so to their sorrow. He put a spell on it so that three separate men could each have three wishes from it.'

His manner was so impressive that his hearers were conscious that their light laughter jarred somewhat.

'Well, why don't you have three, sir?' said Herbert White cleverly.

The soldier regarded him in the way that middle age is wont to regard presumptuous youth. 'I have,' he said quietly, and his blotchy face whitened.

'And did you really have the three wishes granted?' asked Mrs White.

'I did,' said the sergeant-major, and his glass tapped against his strong teeth.

'And has anybody else wished?' persisted the old lady.

'The first man had his three wishes. Yes,' was the reply; 'I don't know what the first two were, but the third was for death. That's how I got the paw.'

His tones were so grave that a hush fell upon the group.

'If you've had your three wishes, it's no good to you now, then, Morris,' said the old man at last. 'What do you keep it for?'

The soldier shook his head. 'Fancy, I suppose,' he said slowly. 'I did have some idea of selling it, but I don't think I will. It has caused enough mischief already. Besides, people won't buy. They think it's a fairy tale, some of them; and those who do think anything of it want to try it first and pay me afterward.'

33

'If you could have another three wishes,' said the old man, eyeing him keenly, 'would you have them?'

'I don't know,' said the other. 'I don't know.'

He took the paw, and dangling it between his forefinger and thumb, suddenly threw it upon the fire. White, with a slight cry, stooped down and snatched it off.

'Better let it burn,' said the soldier solemnly.

'If you don't want it, Morris,' said the other, 'give it to me.'

'I won't,' said his friend doggedly. 'I threw it on the fire. If you keep it, don't blame me for what happens. Pitch it on the fire again like a sensible man.'

The other shook his head and examined his new possession closely. 'How do you do it?' he inquired.

'Hold it up in your right hand and wish aloud,' said the sergeant-major, 'but I warn you of the consequences.'

'Sounds like *The Arabian Nights*,' said Mrs White, as she rose and began to set the supper. 'Don't you think you might wish for four pairs of hands for me?'

Her husband drew the talisman from his pocket, and then all three burst into laughter as the sergeant-major, with a look of alarm on his face, caught him by the arm.

'If you must wish,' he said gruffly, 'wish for something sensible.'

Mr White dropped it back in his pocket, and placing chairs, motioned his friend to the table. In the business of supper the talisman was partly forgotten, and afterwards the three sat listening in an enthralled fashion to a second instalment of the soldier's adventures in India.

'If the tale about the monkey's paw is not more truthful than those he has been telling us,' said Herbert, as the door closed behind their guest, just in time for him to catch the last train, 'we shan't make much out of it.'

'Did you give him anything for it, father?' inquired Mrs White, regarding her husband closely.

'A trifle,' said he, colouring slightly. 'He didn't want it, but I made him take it. And he pressed me again to throw it away.'

'Likely,' said Herbert, with pretended horror. 'Why, we're

34

going to be rich, and famous, and happy. Wish to be an emperor, father, to begin with; then you can't be henpecked.'

He darted round the table, pursued by the maligned Mrs White armed with an antimacassar.

Mr White took the paw from his pocket and eyed it dubiously. 'I don't know what to wish for, and that's a fact,' he said slowly. 'It seems to me I've got all I want.'

'If you only cleared the house, you'd be quite happy, wouldn't you?' said Herbert, with his hand on his shoulder. 'Well, wish for two hundred pounds, then; that'll just do it.'

His father, smiling shamefacedly at his own credulity, held up the talisman, as his son, with a solemn face, somewhat marred by a wink at his mother, sat down at the piano and struck a few impressive chords.

'I wish for two hundred pounds,' said the old man distinctly.

A fine crash from the piano greeted the words, interrupted by a shuddering cry from the old man. His wife and son ran toward him.

'It moved,' he cried, with a glance of disgust at the object as it lay on the floor. 'As I wished, it twisted in my hand like a snake.'

'Well, I don't see the money,' said his son, as he picked it up and placed it on the table, 'and I bet I never shall.'

'It must have been your fancy, father,' said his wife, regarding him anxiously.

He shook his head. 'Never mind, though; there's no harm done, but it gave me a shock all the same.'

They sat down by the fire again while the two men finished their pipes. Outside, the wind was higher than ever, and the old man started nervously at the sound of a door banging upstairs. A silence unusual and depressing settled upon all three, which lasted until the old couple rose to retire for the night.

'I expect you'll find the cash tied up in a big bag in the middle of your bed,' said Herbert, as he bade them good-night, 'and something horrible squatting up on top of the wardrobe watching you as you pocket your ill-gotten gains.'

He sat alone in the darkness, gazing at the dying fire, and seeing faces in it. The last face was so horrible and so simian that he gazed at it in amazement. It got so vivid that, with a little uneasy laugh, he felt on the table for a glass containing a little water to throw over it. His hand grasped the monkey's paw, and with a little shiver he wiped his hand on his coat and went up to bed.

II

In the brightness of the wintry sun next morning as it streamed over the breakfast table he laughed at his fears. There was an air of prosaic wholesomeness about the room which it had lacked on the previous night, and the dirty, shrivelled little paw was pitched on the sideboard with a carelessness which betokened no great belief in its virtues.

'I suppose all old soldiers are the same,' said Mrs White. 'The idea of our listening to such nonsense! How could wishes be granted in these days? And if they could, how could two hundred pounds hurt you, father?'

'Might drop on his head from the sky,' said the frivolous Herbert.

'Morris said the things happened so naturally,' said his father, 'that you might if you so wished attribute it to coincidence.'

'Well, don't break into the money before I come back,' said Herbert as he rose from the table. 'I'm afraid it'll turn you into a mean, avaricious man, and we shall have to disown you.'

His mother laughed, and following him to the door, watched him down the road; and returning to the breakfast table, was very happy at the expense of her husband's credulity. All of which did not prevent her from scurrying to the door at the postman's knock, nor prevent her from referring somewhat shortly to retired sergeant-majors of bibulous habits when she found that the post brought a tailor's bill.

'Herbert will have some more of his funny remarks, I expect, when he comes home,' she said, as they sat at dinner.

'I dare say,' said Mr White, pouring himself out some beer; 'but for all that, the thing moved in my hand; that I'll swear to.'

'You thought it did,' said the old lady soothingly.

'I say it did,' replied the other. 'There was no thought about it; I had just—— What's the matter?'

His wife made no reply. She was watching the mysterious movements of a man outside, who, peering in an undecided fashion at the house, appeared to be trying to make up his mind to enter. In mental connection with the two hundred pounds, she noticed that the stranger was well dressed, and wore a silk hat of glossy newness. Three times he paused at the gate, and then walked on again. The fourth time he stood with his hand upon it, and then with sudden resolution flung it open and walked up the path. Mrs White at the same moment placed her hands behind her, and hurriedly unfastening the strings of her apron, put that useful article of apparel beneath the cushion of her chair.

She brought the stranger, who seemed ill at ease, into the room. He gazed at her furtively, and listened in a preoccupied fashion as the old lady apologised for the appearance of the room, and her husband's coat, a garment which he usually reserved for the garden. She then waited as patiently as her sex would permit, for him to broach his business, but he was at first strangely silent.

'I—was asked to call,' he said at last, and stooped and picked a piece of cotton from his trousers. 'I come from Maw and Meggins.'

The old lady started. 'Is anything the matter?' she asked breathlessly. 'Has anything happened to Herbert? What is it? What is it?'

Her husband interposed. 'There, there, mother,' he said hastily. 'Sit down, and don't jump to conclusions. You've not

37

brought bad news, I'm sure, sir;' and he eyed the other wistfully.

'I'm sorry—' began the visitor.

'Is he hurt?' demanded the mother wildly.

The visitor bowed in assent. 'Badly hurt,' he said quietly, 'but he is not in any pain.'

'Oh, thank God!' said the old woman, clasping her hands. 'Thank God for that! Thank——'

She broke off suddenly as the sinister meaning of the assurance dawned upon her and she saw the awful confirmation of her fears in the other's averted face. She caught her breath, and turning to her slower-witted husband, laid her trembling old hand upon his. There was a long silence.

'He was caught in the machinery,' said the visitor at length in a low voice.

'Caught in the machinery,' repeated Mr White, in a dazed fashion, 'yes.'

He sat staring blankly out at the window, and taking his wife's hand between his own, pressed it as he had been wont to do in their old courting days nearly forty years before.

'He was the only one left to us,' he said, turning gently to the visitor. 'It is hard.'

The other coughed, and rising, walked slowly to the window. 'The firm wished me to convey their sincere sympathy with you in your great loss,' he said, without looking round. 'I beg that you will understand I am only their servant and merely obeying orders.'

There was no reply; the old woman's face was white, her eyes staring, and her breath inaudible; on the husband's face was a look such as his friend the sergeant might have carried into his first action.

'I was to say that Maw and Meggins disclaim all responsibility,' continued the other. 'They admit no liability at all, but in consideration of your son's services, they wish to present you with a certain sum as compensation.'

Mr White dropped his wife's hand, and rising to his feet,

gazed with a look of horror at his visitor. His dry lips shaped the words, 'How much?'

'Two hundred pounds,' was the answer.

Unconscious of his wife's shriek, the old man smiled faintly, put out his hands like a sightless man, and dropped, a senseless heap, to the floor.

III

In the huge new cemetery, some two miles distant, the old people buried their dead, and came back to a house steeped in shadow and silence. It was all over so quickly that at first they could hardly realise it, and remained in a state of expectation as though of something else to happen—something else which was to lighten this load, too heavy for old hearts to bear.

But the days passed, and expectation gave place to resignation—the hopeless resignation of the old, sometimes miscalled apathy. Sometimes they hardly exchanged a word, for now they had nothing to talk about, and their days were long to weariness.

It was about a week after that the old man, waking suddenly in the night, stretched out his hand and found himself alone. The room was in darkness, and the sound of subdued weeping came from the window. He raised himself in bed and listened.

'Come back,' he said tenderly. 'You will be cold.'

'It is colder for my son,' said the old woman, and wept afresh.

The sound of her sobs died away on his ears. The bed was warm, and his eyes heavy with sleep. He dozed fitfully, and then slept until a sudden wild cry from his wife awoke him with a start.

'*The paw!*' she cried wildly. 'The monkey's paw!'

He started up in alarm. 'Where? Where is it? What's the matter?'

She came stumbling across the room toward him. 'I want it,' she said quietly. 'You've not destroyed it?'

'It's in the parlour, on the bracket,' he replied, marvelling. 'Why?'

She cried and laughed together, and bending over, kissed his cheek.

'I only just thought of it,' she said hysterically. 'Why didn't I think of it before? Why didn't *you* think of it?'

'Think of what?' he questioned.

'The other two wishes,' she replied rapidly. 'We've only had one.'

'Was not that enough?' he demanded fiercely.

'No,' she cried triumphantly; 'we'll have one more. Go down and get it quickly, and wish our boy alive again.'

The man sat up in bed and flung the bedclothes from his quaking limbs. 'Good God, you are mad!' he cried, aghast.

'Get it,' she panted; 'get it quickly, and wish—— Oh, my boy, my boy!'

Her husband struck a match and lit the candle. 'Get back to bed,' he said unsteadily. 'You don't know what you are saying.'

'We had the first wish granted,' said the old woman feverishly; 'why not the second?'

'A coincidence,' stammered the old man.

'Go and get it and wish,' cried his wife, quivering with excitement.

The old man turned and regarded her, and his voice shook. 'He has been dead ten days, and besides he—I would not tell you else, but—I could only recognise him by his clothing. If he was too terrible for you to see then, how now?'

'Bring him back,' cried the old woman, and dragged him toward the door. 'Do you think I fear the child I have nursed?'

He went down in the darkness, and felt his way to the parlour, and then to the mantelpiece. The talisman was in its place, and a horrible fear that the unspoken wish might bring his mutilated son before him ere he could escape from the room seized upon him, and he caught his breath as he found that he had lost the direction of the door. His brow cold with sweat, he felt his way round the table, and groped along the wall until he found himself in the small passage with the unwholesome thing in his hand.

Even his wife's face seemed changed as he entered the room. It was white and expectant, and to his fears seemed to have an unnatural look upon it. He was afraid of her.

'*Wish!*' she cried, in a strong voice.

'It is foolish and wicked,' he faltered.

'*Wish!*' repeated his wife.

He raised his hand. 'I wish my son alive again.'

The talisman fell to the floor, and he regarded it fearfully. Then he sank trembling into a chair as the old woman, with burning eyes, walked to the window and raised the blind.

He sat until he was chilled with the cold, glancing occasionally at the figure of the old woman peering through the window. The candle-end, which had burned below the rim of the china candlestick, was throwing pulsating shadows on the ceiling and walls, until, with a flicker larger than the rest, it expired. The old man, with an unspeakable sense of relief at the failure of the talisman, crept back to his bed, and a minute or two afterward the old woman came silently and apathetically beside him.

Neither spoke, but lay silently listening to the ticking of the clock. A stair creaked, and a squeaky mouse scurried noisily through the wall. The darkness was oppressive, and after lying for some time screwing up his courage, he took the box of matches, and striking one, went downstairs for a candle.

At the foot of the stairs the match went out, and he paused to strike another; and at the same moment a knock, so quiet and stealthy as to be scarcely audible, sounded on the front door.

The matches fell from his hand and spilled in the passage. He stood motionless, his breath suspended until the knock was repeated. Then he turned and fled swiftly back to his room, and closed the door behind him. A third knock sounded through the house.

'*What's that?*' cried the old woman, starting up.

'A rat,' said the old man in shaking tones—'a rat. It passed me on the stairs.'

His wife sat up in bed listening. A loud knock resounded through the house.

'It's Herbert!' she screamed. 'It's Herbert!'

She ran to the door, but her husband was before her, and catching her by the arm, held her tightly.

'What are you going to do?' he whispered hoarsely.

'It's my boy; it's Herbert!' she cried, struggling mechanically. 'I forgot it was two miles away. What are you holding me for? Let go. I must open the door.'

'For God's sake don't let it in,' cried the old man, trembling.

'You're afraid of your own son,' she cried, struggling. 'Let me go. I'm coming, Herbert; I'm coming.'

There was another knock, and another. The old woman with a sudden wrench broke free and ran from the room. Her husband followed to the landing, and called after her appealingly as she hurried downstairs. He heard the chain rattle back and the bottom bolt drawn slowly and stiffly from the socket. Then the old woman's voice, strained and panting.

'The bolt,' she cried loudly. 'Come down. I can't reach it.'

But her husband was on his hands and knees groping wildly on the floor in search of the paw. If he could only find it before the thing outside got in. A perfect fusillade of knocks reverberated through the house, and he heard the scraping of a chair as his wife put it down in the passage against the door. He heard the creaking of the bolt as it came slowly back, and at the same moment he found the monkey's paw, and frantically breathed his third and last wish.

The knocking ceased suddenly, although the echoes of it were still in the house. He heard the chair drawn back, and the door opened. A cold wind rushed up the staircase, and a long loud wail of disappointment and misery from his wife gave him courage to run down to her side, and then to the gate beyond. The street lamp flickering opposite shone on a quiet and deserted road.

Bill's Paper Chase

Sailormen 'ave their faults, said the night watchman frankly. I'm not denying of it. I used to 'ave myself when I was at sea, but being close with their money is a fault as can seldom be brought ag'in 'em.

I saved some money once—two golden sovereigns, owing to a 'ole in my pocket. Before I got another ship I slept two nights on a doorstep and 'ad nothing to eat, and I found them two sovereigns in the lining o' my coat when I was over two thousand miles away from the nearest pub.

I on'y knew one miser all the years I was at sea. Thomas Geary 'is name was, and we was shipmates aboard the barque *Grenada*, homeward bound from Sydney to London.

Thomas was a man that was getting into years; sixty, I think 'e was, and old enough to know better. 'E'd been saving 'ard for over forty years, and as near as we could make out 'e was worth a matter o' six 'undered pounds. He used to be fond o' talking about it, and letting us know how much better off 'e was than any of the rest of us.

We was about a month out from Sydney when old Thomas took sick. Bill Hicks said that it was owing to a ha'penny he couldn't account for; but Walter Jones, whose family was always ill, and thought 'e knew a lot about it, said that 'e knew wot it was, but 'e couldn't remember the name of it, and that when we got to London and Thomas saw a doctor, we should see as 'ow 'e was right.

Whatever it was, the old man got worse and worse. The skipper came down and gave 'im some physic and looked at 'is tongue, and then 'e looked at our tongues to see wot the difference was. Then 'e left the cook in charge of 'im and went off.

43

The next day Thomas was worse, and it was soon clear to everybody but 'im that 'e was slipping 'is cable. He wouldn't believe it at first, though the cook told 'im, Bill Hicks told him, and Walter Jones 'ad a grandfather that went off in just the same way.

'I'm not going to die,' says Thomas. 'How can I die and leave all that money?'

'It'll be good for your relations, Thomas,' says Walter Jones.

'I ain't got any,' says the old man.

'Well, your friends, then, Thomas,' says Walter, soft-like.

'Ain't got any,' says the old man ag'in.

'Yes, you 'ave, Thomas,' says Walter, with a kind smile; 'I could tell you one you've got.'

Thomas shut his eyes at 'im and began to talk pitiful about 'is money and the 'ard work 'e'd 'ad saving of it. And by-and-by 'e got worse, and didn't reckernise us, but thought we was a pack o' greedy, drunken sailormen. He thought Walter Jones was a shark, and told 'im so, and, try all 'e could, Walter couldn't persuade 'im different.

He died the day arter. In the morning 'e was whimpering about 'is money ag'in, and angry with Bill when 'e reminded 'im that 'e couldn't take it with 'im, and 'e made Bill promise that 'e should be buried just as 'e was. Bill tucked him up arter that, and when 'e felt a canvas belt tied round the old man's waist 'e began to see wot 'e was driving at.

The weather was dirty that day and there was a bit o' sea running, consequently all 'ands was on deck, and a boy about sixteen wot used to 'elp the steward down aft was lookin' arter Thomas. Me and Bill just run down to give a look at the old man in time.

'I *am* going to take it with me, Bill,' says the old man.

'That's right,' says Bill.

'My mind's—easy now,' says Thomas. 'I gave it to Jimmy —to—to—throw overboard for me.'

'*Wot?*' says Bill, staring.

'That's right, Bill,' says the boy. 'He told me to. It was a little packet o' banknotes. He gave me tuppence for doing it.'

44

Old Thomas seemed to be listening. 'Is eyes was open, and 'e looked artful at Bill to think what a clever thing 'e'd done.

'Nobody's goin'—to spend—*my* money,' 'e says. 'Nobody's——'

We drew back from 'is bunk and stood staring at 'im. Then Bill turned to the boy.

'Go and tell the skipper 'e's gone,' 'e says, 'and mind, for your own sake, don't tell the skipper or anybody else that you've thrown all that money overboard.'

'Why not?' says Jimmy.

'Becos you'll be locked up for it,' says Bill; 'you'd no business to do it. You've been and broke the law. It ought to ha' been left to somebody.'

Jimmy looked scared, and arter 'e was gone I turned to Bill, and I looks at 'im and I says, 'What's the little game, Bill?'

'*Game?*' said Bill, snorting at me. 'I don't want the pore boy to get into trouble, do I? Pore little chap. You was young yourself once.'

'Yes,' I says; 'but I'm a bit older now, Bill, and unless you tell me what your little game is, I shall tell the skipper myself, and the chaps too. Pore old Thomas told 'im to do it, so where's the boy to blame?'

'Do you think Jimmy *did?*' says Bill, screwing up his nose at me. 'That little varmint is walking about worth six 'undered quid. Now you keep your mouth shut and I'll make it worth your while.'

Then I see Bill's game. 'All right, I'll keep quiet for the sake of my half,' I says, looking at 'im.

I thought he'd ha' choked, and the langwidge 'e see fit to use was a'most as much as I could answer.

'Very well, then,' 'e says, at last, 'halves it is. It ain't robbery becos it belongs to nobody, and it ain't the boy's becos 'e was told to throw it overboard.'

They buried pore old Thomas next morning, and arter it was all over Bill put 'is 'and on the boy's shoulder as they walked for'ard and 'e says, 'Poor old Thomas 'as gone to look for 'is money,' he says; 'wonder whether 'e'll find it! Was it a big bundle, Jimmy?'

'No,' says the boy, shaking 'is 'ead. 'They was six 'undered pound notes and two sovereigns, and I wrapped the sovereigns up in the notes to make 'em sink. Fancy throwing money away like that, Bill: seems a sin, don't it?'

Bill didn't answer 'im, and that afternoon the other chaps below being asleep we searched 'is bunk through and through without any luck, and at last Bill sat down and swore 'e must ha' got it about 'im.

We waited till night, and when everybody was snoring 'ard we went over to the boy's bunk and went all through 'is pockets and felt the linings, and then we went back to our side and Bill said wot 'e thought about Jimmy in whispers.

'He must ha' got it tied round 'is waist next to 'is skin, like Thomas 'ad,' I says.

We stood there in the dark whispering, and then Bill couldn't stand it any longer, and 'e went over on tiptoe to the bunk ag'in. He was tremblin' with excitement and I wasn't much better, when all of a sudden the cook sat up in 'is bunk with a dreadful laughing scream and called out that somebody was ticklin' 'im.

I got into my bunk and Bill got into 'is, and we lay there listening while the cook, who was a terrible ticklish man, leaned out of 'is bunk and said wot 'e'd do if it 'appened ag'in.

'Go to sleep,' says Walter Jones; 'you're dreamin'. Who d'you think would want to tickle you?'

'I tell you,' says the cook, 'somebody come over and tickled me with a 'and the size of a leg o' mutton. I feel creepy all over.'

Bill gave it up for that night, but the next day 'e pretended to think Jimmy was gettin' fat an' 'e caught 'old of 'im and prodded 'im all over. He thought 'e felt something round 'is waist, but 'e couldn't be sure, and Jimmy made such a noise that the other chaps interfered and told Bill to leave 'im alone.

For a whole week we tried to find that money, and couldn't, and Bill said it was a suspicious thing that Jimmy kept aft a good deal more than 'e used to, and 'e got an idea that the boy might ha' 'idden it somewhere there. At the end of that time, 'owever, owing to our being short-'anded, Jimmy was sent for'ard to work as ordinary seaman, and it began to be quite noticeable the way 'e avoided Bill.

At last one day we got 'im alone down the fo'c'sle, and Bill put 'is arm round 'im and got 'im on the locker and asked 'im straight out where the money was.

'Why, I chucked it overboard,' he says. 'I told you so afore. What a memory you've got, Bill!'

Bill picked 'im up and laid 'im on the locker, and we searched 'im thoroughly. We even took 'is boots off, and then we 'ad another look in 'is bunk while 'e was putting 'em on ag'in.

'If you're innercent,' says Bill, 'why don't you call out?—eh?'

'Because you told me not to say anything about it, Bill,' says the boy. 'But I will next time. Loud, I will.'

'Look 'ere,' says Bill, 'you tell us where it is, and the three of us'll go shares in it. That'll be two 'undered pounds each, and we'll tell you 'ow to get yours changed without getting caught. We're cleverer than you are, you know.'

'I know that, Bill,' says the boy; 'but it's no good me telling you lies. I chucked it overboard.'

'Very good, then,' says Bill, getting up. 'I'm going to tell the skipper.'

'Tell 'im,' says Jimmy. 'I don't care.'

'Then you'll be searched *arter you've stepped ashore*,' says Bill, 'and you won't be allowed on the ship ag'in. You'll lose it all by being greedy, whereas if you go shares with us you'll 'ave two 'undered pounds.'

I could see as 'ow the boy 'adn't thought of that, and try as 'e would 'e couldn't 'ide 'is feelin's. He called Bill a red-nosed shark, and 'e called me somethin' I've forgotten now.

'Think it over,' says Bill; 'mind, you'll be collared as soon as you've left the gangway and searched by the police.'

47

'And will they tickle the cook too, I wonder?' says Jimmy savagely.

'And if they find it you'll go to prison,' says Bill, giving 'im a clump o' the side o' the 'ead, 'and you won't like that, I can tell you.'

'Why, ain't it nice, Bill?' says Jimmy, holding 'is ear.

Bill looked at 'im and then 'e steps to the ladder. 'I'm not going to talk to you any more, my lad,' 'e says. 'I'm going to tell the skipper.'

He went up slowly, and just as 'e reached the deck Jimmy started up and called 'im. Bill pretended not to 'ear, and the boy ran up on deck and follered 'im; and arter a little while they both came down again together.

'Did you wish to speak to me, my lad?' says Bill, 'olding 'is 'ead up.

'Yes,' says the boy, fiddling with 'is fingers; 'if you keep your ugly mouth shut, we'll go shares.'

'Ho!' says Bill, 'I thought you throwed it overboard!'

'I thought so, too, Bill,' says Jimmy, very softly, 'and when I came below ag'in I found it in my trousers pocket.'

'Where is it now?' says Bill.

'Never mind where it is,' says the boy; 'you couldn't get it if I was to tell you. It'll take me all my time to do it myself.'

'Where is it?' says Bill, ag'in. 'I'm goin' to take care of it. I won't trust you.'

'And I can't trust you,' says Jimmy.

'If you don't tell me where it is this minute,' says Bill, moving to the ladder ag'in, 'I'm off to tell the skipper. I want it in my 'ands, or at any rate my share of it. Why not share it out now?'

'Because I 'aven't got it,' says Jimmy, stamping 'is foot, 'that's why, and it's all your silly fault. Arter you came pawing through my pockets when you thought I was asleep I got frightened and 'id it.'

'Where?' says Bill.

'In the second mate's mattress,' says Jimmy. 'I was tidying up down aft and I found a 'ole in the underneath side of 'is mattress and I shoved it in there, and poked it in with a bit o' stick.'

'And 'ow are you going to get it?' says Bill, scratching 'is 'ead.

'That's wot I don't know, seeing that I'm not allowed aft now,' says Jimmy. 'One of us'll 'ave to make a dash for it when we get to London. And mind if there's any 'anky-panky on your part, Bill, I'll give the show away myself.'

The cook came down just then and we 'ad to leave off talking, and I could see that Bill was so pleased at finding that the money 'adn't been thrown overboard that 'e was losing sight o' the difficulty o' getting at it. In a day or two, 'owever, 'e see it as plain as me and Jimmy did, and, as time went by, he got desprit, and frightened us both by 'anging about aft every chance 'e got.

The companion-way faced the wheel, and there was about as much chance o' getting down there without being seen as there would be o' taking a man's false teeth out of 'is mouth without 'is knowing it. Jimmy went down one day while Bill was at the wheel to look for 'is knife, wot 'e thought e'd left down there, and 'e'd 'ardly got down afore Bill saw 'im come up ag'in, 'olding on to the top of a mop which the steward was using.

We couldn't figure it out nohow, and to think o' the second mate, a little man with a large fam'ly, who never 'ad a penny in 'is pocket, sleeping every night on a six 'undered pound mattress, sent us pretty near crazy. We used to talk it over whenever we got a chance, and Bill and Jimmy could scarcely be civil to each other. The boy said it was Bill's fault, and 'e said it was the boy's.

'The on'y thing I can see,' says the boy, one day, 'is for Bill to 'ave a touch of sunstroke as 'e's leaving the wheel one day, tumble 'ead-first down the companion-way, and injure 'isself so severely that 'e can't be moved. Then they'll put 'im in a cabin down aft, and p'raps I'll 'ave to go and nurse 'im. Anyway, *he'll* be down there.'

'It's a very good idea, Bill,' I says.

'Ho,' says Bill, looking at me as if 'e would eat me. 'Why don't you do it, then?'

'I'd sooner you did it, Bill,' says the boy; 'still, I don't mind which it is. Why not toss up for it?'

'Get away,' says Bill. 'Get away afore I do something you won't like, you bloodthirsty little murderer.'

'I've got a plan myself,' he says, in a low voice, after the boy 'ad 'opped off, 'and if I can't think of nothing better I'll try it, and mind, not a word to the boy.'

He didn't think o' nothing better, and one night just as we was making the Channel 'e tried 'is plan. He was in the second mate's watch, and by-and-by 'e leans over the wheel and says to 'im in a low voice, 'This is my last v'y'ge, sir.'

'Oh,' says the second mate, who was a man as didn't mind talking to a man before the mast. 'How's that?'

'I've got a berth ashore, sir,' says Bill, 'and I wanted to ask a favour, sir.'

The second mate growled and walked off a pace or two.

'I've never been so 'appy as I've been on this ship,' says Bill; 'none of us 'ave. We was saying so the other night, and everybody agreed as it was owing to you, sir, and your kindness to all of us.'

The second mate coughed, but Bill could see as 'e was a bit pleased.

'The feeling came over me,' says Bill, 'that when I leave the sea for good I'd like to 'ave something o' yours to remember you by, sir. And it seemed to me that if I 'ad your mattress I should think of you ev'ry night o' my life.'

'My *wot?*' says the second mate, staring at 'im.

'Your mattress, sir,' says Bill. 'If I might make so bold as to offer a pound for it, sir. I want something wot's been used by you, and I've got a fancy for that as a keepsake.'

The second mate shook 'is 'ead. 'I'm sorry, Bill,' 'e says gently, 'but I couldn't let it go at that.'

'I'd sooner pay thirty shillin's than not 'ave it, sir,' says Bill 'umbly.

'I gave a lot of money for that mattress,' says the mate,

ag'in. 'I forgit 'ow much, but a lot. You don't know 'ow valuable that mattress is.'

'I know it's a good one, sir, else you wouldn't 'ave it,' says Bill. 'Would a couple o' pounds buy it, sir?'

The second mate hum'd and ha'd, but Bill was afear'd to go any 'igher. So far as 'e could make out from Jimmy, the mattress was worth about eighteenpence—to anybody who wasn't pertiklar.

'I've slept on that mattress for years,' says the second mate, looking at 'im from the corner of 'is eye. 'I don't believe I could sleep on another. Still, to oblige you, Bill, you shall 'ave it at that if you don't want it till we go ashore?'

'Thankee, sir,' says Bill, 'ardly able to keep from dancing, 'and I'll 'and over the two pounds when we're paid off. I shall keep it all my life, sir, in memory of you and your kindness.'

'And mind you keep quiet about it,' says the second mate, who didn't want the skipper to know wot 'e'd been doing, 'because I don't want to be bothered by other men wanting to buy things as keepsakes.'

Bill promised 'im like a shot, and when 'e told me about it 'e was nearly crying with joy.

'And mind,' 'e says, 'I've bought that mattress, bought it as it stands, and it's got nothing to do with Jimmy. We'll each pay a pound and halve wot's in it.'

He persuaded me at last, but that boy watched us like a cat watching a couple of canaries, and I could see we should 'ave all we could do to deceive *'im*. He seemed more suspicious o' Bill than me, and 'e kep' worrying us nearly every day to know what we were going to do.

We beat about in the Channel with a strong 'ead-wind for four days, and then a tug picked us up and towed us to London.

The excitement of that last little bit was 'orrible. Fust of all we 'ad got to get the mattress, and then in some way we 'ad got to get rid o' Jimmy. Bill's idea was for me to take 'im ashore with me and tell 'im that Bill would join us arterwards, and then lose 'im; but I said that till I'd got my share I couldn't bear to lose sight o' Bill's honest face for 'alf a second.

And, besides, Jimmy wouldn't 'ave gone. All the way up the river 'e stuck to Bill, and kept asking 'im wot we were to do. 'E was 'alf crying, and so excited that Bill was afraid the other chaps would notice it.

We got to our berth in the East India Docks at last, and arter we were made fast we went below to 'ave a wash and change into our shore-going togs. Jimmy watched us all the time, and then 'e comes up to Bill biting 'is nails, and says,

'How's it to be done, Bill?'

'Hang about arter the rest 'ave gone ashore, and trust to luck,' says Bill, looking at me. 'We'll see 'ow the land lays when we draw our advance.'

We went down aft to draw ten shillings each to go ashore with. Bill and me got ours fust, and then the second mate, who 'ad tipped 'im the wink, followed us out unconcerned-like and 'anded Bill the mattress rolled up in a sack.

''Ere you are, Bill,' 'e says.

'Much obliged, sir,' says Bill, and 'is 'ands trembled so as 'e could 'ardly 'old it, and 'e made to go off afore Jimmy come on deck.

Then that fool of a mate kept us there while 'e made a little speech. Twice Bill made to go off, but 'e put 'is 'and on 'is arm and kept 'im there while 'e told 'im 'ow he'd always tried to be liked by the men, and 'ad generally succeeded, and in the middle of it up popped Master Jimmy.

He gave a start as he saw the bag, and 'is eyes opened wide, and then as we walked for'ard 'e put 'is arm through Bill's and called 'im all the names 'e could think of.

'You'd steal the milk out of a cat's saucer,' 'e says; 'but mind, you don't leave this ship till I've got my share.'

'I meant it for a pleasant surprise for you, Jimmy,' says Bill, trying to smile.

'I don't like your surprises, Bill, so I don't deceive you,' says the boy. 'Where are you going to open it?'

'I was thinking of opening it in my bunk,' says Bill. 'The

52

perlice might want to examine it if we took it through the dock. Come on, Jimmy, old man.'

'Yes; all right,' says the boy, nodding 'is 'ead at 'im. 'I'll stay up 'ere. You might forget yourself, Bill, if I trusted myself down there with you alone. You can throw my share up to me, and then you'll leave the ship afore I do. See?'

'Go to blazes,' says Bill; and then, seeing that the last chance 'ad gone, we went below, and 'e chucked the bundle in 'is bunk. There was only one chap down there, and arter spending best part o' ten minutes doing 'is hair 'e nodded to us and went off.

Half a minute later Bill cut open the mattress and began to search through the stuffing, while I struck matches and watched 'im. It wasn't a big mattress and there wasn't much stuffing, but we couldn't seem to see that money. Bill went all over it ag'in and ag'in, and then 'e stood up and looked at me and caught 'is breath painful.

'Do you think the mate found it?' 'e says, in a 'usky voice.

We went through it ag'in, and then Bill went half-way up the fo'c's'le ladder and called softly for Jimmy. He called three times, and then, with a sinking sensation in 'is stummick, 'e went up on deck and I follered 'im. The boy was nowhere to be seen. All we saw was the ship's cat 'aving a wash and brush-up afore going ashore, and the skipper standing aft talking to the owner.

We never saw that boy ag'in. He never turned up for 'is box, and 'e didn't show up to draw 'is pay. Everybody else was there, of course, and arter I'd got mine and come outside I see pore Bill with 'is back up ag'in a wall, staring 'ard at the second mate, who was looking at 'im with a kind smile, and asking 'im 'ow he'd slept. The last thing I saw of Bill, the pore chap 'ad got 'is 'ands in 'is trousers pockets, and was trying 'is hardest to smile back.

A Tiger's Skin

The travelling sign-painter who was repainting the sign of the 'Cauliflower' was enjoying a well-earned respite from his labours. On the old table under the shade of the elms mammoth sandwiches and a large slice of cheese waited in an untied handkerchief until such time as his thirst should be satisfied. At the other side of the table the oldest man in Claybury, drawing gently at a long clay pipe, turned a dim and regretful eye up at the old signboard.

I've drunk my beer under it for pretty near seventy years, he said, with a sigh. It's a pity it couldn't ha' lasted my time.

The painter, slowly pushing a wedge of sandwich into his mouth, regarded him indulgently.

It's all through two young gentlemen as was passing through 'ere a month or two ago, continued the old man; they told Smith, the landlord, they'd been looking all over the place for the 'Cauliflower', and when Smith showed 'em the sign they said they thought it was the 'George the Fourth', and a very good likeness, too.

The painter laughed and took another look at the old sign; then, with the nervousness of the true artist, he took a look at his own. One or two shadows—

He flung his legs over the bench and took up his brushes. In ten minutes the most fervent loyalist would have looked in vain for any resemblance, and with a sigh at the pitfalls which beset the artist he returned to his interrupted meal and hailed the house for more beer.

There's nobody could mistake your sign for anything but a cauliflower, said the old man; it looks good enough to eat.

The painter smiled and pushed his mug across the table.

He was a tender-hearted man, and once—when painting the sign of the 'Sir Wilfrid Lawson'—knew himself what it was to lack beer. He began to discourse on art, and spoke somewhat disparagingly of the cauliflower as a subject. With a shake of his head he spoke of the possibilities of a spotted cow or a blue lion.

Talking of lions, said the ancient musingly, I s'pose as you never 'eard tell of the Claybury tiger? It was afore your time in these parts, I expect.

The painter admitted his ignorance, and, finding that the allusion had no reference to an inn, pulled out his pipe and prepared to listen.

It's a while ago now, said the old man slowly, and the circus the tiger belonged to was going through Claybury to get to Wickham, when, just as they was passing Gill's farm, a steam-ingine they 'ad to draw some o' the vans broke down, and they 'ad to stop while the blacksmith mended it. That being so, they put up a big tent and 'ad the circus 'ere.

I was one o' them as went, and I must say it was worth the money, though Henery Walker was disappointed at the man who put 'is 'ead in the lion's mouth. He said that the man frightened the lion first, before 'e did it.

It was a great night for Claybury, and for about a week nothing else was talked of. All the children was playing at being lions and tigers and such-like, and young Roberts pretty near broke 'is back trying to see if he could ride horseback standing up.

It was about two weeks after the circus 'ad gone when a strange thing 'appened: the big tiger broke loose. Bill Chambers brought the news first, 'aving read it in the newspaper while 'e was 'aving his tea. He brought out the paper and showed us, and soon after we 'eard all sorts o' tales of its doings.

At first we thought the tiger was a long way off, and we was rather amused at it. Frederick Scott laughed 'imself silly a'most up 'ere one night thinking 'ow surprised a man would be if 'e come 'ome one night and found the tiger sitting in his armchair eating the baby. It didn't seem much of a laughing matter to me, and I said so; none of us liked it, and even Sam Jones, as 'ad got twins for the second time, said 'Shame!' But Frederick Scott was a man as would laugh at anything.

When we 'eard that the tiger 'ad been seen within three miles of Claybury things began to look serious, and Peter Gubbins said that something ought to be done, but before we could think of anything to do something 'appened.

We was sitting up 'ere one evening 'aving a mug o' beer and a pipe—same as I might be now if I'd got any baccy left —and talking about it, when we 'eard a shout and saw a ragged-looking tramp running toward us as 'ard as he could run. Every now and then he'd look over 'is shoulder and give a shout, and then run 'arder than afore.

'It's the *tiger!*' ses Bill Chambers, and afore you could wink a'most he was inside the house, 'aving first upset Smith and a pot o' beer in the doorway.

Before he could get up, Smith 'ad to wait till we was all in. His langwidge was awful for a man as 'ad a license to lose, and everybody shouting 'Tiger!' as they trod on 'im didn't ease 'is mind. He was inside a'most as soon as the last man, though, and in a flash he 'ad the door bolted just as the tramp flung 'imself agin it, all out of breath and sobbing 'is hardest to be let in.

'Open the door,' he ses, banging on it.

'Go away,' ses Smith.

'It's the tiger,' screams the tramp; 'open the door.'

'You go away,' ses Smith, 'you're attracting it to my place; run up the road and draw it off.'

Just at that moment John Biggs, the blacksmith, came in from the taproom, and as soon as he 'eard wot was the matter 'e took down Smith's gun from behind the bar and said he was going out to look after the wimmen and children.

'Open the door,' he ses.

He was trying to get out and the tramp outside was trying to get in, but Smith held on to that door like a Briton. Then John Biggs lost 'is temper, and he ups with the gun—Smith's own gun, mind you—and fetches 'im a bang over the 'ead

with it. Smith fell down at once, and afore we could 'elp ourselves the door was open, the tramp was inside, and John
Biggs was running up the road, shouting 'is hardest.

We 'ad the door closed afore you could wink a'most, and
then, while the tramp lay in a corner 'aving brandy, Mrs
Smith got a bowl of water and a sponge and knelt down bath-
ing 'er husband's 'ead with it.

'Did you see the tiger?' ses Bill Chambers.

'See it?' ses the tramp, with a shiver. 'Oh, Lord!'

He made signs for more brandy, and Henery Walker, wot
was acting as landlord, without being asked, gave it to 'im.

'It chased me for over a mile,' ses the tramp; 'my 'eart's
breaking.'

He gave a groan and fainted right off. A terrible faint it
was, too, and for some time we thought 'e'd never come round
agin. First they poured brandy down 'is throat, then gin, and
then beer, and still 'e didn't come round, but lay quiet with
'is eyes closed and a horrible smile on 'is face.

He come round at last, and with nothing stronger than
water, which Mrs Smith kept pouring into 'is mouth. First
thing we noticed was that the smile went, then 'is eyes opened,
and suddenly 'e sat up with a shiver and gave such a dreadful
scream that we thought at first the tiger was on top of us.

Then 'e told us 'ow he was sitting washing 'is shirt in a
ditch, when he 'eard a snuffling noise and saw the 'ead of a
big tiger sticking through the hedge the other side. He left 'is
shirt and ran, and 'e said that, fortunately, the tiger stopped
to tear the shirt to pieces, else 'is last hour would 'ave arrived.

When 'e 'ad finished Smith went upstairs and looked out
of the bedroom winders, but 'e couldn't see any signs of the
tiger, and 'e said no doubt it 'ad gone down to the village to
see wot it could pick up, or p'raps it 'ad eaten John Biggs.

However that might be, nobody cared to go outside to see,
and after it got dark we liked going 'ome less than ever.

Up to ten o'clock we did very well, and then Smith began
to talk about 'is license. He said it was all rubbish being afraid
to go 'ome, and that, at any rate, the tiger couldn't eat more

than one of us, and while 'e was doing that there was the chance for the others to get 'ome safe. Two or three of 'em took a dislike to Smith that night and told 'im so.

The end of it was we all slept in the taproom that night. It seemed strange at first, but anything was better than going 'ome in the dark, and we all slept till about four next morning, when we woke up and found the tramp 'ad gone and left the front door standing wide open.

We took a careful look-out, and by-and-by first one started off and then another to see whether their wives and children 'ad been eaten or not. Not a soul 'ad been touched, but the wimmen and children was that scared there was no doing anything with 'em. None o' the children would go to school, and they sat at 'ome all day with the front winder blocked up with a mattress to keep the tiger out.

Nobody liked going to work, but it 'ad to be done, and as Farmer Gill said that tigers went to sleep all day and only came out toward evening we was a bit comforted. Not a soul went up to the 'Cauliflower' that evening for fear of coming 'ome in the dark, but as nothing 'appened that night we began to 'ope as the tiger 'ad travelled further on.

Bob Pretty laughed at the whole thing and said 'e didn't believe there was a tiger; but nobody minded wot 'e said, Bob Pretty being, as I've often told people, the black sheep o' Claybury, wot with poaching and, wot was worse, 'is artfulness.

But the very next morning something 'appened that made Bob Pretty look silly and wish 'e 'adn't talked quite so fast; for at five o'clock Frederick Scott, going down to feed 'is hins, found as the tiger 'ad been there afore 'im and 'ad eaten no less than seven of 'em. The side of the hin-'ouse was all broke in, there was a few feathers lying on the ground, and two little chicks smashed and dead beside 'em.

The way Frederick Scott went on about it you'd 'ardly believe. He said that Govinment 'ud 'ave to make it up to 'im, and instead o' going to work 'e put the two little chicks and the feathers into a pudding basin and walked to Cudford, four miles off, where they 'ad a policeman.

He saw the policeman, William White by name, standing at the back door of the 'Fox and Hounds' public-house, throwing a 'andful o' corn to the landlord's fowls, and the first thing Mr White ses was, 'It's off my beat,' he ses.

'But you might do it in your spare time, Mr White,' ses Frederick Scott. 'It's very likely that the tiger'll come back to my hin-'ouse for the rest of 'em, and he'd be very surprised if 'e popped 'is 'ead in and see you there waiting for 'im.'

'He'd 'ave reason to be,' ses Policeman White, staring at 'im.

'Think of the praise you'd get,' said Frederick Scott, coaxing like.

'Look 'ere,' ses Policeman White, 'if you don't take yourself and that pudding basin off pretty quick, you'll come along o' me, d'ye see? You've been drinking and you're in a excited state.'

He gave Frederick Scott a push and follered 'im along the road, and every time Frederick stopped to ask 'im wot 'e was doing of 'e gave 'im another push to show 'im.

Frederick Scott told us all about it that evening, and some of the bravest of us went up to the 'Cauliflower' to talk over wot was to be done, though we took care to get 'ome while it was quite light. That night Peter Gubbins's two pigs went. They were two o' the likeliest pigs I ever seed, and all Peter Gubbins could do was to sit up in bed shivering and listening to their squeals as the tiger dragged 'em off. Pretty near all Claybury was round that sty next morning looking at the broken fence. Some of them looked for the tiger's footmarks, but it was dry weather and they couldn't see any. Nobody knew whose turn it would be next, and the most sensible man there, Sam Jones, went straight off 'ome and killed his pig afore 'e went to work.

Nobody knew what to do; Farmer Hall said as it was a soldier's job, and 'e drove over to Wickham to tell the police so, but nothing came of it, and that night at ten minutes to twelve Bill Chambers's pig went. It was one o' the biggest pigs ever raised in Claybury, but the tiger got it off as easy as possible. Bill 'ad the bravery to look out of the winder when 'e 'eard the pig squeal, but there was such a awful snarling noise that 'e daresn't move 'and or foot.

Dicky Weed's idea was for people with pigs and such-like to keep 'em in the house of a night, but Peter Gubbins and Bill Chambers both pointed out that the tiger could break a back door with one blow of 'is paw, and that if 'e got inside he might take something else instead o' pig. And they said that it was no worse for other people to lose pigs than wot it was for them.

The odd thing about it was that all this time nobody 'ad ever seen the tiger except the tramp, and people sent their children back to school agin and felt safe going about in the daytime till little Charlie Gubbins came running 'ome crying and saying that 'e'd seen it. Next morning a lot more children see it and was afraid to go to school, and people began to wonder wot 'ud happen when all the pigs and poultry was eaten.

Then Henery Walker see it. We was sitting inside 'ere with scythes, and pitchforks, and such-like things handy, when we see 'im come in without 'is hat. His eyes were staring and 'is hair was all rumpled. He called for a pot o' ale and drank it nearly off, and then 'e sat gasping and 'olding the mug be- tween 'is legs and shaking 'is 'ead at the floor till everybody 'ad left off talking to look at 'im.

'Wot's the matter, Henery?' ses one of 'em.

'Don't ask me,' ses Henery Walker, with a shiver.

'You don't mean to say as 'ow you've seen the tiger?' ses Bill Chambers.

Henery Walker didn't answer 'im. He got up and walked back'ards and for'ards, still with that frightened look in 'is eyes, and once or twice 'e give such a terrible start that 'e frightened us 'arf out of our wits. Then Bill Chambers took and forced 'im into a chair and give 'im two o' gin and patted 'im on the back, and at last Henery Walker got 'is senses back agin and told us 'ow the tiger 'ad chased 'im all round and round the trees in Plashett's Wood until 'e managed to climb up a tree and escape it. He said the tiger 'ad kept 'im there for over an hour, and then suddenly turned round and bolted off up the road to Wickham.

It was a merciful escape, and everybody said so except Sam Jones, and 'e asked so many questions that at last Henery Walker asked 'im outright if 'e disbelieved 'is word.

'It's all right, Sam,' ses Bob Pretty, as 'ad come in just after Henery Walker. 'I see 'im with the tiger after 'im.'

'Wot?' ses Henery, staring at him.

'I see it all, Henery,' ses Bob Pretty, 'and I see your pluck. It was all you could do to make up your mind to run from it. I believe if you'd 'ad a fork in your 'and you'd 'ave made a fight for it.'

Everybody said 'Bravo!' but Henery Walker didn't seem to like it at all. He sat still, looking at Bob Pretty, and at last 'e ses, 'Where was you?' 'e ses.

'Up another tree, Henery, where you couldn't see me,' ses Bob Pretty, smiling at 'im.

Henery Walker, wot was drinking some beer, choked a bit, and then 'e put the mug down and went straight off 'ome without saying a word to anybody. I knew 'e didn't like Bob Pretty, but I couldn't see why 'e should be cross about 'is speaking up for 'im as 'e had done, but Bob said as it was 'is modesty, and 'e thought more of 'im for it.

After that things got worse than ever; the wimmen and children stayed indoors and kept the doors shut, and the men never knew when they went out to work whether they'd come 'ome agin. They used to kiss their children afore they went out of a morning, and their wives too, some of 'em; even men who'd been married for years did. And several more of 'em see the tiger while they was at work, and came running 'ome to tell about it.

The tiger 'ad been making free with Claybury pigs and such-like for pretty near a week, and nothing 'ad been done to try and catch it, and wot made Claybury men madder than anything else was folks at Wickham saying it was all a mistake, and the tiger 'adn't escaped at all. Even parson, who'd been away for a holiday, said so, and Henery Walker told 'is wife that if she ever set foot inside the church agin 'e'd ask 'is old mother to come and live with 'em.

It was all very well for parson to talk, but the very night he come back Henery Walker's pig went, and at the same time George Kettle lost five or six ducks.

He was a quiet man, was George, but when 'is temper was up 'e didn't care for anything. Afore he came to Claybury 'e 'ad been in the Militia, and that evening at the 'Cauliflower' 'e turned up with a gun over 'is shoulder and made a speech, and asked who was game to go with 'im and hunt the tiger. Bill Chambers, who was still grieving after 'is pig, said 'e would, then another man offered, until at last there was seventeen of 'em. Some of 'em 'ad scythes and some pitchforks, and one or two of 'em guns, and it was one o' the finest sights I ever seed when George Kettle stood 'em in rows of four and marched 'em off.

They went straight up the road, then across Farmer Gill's fields to get to Plashett's Wood, where they thought the tiger 'ud most likely be, and the nearer they got to the wood the slower they walked. The sun 'ad just gone down and the wood looked very quiet and dark, but John Biggs, the black-smith, and George Kettle walked in first and the others fol-lered, keeping so close together that Sam Jones 'ad a few words over his shoulder with Bill Chambers about the way 'e was carrying 'is pitchfork.

Every now and then somebody 'ud say, '*Wot's that?*' and they'd all stop and crowd together and think the time 'ad come, but it 'adn't, and then they'd go on agin, trembling, until they'd walked all round the wood without seeing any-thing but one or two rabbits. John Biggs and George Kettle wanted for to stay there till it was dark, but the others wouldn't 'ear of it for fear of frightening their wives, and just as it was getting dark they all come tramp, tramp, back to the 'Cauliflower' agin.

Smith stood 'em 'arf a pint apiece, and they was all outside 'ere fancying theirselves a bit for wot they'd done when we see old man Parsley coming along on two sticks as fast as 'e could come.

62

'Are you brave lads a-looking for the tiger?' he asks.

'Yes,' ses John Biggs.

'Then 'urry up, for the sake of mercy,' ses old Mr Parsley, putting 'is 'and on the table and going off into a fit of coughing; 'it's just gone into Bob Pretty's cottage. I was passing and saw it.'

George Kettle snatches up 'is gun and shouts out to 'is men to come along. Some of 'em was for 'anging back at first, some because they didn't like the tiger and some because they didn't like Bob Pretty, but John Biggs drove 'em in front of 'im like a flock o' sheep and then they gave a cheer and ran after George Kettle, full pelt up the road.

A few wimmen and children was at their doors as they passed, but they took fright and went indoors screaming. There was a lamp in Bob Pretty's front room, but the door was closed and the 'ouse was silent as the grave.

George Kettle and the men with the guns went first, then came the pitchforks, and last of all the scythes. Just as George Kettle put 'is 'and on the door he 'eard something moving inside, and the next moment the door opened and there stood Bob Pretty.

'What the dickens!' 'e ses, starting back as 'e see the guns and pitchforks pointing at 'im.

''Ave you killed it, Bob?' ses George Kettle.

'Killed *wot?*' ses Bob Pretty. 'Be careful o' them guns. Take your fingers off the triggers.'

'The tiger's in your 'ouse, Bob,' ses George Kettle, in a whisper. ' 'Ave you on'y just come in?'

'Look 'ere,' ses Bob Pretty. 'I don't want any o' your games. You go and play 'em somewhere else.'

'It ain't a game,' ses John Biggs; 'the tiger's in your 'ouse and we're going to kill it. Now, then, lads.'

They all went in in a 'eap, pushing Bob Pretty in front of 'em, till the room was full. Only one man with a scythe got in, and they wouldn't 'ave let 'im in if they'd known. It a'most made 'em forget the tiger for the time.

George Kettle opened the door wot led into the kitchen,

63

and then 'e sprang back with such a shout that the man with the scythe tried to escape, taking Henery Walker along with 'im. George Kettle tried to speak, but couldn't. All 'e could do was to point with 'is finger at Bob Pretty's kitchen—*and Bob Pretty's kitchen was for all the world like a pork-butcher's shop*. There was joints o' pork 'anging from the ceiling, two brine tubs as full as they could be, and quite a string of fowls and ducks all ready for market.

'Wot d'ye mean by coming into my 'ouse?' ses Bob Pretty, blustering. 'If you don't clear out pretty quick, I'll make you.'

Nobody answered 'im; they was all examining 'ands o' pork and fowls and such-like.

'There's the tiger,' ses Henery Walker, pointing at Bob Pretty; 'that's wot old man Parsley meant.'

'Somebody go and fetch Policeman White,' ses a voice.

'I wish they would,' ses Bob Pretty. 'I'll 'ave the law on you all for breaking into my 'ouse like this, see if I don't.'

'Where'd you get all this pork from?' ses the blacksmith.

'And them ducks and hins?' ses George Kettle.

'That's my bisness,' ses Bob Pretty, staring 'em full in the face. 'I just 'ad a excellent opportunity offered me of going into the pork and poultry line and I took it. Now, all them as doesn't want to buy any pork or fowls go out o' my house.'

'You're a thief, Bob Pretty!' says Henery Walker. 'You stole it all.'

'Take care wot you're saying, Henery,' ses Bob Pretty, 'else I'll make you prove your words.'

'You stole my pig,' ses Herbert Smith.

'Oh, 'ave I?' ses Bob, reaching down a 'and o' pork. 'Is that your pig?' he ses.

'It's just about the size o' my pore pig,' ses Herbert Smith.

'Very usual size, I call it,' ses Bob Pretty; 'and them ducks and hins very usual-looking hins and ducks, I call 'em, except that they don't grow 'em so fat in these parts. It's a

64

fine thing when a man's doing a honest bisness to 'ave these charges brought agin 'im. Dis'eartening, I call it. I don't mind telling you that the tiger got in at my back winder the other night and took 'arf a pound o' sausage, but you don't 'ear me complaining and going about calling other people thieves.'

'Tiger be hanged,' ses Henery Walker, who was almost certain that a loin o' pork on the table was off 'is pig; 'you're the only tiger in these parts.'

'Why, Henery,' ses Bob Pretty, 'wot are you a-thinkin' of? Where's your memory? Why, it's on'y two or three days ago you see it and 'ad to get up a tree out of its way.'

He smiled and shook 'is 'ead at 'im, but Henery Walker on'y kept opening and shutting 'is mouth, and at last 'e went outside without saying a word.

'And Sam Jones see it too,' ses Bob Pretty; 'didn't you, Sam?'

Sam didn't answer 'im.

'And Charlie Hall and Jack Minns and a lot more,' ses Bob; 'besides, I see it myself. I can believe my own eyes, I s'pose?'

'We'll have the law on you,' ses Sam Jones.

'As *you* like,' ses Bob Pretty; 'but I tell you plain, I've got all the bills for this properly made out, upstairs. And there's pretty near a dozen of you as'll 'ave to go in the box and swear as you saw the tiger. Now, can I sell any of you a bit o' pork afore you go? It's delicious eating, and as soon as you taste it you'll know it wasn't grown in Claybury. Or a pair o' ducks wot 'ave come from two 'undered miles off, and yet look as fresh as if they was on'y killed last night.'

George Kettle, whose ducks 'ad gone the night afore, went into the front room and walked up and down fighting for 'is breath, but it was all no good; nobody ever got the better o' Bob Pretty. None of 'em could swear to their property, and even when it became known a month later that Bob Pretty and the tramp knew each other, nothing was done. But nobody ever 'eard any more of the tiger from that day to this.

The Money Box

Sailormen are not good 'ands at saving money as a rule, said the night watchman, as he wistfully toyed with a bad shilling on his watch-chain, though to 'ear 'em talk of saving when they're at sea and there isn't a pub within a thousand miles of 'em, you might think different.

It ain't for the want of trying either with some of 'em, and I've known men do all sorts o' things as soon as they was paid off, with a view to saving. I knew one man as used to keep all but a shilling or two in a belt next to 'is skin so that he couldn't get at it easy, but it was all no good. He was always running short in the most inconvenient places. I've seen 'im wriggle for five minutes right off, with a tramcar conductor standing over 'im and the other people in the tram reading their papers with one eye and watching him with the other.

Ginger Dick and Peter Russet—two men I've spoke of to you afore—tried to save their money once. They'd got so sick and tired of spending it all in p'r'aps a week or ten days arter coming ashore, and 'aving to go to sea agin sooner than they'd intended, that they determined some way or other to 'ave things different.

They was homeward bound on a steamer from Melbourne when they made their minds up; and Isaac Lunn, the oldest fireman aboard—a very steady old teetotaller—gave them a lot of good advice about it. They all wanted to rejoin the ship when she sailed agin, and 'e offered to take a room ashore with them and mind their money, giving 'em what 'e called a moderate amount each day.

They would ha' laughed at any other man, but they knew that old Isaac was as honest as could be and that their money would be safe with 'im, and at last, after a lot of palaver, they wrote out a paper saying as they were willing for 'im to 'ave their money and give it to 'em bit by bit, till they went to sea agin.

Anybody but Ginger Dick and Peter Russet or a fool would ha' known better than to do such a thing, but old Isaac 'ad got such a oily tongue and seemed so fair-minded about what 'e called moderate drinking that they never thought wot they was letting themselves in for, and when they took their pay—close on sixteen pounds each—they put the odd change in their pockets and 'anded the rest over to him.

The first day they was as pleased as Punch. Old Isaac got a nice, respectable bedroom for them all, and arter they'd 'ad a few drinks they humoured 'im by 'aving a nice 'ot cup o' tea, and then goin' off with 'im to see a magic-lantern performance.

It was called 'The Drunkard's Downfall', and it begun with a young man going into a nice-looking pub and being served by a nice-looking barmaid with a glass of ale. Then it got on to 'arf pints and pints in the next picture, and arter Ginger 'ad seen the lost young man put away six pints in about 'arf a minute, 'e got such a raging thirst on 'im that 'e couldn't sit still, and 'e whispered to Peter Russet to go out with 'im.

'You'll lose the best of it if you go now,' ses old Isaac, in a whisper; 'in the next picture there's little frogs and devils sitting on the edge of the pot as 'e goes to drink.'

Ginger Dick got up and nodded to Peter.

'Arter that 'e kills 'is mother with a razor,' ses old Isaac, pleading with 'im and 'olding on to 'is coat.

Ginger Dick sat down agin, and when the murder was over 'e said it made 'im feel faint, and 'im and Peter Russet went out for a breath of fresh air. They 'ad three at the first place, and then they moved on to another and forgot all about Isaac and the dissolving views until ten o'clock, when Ginger, who 'ad been very liberal to some friends 'e'd made in a pub, found 'e'd spent 'is last penny.

'This comes o' listening to a parcel o' teetotallers,' 'e ses, very cross, when 'e found that Peter 'ad spent all 'is money too. 'Here we are just beginning the evening and not a farthing in our pockets.'

They went off 'ome in a very bad temper. Old Isaac was asleep in 'is bed, and when they woke 'im up and said that they was going to take charge of their money themselves 'e kept dropping off to sleep agin and snoring that 'ard they could scarcely hear themselves speak. Then Peter tipped Ginger a wink and pointed to Isaac's trousers, which were 'anging over the foot of the bed.

Ginger Dick smiled and took 'em up softly, and Peter Russet smiled too; but 'e wasn't best pleased to see old Isaac a'-smiling in 'is sleep, as though 'e was 'aving amusing dreams. All Ginger found was a ha'penny, a bunch o' keys, and a cough lozenge. In the coat and waistcoat 'e found a few tracks folded up, a broken pen-knife, a ball of string, and some other rubbish. Then 'e set down on the foot o' the bed and made eyes over at Peter.

'Wake 'im up agin,' ses Peter, in a temper.

Ginger Dick got up and, leaning over the bed, took old Isaac by the shoulders and shook 'im as if 'e'd been a bottle o' medicine.

'Time to get up, lads?' ses old Isaac, putting one leg out o' bed.

'No, it ain't,' ses Ginger, very rough; 'we ain't been to bed yet. We want our money back.'

Isaac drew 'is leg back into bed agin. 'Goo' night,' he ses, and fell fast asleep.

'He's shamming, that's wot 'e is,' ses Peter Russet. 'Let's look for it. It must be in the room somewhere.'

They turned the room upside down pretty near, and then Ginger Dick struck a match and looked up the chimney, but all 'e found was that it 'adn't been swept for about twenty years, and wot with temper and soot 'e looked so frightful that Peter was arf afraid of 'im.

'I've 'ad enough of this,' ses Ginger, running up to the bed and 'olding his sooty fist under old Isaac's nose. 'Now, then, where's that money? If you don't give us our money, our 'ard-earned money, inside o' two minutes, I'll break every bone in your body.'

'This is wot comes o' trying to do you a favour, Ginger,' ses the old man, reproachfully.

'Don't talk to me,' ses Ginger, ''cos I won't have it. Come on; where is it?'

Old Isaac looked at 'im, and then he gave a sigh and got up and put on 'is boots and 'is trousers.

'I thought I should 'ave a little trouble with you,' he ses, slowly, 'but I was prepared for that.'

'You'll 'ave more if you don't hurry up,' ses Ginger, glaring at 'im.

'We don't want to 'urt you, Isaac,' ses Peter Russet, 'we on'y want our money.'

'I know that,' ses Isaac; 'you keep still, Peter, and see fair-play, and I'll knock you silly arterwards.'

He pushed some o' the things into a corner and then 'e spat on 'is 'ands, and began to prance up and down, and duck his 'ead about and hit the air in a way that surprised 'em.

'I ain't hit a man for five years,' 'e ses, still dancing up and down—'fighting's sinful except in a good cause—but afore I got a new 'art, Ginger, I'd lick three men like you afore breakfast, just to git up a appetite.'

'Look 'ere,' ses Ginger; 'you're an old man and I don't want to 'urt you; tell us where our money is, our 'ard-earned money, and I won't lay a finger on you.'

'I'm taking care of it for you,' ses the old man.

Ginger Dick gave a howl and rushed at him, and the next moment Isaac's fist shot out and gave 'im a drive that sent 'im spinning across the room until 'e fell in a heap in the fire-place. It was like a kick from a 'orse, and Peter looked very serious as 'e picked 'im up and dusted him down.

'You should keep your eye on 'is fist,' he ses, sharply.

It was a silly thing to say, seeing that that was just wot 'ad 'appened, and Ginger told 'im wot 'e'd do for 'im when 'e'd finished with Isaac. He went at the old man agin, but 'e never 'ad a chance, and in about three minutes 'e was very glad to let Peter 'elp 'im into bed.

'It's your turn to fight him now, Peter,' he ses. 'Just move this piller so as I can see.'

'Come on, lad,' ses the old man.

Peter shook 'is 'ead. 'I have no wish to 'urt you, Isaac,' he ses, kindly; 'excitement like fighting is dangerous for an old man. Give us our money and we'll say no more about it.'

'No, my lads,' ses Isaac. 'I've undertook to take charge o' this money and I'm going to do it; and I 'ope that when we all sign on aboard the *Planet* there'll be a matter o' twelve pounds each left. Now, I don't want to be 'arsh with you, but I'm going back to bed, and if I 'ave to get up and dress agin you'll wish yourselves dead.'

He went back to bed agin, and Peter, taking no notice of Ginger Dick, who kept calling 'im a coward, got into bed alongside of Ginger and fell fast asleep.

They all 'ad breakfast in a coffee-shop next morning, and arter it was over Ginger, who 'adn't spoke a word till then, said that 'e and Peter Russet wanted a little money to go on with. He said they preferred to get their meals alone, as Isaac's face took their appetite away.

'Very good,' ses the old man. 'I don't want to force my company on nobody,' and after thinking 'ard for a minute or two he put 'is 'and in 'is trouser-pocket and gave them eighteen-pence each.

'Wot's this for?' ses Ginger, staring at the money. 'Matches?'

'That's your day's allowance,' ses Isaac, 'and it's plenty. There's ninepence for your dinner, fourpence for your tea, and twopence for a crust o' bread and cheese for supper. And if you must go and drown yourselves in beer, that leaves threepence each to go and do it with.'

Ginger tried to speak to 'im, but 'is feelings was too much for 'im, and 'e couldn't. Then Peter Russet swallered something 'e was going to say and asked old Isaac very perlite to make it a quid for '*im* because he was going down to Colchester to see 'is mother, and 'e didn't want to go empty-'anded.

'You're a good son, Peter,' ses old Isaac, 'and I wish there was more like you. I'll come down with you, if you like; I've got nothing to do.'

Peter said it was very kind of 'im, but 'e'd sooner go alone, owing to his mother being very shy afore strangers.

'Well, I'll come down to the station and take a ticket for you,' ses Isaac.

Then Peter lost 'is temper altogether, and banged 'is fist on the table and smashed 'arf the crockery. He asked Isaac whether 'e thought 'im and Ginger Dick was a couple o' children, and 'e said if 'e didn't give 'em all their money right away 'e'd give 'im in charge to the first policeman they met.

'I'm afraid you didn't intend for to go and see your mother, Peter,' ses the old man.

'Look 'ere,' ses Peter, 'are you going to give us that money?'

'Not if you went down on your bended knees,' ses the old man.

'Very good,' ses Peter, getting up and walking outside; 'then come along o' me to find a policeman.'

'I'm agreeable,' ses Isaac, 'but I've got the paper you signed.'

Peter said 'e didn't care twopence if 'e'd got fifty papers, and they walked along looking for a policeman, which was a very unusual thing for them to do.

'I 'ope for your sakes it won't be the same policeman that you and Ginger Dick set on in Gun Alley the night afore you shipped on the *Planet*,' ses Isaac, pursing up 'is lips.

'"Tain't likely to be,' ses Peter, beginning to wish 'e 'adn't been so free with 'is tongue.

'Still, if I tell 'im, I dessay he'll soon find 'im,' ses Isaac; 'there's one coming along now, Peter; shall I stop 'im?'

Peter Russet looked at 'im and then he looked at Ginger, and they walked by grinding their teeth. They stuck to Isaac all day, trying to get their money out of 'im, and the names they called 'im was a surprise even to themselves. And at night they turned the room topsy-turvy agin looking for their money, and 'ad more unpleasantness when they wanted Isaac to get up and let 'em search the bed.

They 'ad breakfast together agin next morning, and Ginger tried another tack. He spoke quite nice to Isaac, and 'ad three large cups o' tea to show 'im 'ow 'e was beginning to like it, and when the old man gave 'em their eighteenpences 'e smiled and said 'e'd like a few shillings extra that day.

'It'll be all right, Isaac,' he ses. 'I wouldn't 'ave a drink if you asked me to. Don't seem to care for it now. I was saying so to you on'y last night, wasn't I, Peter?'

'You was,' ses Peter; 'so was I.'

'Then I've done you good, Ginger,' ses Isaac, clapping 'im on the back.

'You 'ave,' ses Ginger, speaking between his teeth, 'and I thank you for it. I don't want drink; but I thought of going to a music-'all this evening.'

'Going to a *wot?*' ses old Isaac, drawing 'imself up and looking very shocked.

'A music-'all,' ses Ginger, trying to keep 'is temper.

'A music-'all?' ses Isaac; 'why, it's worse than a pub, Ginger. I should be a very poor friend o' yours if I let you go there—I couldn't think of it.'

'Wot's it got to do with you, you grey-whiskered serpent?' screams Ginger, arf mad with rage. 'Why don't you leave us alone? Why don't you mind your own business? It's our money.'

Isaac tried to talk to 'im, but 'e wouldn't listen, and he made such a fuss that at last the coffee-shop keeper told 'im to go outside. Peter follered 'im out, and being very upset they went and spent their day's allowance in the first hour, and then they walked about the streets quarrelling as to the death they'd like old Isaac to 'ave when 'is time came.

They went back to their lodgings at dinner-time; but there was no sign of the old man, and, being 'ungry and thirsty, they took all their spare clothes to a pawnbroker, and got enough money to go on with. Just to show their independence they went to two music-'alls, and with a sort of an idea that they was doing Isaac a bad turn they spent every farthing afore they got 'ome, and sat up in bed telling 'im about the spree they'd 'ad.

At five o'clock in the morning Peter woke up and saw, to 'is surprise, that Ginger Dick was dressed and carefully folding up old Isaac's clothes. At first 'e thought that Ginger 'ad gone mad, taking care of the old man's things like that, but afore 'e could speak Ginger noticed that 'e was awake, and stepped over to 'im and whispered to 'im to dress without making a noise. Peter did as 'e was told, and, more puzzled than ever, saw Ginger make up all the old man's clothes in a bundle and creep out of the room on tiptoe.

'Going to 'ide 'is clothes?' 'e ses.

'Yes,' ses Ginger, leading the way downstairs; 'in a pawn-shop. We'll make the old man pay for today's amusements.'

Then Peter saw the joke, and 'e begun to laugh so 'ard that Ginger 'ad to threaten to knock 'is 'ead off to quiet 'im. Ginger laughed 'imself when they got outside, and at last, arter walking about till the shops opened, they got into a pawn-broker's and put old Isaac's clothes up for fifteen shillings.

First thing they did was to 'ave a good breakfast, and after that they came out smiling all over and began to spend a 'appy day. Ginger was in tip-top spirits, and so was Peter, and the idea that old Isaac was in bed while they was drinking 'is clothes pleased them more than anything. Twice that evening policemen spoke to Ginger for dancing on the pavement, and by the time the money was spent it took Peter all 'is time to get 'im 'ome.

Old Isaac was in bed when they got there, and the temper 'e was in was shocking; but Ginger sat on 'is bed and smiled at 'im as if 'e was saying compliments to 'im.

'Where's my clothes?' ses the old man, shaking 'is fist at the two of 'em.

Ginger smiled at 'im, then 'e shut 'is eyes and dropped off to sleep.

'Where's my clothes?' ses Isaac, turning to Peter.

'Closhe?' says Peter, staring at 'im.

'Where are they?' ses Isaac.

It was a long time afore Peter could understand wot 'e meant, but as soon as 'e did 'e started to look for 'em. Drink takes people in different ways, and the way it always took Peter was to make 'im one o' the most obliging men that ever lived. 'E spent arf the night crawling about on all fours looking for the clothes, and four or five times old Isaac woke up from dreams of earthquakes to find Peter 'ad got jammed under 'is bed, and was wondering what 'ad 'appened to 'im.

None of 'em was in the best o' tempers when they woke up next morning, and Ginger 'ad 'ardly got 'is eyes open before Isaac was asking 'im about 'is clothes agin.

'Don't bother me about your clothes,' ses Ginger; 'talk about something else for a change.'

'Where are they?' ses Isaac, sitting on the edge of 'is bed.

Ginger yawned and felt in 'is waistcoat pocket—for neither of 'em 'ad undressed—and then 'e took the pawn-ticket out and threw it on the floor. Isaac picked it up, and then 'e began to dance about the room as if 'e'd gone mad.

'Do you mean to tell me you've pawned my clothes?' he shouts.

'Me and Peter did,' ses Ginger, sitting up in bed and getting ready for a row.

Isaac dropped on the bed agin all of a 'eap. 'And wot am I to do?' he ses.

'If you be'ave yourself,' ses Ginger, 'and give us our money, me and Peter'll go and get 'em out agin. When we've 'ad breakfast, that is. There's no hurry.'

'But I 'aven't got the money,' ses Isaac; 'it was all sewn up in the lining of the coat. I've on'y got about five shillings. You've made a nice mess of it, Ginger, you 'ave.'

'You're a silly fool, Ginger, that's wot you are,' ses Peter.

'*Sewn up in the lining of the coat?*' ses Ginger, staring.

'The bank-notes was,' ses Isaac, 'and three pounds in gold 'idden in the cap. Did you pawn that too?'

74

Ginger got up in 'is excitement and walked up and down the room. 'We must go and get 'em out at once,' he ses.

'And where's the money to do it with?' ses Peter.

Ginger 'adn't thought of that, and it struck 'im all of a 'eap. None of 'em seemed to be able to think of a way of getting the other ten shillings wot was wanted, and Ginger was so upset that 'e took no notice of the things Peter kept saying to 'im.

'Let's go and ask to see 'em, and say we left a railway-ticket in the pocket,' ses Peter.

Isaac shook 'is 'ead. 'There's on'y one way to do it,' he ses. 'We shall 'ave to pawn your clothes, Ginger, to get mine out with.'

'That's the on'y way, Ginger,' ses Peter, brightening up. 'Now, wot's the good o' carrying on like that? It's no worse for you to be without your clothes for a little while than it was for pore old Isaac.'

It took 'em quite arf an hour afore they could get Ginger to see it. First of all 'e wanted Peter's clothes to be took instead of 'is, and when Peter pointed out that they was too shabby to fetch ten shillings 'e 'ad a lot o' nasty things to say about wearing such old rags, and at last, in a terrible temper, 'e took 'is clothes off and pitched 'em in a 'eap on the floor.

'If you ain't back in arf an hour, Peter,' 'e ses, scowling at 'im, 'you'll 'ear from me, I can tell you.'

'Don't you worry about that,' ses Isaac, with a smile. '*I'm* going to take 'em.'

'You?' ses Ginger; 'but you can't. You ain't got no clothes.'

'I'm going to wear Peter's,' ses Isaac, with another smile.

Peter asked 'im to listen to reason, but it was all no good. He'd got the pawn-ticket, and at last Peter, forgetting all he'd said to Ginger Dick about using bad langwidge, took 'is clothes off, one by one, and dashed 'em on the floor, and told Isaac some of the things 'e thought of 'im.

The old man didn't take any notice of 'im. He dressed 'imself up very slow and careful in Peter's clothes, and then 'e drove 'em nearly crazy by wasting time making 'is bed.

'Be as quick as you can, Isaac,' ses Ginger, at last; 'think of us two a-sitting 'ere waiting for you.'

'I sha'n't forget it,' ses Isaac, and 'e came back to the door after 'e'd gone arf-way down the stairs to ask 'em not to go out on the drink while 'e was away.

It was nine o'clock when he went, and at ha'-past nine Ginger began to get impatient and wondered wot 'ad 'appened to 'im, and when ten o'clock came and no Isaac they was both leaning out of the winder with blankets over their shoulders looking up the road. By eleven o'clock Peter was in very low spirits and Ginger was so mad 'e was afraid to speak to 'im.

They spent the rest o' that day 'anging out of the winder, but it was not till ha'-past four in the afternoon that Isaac, still wearing Peter's clothes and carrying a couple of large green plants under 'is arm, turned into the road, and from the way 'e was smiling they thought it must be all right.

'Wot 'ave you been such a long time for?' ses Ginger, in a low, fierce voice, as Isaac stopped underneath the winder and nodded up to 'em.

'I met an old friend,' ses Isaac.

'Met an old friend?' ses Ginger, in a passion. 'Wot d'ye mean, wasting time like that while we was sitting up 'ere waiting and starving?'

'I 'adn't seen him for years,' ses Isaac, 'and time slipped away afore I noticed it.'

'I dessay,' ses Ginger, in a bitter voice. 'Well, is the money all right?'

'I don't know,' ses Isaac; 'I ain't got the clothes.'

'*Wot?*' ses Ginger, nearly falling out of the winder. 'Well, wot 'ave you done with mine, then? Where are they? Come upstairs.'

'I won't come upstairs, Ginger,' ses Isaac, 'because I'm not quite sure whether I've done right. But I'm not used to going into pawnshops, and I walked about trying to make up my mind to go in and couldn't.'

'Well, wot did you do then?' ses Ginger, 'ardly able to contain hisself.

76

'While I was trying to make up my mind,' ses old Isaac, 'I see a man with a barrer of lovely plants. 'E wasn't asking money for 'em, only old clothes.'

'*Old clothes?*' ses Ginger, in a voice as if 'e was being suffocated.

'I thought they'd be a bit o' green for you to look at,' ses the old man, 'olding the plants up; 'there's no knowing 'ow long you'll be up there. The big one is yours, Ginger, and the other is for Peter.'

''Ave you gone mad, Isaac?' ses Peter, in a trembling voice, arter Ginger 'ad tried to speak and couldn't.

Isaac shook 'is 'ead and smiled up at 'em, and then, arter telling Peter to put Ginger's blanket a little more round 'is shoulders, for fear 'e should catch cold, 'e said 'e'd ask the landlady to send 'em up some bread and butter and a cup o' tea.

They 'eard 'im talking to the landlady at the door, and then 'e went off in a hurry without looking behind 'im, and the landlady walked up and down on the other side of the road with 'er apron stuffed in 'er mouth, pretending to be looking at 'er chimney-pots.

Isaac didn't turn up at all that night, and by next morning those two unfortunate men see 'ow they'd been done. It was quite plain to them that Isaac 'ad been deceiving them, and Peter was pretty certain that 'e took the money out of the bed while 'e was fussing about making it. Old Isaac kept 'em there for three days, sending 'em in their clothes bit by bit and two shillings a day to live on; but they didn't set eyes on 'im agin until they all signed on aboard the *Planet*, and they didn't set eyes on their money until they was two miles below Gravesend.

Bill's Lapse

Strength and good-nature—said the night watchman, mus-ingly, as he felt his biceps—strength and good-nature always go together. Sometimes you find a strong man who is not good-natured, but then, as everybody he comes in contact with is, it comes to the same thing.

The strongest and kindest-'earted man I ever come across was a man o' the name of Bill Burton, a shipmate of Ginger Dick's. For that matter 'e was a shipmate o' Peter Russet's and old Sam Small's too. Not over and above tall; just about my height, his arms was like another man's legs for size, and 'is chest and his back and shoulders might ha' been made for a giant. And with all that he'd got a soft blue eye like a gal's (blue's my favourite colour for gals' eyes), and a nice, soft, curly brown beard. He was an A.B. too, and that showed 'ow good-natured he was, to pick up with firemen.

He got so fond of 'em that when they was all paid off from the *Ocean King* he asked to be allowed to join them in taking a room ashore. It pleased everybody, four coming cheaper than three, and Bill being that good-tempered that 'e'd put up with anything, and when any of the three quarrelled he used to act the part of peacemaker.

The only thing about 'im that they didn't like was that 'e was a teetotaller. He'd go into public-'ouses with 'em, but he wouldn't drink; leastways, that is to say, he wouldn't drink beer, and Ginger used to say that it made 'im feel uncom-fortable to see Bill put away a bottle o' lemonade every time they 'ad a drink. One night arter 'e had 'ad seventeen bottles he could 'ardly get home, and Peter Russet, who knew a lot about pills and such-like, pointed out to 'im 'ow bad it was for his constitushon. He proved that the lemonade would eat away the coats o' Bill's stomach, and that if he kept on 'e might drop down dead at any moment.

That frightened Bill a bit, and the next night, instead of 'aving lemonade, 'e had five bottles o' stone ginger-beer, six of different kinds of teetotal beer, three of soda-water, and two cups of coffee. I'm not counting the drink he 'ad at the chemist's shop arterwards, because he took that as medicine, but he was so queer in 'is inside next morning that 'e began to be afraid he'd 'ave to give up drink altogether.

He went without the next night, but 'e was such a generous man that 'e would pay every fourth time, and there was no pleasure to the other chaps to see 'im pay and 'ave nothing out of it. It spoilt their evening, and owing to 'aving only about 'arf wot they was accustomed to they all got up very disagreeable next morning.

'Why not take just a *little* beer, Bill?' asks Ginger.

Bill 'ung his 'ead and looked a bit silly. 'I'd rather not, mate,' he ses, at last. 'I've been teetotal for eleven months now.'

'Think of your 'ealth, Bill,' ses Peter Russet; 'your 'ealth is more important than the pledge. Wot made you take it?'

Bill coughed. 'I 'ad reasons,' he ses, slowly. 'A mate o' mine wished me to.'

'He ought to ha' known better,' ses Sam.

'He 'ad 'is reasons,' ses Bill.

'Well, all I can say is, Bill,' ses Ginger, 'all I can say is, it's very disobligin' of you.'

'Disobligin'?' ses Bill, with a start; 'don't say that, mate.'

'I must say it,' ses Ginger, speaking very firm.

'You needn't take a lot, Bill,' ses Sam; 'nobody wants you to do that. Just drink in moderation, same as wot we do.'

'It gets into my 'ead,' ses Bill, at last.

'Well, and wot of it?' ses Ginger; 'it gets into everybody's 'ead occasionally. Why, one night old Sam 'ere went up behind a policeman and tickled him under the arms; didn't you, Sam?'

'I did nothing o' the kind,' ses Sam, firing up.

'Well, you was fined ten bob for it next morning, that's all I know,' ses Ginger.

'I was fined ten bob for punching 'im,' ses old Sam, very wild. 'I never tickled a policeman in my life. I never thought o' such a thing. I'd no more tickle a policeman than I'd fly. Anybody that ses I did is a liar. Why should I? Where does the sense come in? What should I want to do it for?'

'All right, Sam,' ses Ginger, sticking 'is fingers in 'is ears, 'you didn't, then.'

'No, I didn't,' ses Sam, 'and don't you forget it. This ain't the fust time you've told that lie about me. I can take a joke with any man; but anybody that goes and ses I tickled——'

'All *right*,' ses Ginger and Peter Russet together. 'You'll have tickled policemen on the brain if you ain't careful, Sam,' ses Peter.

Old Sam sat down growling, and Ginger Dick turned to Bill agin. 'It gets into everybody's 'ead at times,' he ses, 'and where's the 'arm? It's wot it was meant for.'

Bill shook his 'ead, but when Ginger called 'im disobligin' agin he gave way and he broke the pledge that very evening with a pint o' six 'arf.

Ginger was surprised to see the way 'e took his liquor. Arter three or four pints he'd expected to see 'im turn a bit silly, or sing, or do something o' the kind, but Bill kept on as if 'e was drinking water.

'Think of the 'armless pleasure you've been losing all these months, Bill,' ses Ginger, smiling at him.

Bill said it wouldn't bear thinking of, and the next place they came to he said some rather 'ard things of the man who'd persuaded 'im to take the pledge. He 'ad two or three more there, and then they began to see that it was beginning to have an effect on 'im. The first one that noticed it was Ginger Dick. Bill 'ad just lit 'is pipe, and as he threw the match down he ses, 'I don't like these 'ere safety matches,' 'e ses.

'Don't you, Bill?' ses Ginger. 'I do, rather.'

'Oh, you do, do you?' ses Bill, turning on 'im like lightning;

'well, take that for contradictin',' he ses, an' he gave Ginger smack that nearly knocked his 'ead off.

It was so sudden that old Sam and Peter put their beer down and stared at each other as if they couldn't believe their eyes. Then they stooped down and helped pore Ginger on to 'is legs agin and began to brush 'im down.

'Never mind about 'im, mates,' ses Bill, looking at Ginger very wicked. 'P'r'aps he won't be so ready to give me 'is lip next time. Let's come to another pub and enjoy ourselves.'

Sam and Peter followed 'im out like lambs, 'ardly daring to look over their shoulder at Ginger, who was staggering arter them some distance behind a 'olding a handkerchief to 'is face.

'It's your turn to pay, Sam,' ses Bill, when they'd got inside the next place. 'Wot's it to be? Give it a name?'

'Three 'arf pints o' four ale, miss,' ses Sam, not because 'e was mean, but because it wasn't 'is turn.

'Three wot?' ses Bill, turning on 'im.

'Three pots o' six ale, miss,' ses Sam, in a hurry.

'That wasn't wot you said afore,' ses Bill. 'Take that,' he ses, giving pore old Sam a wipe in the mouth and knocking 'im over a stool; 'take that for your sauce.'

Peter Russet stood staring at Sam and wondering wot Bill 'ud be like when he'd 'ad a little more. Sam picked hisself up arter a time and went outside to talk to Ginger about it, and then Bill put 'is arm round Peter's neck and began to cry a bit and say 'e was the only pal he'd got left in the world. It was very awkward for Peter, and more awkward still when the barman came up and told 'im to take Bill outside.

'Go on,' 'e ses, 'out with 'im.'

'He's all right,' ses Peter, trembling; ''e's the truest-'arted gentleman in London. Ain't you, Bill?'

Bill said he was, and 'e asked the barman to go and hide 'is face because it reminded 'im of a little dog 'e had 'ad once wot 'ad died.

'You get outside afore you're hurt,' ses the barman.

Bill punched at 'im over the bar, and not being able to reach 'im threw Peter's pot o' beer at 'im. There was a fearful

81

to-do then, and the landlord jumped over the bar and stood in the doorway, whistling for the police. Bill struck out right and left, and the men in the bar went down like skittles, Peter among them. Then they got outside, and Bill, arter giving the landlord a thump in the back wot nearly made him swallow the whistle, jumped into a cab and pulled Peter Russet in arter 'im.

'I'll talk to you by-and-by,' he ses, as the cab drove off at a gallop; 'there ain't room in this cab. You wait, my lad, that's all. You just wait till we get out, and I'll knock you silly.'

'Wot for, Bill?' ses Peter, staring.

'Don't you talk to me,' roars Bill. 'If I choose to knock you about that's my business, ain't it? Besides, you know very well.'

He wouldn't let Peter say another word, but coming to a quiet place near the docks he stopped the cab and pulling 'im out gave 'im such a dressing down that Peter thought 'is last hour 'ad arrived. He let 'im go at last, and after first making him pay the cabman took 'im along till they came to a public-'ouse and made 'im pay for drinks.

They stayed there till nearly eleven o'clock, and then Bill set off home 'olding the unfortunit Peter by the scruff o' the neck, and wondering out loud whether 'e ought to pay 'im a bit more or not. Afore 'e could make up 'is mind, however, he turned sleepy, and, throwing 'imself down on the bed which was meant for the two of 'em, fell into a peaceful sleep.

Sam and Ginger Dick came in a little while arterwards, both badly marked where Bill 'ad hit them, and sat talking to Peter in whispers as to wot was to be done. Ginger, who 'ad plenty of pluck, was for them all to set on to 'im, but Sam wouldn't 'ear of it, and as for Peter he was so sore he could 'ardly move.

They all turned in to the other bed at last, 'arf afraid to move for fear of disturbing Bill, and when they woke up in the morning and see 'im sitting up in 'is bed they lay as still as mice.

'Why, Ginger, old chap,' ses Bill, with a 'earty smile, 'wot are you all three in one bed for?'

'We was a bit cold,' ses Ginger.

'*Cold?*' ses Bill. 'Wot, this weather? We 'ad a bit of a spree last night, old man, didn't we? My throat's as dry as a cinder.'

'It ain't my idea of a spree,' ses Ginger, sitting up and looking at 'im.

'Good 'eavens, Ginger!' ses Bill, starting back, 'wotever 'ave you been a-doing to your face? Have you been tumbling off of a 'bus?'

Ginger couldn't answer; and Sam Small and Peter sat up in bed alongside of 'im, and Bill, getting as far back on 'is bed as he could, sat staring at their pore faces as if 'e was having a 'orrible dream.

'And there's Sam,' he ses. 'Where ever did you get that mouth, Sam?'

'Same place as Ginger got 'is eye and pore Peter got 'is face,' ses Sam, grinding his teeth.

'You don't mean to tell me,' ses Bill, in a sad voice—'you don't mean to tell me that I did it?'

'You know well enough,' ses Ginger.

Bill looked at 'em, and 'is face got as long as a yard measure.

'I'd 'oped I'd growed out of it, mates,' he ses, at last, 'but drink always takes me like that. I can't keep a pal.'

'You sur-prise me,' ses Ginger, sarcastic-like.

'Don't talk like that, Ginger,' ses Bill, 'arf crying. 'It ain't my fault; it's my weakness. Wot did I do it for?'

'I don't know,' ses Ginger, 'but you won't get the chance of doing it agin, I'll tell you that much.'

'I daresay I shall be better tonight, Ginger,' ses Bill, very humble; 'it don't always take me that way.'

'Well, we don't want you with us any more,' ses old Sam, 'olding his 'ead very high.

'You'll 'ave to go and get your beer by yourself, Bill,' ses Peter Russet, feeling 'is bruises with the tips of 'is fingers.

'But then I should be worse,' ses Bill. 'I want cheerful company when I'm like that. I should very likely come 'ome and 'arf kill you all in your beds. You don't 'arf know wot

I'm like. Last night was nothing, else I should 'ave remembered it.'

'*Cheerful company?*' ses old Sam. ''Ow do you think company's going to be cheerful when you're carrying on like that, Bill? Why don't you go away and leave us alone?'

'Because I've got a 'art,' ses Bill. '*I* can't chuck up pals in that free-and-easy way. Once I take a liking to anybody I'd do anything for 'em, and I've never met three chaps I like better than wot I do you. Three nicer, straightforrard, free-'anded mates I've never met afore.'

'Why not take the pledge agin, Bill?' ses Peter Russet.

'No, mate,' ses Bill, with a kind smile; 'it's just a weakness, and I must try and grow out of it. I'll tie a bit o' string round my little finger tonight as a reminder.'

He got out of bed and began to wash 'is face, and Ginger Dick, who was doing a bit o' thinking, gave a whisper to Sam and Peter Russet.

'All right, Bill, old man,' he ses, getting out of bed and beginning to put his clothes on; 'but first of all we'll try and find out 'ow the landlord is.'

'Landlord?' ses Bill, puffing and blowing in the basin. 'Wot landlord?'

'Why, the one you bashed,' ses Ginger, with a wink at the other two. 'He 'adn't got 'is senses back when me and Sam came away.'

Bill gave a groan and sat on the bed while 'e dried himself, and Ginger told 'im 'ow he 'ad bent a quart pot on the landlord's 'ead, and 'ow the landlord 'ad been carried upstairs and the doctor sent for. He began to tremble all over, and when Ginger said he'd go out and see 'ow the land lay 'e could 'ardly thank 'im enough.

Ginger was gone about two hours, and when 'e came back he looked so solemn that old Sam asked 'im whether he 'ad seen a ghost. Ginger didn't answer 'im; he set down on the side o' the bed and sat thinking.

'I s'pose—I s'pose it's nice and fresh in the streets this morning?' ses Bill at last, in a trembling voice.

Ginger started and looked at 'im. 'I didn't notice, mate,' he ses. Then 'e got up and patted Bill on the back, very gentle, and sat down again.

'Anything wrong, Ginger?' asks Peter Russet, staring at 'im.

'It's that landlord,' ses Ginger; 'there's straw down in the road outside, and they say that he's dying. Pore old Bill don't know 'is own strength. The best thing you can do, old pal, is to go as far away as you can, at once.'

'I shouldn't wait a minnit if it was me,' ses old Sam.

Bill groaned and hid 'is face in his 'ands, and then Peter Russet went and spoilt things by saying that the safest place for a murderer to 'ide in was London. Bill gave a dreadful groan when 'e said murderer, but 'e up and agreed with Peter, and all Sam and Ginger Dick could do wouldn't make 'im alter his mind. He said that he would shave off 'is beard and moustache, and when night came 'e would creep out and take a lodging somewhere right the other end of London.

He stayed in the bedroom all day, with the blinds down, and wouldn't eat anything, and when Ginger looked in about eight o'clock to find out whether he 'ad gone, he found 'im sitting on the bed clean shaved, and 'is face cut about all over where the razor 'ad slipped.

'It'll soon be dark,' ses Ginger, 'and your own brother wouldn't know you now, Bill. Where d'you think of going?'

Bill shook his 'ead. 'Nobody must know that, mate,' he ses. 'I must go into hiding for as long as I can—as long as my money lasts; I've only got six pounds left.'

'That'll last a long time if you're careful,' ses Ginger.

'I want a lot more,' ses Bill. 'I want you to take this silver ring as a keepsake, Ginger. If I 'ad another six pounds or so I should feel much safer. 'Ow much 'ave you got, Ginger?'

'Not much,' ses Ginger, shaking his 'ead.

'Lend it to me, mate,' ses Bill, stretching out his 'and. 'You can easy get another ship. Ah, I wish I was you; I'd be as 'appy as 'appy if I hadn't got a penny.'

'I'm very sorry, Bill,' ses Ginger, trying to smile, 'but I've

85

already promised to lend it to a man wot we met this evening. A promise is a promise, else I'd lend it to you with pleasure.'

'Would you let me be 'ung for the sake of a few pounds, Ginger?' ses Bill, looking at 'im reproachfully. 'I'm a desprit man, Ginger, and I must 'ave that money.'

Afore pore Ginger could move he suddenly clapped 'is hand over 'is mouth and flung 'im on the bed. Ginger was like a child in 'is hands, although he struggled like a madman, and in five minutes 'e was laying there with a towel tied round his mouth and 'is arms and legs tied up with the cord off of Sam's chest.

'I'm very sorry, Ginger,' ses Bill, as 'e took a little over eight pounds out of Ginger's pocket. 'I'll pay you back one o' these days, if I can. If you'd got a rope round your neck same as I 'ave you'd do the same as I've done.'

He lifted up the bedclothes and put Ginger inside and tucked 'im up. Ginger's face was red with passion and 'is eyes starting out of his 'ead.

'Eight and six is fifteen,' ses Bill, and just then he 'eard somebody coming up the stairs. Ginger 'eard it, too, and as Peter Russet came into the room 'e tried all 'e could to attract 'is attention by rolling 'is 'ead from side to side.

'Why 'as Ginger gone to bed?' ses Peter. 'Wot's up, Ginger?'

'He's all right,' ses Bill; 'just a bit of a 'eadache.'

Peter stood staring at the bed, and then 'e pulled the clothes off and saw pore Ginger all tied up, and making awful eyes at 'im to undo him.

'I 'ad to do it, Peter,' ses Bill. 'I wanted some more money to escape with, and 'e wouldn't lend it to me. I 'aven't got as much as I want now. You just came in in the nick of time. Another minute and you'd ha' missed me. 'Ow much 'ave you got?'

'Ah, I wish I could lend you some, Bill,' ses Peter Russet, turning pale, 'but I've 'ad my pocket picked; that's wot I come back for, to get some from Ginger.'

Bill didn't say a word.

'You see 'ow it is, Bill,' ses Peter, edging back towards the door; 'three men laid 'old of me and took every farthing I'd got.'

'Well, I can't rob you, then,' ses Bill, catching 'old of 'im. 'Whoever's money this is,' he ses, pulling a handful out o' Peter's pocket, 'it can't be yours. Now, if you make another sound I'll knock your 'ead off afore I tie you up.'

'Don't tie me up, Bill,' ses Peter, struggling.

'I can't trust you,' ses Bill, dragging 'im over to the wash-stand and taking up the other towel; 'turn round.'

Peter was a much easier job than Ginger Dick, and arter Bill 'ad done 'im 'e put 'im in alongside o' Ginger and covered 'em up, arter first tying both the gags round with some string to prevent 'em slipping.

'Mind, I've only borrowed it,' he ses, standing by the side o' the bed; 'but I must say, mates, I'm disappointed in both of you. If either of you 'ad 'ad the misfortune wot I've 'ad, I'd have sold the clothes off my back to 'elp you. And I wouldn't 'ave waited to be asked neither.'

He stood there for a minute very sorrowful, and then 'e patted both their 'eads and went downstairs. Ginger and Peter lay listening for a bit, and then they turned their pore bound-up faces to each other and tried to talk with their eyes.

Then Ginger began to wriggle and try and twist the cords off, but 'e might as well 'ave tried to wriggle out of 'is skin. The worst of it was they couldn't make known their intentions to each other, and when Peter Russet leaned over 'im and tried to work 'is gag off by rubbing it up agin 'is nose, Ginger pretty near went crazy with temper. He banged Peter with his 'ead, and Peter banged back, and they kept it up till they'd both got splitting 'eadaches, and at last they gave up in despair and lay in the darkness waiting for Sam.

And all this time Sam was sitting in the Red Lion, waiting for them. He sat there quite patient till twelve o'clock and then walked slowly 'ome, wondering wot 'ad happened and whether Bill 'ad gone.

Ginger was the fust to 'ear 'is foot on the stairs, and as he came into the room, in the darkness, him an' Peter Russet started shaking their bed in a way that scared old Sam nearly to death. He thought it was Bill carrying on agin, and 'e was out o' that door and 'arf-way downstairs afore he stopped to take breath. He stood there trembling for about ten minutes, and then, as nothing 'appened, he walked slowly upstairs agin on tiptoe, and as soon as they heard the door creak Peter and Ginger made that bed do everything but speak.

'Is that you, Bill?' ses old Sam, in a shaky voice, and standing ready to dash downstairs agin.

There was no answer except for the bed, and Sam didn't know whether Bill was dying or whether 'e 'ad got delirium trimmings. All 'e did know was that 'e wasn't going to sleep in that room. He shut the door gently and went downstairs agin, feeling in 'is pocket for a match, and, not finding one, 'e picked out the softest stair he could find and, leaning his 'ead agin the banisters, went to sleep.

It was about six o'clock when 'e woke up, and broad daylight. He was stiff and sore all over, and feeling braver in the light 'e stepped softly upstairs and opened the door. Peter and Ginger was waiting for 'im, and as he peeped in 'e saw two things sitting up in bed with their 'air standing up all over like mops and their faces tied up with bandages. He was that startled 'e nearly screamed, and then 'e stepped into the room and stared at 'em as if he couldn't believe 'is eyes.

'Is that you, Ginger?' he ses. 'Wot d'ye mean by making sights of yourselves like that? 'Ave you took leave of your senses?'

Ginger and Peter shook their 'eads and rolled their eyes, and then Sam see wot was the matter with 'em. Fust thing 'e did was to pull out 'is knife and cut Ginger's gag off, and the fust thing Ginger did was to call 'im every name 'e could lay his tongue to.

'You wait a moment,' he screams, 'arf crying with rage. 'You wait till I get my 'ands loose and I'll pull you to pieces. The idea o' leaving us like this all night, you old crocodile. I 'eard you come in. I'll pay you!'

Sam didn't answer 'im. He cut off Peter Russet's gag, and Peter Russet called 'im 'arf a score o' names without taking breath.

'And when Ginger's finished I'll 'ave a go at you,' he ses. 'Cut off these cords!'

'At once, d'ye 'ear?' ses Ginger. 'Oh, you wait till I get my 'ands on you!'

Sam didn't answer 'em; he shut up 'is knife with a click and then 'e sat at the foot o' the bed on Ginger's feet and looked at 'em. It wasn't the fust time they'd been rude to 'im, but as a rule he'd 'ad to put up with it. He sat and listened while Ginger swore 'imself faint.

'That'll do,' he ses, at last; 'another word and I shall put the bedclothes over your 'ead. Afore I do anything more I want to know wot it's all about.'

Peter told 'im, arter fust calling 'im some more names, because Ginger was past it, and when 'e'd finished old Sam said 'ow surprised he was at them for letting Bill do it, and told 'em how they ought to 'ave prevented it. He sat there talking as though 'e enjoyed the sound of 'is own voice, and he told Peter and Ginger all their faults and said wot sorrow it caused their friends. Twice he 'ad to throw the bedclothes over their 'eads because o' the noise they was making.

'*Are—you—going—to undo—us?*' ses Ginger, at last.

'No, Ginger,' ses old Sam; 'in justice to myself I couldn't do it. Arter wot you've said—and arter wot I've said—my life wouldn't be safe. Besides which, you'd want to go shares in my money.'

He took up 'is chest and marched downstairs with it, and about 'arf an hour arterwards the landlady's 'usband came up and set 'em free. As soon as they'd got the use of their legs back they started out to look for Sam, but they didn't find 'im for nearly a year, and as for Bill, they never set eyes on 'im agin.

The Persecution of Bob Pretty

The old man sat on his accustomed bench outside the 'Cauliflower'. A generous measure of beer stood in a blue and white jug by his elbow, and little wisps of smoke curled slowly upwards from the bowl of his churchwarden pipe. The knapsacks of two young men lay where they were flung on the table, and the owners, taking a noontide rest, turned a polite, if bored, ear to the reminiscences of grateful old age.

Poaching, said the old man, who had tried topics ranging from early turnips to horse-shoeing—poaching ain't wot it used to be, poaching nor anything else; but that there man you might ha' noticed as went out about ten minutes ago and called me 'Old Truthfulness' as 'e passed is the worst one I know. Bob Pretty 'is name is, and of all the sly, artful, deceiving men that ever lived in Claybury 'e is the worst—never did a honest day's work in 'is life, and never wanted the price of a glass of ale.

Bob Pretty's worst time was just after old Squire Brown died. The old squire couldn't afford to preserve much, but by-and-by a gentleman with plenty of money, from London, named Rockett, took 'is place and things began to look up. Pheasants was 'is favourites, and 'e spent no end o' money rearing of 'em, but anything that could be shot at suited 'im, too.

He started by sneering at the little game that Squire Brown 'ad left, but all 'e could do didn't seem to make much difference; things disappeared in a most eggstrordinary way, and the keepers went pretty near crazy, while the things the squire said about Claybury and Claybury men was disgraceful.

Everybody knew as it was Bob Pretty and one or two of 'is

mates from other places, but they couldn't prove it. They couldn't catch 'im nohow, and at last the squire 'ad two keepers set off to watch 'im by night and by day.

Bob Pretty wouldn't believe it; he said 'e couldn't. And even when it was pointed out to 'im that Keeper Lewis was follering of 'im he said that it just 'appened he was going the same way, that was all. And sometimes he'd get up in the middle of the night and go for a fifteen-mile walk 'cos 'e'd got the toothache, and Mr Lewis, who 'adn't got it, had to tag along arter 'im till he was fit to drop. O' course, it was one keeper the less to look arter the game, and by-and-by the squire see that and took 'im off.

All the same they kept a pretty close watch on Bob, and at last one arternoon they sprang out on 'im as he was walking past Gray's farm, and asked him wot it was he 'ad got in his pockets.

'That's my bisness, Mr Lewis,' ses Bob Pretty.

Mr Smith, the other keeper, passed 'is hands over Bob's coat and felt something soft and bulgy.

'You take your 'ands off of me,' ses Bob; 'you don't know 'ow partikler I am.'

He jerked 'imself away, but they caught 'old of 'im agin, and Mr Lewis put 'is hand in his inside pocket and pulled out two brace o' partridges.

'You'll come along of us,' he ses, catching 'im by the arm.

'We've been looking for you a long time,' ses Keeper Smith, 'and it's a pleasure for us to 'ave your company.'

Bob Pretty said 'e wouldn't go, but they forced 'im along and took 'im all the way to Cudford, four miles off, so that Policeman White could lock 'im up for the night. Mr White was a'most as pleased as the keepers, and 'e warned Bob solemn not to speak becos all 'e said would be used agin 'im.

'Never mind about that,' ses Bob Pretty. 'I've got a clear conscience, and talking can't 'urt me. I'm very glad to see you, Mr White; if these two clever, experienced keepers hadn't brought me I should 'ave looked you up myself. They've been and stole my partridges.'

Them as was standing round laughed, and even Policeman White couldn't 'elp giving a little smile.

'There's nothing to laugh at,' ses Bob, 'olding his 'ead up. 'It's a fine thing when a working man—a 'ardworking man—can't take home a little game for 'is family without being stopped and robbed.'

'I s'pose they flew into your pocket?' ses Policeman White.

'No, they didn't,' ses Bob. 'I'm not going to tell any lies about it; I put 'em there. The partridges in my inside coat-pocket and the bill in my waistcoat-pocket.'

'The *bill?*' ses Keeper Lewis, staring at 'im.

'Yes, the bill,' ses Bob Pretty, staring back; 'the bill from Mr Keen, the poulterer, at Wickham.'

He fetched it out of 'is pocket and showed it to Mr White, and the keepers was like madmen a'most 'cos it was plain to see that Bob Pretty 'ad been and bought them partridges just for to play a game on 'em.

'I was curious to know wot they tasted like,' he ses to the policeman. 'Worst of it is, I don't s'pose my pore wife'll know 'ow to cook 'em.'

'You get off 'ome,' ses Policeman White, staring at 'im.

'But ain't I goin' to be locked up?' ses Bob. ''Ave I been brought all this way just to 'ave a little chat with a policeman I don't like?'

'You go 'ome,' ses Policeman White, handing the partridges back to 'im.

'All right,' ses Bob, 'and I may 'ave to call you to witness that these 'ere two men laid hold o' me and tried to steal my partridges. I shall go up and see my loryer about it.'

He walked off 'ome with his 'ead up as high as 'e could hold it, and the airs 'e used to give 'imself arter this was terrible for to behold. He got 'is eldest boy to write a long letter to the squire about it, saying that 'e'd overlook it this time, but 'e couldn't promise for the future. Wot with Bob Pretty on one side and Squire Rockett on the other, them two keepers' lives was 'ardly worth living.

Then the squire got a head-keeper named Cutts, a man as

was said to know more about the ways of poachers than they did themselves. He was said to 'ave cleared out all the poachers for miles round the place 'e came from, and pheasants could walk into people's cottages and not be touched.

He was a sharp-looking man, tall and thin, with screwed-up eyes and a little red beard. The second day 'e came 'e was up here at this 'ere 'Cauliflower', having a pint o' beer and looking round at the chaps as he talked to the landlord. The odd thing was that men who'd never taken a hare or a pheasant in their lives could 'ardly meet 'is eye, while Bob Pretty stared at 'im as if 'e was a wax-works.

'I 'ear you 'ad a little poaching in these parts afore I came,' ses Mr Cutts to the landlord.

'I think I 'ave 'eard something o' the kind,' ses the landlord, staring over his 'ead with a far-away look in 'is eyes.

'You won't hear of much more,' ses the keeper. 'I've invented a new way of catching the dirty rascals; afore I came 'ere I caught all the poachers on three estates. I clear 'em out just like a ferret clears out rats.'

'Sort o' man-trap?' ses the landlord.

'Ah, that's tellings,' ses Mr Cutts.

'Well, I 'ope you'll catch 'em here,' ses Bob Pretty; 'there's far too many of 'em about for my liking. Far too many.'

'I shall 'ave 'em afore long,' ses Mr Cutts, nodding his 'ead.

'Your good 'ealth,' ses Bob Pretty, holding up 'is mug. 'We've been wanting a man like you for a long time.'

'I don't want any of your impidence, my man,' ses the keeper. 'I've 'eard about you, and nothing good either. You be careful.'

'I am careful,' ses Bob, winking at the others. 'I 'ope you'll catch all them low poaching chaps; they give the place a bad name, and I'm a'most afraid to go out arter dark for fear o' meeting 'em.'

Peter Gubbins and Sam Jones began to laugh, but Bob Pretty got angry with 'em and said he didn't see there was anything to laugh at. He said that poaching was a disgrace to their native place, and instead o' laughing they ought to be thankful to Mr Cutts for coming to do away with it all.

'Any help I can give you shall be given cheerful,' he ses to the keeper.

'When I want your help I'll ask you for it,' ses Mr Cutts.

'Thankee,' ses Bob Pretty. 'I on'y 'ope I sha'n't get my face knocked about like yours 'as been, that's all; cos my wife's so partikler.'

'Wot d'ye mean?' ses Mr Cutts, turning on him. 'My face ain't been knocked about.'

'Oh, I beg your pardin,' ses Bob; 'I didn't know it was natural.'

Mr Cutts went black in the face a'most and stared at Bob Pretty as if 'e was going to eat 'im, and Bob stared back, looking fust at the keeper's nose and then at 'is eyes and mouth, and then at 'is nose agin.

'You'll know me agin, I s'pose?' ses Mr Cutts, at last.

'Yes,' ses Bob, smiling; 'I should know you a mile off—on the darkest night.'

'We shall see,' ses Mr Cutts, taking up 'is beer and turning 'is back on him. 'Those of us as live the longest 'll see the most.'

'I'm glad I've lived long enough to see 'im,' ses Bob to Bill Chambers. 'I feel more satisfied with *myself* now.'

Bill Chambers coughed, and Mr Cutts, arter finishing 'is beer, took another look at Bob Pretty, and went off boiling a'most.

The trouble he took to catch Bob Pretty arter that you wouldn't believe, and all the time the game seemed to be simply melting away, and Squire Rockett was finding fault with 'im all day long. He was worn to a shadder a'most with watching, and Bob Pretty seemed to be more prosperous than ever.

Sometimes Mr Cutts watched in the plantations, and sometimes 'e hid 'imself near Bob's house, and at last one night, when 'e was crouching behind the fence of Frederick Scott's front garden, 'e saw Bob Pretty come out of 'is house and, arter a careful look round, walk up the road. He held 'is breath as Bob passed 'im, and was just getting up to foller 'im when Bob stopped and walked slowly back agin, sniffing.

'Wot a delicious smell o' roses!' he ses out loud.

He stood in the middle o' the road nearly opposite where the keeper was hiding, and sniffed so that you could ha' heard him the other end o' the village.

'It can't be roses,' he ses, in a puzzled voice, 'becos there ain't no roses hereabouts, and besides, it's too late for 'em. It must be Mr Cutts, the clever new keeper.'

He put his 'ead over the fence and bid 'im good evening, and said wot a fine night for a stroll it was, and asked 'im whether 'e was waiting for Frederick Scott's aunt. Mr Cutts didn't answer 'im a word; 'e was pretty near bursting with passion. He got up and shook 'is fist in Bob Pretty's face, and then 'e went off stamping down the road as if 'e was going mad.

And for a time Bob Pretty seemed to 'ave all the luck on 'is side. Keeper Lewis got rheumatic fever, which 'e put down to sitting about night arter night in damp places watching for Bob, and, while 'e was in the thick of it, with the doctor going every day, Mr Cutts fell in getting over a fence and broke 'is leg. Then all the work fell on Keeper Smith, and to 'ear 'im talk you'd think that rheumatic fever and broken legs was better than anything else in the world. He asked the squire for 'elp, but the squire wouldn't give it to 'im, and he kept telling 'im wot a feather in 'is cap it would be if 'e did wot the other two couldn't do, and caught Bob Pretty. It was all very well, but, as Smith said, wot 'e wanted was feathers in 'is piller, instead of 'aving to snatch a bit o' sleep in 'is chair or sitting down with his 'ead agin a tree. When I tell you that 'e fell asleep in this public-'ouse one night while the landlord was drawing a pint o' beer he 'ad ordered, you'll know wot 'e suffered.

O' course, all this suited Bob Pretty as well as could be, and he was that good-tempered 'e'd got a nice word for every-body, and when Bill Chambers told 'im 'e was foolhardy 'e only laughed and said 'e knew wot 'e was about.

But the very next night 'e had reason to remember Bill Chambers's words. He was walking along Farmer Hall's field —the one next to the squire's plantation—and, so far from being nervous, 'e was actually a-whistling. He'd got a sack over 'is shoulder, loaded as full as it could be, and 'e 'ad just stopped to light 'is pipe when three men burst out o' the plantation and ran towards 'im as 'ard as they could run.

Bob Pretty just gave one look and then 'e dropped 'is pipe and set off like a hare. It was no good dropping the sack, because Smith, the keeper, 'ad recognised 'im and called 'im by name, so 'e just put 'is teeth together and did the best he could, and there's no doubt that if it 'adn't ha' been for the sack 'e could 'ave got clear away.

As it was, 'e ran for pretty near a mile, and they could 'ear 'im breathing like a pair o' bellows; but at last 'e saw that the game was up. He just managed to struggle as far as Farmer Pinnock's pond, and then, waving the sack round his 'ead, 'e flung it into the middle of it, and fell down gasping for breath.

'Got—you—this time—Bob Pretty,' ses one o' the men, as they came up.

'Wot—*Mr Cutts?*' ses Bob, with a start.

'That's me, my man,' ses the keeper.

'Why—I thought—you was——. Is that *Mr Lewis?* It can't be.'

'That's me,' ses Keeper Lewis. 'We both got well sudden-like, Bob Pretty, when we 'eard you was out. You ain't so sharp as you thought you was.'

Bob Pretty sat still, getting 'is breath back and doing a bit o' thinking at the same time.

'You give me a start,' he ses, at last. 'I thought you was both in bed, and, knowing 'ow hard worked Mr Smith 'as been, I just came round to 'elp 'im keep watch like. I promised to 'elp you, Mr Cutts, if you remember.'

'Wot was that you threw in the pond just now?' ses Mr Cutts.

'A sack,' ses Bob Pretty; 'a sack I found in Farmer Hall's field. It felt to me as though it might 'ave birds in it, so I picked it up, and I was just on my way to your 'ouse with it, Mr Cutts, when you started arter me.'

'Ah!' ses the keeper, 'and wot did you run for?'

Bob Pretty tried to laugh. 'Becos I thought it was the poachers arter me,' he ses. 'It seems ridiklous, don't it?'

'Yes, it does,' ses Lewis.

'I thought you'd know me a mile off,' ses Mr Cutts. 'I should ha' thought the smell o' roses would ha' told you I was near.'

Bob Pretty scratched 'is 'ead and looked at 'im out of the corner of 'is eye, but he 'adn't got any answer. Then 'e sat biting his finger-nails and thinking, while the keepers stood argyfying as to who should take 'is clothes off and go into the pond arter the pheasants. It was a very cold night and the pond was pretty deep in places, and none of 'em seemed anxious.

'Make 'im go in for it,' ses Lewis, looking at Bob; ''e chucked it in.'

'On'y becos I thought you was poachers,' ses Bob. 'I'm sorry to have caused so much trouble.'

'Well, you go in and get it out,' ses Lewis, who pretty well guessed who'd 'ave to do it if Bob didn't. 'It'll look better for you, too.'

'I've got my defence all right,' ses Bob Pretty. 'I ain't set a foot on the squire's preserves, and I found this sack a 'undered yards away from it.'

'Don't waste more time,' ses Mr Cutts to Lewis. 'Off with your clothes and in with you. Anybody'd think you was afraid of a little cold water.'

'Whereabouts did 'e pitch it in?' ses Lewis.

Bob Pretty pointed with 'is finger exactly where 'e thought it was, but they wouldn't listen to 'im, and then Lewis, arter twice saying wot a bad cold he'd got, took 'is coat off very slow and careful.

'I wouldn't mind going in to oblige you,' ses Bob Pretty, 'but the pond is so full o' them cold, slimy efts; I don't fancy them crawling up agin me, and, besides that, there's such a lot o' deep holes in it. And wotever you do don't put your 'ead under; you know 'ow foul that water is.'

Keeper Lewis pretended not to listen to 'im. He took off 'is clothes very slowly and then 'e put one foot in and stood shivering, although Smith, who felt the water with his 'and, said it was quite warm. Then Lewis put the other foot in and began to walk about careful, arf-way up to 'is knees.

'I can't find it,' he ses, with 'is teeth chattering.

'You 'aven't looked,' ses Mr Cutts; 'walk about more; you can't expect to find it all at once. Try the middle.'

Lewis tried the middle, and 'e stood there up to 'is neck, feeling about with his foot and saying things out loud about Bob Pretty, and other things under 'is breath about Mr Cutts.

'Well, I'm going off 'ome,' ses Bob Pretty, getting up. 'I'm too tender-'earted to stop and see a man drownded.'

'You stay 'ere,' ses Mr Cutts, catching 'old of him.

'Wot for?' ses Bob; 'you've got no right to keep me 'ere.'

'Catch 'old of 'im, Joe,' ses Mr Cutts, quick-like.

Smith caught 'old of his other arm, and Lewis left off trying to find the sack to watch the struggle. Bob Pretty fought 'ard, and once or twice 'e nearly tumbled Mr Cutts into the pond, but at last he gave in and lay down panting and talking about 'is loryer. Smith 'eld him down on the ground while Mr Cutts kept pointing out places with 'is finger for Lewis to walk to. The last place 'e pointed to wanted a much taller man, but it wasn't found out till too late, and the fuss Keeper Lewis made when 'e could speak agin was terrible.

'You'd better come out,' ses Mr Cutts; 'you ain't doing no good. We know where they are and we'll watch the pond till daylight—that is, unless Smith 'ud like to 'ave a try.'

'It's pretty near daylight now, I think,' ses Smith.

Lewis came out and ran up and down to dry 'imself, and finished off on his pocket-'andkerchief, and then with 'is teeth chattering 'e began to dress 'imself. He got 'is shirt on, and then 'e stood turning over 'is clothes as if 'e was looking for something.

'Never mind about your stud now,' ses Mr Cutts; 'hurry up and dress.'

'*Stud?*' ses Lewis, very snappish. 'I'm looking for my trowsis.'

'Your trowsis?' ses Smith, 'elping 'im look.

'I put all my clothes together,' ses Lewis, a'most shouting. 'Where are they? I'm 'arf perished with cold. Where are they?'

'He 'ad 'em on this evening,' ses Bob Pretty, "cos I remember noticing 'em.'

'They must be somewhere about,' ses Mr Cutts; 'why don't you use your eyes?'

He walked up and down, peering about, and as for Lewis he was 'opping round 'arf crazy.

'I wonder,' ses Bob Pretty, in a thoughtful voice, to Smith —'I wonder whether you or Mr Cutts kicked 'em in the pond while you was struggling with me. Come to think of it, I seem to remember 'earing a splash.'

'He's done it, Mr Cutts,' ses Smith; 'never mind, it'll go all the 'arder with 'im.'

'But I do mind,' ses Lewis shouting. 'I'll be even with you for this, Bob Pretty. I'll make you feel it. You wait till I've done with you. You'll get a month extra for this, you see if you don't.'

'Don't you mind about me,' ses Bob; 'you run off 'ome and cover them legs of yours. I found that sack, so my conscience is clear.'

Lewis put on 'is coat and waistcoat and set off, and Mr Cutts and Smith, arter feeling about for a dry place, set theirselves down and began to smoke.

'Look 'ere,' ses Bob Pretty, 'I'm not going to sit 'ere all night to please you; I'm going off 'ome. If you want me you'll know where to find me.'

'You stay where you are,' ses Mr Cutts. 'We ain't going to let you out of our sight.'

'Very well, then, you take me 'ome,' ses Bob. 'I'm not going to catch my death o' cold sitting 'ere. I'm not used to being out of a night like you are. I was brought up respectable.'

'I daresay,' ses Mr Cutts. 'Take you 'ome, and then 'ave one o' your mates come and get the sack while we're away.'

Then Bob Pretty lost 'is temper, and the things 'e said about Mr Cutts wasn't fit for Smith to hear. He threw 'imself down at last full length on the ground and sulked till the day broke.

Keeper Lewis was there a'most as soon as it was light, with some long hay-rakes he borrowed, and I should think that pretty near 'arf the folks in Claybury 'ad turned up to see the fun. Mrs Pretty was crying and wringing 'er 'ands; but most folk seemed to be rather pleased that Bob 'ad been caught at last.

In next to no time 'arf-a-dozen rakes was at work and the things they brought out o' that pond you wouldn't believe. The edge of it was all littered with rusty tin pails and sauce-pans and such-like, and by-and-by Lewis found the things he'd 'ad to go 'ome without a few hours afore, but they didn't seem to find that sack, and Bob Pretty, wot was talking to 'is wife, began to look 'opeful.

But just then the squire came riding up with two friends as was staying with 'im, and he offered a reward of five shillings to the man wot found it. Three or four of 'em waded in up to their middle then and raked their 'ardest, and at last Henery Walker give a cheer and brought it to the side, all heavy with water.

'That's the sack I found, sir,' ses Bob, starting up. 'It wasn't on your land at all, but on the field next to it. I'm an honest, 'ardworking man, and I've never been in trouble afore. Ask anybody 'ere and they'll tell you the same.'

Squire Rockett took no notice of 'im. 'Is that the sack?' he asks, turning to Mr Cutts.

'That's the one, sir,' ses Mr Cutts. 'I'd swear to it anywhere.'

'You'd swear a man's life away,' ses Bob. ''Ow can you swear to it when it was dark?'

Mr Cutts didn't answer 'im. He went down on 'is knees and cut the string that tied up the mouth o' the sack, and then 'e started back as if 'e'd been shot, and 'is eyes a'most started out of 'is 'ead.

'What's the matter?' ses the squire.

Mr Cutts couldn't speak; he could only stutter and point at the sack with 'is finger, and Henery Walker, as was getting curious, lifted up the other end of it and out rolled about a score of as fine cabbages as you could wish to see.

I never see people so astonished afore in all my born days, and as for Bob Pretty 'e stood staring at them cabbages as if 'e couldn't believe 'is eyesight.

'And that's wot I've been kept 'ere all night for,' he ses at last, shaking his 'ead. 'That's wot comes o' trying to do a kindness to keepers, and 'elping of 'em in their difficult work. P'r'aps that ain't the sack arter all, Mr Cutts. I could ha' sworn they was pheasants in the one I found, but I may be mistook, never 'aving 'ad one in my 'ands afore. Or p'r'aps somebody was trying to 'ave a game with you, Mr Cutts, and deceived me instead.'

The keepers on'y stared at 'im.

'You ought to be more careful,' ses Bob. 'Very likely while you was taking all that trouble over me, and Keeper Lewis was catching 'is death o' cold, the poachers was up at the plantation taking all they wanted. And, besides, it ain't right for Squire Rockett to 'ave to pay Henery Walker five shillings for finding a lot of old cabbages. I shouldn't like it myself.'

He looked out of the corner of 'is eye at the squire, as was pretending not to notice Henery Walker touching 'is cap to him, and then 'e turns to 'is wife and he ses,

'Come along, old gal,' 'e ses. 'I want my breakfast bad, and arter that I shall 'ave to lose a honest day's work in bed.'

Dixon's Return

Talking about eddication, said the night watchman, thought-fully, the finest eddication you can give a lad is to send 'im to sea. School is all right up to a certain p'int, but arter that comes the sea. I've been there myself and I know wot I'm talking about. All that I am I owe to 'aving been to sea.

There's a saying that boys will be boys. That's all right till they go to sea, and then they 'ave to be men, and good men, too. They get knocked about a bit, o' course, but that's all part o' the eddication, and when they get bigger they pass the eddication they've received on to other boys smaller than wot they are. Arter I'd been at sea a year I spent all my fust time ashore going round and looking for boys wot 'ad knocked me about afore I sailed, and there was only one out o' the whole lot that I wished I 'adn't found.

Most people, o' course, go to sea as boys or else not at all, but I mind one chap as was pretty near thirty years old when 'e started. It's a good many years ago now, and he was land-lord of a public-'ouse as used to stand in Wapping, called the Blue Lion.

His mother, wot had 'ad the pub afore 'im, 'ad brought 'im up very quiet and genteel, and when she died 'e went and married a fine, handsome young woman who 'ad got her eye on the pub without thinking much about 'im. I got to know about it through knowing the servant that lived there. A nice, quiet gal she was, and there wasn't much went on that she didn't hear. I've known 'er to cry for hours with the ear-ache, pore gal.

Not caring much for 'er 'usband, and being spoiled by 'im into the bargain, Mrs Dixon soon began to lead 'im a terrible life. She was always throwing his meek and mildness up into 'is face, and arter they 'ad been married two or three years he was no more like the landlord o' that public-'ouse than I'm like a lord. Not so much. She used to get into such terrible tempers there was no doing anything with 'er, and for the sake o' peace and quietness he gave way to 'er till 'e got into the habit of it and couldn't break 'imself of it.

They 'adn't been married long afore she 'ad her cousin, Charlie Burge, come in as barman, and a month or two arter that 'is brother Bob, who 'ad been spending a lot o' time looking for work instead o' doing it, came too. They was so comfortable there that their father—a 'ouse-painter by trade —came round to see whether he couldn't paint the Blue Lion up a bit and make 'em look smart, so that they'd get more trade. He was one o' these 'ere fust-class 'ouse-painters that can go to sleep on a ladder holding a brush in one hand and a pot o' paint in the other, and by the time he 'ad finished painting the 'ouse it was ready to be done all over agin.

I dare say that George Dixon—that was 'is name— wouldn't ha' minded so much if 'is wife 'ad only been civil, but instead o' that she used to make fun of 'im and order 'im about, and by-and-by the others began to try the same thing. As I said afore, Dixon was a very quiet man, and if there was ever anybody to be put outside Charlie or Bob used to do it. They tried to put me outside once, the two of 'em, but they on'y did it at last by telling me that somebody 'ad gone off and left a pot o' beer standing on the pavement. They was both of 'em fairly strong young chaps with a lot of bounce in 'em, and she used to say to her 'usband wot fine young fellers they was, and wot a pity it was he wasn't like 'em.

Talk like this used to upset George Dixon awful. Having been brought up careful by 'is mother, and keeping a very quiet, respectable 'ouse—I used it myself—he cert'nly was soft, and I remember 'im telling me once that he didn't believe in fighting, and that instead of hitting people you ought to try and persuade them. He was uncommon fond of 'is wife, but at last one day, arter she 'ad made a laughing-stock of 'im in the bar, he up and spoke sharp to her.

'*Wot?*' ses Mrs Dixon, 'ardly able to believe her ears.

'Remember who you're speaking to; that's wot I said,' ses Dixon.

''Ow dare you talk to me like that?' screams 'is wife, turning red with rage. 'Wot d'ye mean by it?'

'Because you seem to forget who is master 'ere,' ses Dixon, in a trembling voice.

'*Master?*' she ses, firing up. 'I'll soon show you who's master. Go out o' my bar; I won't 'ave you in it. D'ye 'ear? Go out of it.'

Dixon turned away and began to serve a customer.

'D'ye hear wot I say?' ses Mrs Dixon, stamping 'er foot. 'Go out o' my bar. Here, Charlie!'

'Hullo!' ses 'er cousin, who 'ad been standing looking on and grinning.

'Take the *master* and put 'im into the parlour,' ses Mrs Dixon, 'and don't let 'im come out till he's begged my pardon.'

'Go on,' ses Charlie, brushing up 'is shirt sleeves; 'in you go. You heard wot she said.'

He caught 'old of George Dixon, who 'ad just turned to the back o' the bar to give a customer change out of 'arf a crown, and ran 'im kicking and struggling into the parlour. George gave 'im a silly little punch in the chest, and got such a bang on the 'ead back that at fust he thought it was knocked off. When 'e came to 'is senses agin the door leading to the bar was shut, and 'is wife's uncle, who 'ad been asleep in the easy chair, was finding fault with 'im for waking 'im up.

'Why can't you be quiet and peaceable?' he ses, shaking his 'ead at him. 'I've been 'ard at work all the morning thinking wot colour to paint the back-door, and this is the second time I've been woke up since dinner. You're old enough to know better.'

'Go and sleep somewhere else, then,' ses Dixon. 'I don't want you 'ere at all, or your boys neither. Go and give somebody else a treat; I've 'ad enough of the whole pack of you.'

He sat down and put 'is feet on the fender, and old Burge, as soon as he 'ad got 'is senses back, went into the bar and complained to 'is niece, and she came into the parlour like a thunderstorm.

'You'll beg my uncle's pardon as well as mine afore you come out o' that room,' she ses to her 'usband; 'mind that.'

George Dixon didn't say a word; the shame of it was a'most more than 'e could stand. Then 'e got up to go out o' the parlour and Charlie pushed 'im back agin. Three times he tried, and then 'e stood up and looked at 'is wife.

'I've been a good 'usband to you,' he ses; 'but there's no satisfying you. You ought to ha' married somebody that would ha' knocked you about, and then you'd ha' been happy. I'm too fond of a quiet life to suit you.'

'Are you going to beg my pardon and my uncle's pardon?' ses 'is wife, stamping 'er foot.

'No,' ses Dixon; 'I am not. I'm surprised at you asking it.'

'Well, you don't come out o' this room till you do,' ses 'is wife.

'That won't hurt me,' ses Dixon. 'I couldn't look anybody in the face arter being pushed out o' my own bar.'

They kept 'im there all the rest o' the day, and, as 'e was still obstinate when bedtime came, Mrs Dixon, who wasn't to be beat, brought down some bed-clothes, and 'ad a bed made up for 'im on the sofa. Some men would ha' 'ad the police in for less than that, but George Dixon 'ad got a great deal o' pride, and 'e couldn't bear the shame of it. Instead o' that 'e acted like a fourteen-year-old boy, and ran away to sea.

They found 'im gone when they came down in the morning, and the side-door on the latch. 'E 'ad left a letter for his wife on the table, telling 'er what he had done. Short and sweet it was, and wound up with telling 'er to be careful that 'er uncle and cousins didn't eat 'er out of house and 'ome.

She got another letter two days arterwards, saying that 'e 'ad shipped as ordinary seaman on an American barque called the *Seabird*, bound for California, and that 'e expected to be away a year or thereabouts.

'It'll do 'im good,' ses old Burge, when Mrs Dixon read the letter to 'em. 'It's a 'ard life is the sea, and 'e'll appreciate 'is 'ome when 'e comes back to it agin. 'E don't know when 'e's well off. It's as comfortable a 'ome as a man could wish to 'ave.'

It was surprising wot a little difference George Dixon's being away made to the Blue Lion. Nobody seemed to miss 'im much, and things went on just the same as afore he went. Mrs Dixon was all right with most people, and 'er relations 'ad a very good time of it; old Burge began to put on flesh at such a rate that the sight of a ladder made 'im ill a'most, and Charlie and Bob went about as if the place belonged to 'em.

They 'eard nothing for eight months, and then a letter came for Mrs Dixon from 'er husband, in which 'e said that 'e had left the *Seabird*, after 'aving 'ad a time which made 'im shiver to think of. He said that the men was the roughest of the rough, and the officers was worse, and that he 'ad 'ardly 'ad a day without a blow from one or other since 'e'd been aboard. He'd been knocked down with a handspike by the second mate, and had 'ad a week in his bunk with a kick given 'im by the boatswain. He said 'e was now on the *Rochester Castle*, bound for Sydney, and he 'oped for better times.

That was all they 'eard for some months, and then they got another letter saying that the men on the *Rochester Castle* was, if anything, worse than those on the *Seabird*, and that he'd began to think that running away to sea was diff'rent to wot he'd expected, and that he supposed 'e'd done it too late in life. He sent 'is love to 'is wife, and asked 'er as a favour to send Uncle Burge and 'is boys away, as 'e didn't want to find them there when 'e came home, because they was the cause of all his sufferings.

'He don't know 'is best friends,' ses old Burge. ''E's got a nasty sperrit I don't like to see.'

'I'll 'ave a word with 'im when 'e does come home,' ses

Bob. 'I s'pose he thinks 'imself safe writing letters thousands o' miles away.'

The last letter they 'ad came from Auckland, and said that he 'ad shipped on the *Monarch*, bound for the Albert Docks, and he 'oped soon to be at 'ome and managing the Blue Lion, same as in the old happy days afore he was fool enough to go to sea.

That was the very last letter, and some time arterwards the *Monarch* was in the missing list, and by-and-by it became known that she 'ad gone down with all hands not long arter leaving New Zealand. The only difference it made at the Blue Lion was that Mrs Dixon 'ad two of 'er dresses dyed black, and the others wore black neckties for a fortnight, and spoke of Dixon as pore George, and said it was a funny world, but they supposed everything was for the best.

It must ha' been pretty near four years since George Dixon 'ad run off to sea, when Charlie, who was sitting in the bar one arternoon reading the paper, things being dull, saw a man's head peep through the door for a minute and then disappear. A'most direckly arterwards it looked in at another door, and then disappeared agin. When it looked in at the third door Charlie 'ad put down 'is paper and was ready for it.

'Who are you looking for?' he ses, rather sharp. 'Wot d'ye want? Are you 'aving a game of peep-bo, or what?'

The man coughed and smiled, and then 'e pushed the door open gently and came in, and stood there fingering 'is beard as though 'e didn't know wot to say.

'I've come back, Charlie,' he ses at last.

'Wot, *George*!' ses Charlie, starting. 'Why, I didn't know you in that beard. We all thought you was dead years ago.'

'I was pretty nearly, Charlie,' ses Dixon, shaking his 'ead. 'Ah! I've 'ad a terrible time since I left 'ome.'

'You don't seem to ha' made your fortune,' ses Charlie, looking down at his clothes. 'I'd ha' been ashamed to come 'ome like that if it 'ad been me.'

'I'm wore out,' ses Dixon, leaning agin the bar. 'I've got no pride left; it's all been knocked out of me. How's Julia?'

'She's all right,' ses Charlie. 'Here, *Ju——*'

'*H'sh!*' ses Dixon, reaching over the bar and laying his 'and on his arm. 'Don't let 'er know too sudden; break it to her gently.'

'Fiddlesticks!' ses Charlie, throwing his 'and off, and calling, 'Here, *Julia! he's come back!*'

Mrs Dixon came running downstairs and into the bar. 'Good gracious!' she ses, staring at her 'usband. 'Whoever'd ha' thought o' seeing you agin? Where 'ave you sprung from?'

'Ain't you glad to see me, Julia?' ses George Dixon.

'Yes, I s'pose so; if you've come back to behave yourself,' ses Mrs Dixon. 'What 'ave you got to say for yourself for running away, and then writing them letters telling me to get rid of my relations?'

'That's a long time ago, Julia,' ses Dixon, raising the flap in the counter and going into the bar. 'I've gone through a great deal o' suffering since then. I've been knocked about till I 'adn't got any feeling left in me; I've been shipwrecked, and I've had to fight for my life with savages.'

'Nobody asked you to run away,' ses his wife, edging away as he went to put his arm round 'er waist. 'You'd better go upstairs and put on some decent clothes.'

Dixon looked at 'er for a moment, and then he 'ung his 'ead.

'I've been thinking o' you and of seeing you agin every·day since I went away, Julia,' he ses. 'You'd be the same to me if you was dressed in rags.'

He went up the stairs without another word, and old Burge, who was coming down, came down five of 'em at once, owing to Dixon speaking to 'im afore 'e knew who 'e was. The old man was still grumbling when Dixon came down agin, and said he believed he'd done it a-purpose.

'You run away from a good 'ome,' he ses, 'and the best wife in Wapping, and you come back and frighten people 'arf out o' their lives. I never see such a feller in all my born days.'

'I was so glad to get 'ome agin I didn't think,' ses Dixon. 'I hope you're not 'urt.'

He started telling them all about his 'ardships while they were at tea, but none of 'em seemed to care much about hearing 'em. Bob said that the sea was all right for men, and that other people were sure not to like it.

'And you brought it all on yourself,' ses Charlie. 'You've only got yourself to thank for it. I 'ad thought o' picking a bone with you over those letters you wrote.'

'Let's 'ope he's come back more sensible than wot 'e was when 'e went away,' ses old Burge, with 'is mouth full o' toast.

By the time he'd been back a couple o' days George Dixon could see that 'is going away 'adn't done any good at all. Nobody seemed to take any notice of 'im or wot he said, and at last, arter a word or two with Charlie about the rough way he spoke to some o' the customers, Charlie came in to Mrs Dixon and said that he was at 'is old tricks of interfering, and he would not 'ave it.

'Well, he'd better keep out o' the bar altogether,' ses Mrs Dixon. 'There's no need for 'im to go there; we managed all right while 'e was away.'

'Do you mean I'm not to go into my own bar?' ses Dixon, stammering.

'Yes, I do,' ses Mrs Dixon. 'You kept out of it for four years to please yourself, and now you can keep out of it to please me.'

'I've put you out o' the bar before,' ses Charlie, 'and if you come messing about with me any more I'll do it agin. So now you know.'

He walked back into the bar whistling, and George Dixon, arter sitting still for a long time thinking, got up and went into the bar, and he'd 'ardly got his foot inside afore Charlie caught 'old of 'im by the shoulder and shoved 'im back into the parlour agin.

'I told you wot it would be,' ses Mrs Dixon, looking up from 'er sewing. 'You've only got your interfering ways to thank for it.'

'This is a fine state of affairs in my own 'ouse,' ses Dixon, ardly able to speak. 'You've got no proper feeling for your' husband, Julia, else you wouldn't allow it. Why, I was happier at sea than wot I am 'ere.'

'Well, you'd better go back to it if you're so fond of it,' ses 'is wife.

'I think I 'ad,' ses Dixon. 'If I can't be master in my own 'ouse I'm better at sea, hard as it is. You must choose between us, Julia—me or your relations. I won't sleep under the same roof as them for another night. Am I to go?'

'Please yourself,' ses 'is wife. 'I don't mind your staying 'ere so long as you behave yourself, but the others won't go; you can make your mind easy on that.'

'I'll go and look for another ship, then,' ses Dixon, taking up 'is cap. 'I'm not wanted here. P'r'aps you wouldn't mind 'aving some clothes packed into a chest for me so as I can go away decent.'

He looked round at 'is wife, as though 'e expected she'd ask 'im not to go, but she took no notice, and he opened the door softly and went out, while old Burge, who 'ad come into the room and 'eard what he was saying, trotted off upstairs to pack 'is chest for 'im.

In two hours 'e was back agin and more cheerful than he 'ad been since he 'ad come 'ome. Bob was in the bar and the others were just sitting down to tea, and a big chest, nicely corded, stood on the floor in the corner of the room.

'That's right,' he ses, looking at it; 'that's just wot I wanted.'

'It's as full as it can be,' ses old Burge. 'I done it for you myself. 'Ave you got a ship?'

'I 'ave,' ses Dixon. 'A jolly good ship. No more hardships for me this time. I've got a berth as captain.'

'*Wot?*' ses 'is wife. '*Captain?* You!'

'Yes,' ses Dixon, smiling at her. 'You can sail with me if you like.'

'Thankee,' ses Mrs Dixon, 'I'm quite comfortable where I am.'

'Do you mean to say *you've* got a master's berth?' ses Charlie, staring at 'im.

'I do,' ses Dixon; 'master and owner.'

Charlie coughed. 'Wot's the name of the ship?' he asks, winking at the others.

'THE BLUE LION,' ses Dixon, in a voice that made 'em all start. 'I'm shipping a new crew and I pay off the old one tonight. You first, my lad.'

'Pay off,' ses Charlie, leaning back in 'is chair and staring at 'im in a puzzled way. '*Blue Lion?*'

'Yes,' ses Dixon, in the same loud voice. 'When I came 'ome the other day I thought p'r'aps I'd let bygones be bygones, and I laid low for a bit to see whether any of you deserved it. I went to sea to get hardened—and I got hard. I've fought men that would eat you at a meal. I've 'ad more blows in a week than you've 'ad in a lifetime, you fat-faced landlubber.'

He walked to the door leading to the bar, where Bob was doing 'is best to serve customers and listen at the same time, and arter locking it put the key in 'is pocket. Then 'e put his 'and in 'is trouser pocket and slapped some money down on the table in front o' Charlie.

'There's a month's pay instead o' notice,' he ses. 'Now git.'

'George!' screams 'is wife. ''Ow dare you. 'Ave you gone crazy?'

'I'm surprised at you,' ses old Burge, who'd been looking on with 'is mouth wide open, and pinching 'imself to see whether 'e wasn't dreaming.

'I don't go for your orders,' ses Charlie, getting up. 'Wot d'ye mean by locking that door?'

'Wot!' roars Dixon. 'D—n it! I mustn't lock a door without asking my barman now. Pack up and be off, you swab, afore I start on you.'

Charlie gave a growl and rushed at 'im and the next moment 'e was down on the floor with the 'ardest bang in the face that he'd ever 'ad in 'is life. Mrs Dixon screamed and ran into the kitchen, follered by old Burge, who went in to tell 'er not to be frightened. Charlie got up and went for Dixon agin; but he 'ad come back as 'ard as nails and 'ad a rushing style o' fighting that took Charlie's breath away. By the time Bob 'ad left the bar to take care of itself, and run round and got in the back way, Charlie had 'ad as much as 'e wanted and was lying on the sea-chest in the corner trying to get 'is breath.

'Yes? Wot d'ye want?' ses Dixon, with a growl, as Bob came in at the door.

He was such a 'orrible figure, with the blood on 'is face and 'is beard sticking out all ways, that Bob, instead of doing wot he 'ad come round for, stood in the doorway staring at 'im without a word.

'I'm paying off,' ses Dixon. ''Ave *you* got anything to say agin it?'

'No,' ses Bob, drawing back.

'You and Charlie'll go now,' ses Dixon, taking out some money. 'The old man can stay on for a month to give 'im time to look round. Don't look at me that way, else I'll knock your 'ead off.'

He started counting out Bob's money just as old Burge and Mrs Dixon, hearing all quiet, came in out of the kitchen.

'Don't you be alarmed on my account, my dear,' he ses, turning to 'is wife; 'it's child's play to wot I've been used to. I'll just see these two mistaken young fellers off the premises, and then we'll 'ave a cup o' tea while the old man minds the bar.'

Mrs Dixon tried to speak, but 'er temper was too much for 'er. She looked from her 'usband to Charlie and Bob and then back at 'im agin and caught 'er breath.

'That's right,' ses Dixon, nodding his 'ead at her. 'I'm master and owner of the Blue Lion and you're first mate. When I'm speaking you keep quiet; that's dis-sipline.'

I was in that bar about three months arterwards, and I never saw such a change in any woman as there was in Mrs Dixon. Of all the nice-mannered, soft-spoken landladies I've ever seen, she was the best, and on'y to 'ear the way she answered her 'usband when he spoke to 'er was a pleasure to every married man in the bar.

The Third String

Love? said the night watchman, as he watched in an abstracted fashion the efforts of a skipper to reach a brother skipper on a passing barge with a boat-hook; don't talk to me about love, because I've suffered enough through it. There ought to be teetotallers for love the same as wot there is for drink, and they ought to wear a piece o' ribbon to show it, the same as the teetotallers do; but not an attractive piece o' ribbon, mind you. I've seen as much mischief caused by love as by drink, and the funny thing is, one often leads to the other. Love, arter it is over, often leads to drink, and drink often leads to love, and to a man committing himself for life afore it *is* over.

Sailormen give way to it most; they see so little o' wimmen that they naturally 'ave a high opinion of 'em. Wait till they become night watchmen, and, having to be at 'ome all day, see the other side of 'em. If people on'y started life as night watchmen there wouldn't be one arf the falling in love that there is now.

I remember one chap, as nice a fellow as you could wish to meet, too. He always carried his sweetheart's photograph about with 'im, and it was the on'y thing that cheered 'im up during the fourteen years he was cast away on a deserted island. He was picked up at last and taken 'ome, and there she was still single and waiting for 'im; and arter spending fourteen years on a deserted island, he got another ten in quod for shooting 'er, because she 'ad altered so much in 'er looks.

Then there was Ginger Dick, a red-'aired man I've spoken about to you before. He went and fell in love one time when he was lodging in Wapping 'ere with old Sam Small and Peter Russet, and a nice mess 'e made of it.

They was just back from a v'y'ge, and they 'adn't been ashore a week afore both of 'em noticed a change for the worse in Ginger. He turned quiet and peaceful, and lost 'is taste for beer. He used to play with 'is food instead of eating it, and, in place of going out of an evening with Sam and Peter, took to going off by 'imself.

'It's love,' ses Peter Russet, shaking his 'ead, 'and he'll be worse afore he's better.'

'Who's the gal?' ses old Sam.

Peter didn't know, but when they came 'ome that night 'e asked. Ginger, who was sitting up in bed with a far-off look in 'is eyes, cuddling 'is knees, went on staring, but didn't answer.

'Who is it making a fool of you this time, Ginger?' ses old Sam.

'You mind your bisness and I'll mind mine,' ses Ginger, suddenly waking up and looking very fierce.

'No offence, mate,' ses Sam, winking at Peter. 'I on'y asked in case I might be able to do you a good turn.'

'Well, you can do that by not letting her know you're a pal o' mine,' ses Ginger, very nasty.

Old Sam didn't understand at fust, and when Peter explained to 'im he wanted to hit 'im for trying to twist Ginger's words about.

'She don't like fat old men,' ses Ginger.

'Ho!' ses old Sam, who couldn't think of anything else to say. 'Ho! don't she? Ho! Ho, indeed!'

He undressed 'imself, and got into the bed he shared with Peter, and kept 'im awake for hours by telling 'im in a loud voice about all the gals he'd made love to in his life, and in partikler about one gal that always fainted dead away whenever she saw either a red-'aired man or a monkey.

Peter Russet found out all about it next day, and told Sam that it was a barmaid with black 'air and eyes at the Jolly Pilots, and that she wouldn't 'ave anything to say to Ginger.

He spoke to Ginger about it agin when they were going to bed that night, and, to 'is surprise, found that he was quite civil. When 'e said that he would do anything he could for 'im, Ginger was quite affected.

'I can't eat or drink,' he ses, in a miserable voice; 'I lay awake all last night thinking of her. She's so diff'rent to other gals; she's got—— If I start on you, Sam Small, you'll know it. You go and make that choking noise to them as likes it.'

'It's a bit o' egg-shell I got in my throat at breakfast this morning, Ginger,' ses Sam. 'I wonder whether she lays awake all night thinking of you?'

'I dare say she does,' ses Peter Russet, giving 'im a little push.

'Keep your 'eart up, Ginger,' ses Sam; 'I've known girls to 'ave the most extr'ordinary likings afore now.'

'Don't take no notice of 'im,' ses Peter, holding Ginger back. ''Ow are you getting on with her?'

Ginger groaned and sat down on 'is bed and looked at the floor, and Sam went and sat on his till it shook so that Ginger offered to step over and break 'is neck for 'im.

'I can't 'elp the bed shaking,' ses Sam; 'it ain't my fault. I didn't make it. If being in love is going to make you so dis- agreeable to your best friends, Ginger, you'd better go and live by yourself.'

'I 'eard something about her today, Ginger,' ses Peter Russet. 'I met a chap I used to know at Bull's Wharf, and he told me that she used to keep company with a chap named Bill Lumm, a bit of a prize-fighter, and since she gave 'im up she won't look at anybody else.'

'Was she very fond of 'im, then?' asks Ginger.

'I don't know,' ses Peter; 'but this chap told me that she won't walk out with anybody agin, unless it's another prize- fighter. Her pride won't let her, I s'pose.'

'Well, that's all right, Ginger,' ses Sam; 'all you've got to do is to go and be a prize-fighter.'

'If I 'ave any more of your nonsense——' ses Ginger, starting up.

'That's right,' ses Sam; 'jump down anybody's throat when they're trying to do you a kindness. That's you all over,

Ginger, that is. Wot's to prevent you telling 'er that you're a prize-fighter from Australia or somewhere? She won't know no better.'

He got up off the bed, and put his 'ands up as Ginger walked across the room to 'im; but Ginger on'y wanted to shake 'ands, and arter he 'ad done that 'e patted 'im on the back, and smiled at 'im.

'I'll try it,' he ses. 'I'd tell any lies for 'er sake. Ah! you don't know wot love is, Sam.'

'I used to,' ses Sam; and then he sat down agin, and began to tell 'em all the love affairs he could remember, until at last Peter Russet got tired, and said it was 'ard to believe, looking at 'im now, wot a perfick terror he'd been with gals, and said that the face he'd got now was a judgment on 'im. Sam shut up arter that, and got into trouble with Peter in the middle o' the night by waking him up to tell 'im something that he 'ad just thought of about *his* face.

The more Ginger thought o' Sam's idea the more he liked it, and the very next evening 'e took Peter Russet into the private bar o' the Jolly Pilots. He ordered port wine, which he thought seemed more 'igh-class than beer, and then Peter Russet started talking to Miss Tucker, and told her that Ginger was a prize-fighter from Sydney, where he'd beat everybody that stood up to 'im.

The gal seemed to change towards Ginger all in a flash, and her beautiful black eyes looked at 'im so admiring that he felt quite faint. She started talking to 'im about his fights at once, and when at last 'e plucked up courage to ask 'er to go for a walk with 'im on Sunday afternoon she seemed quite delighted.

'It'll be a nice change for me,' she ses, smiling. 'I used to walk out with a prize-fighter once before, and since I gave 'im up I began to think I was never going to 'ave a young man agin. You can't think how dull it's been.'

'Must ha' been,' ses Ginger.

'I s'pose you've got a taste for prize-fighters, miss,' ses Peter Russet.

'No,' ses Miss Tucker; 'I don't think that it's that exactly, but, you see, I couldn't 'ave anybody else. Not for their own sakes.'

'Why not?' ses Ginger, looking puzzled.

'Why not?' ses Miss Tucker. 'Why, because o' Bill. He's such a 'orrid jealous disposition. After I gave 'im up I walked out with a young fellow named Smith; fine, big, strapping chap 'e was, too, and I never saw such a change in any man as there was in 'im after Bill 'ad done with 'im. I couldn't believe it was 'im. I told Bill he ought to be ashamed of 'imself.'

'Wot did 'e say?' asks Ginger.

'Don't ask me wot 'e said,' ses Miss Tucker, tossing her 'ead. 'Not liking to be beat, I 'ad one more try with a young fellow named Charlie Webb.'

'Wot 'appened to him?' ses Peter Russet, arter waiting a bit for 'er to finish.

'I can't bear to talk of it,' ses Miss Tucker, holding up Ginger's glass and giving the counter a wipe down. '*He* met Bill, and I saw 'im six weeks afterwards just as 'e was being sent away from the 'ospital to a seaside home. Bill disappeared after that.'

'Has he gone far away?' ses Ginger, trying to speak in a off'and way.

'Oh, he's back now,' ses Miss Tucker. 'You'll see 'im fast enough, and, wotever you do, don't let 'im know you're a prize-fighter.'

'Why not?' ses pore Ginger.

'Because o' the surprise it'll be to 'im,' ses Miss Tucker. 'Let 'im rush on to 'is doom. He'll get a lesson 'e don't expect, the bully. Don't be afraid of hurting 'im. Think o' pore Smith and Charlie Webb.'

'I am thinkin' of 'em,' ses Ginger, slow-like. 'Is—is Bill—very quick—with his 'ands?'

'*Rather*,' ses Miss Tucker; 'but o' course he ain't up to your mark; he's on'y known in these parts.'

She went off to serve a customer, and Ginger Dick tried to

117

catch Peter's eye, but couldn't, and when Miss Tucker came back he said 'e must be going.

'Sunday afternoon at a quarter past three sharp, outside 'ere,' she ses. 'Never mind about putting on your best clothes, because Bill is sure to be hanging about. I'll take care o' that.'

She reached over the bar and shook 'ands with 'im, and Ginger felt a thrill go up 'is arm which lasted 'im all the way 'ome.

He didn't know whether to turn up on Sunday or not, and if it 'adn't ha' been for Sam and Peter Russet he'd ha' most likely stayed at home. Not that 'e was a coward, being always ready for a scrap and gin'rally speaking doing well at it, but he made a few inquiries about Bill Lumm and 'e saw that 'e had about as much chance with 'im as a kitten would 'ave with a bulldog.

Sam and Peter was delighted, and they talked about it as if it was a pantermime, and old Sam said that when *he* was a young man he'd ha' fought six Bill Lumms afore *he'd* ha' given a gal up. He brushed Ginger's clothes for 'im with 'is own hands on Sunday arternoon, and, when Ginger started, 'im and Peter follered some distance behind to see fair play.

The on'y person outside the Jolly Pilots when Ginger got there was a man; a strong-built chap with a thick neck, very large 'ands, and a nose which 'ad seen its best days some time afore. He looked 'ard at Ginger as 'e came up, and then stuck his 'ands in his trouser pockets and spat on the pavement. Ginger walked a little way past and then back agin, and just as he was thinking that 'e might venture to go off, as Miss Tucker 'adn't come, the door opened and out she came.

'I couldn't find my 'at-pins,' she ses, taking Ginger's arm and smiling up into his face.

Before Ginger could say anything the man he 'ad noticed took his 'ands out of 'is pockets and stepped up to 'im.

'Let go o' that young lady's arm,' he ses.

'Sha'n't,' ses Ginger, holding it so tight that Miss Tucker nearly screamed.

'Let go 'er arm and put your hands up,' ses the chap agin.

'Not 'ere,' ses Ginger, who 'ad laid awake the night afore thinking wot to do if he met Bill Lumm. 'If you wish to 'ave a spar with me, my lad, you must 'ave it where we can't be interrupted. When I start on a man I like to make a good job of it.'

'Good job of it!' ses the other, starting. 'Do you know who I am?'

'No, I don't,' ses Ginger, 'and, wot's more, I don't care.'

'My name,' ses the chap, speaking in a slow, careful voice, 'is Bill Lumm.'

'Wot a 'orrid name!' ses Ginger.

'Otherwise known as the Wapping Basher,' ses Bill, shoving 'is face into Ginger's and glaring at 'im.

'Ho!' ses Ginger, sniffing, 'a amatoor.'

'*Amatoor?*' ses Bill, shouting.

'That's wot we should call you over in Australia,' ses Ginger; '*my* name is Dick Duster, likewise known as the Sydney Puncher. I've killed three men in the ring and 'ave never 'ad a defeat.'

'Well, put 'em up,' ses Bill, doubling up 'is fists and shaping at 'im.

'Not in the street, I tell you,' ses Ginger, still clinging tight to Miss Tucker's arm. 'I was fined five pounds the other day for punching a man in the street, and the magistrate said it would be 'ard labour for me next time. You find a nice, quiet spot for some arternoon, and I'll knock your 'ead off with pleasure.'

'I'd sooner 'ave it knocked off now,' ses Bill; 'I don't like waiting for things.'

'Thursday arternoon,' ses Ginger, very firm; 'there's one or two gentlemen want to see a bit o' my work afore backing me, and we can combine bisness with pleasure.'

He walked off with Miss Tucker, leaving Bill Lumm standing on the pavement scratching his 'ead and staring arter 'im as though 'e didn't quite know wot to make of it. Bill stood there for pretty near five minutes, and then arter asking Sam and Peter, who 'ad been standing by listening, whether they wanted anything for themselves, walked off to ask 'is pals wot they knew about the Sydney Puncher.

Ginger Dick was so quiet and satisfied about the fight that old Sam and Peter couldn't make 'im out at all. He wouldn't even practise punching at a bolster that Peter rigged up for 'im, and when 'e got a message from Bill Lumm naming a quiet place on the Lea Marshes he agreed to it as comfortable as possible.

'Well, I must say, Ginger, that I like your pluck,' ses Peter Russet.

'I always 'ave said that for Ginger; 'e's got pluck,' ses Sam.

Ginger coughed and tried to smile at 'em in a superior sort o' way. 'I thought you'd got more sense,' he ses at last. 'You don't think I'm going, do you?'

'*Wot?*' ses old Sam, in a shocked voice.

'You're never going to back out of it, Ginger?' ses Peter.

'I am,' ses Ginger. 'If you think I'm going to be smashed up by a prize-fighter just to show my pluck you're mistook.'

'You must go, Ginger,' ses old Sam, very severe. 'It's too late to back out of it now. Think of the gal. Think of '*er* feelings.'

'For the sake of your good name,' ses Peter.

'I should never speak to you agin, Ginger,' ses old Sam, pursing up 'is lips.

'Nor me neither,' ses Peter Russet.

'To think of our Ginger being called a coward,' ses old Sam, with a shudder, 'and afore a gal, too.'

'The loveliest gal in Wapping,' ses Peter.

'Look 'ere,' ses Ginger, 'you can shut up, both of you. I'm not going, and that's the long and short of it. I don't mind an ordinary man, but I draw the line at prize-fighters.'

Old Sam sat down on the edge of 'is bed and looked the picture of despair. 'You must go, Ginger,' he ses, 'for my sake.'

'Your sake?' ses Ginger, staring.

'I've got money on it,' ses Sam, 'so's Peter. If you don't turn up all bets'll be off.'

'Good job for you, too,' ses Ginger. 'If I did turn up you'd lose it to a dead certainty.'

Old Sam coughed and looked at Peter, and Peter 'e coughed and looked at Sam.

'You don't understand, Ginger,' ses Sam, in a soft voice; 'it ain't often a chap gets the chance o' making a bit o' money these 'ard times.'

'So we've put all our money on Bill Lumm,' ses Peter. 'It's the safest and easiest way o' making money I ever 'eard of. You see, we know you're not a prize-fighter and the others don't.'

Pore Ginger looked at 'em, and then 'e called 'em all the names he could lay 'is tongue to, but, with the idea o' the money they was going to make, they didn't mind a bit. They let him 'ave 'is say, and that night they brought 'ome two other sailormen wot 'ad bet agin Ginger to share their room, and, though they 'ad bet agin 'im, they was so fond of 'im that it was evident that they wasn't going to leave 'im till the fight was over.

Ginger gave up then, and at twelve o'clock next day they started off to find the place. Mr Webson, the landlord of the Jolly Pilots, a short, fat man o' fifty, wot 'ad spoke to Ginger once or twice, went with 'em, and all the way to the station he kept saying wot a jolly spot it was for that sort o' thing. Perfickly private; nice soft green grass to be knocked down on, and larks up in the air singing away as if they'd never leave off.

They took the train to Homerton, and, being a slack time o' the day, the porters was surprised to see wot a lot o' people was travelling by it. So was Ginger. There was the landlords of 'arf the public-'ouses in Wapping, all smoking big cigars; two dock policemen in plain clothes wot 'ad got the arternoon off—one with a raging toothache and the other with a baby wot wasn't expected to last the day out. They was as full o' fun as kittens, and the landlord o' the Jolly Pilots pointed out to Ginger wot reasonable 'uman beings policemen was at 'art. Besides them there was quite a lot o' sailormen, even skippers and mates, nearly all of 'em smoking big cigars, too, and looking at Ginger out of the corner of one eye and at the Wapping Basher out of the corner of the other.

'Hit 'ard and hit straight,' ses the landlord to Ginger in a low voice, as they got out of the train and walked up the road. ''Ow are you feeling?'

'I've got a cold coming on,' ses pore Ginger, looking at the Basher, who was on in front, 'and a splitting 'eadache, and a sharp pain all down my left leg. I don't think——'

'Well, it's a good job it's no worse,' ses the landlord; 'all you've got to do is to hit 'ard. If you win it's a 'undred pounds in my pocket, and I'll stand you a fiver of it. D'ye understand?'

They turned down some little streets, several of 'em going diff'rent ways, and arter crossing the River Lea got on to the marshes, and, as the landlord said, the place might ha' been made for it.

A little chap from Mile End was the referee, and Bill Lumm, 'aving peeled, stood looking on while Ginger took 'is things off and slowly and carefully folded of 'em up. Then they stepped towards each other, Bill taking longer steps than Ginger, and shook 'ands; immediately arter which Bill knocked Ginger head over 'eels.

'Time!' was called, and the landlord o' the Jolly Pilots, who was nursing Ginger on 'is knee, said that it was nothing at all, and that bleeding at the nose was a sign of 'ealth. But as it happened Ginger was that mad 'e didn't want any encouragement, he on'y wanted to kill Bill Lumm.

He got two or three taps in the next round which made his 'ead ring, and then he got 'ome on the mark and follered it up by a left-'anded punch on Bill's jaw that surprised 'em both —Bill because he didn't think Ginger could hit so 'ard, and Ginger because 'e didn't think that prize-fighters 'ad any feelings.

They clinched and fell that round, and the landlord patted Ginger on the back and said that if he ever 'ad a son he 'oped he'd grow up like 'im.

Ginger was surprised at the way 'e was getting on, and so was old Sam and Peter Russet, and when Ginger knocked Bill down in the sixth round Sam went as pale as death. Ginger was getting marked all over, but he stuck to 'is man, and the two dock policemen, wot 'ad put their money on Bill Lumm, began to talk of their dooty, and say as 'ow the fight ought to be stopped.

At the tenth round Bill couldn't see out of 'is eyes, and kept wasting his strength on the empty air, and once on the referee. Ginger watched 'is opportunity, and at last, with a terrific smash on the point o' Bill's jaw, knocked 'im down and then looked round for the landlord's knee.

Bill made a game try to get up when 'Time!' was called, but couldn't; and the referee, who was 'olding a 'andkerchief to 'is nose, gave the fight to Ginger.

It was the proudest moment o' Ginger Dick's life. He sat there like a king, smiling 'orribly, and Sam's voice as he paid 'is losings sounded to 'im like music, in spite o' the words the old man see fit to use. It was so 'ard to get Peter Russet's money that it a'most looked as though there was going to be another prize fight, but 'e paid up at last and went, arter fust telling Ginger part of wot he thought of 'im.

There was a lot o' quarrelling, but the bets was all settled at last, and the landlord o' the Jolly Pilots, who was in 'igh feather with the money he'd won, gave Ginger the five pounds he'd promised and took him 'ome in a cab.

'You done well, my lad,' he ses. 'No, don't smile. It looks as though your 'ead's coming off.'

'I 'ope you'll tell Miss Tucker 'ow I fought,' ses Ginger.

'I will, my lad,' ses the landlord; 'but you'd better not see 'er for some time, for both your sakes.'

'I was thinking of 'aving a day or two in bed,' ses Ginger.

'Best thing you can do,' ses the landlord; 'and mind, don't you ever fight Bill Lumm agin. Keep out of 'is way.'

'Why? I beat 'im once, an' I can beat 'im agin,' ses Ginger, offended.

'*Beat 'im?*' ses the landlord. He took 'is cigar out of 'is mouth as though 'e was going to speak, and then put it back agin and looked out of the window.

'Yes, beat 'im,' ses Ginger. 'You was there and saw it.'

'He lost the fight a-purpose,' ses the landlord, whispering. 'Miss Tucker found out that you wasn't a prize-fighter—leastways, I did for 'er—and she told Bill that, if 'e loved 'er so much that he'd 'ave 'is sinful pride took down by letting you beat 'im, she'd think diff'rent of 'im. Why, 'e could 'ave settled you in a minute if he'd liked. He was on'y playing with you.'

Ginger stared at 'im as if 'e couldn't believe 'is eyes. '*Playing?*' he ses, feeling 'is face very gently with the tips of his fingers.

'Yes,' ses the landlord; 'and if he ever hits you agin you'll know I'm speaking the truth.'

Ginger sat back all of a heap and tried to think. 'Is Miss Tucker going to keep company with 'im agin, then?' he ses, in a faint voice.

'No,' ses the landlord; 'you can make your mind easy on that point.'

'Well, then, if I walk out with 'er I shall 'ave to fight Bill all over agin,' ses Ginger.

The landlord turned to 'im and patted 'im on the shoulder. 'Don't you take up your troubles afore they come, my lad,' he ses, kindly; 'and mind and keep wot I've told you dark, for all our sakes.'

He put 'im down at the door of 'is lodgings and, arter shaking 'ands with 'im, gave the landlady a shilling and told 'er to get some beefsteak and put on 'is face, and went home. Ginger went straight off to bed, and the way he carried on when the landlady fried the steak afore bringing it up showed 'ow upset he was.

It was over a week afore he felt 'e could risk letting Miss Tucker see 'im, and then at seven o'clock one evening he felt 'e couldn't wait any longer, and arter spending an hour cleaning 'imself he started out for the Jolly Pilots.

He felt so 'appy at the idea o' seeing her agin that 'e forgot all about Bill Lumm, and it gave 'im quite a shock when 'e saw 'im standing outside the Pilots. Bill took his 'ands out of 'is pockets when he saw 'im and came towards 'im.

'It's no good tonight, mate,' he ses; and to Ginger's great surprise shook 'ands with 'im.

'No good?' ses Ginger, staring.

'No,' ses Bill; 'he's in the little back-parlour, like a whelk in 'is shell; but we'll 'ave 'im sooner or later.'

'Him? Who?' ses Ginger, more puzzled than ever.

'*Who?*' ses Bill; 'why, Webson, the landlord. You don't mean to tell me you ain't heard about it?'

'Heard wot?' ses Ginger. 'I haven't 'eard anything. I've been indoors with a bad cold all the week.'

'Webson and Julia Tucker was married at eleven o'clock yesterday morning,' ses Bill Lumm, in a hoarse voice. 'When I think of the way I've been done, and wot I've suffered, I feel arf crazy. He won a 'undred pounds through me, and then got the gal I let myself be disgraced for. I 'ad an idea some time ago that he'd got 'is eye on her.'

Ginger Dick didn't answer 'im a word. He staggered back and braced 'imself up agin the wall for a bit, and arter staring at Bill Lumm in a wild way for pretty near three minutes, he crawled back to 'is lodgings and went straight to bed agin.

Captains All

Every sailorman grumbles about the sea, said the night watchman, thoughtfully. It's human nature to grumble, and I s'pose they keep on grumbling and sticking to it because there ain't much else they can do. There's not many shore-going berths that a sailorman is fit for, and those that there are —such as a night watchman's, for instance—wants such a good character that there's few as are equal to it.

Sometimes they get things to do ashore. I knew one man that took up butchering, and 'e did very well at it till the police took *him* up. Another man I knew gave up the sea to marry a washerwoman, and they hadn't been married six months afore she died, and back he 'ad to go to sea agin, pore chap.

A man who used to grumble awful about the sea was old Sam Small—a man I've spoke of to you before. To hear 'im go on about the sea, arter he 'ad spent four or five months' money in a fortnight, was 'artbreaking. He used to ask us wot was going to happen to 'im in his old age, and when we pointed out that he wouldn't be likely to 'ave any old age if he wasn't more careful of 'imself he used to fly into a temper and call us everything 'e could lay his tongue to.

One time when 'e was ashore with Peter Russet and Ginger Dick he seemed to 'ave got it on the brain. He started being careful of 'is money instead o' spending it, and three mornings running he bought a newspaper and read the advertisements, to see whether there was any comfortable berth for a strong, good-'arted man wot didn't like work.

He actually went arter one situation, and, if it hadn't ha' been for seventy-nine other men, he said he believed he'd ha' had a good chance of getting it. As it was, all 'e got was a black eye for shoving another man, and for a day or two he was so down-'arted that 'e was no company at all for the other two. For three or four days 'e went out by 'imself, and then, all of a sudden, Ginger Dick and Peter began to notice a great change in him. He seemed to 'ave got quite cheerful and 'appy. He answered 'em back pleasant when they spoke to 'im, and one night he lay in 'is bed whistling comic songs until Ginger and Peter Russet 'ad to get out o' bed to him. When he bought a new necktie and a smart cap and washed 'imself twice in one day they fust began to ask each other wot was up, and then they asked him.

'Up?' ses Sam; 'nothing.'

'He's in love,' ses Peter Russet.

'You're a liar,' ses Sam, without turning round.

'He'll 'ave it bad at 'is age,' ses Ginger.

Sam didn't say nothing, but he kept fidgeting about as though 'e'd got something on his mind. Fust he looked out o' the winder, then he 'ummed a tune, and at last, looking at 'em very fierce, he took a tooth-brush wrapped in paper out of 'is pocket and began to clean 'is teeth.

'He *is* in love,' ses Ginger, as soon as he could speak.

'Or else 'e's gorn mad,' ses Peter, watching 'im. 'Which is it, Sam?'

Sam made believe that he couldn't answer 'im because o' the tooth-brush, and arter he'd finished he 'ad such a raging toothache that 'e sat in a corner holding 'is face and looking the pictur' o' misery. They couldn't get a word out of him till they asked 'im to go out with them, and then he said 'e was going to bed. Twenty minutes arterwards, when Ginger Dick stepped back for 'is pipe, he found he 'ad gorn.

He tried the same game next night, but the other two wouldn't 'ave it, and they stayed in so long that at last 'e lost 'is temper, and, arter wondering wot Ginger's father and mother could ha' been a-thinking about, and saying that he believed Peter Russet 'ad been changed at birth for a sea-sick monkey, he put on 'is cap and went out. Both of 'em follered 'im sharp, but when he led 'em to a mission-hall, and actually went inside, they left 'im and went off on their own.

They talked it over that night between themselves, and next evening they went out fust and hid themselves round the corner. Ten minutes arterwards old Sam came out, walking as though 'e was going to catch a train; and smiling to think 'ow he 'ad shaken them off. At the corner of Commercial Road he stopped and bought 'imself a button-hole for 'is coat, and Ginger was so surprised that 'e pinched Peter Russet to make sure that he wasn't dreaming.

Old Sam walked straight on whistling, and every now and then looking down at 'is button-hole, until by-and-by he turned down a street on the right and went into a little shop. Ginger Dick and Peter waited for 'im at the corner, but he was inside for so long that at last they got tired o' waiting and crept up and peeped through the winder.

It was a little tobacconist's shop, with newspapers and penny toys and such-like; but, as far as Ginger could see through two rows o' pipes and the *Police News*, it was empty. They stood there with their noses pressed against the glass for some time, wondering wot had 'appened to Sam, but by-and-by a little boy went in and then they began to 'ave an idea wot Sam's little game was.

As the shop-bell went the door of a little parlour at the back of the shop opened, and a stout and uncommon good-looking woman of about forty came out. Her 'ead pushed the *Police News* out o' the way and her 'and came groping into the winder arter a toy. Ginger 'ad a good look at 'er out o' the corner of one eye, while he pretended to be looking at a tobacco-jar with the other. As the little boy came out 'im and Peter Russet went in.

'I want a pipe, please,' he ses, smiling at 'er; 'a clay-pipe—one o' your best.'

The woman handed 'im down a box to choose from, and just then Peter, wot 'ad been staring in at the arf-open door at a boot wot wanted lacing up, gave a big start and ses, 'Why! Halloa!'

'Wot's the matter?' ses the woman, looking at 'im.

'I'd know that foot anywhere,' ses Peter, still staring at it; and the words was hardly out of 'is mouth afore the foot 'ad moved itself away and tucked itself under its chair. 'Why, that's my dear old friend Sam Small, ain't it?'

'Do you know the captin?' ses the woman, smiling at 'im.

'Cap——?' ses Peter. '*Cap*——? Oh, yes; why, he's the biggest friend I've got.'

''Ow strange!' ses the woman.

'We've been wanting to see 'im for some time,' ses Ginger. 'He was kind enough to lend me arf a crown the other day, and I've been wanting to pay 'im.'

'Captin Small,' ses the woman, pushing open the door, 'here's some old friends o' yours.'

Old Sam turned 'is face round and looked at 'em, and if looks could ha' killed, as the saying is, they'd ha' been dead men there and then.

'Oh, yes,' he ses, in a choking voice; ''ow are you?'

'Pretty well, thank you, *captin*,' ses Ginger, grinning at 'im; 'and 'ow's yourself arter all this long time?'

He held out 'is hand and Sam shook it, and then shook 'ands with Peter Russet, who was grinning so 'ard that he couldn't speak.

'These are two old friends o' mine, Mrs Finch,' ses old Sam, giving 'em a warning look; 'Captin Dick and Captin Russet, two o' the oldest and best friends a man ever 'ad.'

'Captin Dick 'as got arf a crown for you,' ses Peter Russet, still grinning.

'There now,' ses Ginger, looking vexed, 'if I ain't been and forgot it; I've on'y got arf a sovereign.'

'I can give you change, sir,' ses Mrs Finch. 'P'r'aps you'd like to sit down for five minutes?'

Ginger thanked 'er, and 'im and Peter Russet took a chair apiece in front o' the fire and began asking old Sam about 'is 'ealth, and wot he'd been doing since they saw 'im last.

'Fancy your reckernising his foot,' ses Mrs Finch, coming in with the change.

'I'd know it anywhere,' ses Peter, who was watching Ginger

129

pretending to give Sam Small the arf-dollar, and Sam pretending in a most lifelike manner to take it.

Ginger Dick looked round the room. It was a comfortable little place, with pictur's on the walls and antimacassars on all the chairs, and a row of pink vases on the mantelpiece. Then 'e looked at Mrs Finch, and thought wot a nice-looking woman she was.

'This is nicer than being aboard ship with a crew o' nasty, troublesome sailormen to look arter, Captin Small,' he ses.

'It's wonderful the way he manages 'em,' ses Peter Russet to Mrs Finch. 'Like a lion he is.'

'A roaring lion,' ses Ginger, looking at Sam. 'He don't know wot fear is.'

Sam began to smile, and Mrs Finch looked at 'im so pleased that Peter Russet, who 'ad been looking at 'er and the room, and thinking much the same way as Ginger, began to think that they was on the wrong tack.

'Afore 'e got stout and old,' he ses, shaking his 'ead, 'there wasn't a smarter skipper afloat.'

'We all 'ave our day,' ses Ginger, shaking his 'ead too.

'I dessay he's good for another year or two afloat, yet,' ses Peter Russet, considering.

'With care,' ses Ginger.

Old Sam was going to say something, but 'e stopped himself just in time. 'They will 'ave their joke,' he ses, turning to Mrs Finch and trying to smile. 'I feel as young as ever I did.'

Mrs Finch said that anybody with arf an eye could see that, and then she looked at a kettle that was singing on the 'ob.

'I s'pose you gentlemen wouldn't care for a cup o' cocoa?' she ses, turning to them.

Ginger Dick and Peter both said that they liked it better than anything else, and, arter she 'ad got out the cups and saucers and a tin o' cocoa, Ginger held the kettle and poured the water in the cups while she stirred them, and old Sam sat looking on 'elpless.

'It does seem funny to see you drinking cocoa, captin,' ses Ginger, as old Sam took his cup.

'Ho!' ses Sam, firing up; 'and why, if I might make so bold as to ask?'

''Cos I've generally seen you drinking something out of a bottle,' ses Ginger.

'Now, look 'ere,' ses Sam, starting up and spilling some of the hot cocoa over 'is lap.

'A ginger-beer bottle,' ses Peter Russet, making faces at Ginger to keep quiet.

'Yes, o' course, that's wot I meant,' ses Ginger, looking surprised.

Old Sam wiped the cocoa off 'is knees without saying a word, but his weskit kept going up and down till Peter Russet felt quite sorry for 'im.

'There's nothing like it,' he ses to Mrs Finch. 'It was by sticking to ginger-beer and milk and such-like that Captain Small 'ad command of a ship afore 'e was twenty-five.'

'Lor'!' ses Mrs Finch.

She smiled at old Sam till Peter got uneasy agin, and began to think p'r'aps 'e'd been praising 'im too much.

'Of course, I'm speaking of long ago now,' he ses.

'Years and years afore you was born, ma'am,' ses Ginger.

Old Sam was going to say something, but Mrs Finch looked so pleased that 'e thought better of it. Some o' the cocoa 'e was drinking went the wrong way, and then Ginger patted 'im on the back and told 'im to be careful not to bring on 'is brown-chitis agin. Wot with temper and being afraid to speak for fear they should let Mrs Finch know that 'e wasn't a captin, he could 'ardly bear 'imself, but he very near broke out when Peter Russet advised 'im to 'ave his weskit lined with red flannel. They all stayed on till closing time, and by the time they left they 'ad made theirselves so pleasant that Mrs Finch said she'd be pleased to see them any time they liked to look in.

Sam Small waited till they 'ad turned the corner, and then he broke out so alarming that they could 'ardly do anything with 'im. Twice policemen spoke to 'im and advised 'im to go home afore they altered their minds; and he 'ad to hold 'imself in and keep quiet while Ginger and Peter Russet took 'is arms and said they were seeing him 'ome.

He started the row agin when they got indoors, and sat up in 'is bed smacking 'is lips over the things he'd like to 'ave done to them if he could. And then, arter saying 'ow he'd like to see Ginger boiled alive like a lobster, he said he knew that 'e was a noble-'arted feller who wouldn't try and cut an old pal out, and that it was a case of love at first sight on top of a tram-car.

'She's too young for you,' ses Ginger; 'and too good-looking besides.'

'It's the nice little bisness he's fallen in love with, Ginger,' ses Peter Russet. 'I'll toss you who 'as it.'

Ginger, who was sitting on the foot o' Sam's bed, said 'no' at fust, but arter a time he pulled out arf a dollar and spun it in the air. That was the last 'e see of it, although he 'ad Sam out o' bed and all the clothes stripped off of it twice. He spent over arf an hour on his 'ands and knees looking for it, and Sam said when he was tired of playing bears p'r'aps he'd go to bed and get to sleep like a Christian.

They 'ad it all over agin next morning, and at last, as nobody would agree to keep quiet and let the others 'ave a fair chance, they made up their minds to let the best man win. Ginger Dick bought a necktie that took all the colour out o' Sam's, and Peter Russet went in for a collar so big that 'e was lost in it.

They all strolled into the widow's shop separate that night. Ginger Dick 'ad smashed his pipe and wanted another; Peter Russet wanted some tobacco; and old Sam Small walked in smiling, with a little silver brooch for 'er, that he said 'e had picked up.

It was a very nice brooch, and Mrs Finch was so pleased with it that Ginger and Peter sat there as mad as they could be because they 'adn't thought of the same thing.

'Captin Small is very lucky at finding things,' ses Ginger, at last.

'He's got the name for it,' ses Peter Russet.

'It's a handy 'abit,' ses Ginger; 'it saves spending money. Who did you give that gold bracelet to you picked up the other night, captin?' he ses, turning to Sam.

'Gold bracelet?' ses Sam. 'I didn't pick up no gold bracelet. Wot are you talking about?'

'All right, captin; no offence,' ses Ginger, holding up his 'and. 'I dreamt I saw one on your mantelpiece, I s'pose. P'r'aps I oughtn't to ha' said anything about it.'

Old Sam looked as though he'd like to eat 'im, especially as he noticed Mrs Finch listening and pretending not to. 'Oh! that one,' he ses, arter a bit o' hard thinking. 'Oh! I found out who it belonged to. You wouldn't believe 'ow pleased they was at getting it back agin.'

Ginger Dick coughed and began to think as 'ow old Sam was sharper than he 'ad given 'im credit for, but afore he could think of anything else to say Mrs Finch looked at old Sam and began to talk about 'is ship, and to say 'ow much she should like to see over it.

'I wish I could take you,' ses Sam, looking at the other two out o' the corner of his eye, 'but my ship's over at Dunkirk, in France. I've just run over to London for a week or two to look round.'

'And mine's there too,' ses Peter Russet, speaking a'most afore old Sam 'ad finished; 'side by side they lay in the harbour.'

'Oh, dear,' ses Mrs Finch, folding her 'ands and shaking her 'ead. 'I *should* like to go over a ship one arternoon. I'd quite made up my mind to it, knowing three captins.'

She smiled and looked at Ginger; and Sam and Peter looked at 'im too, wondering whether he was going to berth his ship at Dunkirk alongside o' theirs.

'Ah, I wish I 'ad met you a fortnight ago,' ses Ginger, very sad. 'I gave up my ship, the *Highflyer*, then, and I'm waiting for one my owners are 'aving built for me at Newcastle. They said the *Highflyer* wasn't big enough for me. She was a nice little ship, though. I believe I've got 'er pictur' somewhere about me!'

He felt in 'is pocket and pulled out a little, crumpled-up photograph of a ship he'd been fireman aboard of some years afore, and showed it to 'er.

'That's me standing on the bridge,' he ses, pointing out a little dot with the stem of 'is pipe.

'It's your figger,' ses Mrs Finch, straining her eyes. 'I should know it anywhere.'

'You've got wonderful eyes, ma'am,' ses old Sam, choking with 'is pipe.

'Anybody can see that,' ses Ginger. 'They're the largest and the bluest I've ever seen.'

Mrs Finch told 'im not to talk nonsense, but both Sam and Peter Russet could see 'ow pleased she was.

'Truth is truth,' ses Ginger. 'I'm a plain man, and I speak my mind.'

'Blue is my fav'rit' colour,' ses old Sam, in a tender voice. 'True blue.'

Peter Russet began to feel out of it. 'I thought brown was,' he ses.

'Ho!' ses Sam, turning on 'im; 'and why?'

'I 'ad my reasons,' ses Peter, nodding, and shutting 'is mouth very firm.

'I thought brown was 'is fav'rit' colour too,' ses Ginger. 'I don't know why. It's no use asking me; because if you did I couldn't tell you.'

'Brown's a very nice colour,' ses Mrs Finch, wondering wot was the matter with old Sam.

'Blue,' ses Ginger; 'big blue eyes—they're the ones for me. Other people may 'ave their blacks and their browns,' he ses, looking at Sam and Peter Russet, 'but give me blue.'

They went on like that all the evening, and every time the shop-bell went and the widow 'ad to go out to serve a customer they said in w'ispers wot they thought of each other; and once when she came back rather sudden Ginger 'ad to explain to 'er that 'e was showing Peter Russet a scratch on his knuckle.

Ginger Dick was the fust there next night, and took 'er a little chiney teapot he 'ad picked up dirt cheap because it was cracked right acrost the middle; but, as he explained that he 'ad dropped it in hurrying to see 'er, she was just as pleased.

She stuck it up on the mantelpiece, and the things she said about Ginger's kindness and generosity made Peter Russet spend good money that he wanted for 'imself on a painted flower-pot next evening.

With three men all courting 'er at the same time Mrs Finch had 'er hands full, but she took to it wonderful considering. She was so nice and kind to 'em all that even arter a week's 'ard work none of 'em was really certain which she liked best.

They took to going in at odd times o' the day for tobacco and such-like. They used to go alone then, but they all met and did the polite to each other there of an evening, and then quarrelled all the way 'ome.

Then all of a sudden, without any warning, Ginger Dick and Peter Russet left off going there. The fust evening Sam sat expecting them every minute, and was so surprised that he couldn't take any advantage of it; but on the second, beginning by squeezing Mrs Finch's 'and at ha'-past seven, he 'ad got best part of his arm round 'er waist by a quarter to ten. He didn't do more that night because she told him to be'ave 'imself, and threatened to scream if he didn't leave off.

He was arf-way home afore 'e thought of the reason for Ginger Dick and Peter Russet giving up, and then he went along smiling to 'imself to such an extent that people thought 'e was mad. He went off to sleep with the smile still on 'is lips, and when Peter and Ginger came in soon arter closing time and 'e woke up and asked them where they'd been, 'e was still smiling.

'I didn't 'ave the pleasure o' seeing you at Mrs Finch's tonight,' he ses.

'No,' ses Ginger, very short. 'We got tired of it.'

'So un'ealthy sitting in that stuffy little room every evening,' ses Peter.

Old Sam put his 'ead under the bedclothes and laughed till the bed shook; and every now and then he'd put his 'ead out and look at Peter and Ginger and laugh agin till he choked.

'I see 'ow it is,' he ses, sitting up and wiping his eyes on the sheet. 'Well, we can't all win.'

'Wot d'ye mean?' ses Ginger, very disagreeable.

'She wouldn't 'ave you,' ses Sam, 'that's wot I mean. And I don't wonder at it. I wouldn't 'ave you if I was a gal.'

'You're dreaming,' ses Peter Russet, sneering at 'im.

'That flower-pot o' yours'll come in handy,' ses Sam, thinking 'ow he 'ad put 'is arm round the widow's waist; 'and I thank you kindly for the teapot, Ginger.'

'You don't mean to say as you've asked 'er to marry you?' ses Ginger, looking at Peter Russet.

'Not quite; but I'm going to,' ses Sam, 'and I'll bet you even arf-crowns she ses "yes". '

Ginger wouldn't take 'im, and no more would Peter, not even when he raised it to five shillings; and the vain way old Sam lay there boasting and talking about 'is way with the gals made 'em both feel ill.

'I wouldn't 'ave her if she asked me on 'er bended knees,' ses Ginger, holding up his 'ead.

'Nor me,' ses Peter. 'You're welcome to 'er, Sam. When I think of the evenings I've wasted over a fat old woman I feel——'

'That'll do,' ses old Sam, very sharp; 'that ain't the way to speak of a lady, even if she 'as said "no". '

'All right, Sam,' ses Ginger. 'You go in and win if you think you're so precious clever.'

Old Sam said that that was wot 'e was going to do, and he spent so much time next morning making 'imself look pretty that the other two could 'ardly be civil to him.

He went off a'most direckly arter breakfast, and they didn't see 'im agin till twelve o'clock that night. He 'ad brought a bottle o' whisky in with 'im, and he was so 'appy that they see plain wot had 'appened.

'She said "yes" at two o'clock in the arternoon,' ses old Sam, smiling, arter they had 'ad a glass apiece. 'I'd nearly done the trick at one o'clock, and then the shop-bell went and I 'ad to begin all over agin. Still, it wasn't unpleasant.'

'Do you mean to tell us you've asked 'er to marry you?' ses Ginger, 'olding out 'is glass to be filled agin.

'I do,' ses Sam; 'but I 'ope there's no ill-feeling. You never 'ad a chance, neither of you; she told me so.'

Ginger Dick and Peter Russet stared at each other.

'She said she 'ad been in love with me all along,' ses Sam, filling their glasses agin to cheer 'em up. 'We went out arter tea and bought the engagement-ring, and then she got somebody to mind the shop and we went to the Pagoda music-'all.'

'I 'ope you didn't pay much for the ring, Sam,' ses Ginger, who always got very kind-'arted arter two or three glasses o' whisky. 'If I'd known you was going to be in such a hurry I might ha' told you before.'

'We ought to ha' done,' ses Peter, shaking his 'ead.

'Told me?' ses Sam, staring at 'em. 'Told me wot?'

'Why me and Peter gave it up,' ses Ginger; 'but, o' course, p'r'aps you don't mind.'

'Mind wot?' ses Sam.

'It's wonderful 'ow quiet she kept it,' ses Peter.

Old Sam stared at 'em agin, and then he asked 'em to speak in plain English wot they'd got to say, and not to go taking away the character of a woman wot wasn't there to speak up for herself.

'It's nothing agin 'er character,' ses Ginger.

'It's a credit to her, looked at properly,' ses Peter Russet.

'And Sam'll 'ave the pleasure of bringing of 'em up,' ses Ginger.

'*Bringing of 'em up?*' ses Sam, in a trembling voice and turning pale; 'bringing who up?'

'Why, 'er children,' ses Ginger. 'Didn't she tell you? She's got nine of 'em.'

Sam pretended not to believe 'em at fust, and said they was jealous; but next day he crept down to the greengrocer's shop in the same street, where Ginger had 'appened to buy some oranges one day, and found that it was only too true. Nine children, the eldest of 'em only fifteen, was staying with diff'rent relations owing to scarlet-fever next door.

Old Sam crept back 'ome like a man in a dream, with a bag of oranges he didn't want, and, arter making a present of the engagement-ring to Ginger—if 'e could get it—he took the fust train to Tilbury and signed on for a v'y'ge to China.

In the Family

The oldest inhabitant of Claybury sat beneath the sign of the 'Cauliflower' and gazed with affectionate, but dim, old eyes in the direction of the village street.

No; Claybury men ain't never been much of ones for emigrating, he said, turning to the youthful traveller who was resting in the shade with a mug of ale and a cigarette. They know they'd 'ave to go a long way afore they'd find a place as 'ud come up to this.

He finished the tablespoonful of beer in his mug and sat for so long with his head back and the inverted vessel on his face that the traveller, who at first thought it was the beginning of a conjuring trick, coloured furiously, and asked permission to refill it.

Now and then a Claybury man has gone to foreign parts, said the old man, drinking from the replenished mug, and placing it where the traveller could mark progress without undue strain; but they've, gen'rally speaking, come back and wished as they'd never gone.

The on'y man as I ever heard of that made his fortune by emigrating was Henery Walker's great-uncle, Josiah Walker by name, and he wasn't a Claybury man at all. He made his fortune out o' sheep in Australey, and he was so rich and well-to-do that he could never find time to answer the letters that Henery Walker used to send him when he was hard up.

Henery Walker used to hear of 'im through a relation of his up in London, and tell us all about 'im and his money up at this here 'Cauliflower' public-house. And he used to sit and drink his beer and wonder who would 'ave the old man's money arter he was dead.

138

When the relation in London died Henery Walker left off hearing about his uncle, and he got so worried over thinking that the old man might die and leave his money to strangers that he got quite thin. He talked of emigrating to Australey 'imself, and then, acting on the advice of Bill Chambers—who said it was a cheaper thing to do—he wrote to his uncle instead, and, arter reminding 'im that 'e was an old man living in a strange country, 'e asked 'im to come to Claybury and make his 'ome with 'is loving grand-nephew.

It was a good letter, because more than one gave 'im a hand with it, and there was little bits o' Scripture in it to make it more solemn-like. It was wrote on pink paper with pie-crust edges and put in a green envelope, and Bill Chambers said a man must 'ave a 'art of stone if that didn't touch it.

Four months arterwards Henery Walker got an answer to 'is letter from 'is great-uncle. It was a nice letter, and, arter thanking Henery Walker for all his kindness, 'is uncle said that he was getting an old man, and p'r'aps he should come and lay 'is bones in England arter all, and if he did 'e should certainly come and see his grand-nephew, Henery Walker.

Most of us thought Henery Walker's fortune was as good as made, but Bob Pretty, a nasty, low, poaching chap that has done wot he could to give Claybury a bad name, turned up his nose at it.

'I'll believe he's coming 'ome when I see him,' he ses. 'It's my belief he went to Australey to get out o' your way, Henery.'

'As it 'appened he went there afore I was born,' ses Henery Walker, firing up.

'He knew your father,' ses Bob Pretty, 'and he didn't want to take no risks.'

They 'ad words then, and arter that every time Bob Pretty met 'im he asked arter his great-uncle's 'ealth, and used to pretend to think 'e was living with 'im.

'You ought to get the old gentleman out a bit more, Henery,' he would say; 'it can't be good for 'im to be shut up in the 'ouse so much—especially your 'ouse.'

Henery Walker used to get that riled he didn't know wot to do with 'imself, and as time went on, and he began to be afraid that 'is uncle never would come back to England, he used to get quite nasty if anybody on'y so much as used the word 'uncle' in 'is company.

It was over six months since he 'ad had the letter from 'is uncle, and 'e was up here at the 'Cauliflower' with some more of us one night, when Dicky Weed, the tailor, turns to Bob Pretty and ses, 'Who's the old gentleman that's staying with you, Bob?'

Bob Pretty puts down 'is beer very careful and turns round on 'im.

'Old gentleman?' he ses, very slow. 'Wot are you talking about?'

'I mean the little old gentleman with white whiskers and a squeaky voice,' ses Dicky Weed.

'You've been dreaming,' ses Bob, taking up 'is beer ag'in.

'I see 'im too, Bob,' ses Bill Chambers.

'Ho, you did, did you?' ses Bob Pretty, putting down 'is mug with a bang. 'And wot d'ye mean by coming spying round my place, eh? Wot d'ye mean by it?'

'Spying?' ses Bill Chambers, gaping at 'im with 'is mouth open; 'I wasn't spying. Anyone 'ud think you 'ad done something you was ashamed of.'

'You mind your business and I'll mind mine,' ses Bob, very fierce.

'I was passing the 'ouse,' ses Bill Chambers, looking round at us, 'and I see an old man's face at the bedroom winder, and while I was wondering who 'e was a hand come and drawed 'im away. I see 'im as plain as ever I see anything in my life, and the hand, too. Big and dirty it was.'

'And he's got a cough,' ses Dicky Weed—'a churchyard cough—I 'eard it.'

'It ain't much you don't hear, Dicky,' ses Bob Pretty, turning on 'im; 'the on'y thing you never did 'ear, and never will 'ear, is any good of yourself.'

He kicked over a chair wot was in 'is way and went off in

such a temper as we'd never seen 'im in afore, and, wot was more surprising still, but I know it's true, 'cos I drunk it up myself, he'd left over arf a pint o' beer in 'is mug.

'He's up to something,' ses Sam Jones, staring arter him; 'mark my words.'

We couldn't make head nor tail out of it, but for some days arterward you'd ha' thought that Bob Pretty's 'ouse was a peep-show. Everybody stared at the winders as they went by, and the children played in front of the 'ouse and stared in all day long. Then the old gentleman was seen one day as bold as brass sitting at the winder, and we heard that it was a pore old tramp Bob Pretty 'ad met on the road and given a home to, and he didn't like 'is good-'artedness to be known for fear he should be made fun of.

Nobody believed that, o' course, and things got more puzzling than ever. Once or twice the old gentleman went out for a walk, but Bob Pretty or 'is missis was always with 'im, and if anybody tried to speak to him they always said 'e was deaf and took 'im off as fast as they could. Then one night up at the 'Cauliflower' here Dicky Weed came rushing in with a bit o' news that took everybody's breath away.

'I've just come from the post-office,' he ses, 'and there's a letter for Bob Pretty's old gentleman! Wot d'ye think o' that?'

'If you could tell us wot's inside it you might 'ave something to brag about,' ses Henery Walker.

'I don't want to see the inside,' ses Dicky Weed; 'the name on the outside was good enough for me. I couldn't hardly believe my own eyes, but there it was: "Mr Josiah Walker", as plain as the nose on your face.'

O' course, we see it all then, and wondered why we hadn't thought of it afore; and we stood quiet listening to the things that Henery Walker said about a man that would go and steal another man's great-uncle from 'im. Three times Smith, the landlord, said, '*Hush!*' and the fourth time he put Henery Walker outside and told 'im to stay there till he 'ad lost his voice.

Henery Walker stayed outside five minutes, and then 'e come back in ag'in to ask for advice. His idea seemed to be that, as the old gentleman was deaf, Bob Pretty was passing 'isself off as Henery Walker, and the disgrace was a'most more than 'e could bear. He began to get excited ag'in, and Smith 'ad just said 'Hush!' once more when he 'eard somebody whistling outside, and in come Bob Pretty.

He 'ad hardly got 'is face in at the door afore Henery Walker started on 'im, and Bob Pretty stood there, struck all of a heap, and staring at 'im as though he couldn't believe his ears.

"Ave you gone mad, Henery?' he ses, at last.

'Give me back my great-uncle,' ses Henery Walker, at the top of 'is voice.

Bob Pretty shook his 'ead at him. 'I haven't got your great-uncle, Henery,' he ses, very gentle. 'I know the name is the same, but wot of it? There's more than one Josiah Walker in the world. This one is no relation to you at all; he's a very respectable old gentleman.'

'I'll go and ask 'im,' ses Henery Walker, getting up, 'and I'll tell 'im wot sort o' man you are, Bob Pretty.'

'He's gone to bed now, Henery,' ses Bob Pretty.

'I'll come in the fust thing tomorrow morning, then,' ses Henery Walker.

'Not in my 'ouse, Henery,' ses Bob Pretty; 'not arter the things you've been sayin' about me. I'm a poor man, but I've got my pride. Besides, I tell you he ain't your uncle. He's a pore old man I'm giving a 'ome to, and I won't 'ave 'im worried.'

"Ow much does 'e pay you a week, Bob?' ses Bill Chambers.

Bob Pretty pretended not to hear 'im.

'Where did your wife get the money to buy that bonnet she 'ad on on Sunday?' ses Bill Chambers. 'My wife ses it's the fust new bonnet she has 'ad since she was married.'

'And where did the new winder curtains come from?' ses Peter Gubbins.

Bob Pretty drank up 'is beer and stood looking at them very thoughtful; then he opened the door and went out without saying a word.

'He's got your great-uncle a prisoner in his 'ouse, Henery,' ses Bill Chambers; 'it's easy for to see that the pore old gentleman is getting past things, and I shouldn't wonder if Bob Pretty don't make 'im leave all 'is money to 'im.'

Henery Walker started raving ag'in, and for the next few days he tried his 'ardest to get a few words with 'is great-uncle, but Bob Pretty was too much for 'im. Everybody in Claybury said wot a shame it was, but it was all no good, and Henery Walker used to leave 'is work and stand outside Bob Pretty's for hours at a time in the 'opes of getting a word with the old man.

He got 'is chance at last, in quite a unexpected way. We was up 'ere at the 'Cauliflower' one evening, and, as it 'appened, we was talking about Henery Walker's great-uncle, when the door opened, and who should walk in but the old gentleman 'imself. Everybody left off talking and stared at 'im, but he walked up to the bar and ordered a glass o' gin and beer as comfortable as you please.

Bill Chambers was the fust to get 'is presence of mind back, and he set off arter Henery Walker as fast as 'is legs could carry 'im, and in a wunnerful short time, considering, he came back with Henery, both of 'em puffing and blowing their 'ardest.

'There—he—is!' ses Bill Chambers, pointing to the old gentleman.

Henery Walker gave one look, and then 'e slipped over to the old man and stood all of a tremble, smiling at 'im. 'Good-evening,' he ses.

'Wot?' ses the old gentleman.

'Good-evening!' ses Henery Walker ag'in.

'I'm a bit deaf,' ses the old gentleman, putting his 'and to his ear.

'GOOD-EVENING!' ses Henery Walker ag'in, shouting. 'I'm your grand-nephew, Henery Walker!'

'Ho, are you?' ses the old gentleman, not at all surprised. 'Bob Pretty was telling me all about you.'

'I 'ope you didn't listen to 'im,' ses Henery Walker, all of a tremble. 'Bob Pretty'd say anything except his prayers.'

'He ses you're arter my money,' ses the old gentleman, looking at 'im.

'He's a liar, then,' ses Henery Walker; 'he's arter it 'imself. And it ain't a respectable place for you to stay at. Anybody'll tell you wot a rascal Bob Pretty is. Why, he's a byword.'

'Everybody is arter my money,' ses the old gentleman, looking round. 'Everybody.'

'I 'ope you'll know me better afore you've done with me, uncle,' ses Henery Walker, taking a seat alongside of 'im. 'Will you 'ave another mug o' beer?'

'Gin and beer,' ses the old gentleman, cocking his eye up very fierce at Smith, the landlord; 'and mind the gin don't get out ag'in, same as it did in the last.'

Smith asked 'im wot he meant, but 'is deafness come on ag'in. Henery Walker 'ad an extra dose o' gin put in, and arter he 'ad tasted it the old gentleman seemed to get more amiable-like, and 'im and Henery Walker sat by theirselves talking quite comfortable.

'Why not come and stay with me?' ses Henery Walker, at last. 'You can do as you please and have the best of everything.'

'Bob Pretty ses you're arter my money,' ses the old gentleman, shaking his 'ead. 'I couldn't trust you.'

'He ses that to put you ag'in me,' ses Henery Walker, pleading-like.

'Well, wot do you want me to come and live with you for, then?' ses old Mr Walker.

'Because you're my great-uncle,' ses Henery Walker, 'and my 'ouse is the proper place for you. Blood is thicker than water.'

'And you don't want my money?' ses the old man, looking at 'im very sharp.

'Certainly not,' ses Henery Walker.

'And 'ow much 'ave I got to pay a week?' ses old Mr Walker. 'That's the question?'

'Pay?' ses Henery Walker, speaking afore he 'ad time to think. 'Pay? Why, I don't want you to pay anything.'

The old gentleman said as 'ow he'd think it over, and Henery started to talk to 'im about his father and an old aunt named Maria, but 'e stopped 'im sharp, and said he was sick and tired of the whole Walker family, and didn't want to 'ear their names ag'in as long as he lived. Henery Walker began to talk about Australey then, and asked 'im 'ow many sheep he'd got, and the words was 'ardly out of 'is mouth afore the old gentleman stood up and said he was arter his money ag'in.

Henery Walker at once gave 'im some more gin and beer, and arter he 'ad drunk it the old gentleman said that he'd go and live with 'im for a little while to see 'ow he liked it.

'But I sha'n't pay anything,' he ses, very sharp; 'mind that.'

'I wouldn't take it if you offered it to me,' ses Henery Walker. 'You'll come straight 'ome with me tonight, won't you?'

Afore old Mr Walker could answer the door opened and in came Bob Pretty. He gave one look at Henery Walker and then he walked straight over to the old gentleman and put his 'and on his shoulder.

'Why, I've been looking for you everywhere, Mr Walker,' he ses. 'I couldn't think wot had 'appened to you.'

'You needn't worry yourself, Bob,' ses Henery Walker; 'he is coming to live with me now.'

'Don't you believe it,' ses Bob Pretty, taking hold of old Mr Walker by the arm; 'he's my lodger, and he's coming with me.'

He began to lead the old gentleman towards the door, but Henery Walker, wot was still sitting down, threw 'is arms round his legs and held 'im tight. Bob Pretty pulled one way and Henery Walker pulled the other, and both of 'em shouted to each other to leave go. The row they made was awful, but old Mr Walker made more noise than the two of 'em put together.

'You leave go o' my lodger,' ses Bob Pretty.

'You leave go o' my great-uncle—my dear great-uncle,' ses Henery Walker, as the old gentleman called 'im a bad name and asked 'im whether he thought he was made of iron.

I believe they'd ha' been at it till closing-time, on'y Smith, the landlord, came running in from the back and told them to go outside. He 'ad to shout to make 'imself heard, and all four of 'em seemed to be trying which could make the most noise.

'He's my lodger,' ses Bob Pretty, 'and he can't go without giving me proper notice; that's the lor—a week's notice.'

They all shouted ag'in then, and at last the old gentleman told Henery Walker to give Bob Pretty ten shillings for the week's notice and ha' done with 'im. Henery Walker 'ad only got four shillings with 'im, but 'e borrowed the rest from Smith, and arter he 'ad told Bob Pretty wot he thought of 'im he took old Mr Walker by the arm and led him 'ome a'most dancing for joy.

Mrs Walker was nearly as pleased as wot 'e was, and the fuss they made of the old gentleman was sinful a'most. He 'ad to speak about it 'imself at last, and he told 'em plain that when 'e wanted arf-a-dozen sore-eyed children to be brought down in their night-gowns to kiss 'im while he was eating sausages, he'd say so.

Arter that Mrs Walker was afraid that 'e might object when her and her 'usband gave up their bedroom to 'im; but he didn't. He took it all as 'is right, and when Henery Walker, who was sleeping in the next room with three of 'is boys, fell out o' bed for the second time, he got up and rapped on the wall.

Bob Pretty came round the next morning with a tin box that belonged to the old man, and 'e was so perlite and nice to 'im that Henery Walker could see that he 'ad 'opes of getting 'im back ag'in. The box was carried upstairs and put under old Mr Walker's bed, and 'e was so partikler about its being locked, and about nobody being about when 'e opened it, that Mrs Walker went arf out of her mind with curiosity.

'I s'pose you've looked to see that Bob Pretty didn't take anything out of it?' ses Henery Walker.

'He didn't 'ave the chance,' ses the old gentleman. 'It's always kep' locked.'

'It's a box that looks as though it might 'ave been made in

146

Australey,' ses Henery Walker, who was longing to talk about them parts.

'If you say another word about Australey to me,' ses old Mr Walker, firing up, 'off I go. Mind that! You're arter my money, and if you're not careful you sha'n't 'ave a farthing of it.'

That was the last time the word 'Australey' passed Henery Walker's lips, and even when 'e saw his great-uncle writing letters there he didn't say anything. And the old man was so suspicious of Mrs Walker's curiosity that all the letters that was wrote to 'im he 'ad sent to Bob Pretty's. He used to call there pretty near every morning to see whether any 'ad come for 'im.

In three months Henery Walker 'adn't seen the colour of 'is money once, and, wot was worse still, he took to giving Henery's things away. Mrs Walker 'ad been complaining for some time of 'ow bad the hens had been laying, and one morning at breakfast-time she told her 'usband that, besides missing eggs, two of 'er best hens 'ad been stolen in the night.

'They wasn't stolen,' ses old Mr Walker, putting down 'is teacup. 'I took 'em round this morning and give 'em to Bob Pretty.'

'Give 'em to Bob Pretty?' ses Henery Walker, arf choking. 'Wot for?'

''Cos he asked me for 'em,' ses the old gentleman. 'Wot are you looking at me like that for?'

Henery couldn't answer 'im, and the old gentleman, looking very fierce, got up from the table and told Mrs Walker to give 'im his hat. Henery Walker clung to 'im with tears in his eyes a'most and begged 'im not to go, and arter a lot of talk old Mr Walker said he'd look over it this time, but it mustn't occur ag'in.

Arter that 'e did as 'e liked with Henery Walker's things, and Henery dursen't say a word to 'im. Bob Pretty used to come up and flatter 'im and beg 'im to go back and lodge with 'im, and Henery was so afraid he'd go that he didn't say a word when old Mr Walker used to give Bob Pretty things to make up for 'is disappointment. He 'eard on the quiet from Bill Chambers, who said that the old man 'ad told it to Bob Pretty as a dead secret, that 'e 'ad left 'im all his money, and he was ready to put up with anything.

The old man must ha' been living with Henery Walker for over eighteen months when one night he passed away in 'is sleep. Henery knew that his 'art was wrong, because he 'ad just paid Dr Green 'is bill for saying that 'e couldn't do anything for 'im, but it was a surprise to 'im all the same. He blew his nose 'ard and Mrs Walker kept rubbing 'er eyes with her apron while they talked in whispers and wondered 'ow much money they 'ad come in for.

In less than ten minutes the news was all over Claybury, and arf the people in the place hanging round in front of the 'ouse waiting to hear 'ow much the Walkers 'ad come in for. Henery Walker pulled the blind on one side for a moment and shook his 'ead at them to go away. Some of them did go back a yard or two, and then they stood staring at Bob Pretty, wot come up as bold as brass and knocked at the door.

'Wot's this I 'ear?' he ses, when Henery Walker opened it. 'You don't mean to tell me that the pore old gentleman has really gone? I told 'im wot would happen if 'e came to lodge with you.'

'You be off,' ses Henery Walker; 'he hasn't left you anything.'

'I know that,' ses Bob Pretty, shaking his 'ead. 'You're welcome to it, Henery, if there is anything. I never bore any malice to you for taking of 'im away from us. I could see you'd took a fancy to 'im from the fust. The way you pretended 'e was your great-uncle showed me that.'

'Wot are you talking about?' ses Henery Walker. 'He *was* my great-uncle!'

'Have it your own way, Henery,' ses Bob Pretty; 'on'y, if you asked me, I should say that he was my wife's grandfather.'

'*Your—wife's—grandfather?*' ses Henery Walker, in a choking voice.

He stood staring at 'im, stupid-like, for a minute or two,

but he couldn't get out another word. In a flash 'e saw 'ow he'd been done, and how Bob Pretty 'ad been deceiving 'im all along, and the idea that he 'ad arf ruined himself keeping Mrs Pretty's grandfather for 'em pretty near sent 'im out of his mind.

'But how is it 'is name was Josiah Walker, same as Henery's great-uncle?' ses Bill Chambers, who 'ad been crowding round with the others. 'Tell me that!'

'He 'ad a fancy for it,' ses Bob Pretty, 'and being a 'armless amusement we let him 'ave his own way. I told Henery Walker over and over ag'in that it wasn't his uncle, but he wouldn't believe me. I've got witnesses to it. Wot did you say, Henery?'

Henery Walker drew 'imself up as tall as he could and stared at him. Twice he opened 'is mouth to speak but couldn't and then he made a odd sort o' choking noise in his throat, and slammed the door in Bob Pretty's face.

The Dreamer

Dreams and warnings are things I don't believe in, said the night watchman. The only dream I ever 'ad that come anything like true was once when I dreamt I came in for a fortune, and next morning I found half a crown in the street, which I sold to a man for fourpence. And once, two days arter my missis 'ad dreamt she 'ad spilt a cup of tea down the front of 'er Sunday dress, she spoilt a pot o' paint of mine by sitting in it.

The only other dream I know of that come true happened to the cook of a barque I was aboard of once, called the *Southern Belle*. He was a silly, pasty-faced sort o' chap, always giving hisself airs about eddication to sailormen who didn't believe in it, and one night, when we was homeward-bound from Sydney, he suddenly sat up in 'is bunk and laughed so loud that he woke us all up.

'Wot's wrong, cookie?' ses one o' the chaps.

'I was dreaming,' ses the cook, 'such a funny dream. I dreamt old Bill Foster fell out o' the foretop and broke 'is leg.'

'Well, wot is there to laugh at in that?' ses old Bill, very sharp.

'It was funny in my dream,' ses the cook. 'You looked so comic with your leg doubled up under you, you can't think. It would ha' made a cat laugh.'

Bill Foster said he'd make 'im laugh the other side of his face if he wasn't careful, and then we went off to sleep ag'in and forgot all about it.

If you'll believe me, on'y three days arterwards pore Bill did fall out o' the foretop and break his leg. He was surprised, but I never see a man so surprised as the cook was. His eyes was nearly starting out of 'is head, but by the time the other chaps 'ad picked Bill up and asked 'im whether he was hurt, cook 'ad pulled 'imself together ag'in and was giving himself such airs it was perfectly sickening.

'My dreams always come true,' he ses. 'It's a kind o' second sight with me. It's a gift, and, being tender-'arted, it worries me terrible sometimes.'

He was going on like that, taking credit for a pure accident, when the second officer came up and told 'em to carry Bill below. He was in agony, of course, but he kept 'is presence of mind, and as they passed the cook he gave 'im such a clip on the side of the 'ead as nearly broke it.

'That's for dreaming about me,' he ses.

The skipper and the fust officer and most of the hands set 'is leg between them, and arter the skipper 'ad made him wot he called comfortable, but wot Bill called something that I won't soil my ears by repeating, the officers went off and the cook came and sat down by the side o' Bill and talked about his gift.

'I don't talk about it as a rule,' he ses, ''cos it frightens people.'

'It's a wonderful gift, cookie,' ses Charlie Epps.

All of 'em thought the same, not knowing wot a fust-class liar the cook was, and he sat there and lied to 'em till he couldn't 'ardly speak, he was so 'oarse.

'My grandmother was a gipsy,' he ses, 'and it's in the family. Things that are going to 'appen to people I know come to me in dreams same as pore Bill's did. It's curious to me sometimes when I look round at you chaps, seeing you going about 'appy and comfortable, and knowing all the time 'orrible things that is going to 'appen to you. Sometimes it gives me the fair shivers.'

'Horrible things to us, slushy?' ses Charlie, staring.

'Yes,' ses the cook, nodding. 'I never was on a ship afore with such a lot of unfortunit men aboard. Never. There's two pore fellers wot'll be dead corpses inside o' six months, sitting 'ere laughing and talking as if they was going to live to ninety. Thank your stars you don't 'ave such dreams.'

'Who—who are the two, cookie?' ses Charlie, arter a bit.

'Never mind, Charlie,' ses the cook, in a sad voice; 'it would do no good if I was to tell you. Nothing can alter it.'

'Give us a hint,' ses Charlie.

'Well, I'll tell you this much,' ses the cook, arter sitting with his 'ead in his 'ands, thinking; 'one of 'em is nearly the ugliest man in the fo'c's'le and the other ain't.'

O' course, that didn't 'elp 'em much, but it caused a lot of argufying, and the ugliest man aboard, instead o' being grateful, behaved more like a wild beast than a Christian when it was pointed out to him that he was safe.

Arter that dream about Bill, there was no keeping the cook in his place. He 'ad dreams pretty near every night, and talked little bits of 'em in his sleep. Little bits that you couldn't make head nor tail of, and when we asked 'im next morning he'd always shake his 'ead and say, 'Never mind.' Sometimes he'd mention a chap's name in 'is sleep and make 'im nervous for days.

It was an unlucky v'y'ge that, for some of 'em. About a week arter pore Bill's accident Ted Jones started playing catch-ball with another chap and a empty beer-bottle, and about the fifth chuck Ted caught it with his face. We thought 'e was killed at fust—he made such a noise; but they got 'im down below, and, arter they 'ad picked out as much broken glass as Ted would let 'em, the second officer did 'im up in sticking-plaster and told 'im to keep quiet for an hour or two.

Ted was very proud of 'is looks, and the way he went on was alarming. Fust of all he found fault with the chap 'e was playing with, and then he turned on the cook.

'It's a pity you didn't see *that* in a dream,' he ses, tryin' to sneer, on'y the sticking-plaster was too strong for 'im.

'But I did see it,' ses the cook, drawin' 'imself up.

'*Wot?*' ses Ted, starting.

'I dreamt it night afore last, just exactly as it 'appened,' ses the cook, in a off-hand way.

'Why didn't you tell me, then?' ses Ted, choking.

'It 'ud ha' been no good,' ses the cook, smiling and shaking his 'ead. 'Wot I see must 'appen. I on'y see the future, and that must be.'

'But you stood there watching me chucking the bottle about,' ses Ted, getting out of 'is bunk. 'Why didn't you stop me?'

'You don't understand,' ses the cook. 'If you'd 'ad more eddication——'

He didn't 'ave time to say any more afore Ted was on him, and cookie, being no fighter, 'ad to cook with one eye for the next two or three days. He kept quiet about 'is dreams for some time arter that, but it was no good, because George Hall, wot was a firm believer, gave 'im a licking for not warning 'im of a sprained ankle he got skylarking, and Bob Law took it out of 'im for not telling 'im that he was going to lose 'is suit of shore-going togs at cards.

The only chap that seemed to show any good feeling for the cook was a young feller named Joseph Meek, a steady young chap wot was goin' to be married to old Bill Foster's niece as soon as we got 'ome. Nobody else knew it, but he told the cook all about it on the quiet. He said she was too good for 'im, but, do all he could, he couldn't get her to see it.

'My feelings 'ave changed,' he ses.

'P'r'aps they'll change ag'in,' ses the cook, trying to comfort 'im.

Joseph shook his 'ead. 'No, I've made up my mind,' he ses, very slow. 'I'm young yet, and, besides, I can't afford it; but 'ow to get out of it I don't know. Couldn't you 'ave a dream ag'in it for me?'

'Wot d'ye mean?' ses the cook, firing up. 'Do you think I make my dreams up?'

'No, no; cert'inly not,' ses Joseph, patting 'im on the shoulder; 'but couldn't you do it just for once? 'Ave a dream that me and Emily are killed a few days arter the wedding. Don't say in wot way, 'cos she might think we could avoid it; just dream we are killed. Bill's always been a superstitious man, and since you dreamt about his leg he'd believe anything; and he's that fond of Emily I believe he'd 'ave the wedding put off, at any rate—if I put him up to it.'

It took 'im three days and a silver watchchain to persuade the cook, but he did at last; and one arternoon, when old Bill, who was getting on fust-class, was resting 'is leg in 'is bunk, the cook went below and turned in for a quiet sleep.

For ten minutes he was as peaceful as a lamb, and old Bill, who 'ad been laying in 'is bunk with an eye open watching 'im, was just dropping off 'imself, when the cook began to talk in 'is sleep, and the very fust words made Bill sit up as though something 'ad bit 'im.

'There they go,' ses the cook, 'Emily Foster and Joseph Meek—and there's old Bill, good old Bill, going to give the bride away. How 'appy they all look, especially Joseph!'

Old Bill put his 'and to his ear and leaned out of his bunk.

'There they go,' ses the cook ag'in; 'but wot is that 'orrible black thing with claws that's 'anging over Bill?'

Pore Bill nearly fell out of 'is bunk, but he saved 'imself at the last moment and lay there as pale as death, listening.

'It must be meant for Bill,' ses the cook. 'Well, pore Bill; he won't know of it, that's one thing. Let's 'ope it'll be sudden.'

He lay quiet for some time and then he began again.

'No,' he ses, 'it isn't Bill; it's Joseph and Emily, stark and stiff, and they've on'y been married a week. 'Ow awful they look! Pore things. Oh! oh! o-oh!'

He woke up with a shiver and began to groan, and then 'e sat up in his bunk and saw old Bill leaning out and staring at 'im.

'You've been dreaming, cook,' ses Bill, in a trembling voice.

''Ave I?' ses the cook. 'How do you know?'

'About me and my niece,' ses Bill; 'you was talking in your sleep.'

'You oughtn't to 'ave listened,' ses the cook, getting out of 'is bunk and going over to 'im. 'I 'ope you didn't 'ear all I dreamt. 'Ow much did you hear.'

Bill told 'im, and the cook sat there, shaking his 'ead. 'Thank goodness, you didn't 'ear the worst of it,' he ses.

'*Worst!*' ses Bill. 'Wot, was there any more of it?'

'Lots more,' ses the cook. 'But promise me you won't tell Joseph, Bill. Let 'im be happy while he can; it would on'y make 'im miserable, and it wouldn't do any good.'

'I don't know so much about that,' ses Bill, thinking about the arguments some of them had 'ad with Ted about the bottle. 'Was it arter they was married, cookie, that it 'appened? Are you sure?'

'Certain sure. It was a week arter,' ses the cook.

'Very well, then,' ses Bill, slapping 'is bad leg by mistake; 'if they didn't marry, it couldn't 'appen, could it?'

'Don't talk foolish,' ses the cook; 'they must marry. I saw it in my dream.'

'Well, we'll see,' ses Bill. 'I'm going to 'ave a quiet talk with Joseph about it, and see wot he ses. I ain't a-going to 'ave my pore gal murdered just to please you and make your dreams come true.'

He 'ad a quiet talk with Joseph, but Joseph wouldn't 'ear of it at fust. He said it was all the cook's nonsense, though 'e owned up that it was funny that the cook should know about the wedding and Emily's name, and at last he said they would put it afore Emily and let her decide.

That was about the last dream the cook had that v'y'ge, although he told old Bill one day that he had 'ad the same dream about Joseph and Emily ag'in, so that he was quite certain they 'ad got to be married and killed. He wouldn't tell Bill 'ow they was to be killed, because 'e said it would make 'im an old man afore his time; but, of course, he 'ad to say that *if* they wasn't married the other part couldn't come true. He said that as he 'ad never told 'is dreams before— except in the case of Bill's leg—he couldn't say for certain that they couldn't be prevented by taking care, but p'r'aps they could; and Bill pointed out to 'im wot a useful man he would be if he could dream and warn people in time.

By the time we got into the London river old Bill's leg was getting on fust-rate, and he got along splendid on a pair of crutches the carpenter 'ad made for him. Him and Joseph and the cook had 'ad a good many talks about the dream, and the old man 'ad invited the cook to come along 'ome with 'em, to be referred to when he told the tale.

'I shall take my opportunity,' he ses, 'and break it to 'er gentle-like. When I speak to you, you chip in, and not afore. D'ye understand?'

We went into the East India Docks that v'y'ge, and got there early on a lovely summer's evening. Everybody was 'arf crazy at the idea o' going ashore ag'in, and working as cheerful and as willing as if they liked it. There was a few people standing on the pier-head as we went in, and among 'em several very nice-looking young wimmen.

'My eye, Joseph,' ses the cook, who 'ad been staring hard at one of 'em, 'there's a fine gal—lively, too. Look 'ere!'

He kissed 'is dirty paw—which is more than I should 'ave liked to 'ave done if it 'ad been mine—and waved it, and the gal turned round and shook her 'ead at 'im.

'Here, that'll do,' ses Joseph, very cross. 'That's my gal; that's my Emily.'

'Eh?' says the cook. 'Well, 'ow was I to know? Besides, you're a-giving of her up.'

Joseph didn't answer 'im. He was staring at Emily, and the more he stared the better-looking she seemed to grow. She really was an uncommon nice-looking gal, and more than the cook was struck with her.

'Who's that chap standing alongside of her?' ses the cook.

'It's one o' Bill's sister's lodgers,' ses Joseph, who was looking very bad-tempered. 'I should like to know wot right he 'as to come 'ere to welcome me 'ome. I don't want 'im.'

'P'r'aps he's fond of 'er,' ses the cook. 'I could be, very easy.'

'I'll chuck 'im in the dock if he ain't careful,' ses Joseph, turning red in the face.

He waved his 'and to Emily, who didn't 'appen to be look-ing at the moment, but the lodger waved back in a careless sort of way and then spoke to Emily, and they both waved to old Bill, who was standing on his crutches further aft.

By the time the ship was berthed and everything snug it was quite dark, and old Bill didn't know whether to take the cook 'ome with 'im and break the news that night, or wait a bit. He made up his mind at last to get it over and done with, and arter waiting till the cook 'ad cleaned 'imself they got a cab and drove off.

Bert Simmons, the lodger, 'ad to ride on the box, and Bill took up so much room with 'is bad leg that Emily found it more comfortable to sit on Joseph's knee; and by the time they got to the 'ouse he began to see wot a silly mistake he was making.

'Keep that dream o' yours to yourself till I make up my mind,' he ses to the cook, while Bill and the cabman were calling each other names.

'Bill's going to speak fust,' whispers the cook.

The lodger and Emily 'ad gone inside, and Joseph stood there, fidgeting, while the cabman asked Bill, as a friend, why he 'adn't paid twopence more for his face, and Bill was wasting his time trying to think of something to say to 'urt the cabman's feelings. Then he took Bill by the arm as the cab drove off and told 'im not to say nothing about the dream, because he was going to risk it.

'Stuff and nonsense,' ses Bill. 'I'm going to tell Emily. It's my dooty. Wot's the good o' being married if you're going to be killed?'

He stumped in on his crutches afore Joseph could say any more, and, arter letting his sister kiss 'im, went into the front room and sat down. There was cold beef and pickles on the table and two jugs o' beer, and arter just telling his sister 'ow he fell and broke 'is leg, they all sat down to supper.

Bert Simmons sat on one side of Emily and Joseph the other, and the cook couldn't 'elp feeling sorry for 'er, seeing as he did that sometimes she was 'aving both hands squeezed at once under the table and could 'ardly get a bite in edgeways.

Old Bill lit his pipe arter supper, and then, taking another glass o' beer, he told 'em about the cook dreaming of his accident three days afore it happened. They couldn't 'ardly believe it at fust, but when he went on to tell 'em the other things the cook 'ad dreamt, and that everything 'ad 'appened just as he dreamt it, they all edged away from the cook and sat staring at him with their mouths open.

'And that ain't the worst of it,' ses Bill.

'That's enough for one night, Bill,' ses Joseph, who was staring at Bert Simmons as though he could eat him. 'Besides, I believe it was on'y chance. When cook told you 'is dream it made you nervous, and that's why you fell.'

'Nervous be blowed!' ses Bill; and then he told 'em about the dream he 'ad heard while he was laying in 'is bunk.

Bill's sister gave a scream when he 'ad finished, and Emily, wot was sitting next to Joseph, got up with a shiver and went and sat next to Bert Simmons and squeezed his coat-sleeve.

'It's all nonsense!' ses Joseph, starting up. 'And if it wasn't, true love would run the risk. I ain't afraid!'

'It's too much to ask a gal,' ses Bert Simmons, shaking 'is 'ead.

'I couldn't dream of it,' ses Emily. 'Wot's the use of being married for a week? Look at uncle's leg—that's enough for me!'

They all talked at once then, and Joseph tried all he could to persuade Emily to prove to the cook that 'is dreams didn't always come true; but it was no good. Emily said she wouldn't marry 'im if he 'ad a million a year, and her aunt and uncle backed her up in it—to say nothing of Bert Simmons.

'I'll go up and get your presents, Joseph,' she ses; and she ran upstairs afore anybody could stop her.

Joseph sat there as if he was dazed, while everybody gave 'im good advice, and said 'ow thankful he ought to be that the cook 'ad saved him by 'is dreaming. And by-and-by Emily came downstairs ag'in with the presents he 'ad given 'er and put them on the table in front of 'im.

'There's everything there but that little silver brooch you gave me, Joseph,' she ses, 'and I lost that the other evening when I was out with—with—for a walk.'

Joseph tried to speak, but couldn't.

'It was six-and-six, 'cos I was with you when you bought it,' ses Emily; 'and as I've lost it, it's on'y fair I should pay for it.'

She put down 'arf a sovereign with the presents, and Joseph sat staring at it as if he 'ad never seen one afore.

'And you needn't mind about the change, Joseph,' ses Emily; 'that'll 'elp to make up for your disappointment.'

Old Bill tried to turn things off with a bit of a laugh. 'Why, you're made o' money, Emily,' he ses.

'Ah! I haven't told you yet,' ses Emily, smiling at him; 'that's a little surprise I was keeping for you. Aunt Emma—pore Aunt Emma, I should say—died while you was away and left me all 'er furniture and two hundred pounds.'

Joseph made a choking noise in his throat and then 'e got up, leaving the presents and the 'arf-sovereign on the table, and stood by the door, staring at them.

'Good-night all,' he ses. Then he went to the front door and opened it, and arter standing there a moment came back as though he 'ad forgotten something.

'Are you coming along now?' he ses to the cook.

'Not just yet,' ses the cook, very quick.

'I'll wait outside for you, then,' ses Joseph, grinding his teeth. 'Don't be long.'

Self Help

The night watchman sat brooding darkly over life and its troubles. A shooting corn on the little toe of his left foot, and a touch of liver, due, he was convinced, to the unlawful cellar-work of the landlord of the Queen's Head, had induced in him a vein of profound depression. A discarded boot stood by his side, and his grey-stockinged foot protruded over the edge of the jetty until a passing waterman gave it a playful rap with his oar. A subsequent inquiry as to the price of pigs' trotters fell on ears rendered deaf by suffering.

I might 'ave expected it, said the watchman at last. I done that man—if you can call him a man—a kindness once, and this is my reward for it. Do a man a kindness, and years arterwards 'e comes along and hits you over your tenderest corn with a oar.

He took up his boot, and, inserting his foot with loving care, stooped down and fastened the laces.

Do a man a kindness, he continued, assuming a safer posture, and 'e tries to borrow money off of you; do a woman a kindness and she thinks you want to marry 'er; do an animal a kindness and it tries to bite you—same as a horse bit a sailorman I knew once, when 'e sat on its head to 'elp it get up. He sat too far for'ard, pore chap.

Kindness never gets any thanks. I remember a man whose pal broke 'is leg while they was working together unloading a barge; and he went off to break the news to 'is pal's wife. A kind-'earted man 'e was as ever you see, and, knowing 'ow she would take on when she 'eard the news, he told her fust of all that 'er husband was killed. She took on like a mad thing, and at last, when she couldn't do anything more and 'ad quieted down a bit, he told 'er that it was on'y a case of a broken leg, thinking that 'er joy would be so great that she wouldn't think anything of that. He 'ad to tell her three times afore she understood 'im, and then, instead of being thankful to 'im for 'is thoughtfulness, she chased him 'arf over Wapping with a chopper, screaming with temper.

I remember Ginger Dick and Peter Russet trying to do old Sam Small a kindness one time when they was 'aving a rest ashore arter a v'y'ge. They 'ad took a room together as usual, and for the fust two or three days they was like brothers. That couldn't last, o' course, and Sam was so annoyed one evening at Ginger's suspiciousness by biting a 'arf-dollar Sam owed 'im and finding it was a bad 'un, that 'e went off to spend the evening all alone by himself.

He felt a bit dull at fust, but arter he had 'ad two or three 'arf-pints 'e began to take a brighter view of things. He found a very nice, cosy little public-'ouse he hadn't been in before, and, arter getting two and threepence and a pint for the 'arf-dollar with Ginger's tooth-marks on, he began to think that the world wasn't 'arf as bad a place as people tried to make out.

There was on'y one other man in the little bar Sam was in —a tall, dark chap, with black side-whiskers and spectacles wot kept peeping round the partition and looking very 'ard at everybody that came in.

'I'm just keeping my eye on 'em, cap'n,' he ses to Sam, in a low voice.

'Ho!' ses Sam.

'They don't know me in this disguise,' ses the dark man, 'but I see as 'ow you spotted me at once. Anybody 'ud have a 'ard time of it to deceive you; and then they couldn't gain nothing by it.'

'Nobody ever 'as yet,' ses Sam, smiling at 'im.

'And nobody ever will,' ses the dark man, shaking his 'ead; 'if they was all as fly as you, I might as well put the shutters up. How did you twig I was a detective officer, cap'n?'

Sam, wot was taking a drink, got some beer up 'is nose with surprise.

'That's my secret,' he says, arter the 'tec 'ad patted 'im on the back and brought 'im round.

'You're a marvel, that's wot you are,' ses the 'tec, shaking his 'ead. 'Have one with me.'

Sam said he didn't mind if 'e did, and arter drinking each other's healths very perlite 'e ordered a couple o' twopenny smokes, and by way of showing off paid for 'em with 'arf a quid.

'That's right, ain't it?' ses the barmaid, as he stood staring very 'ard at the change. 'I ain't sure about that 'arf- crown, now I come to look at it; but it's the one you gave me.'

Pore Sam, with a 'tec standing alongside of 'im, said it was quite right, and put it into 'is pocket in a hurry and began to talk to the 'tec as fast as he could about a murder he 'ad been reading about in the paper that morning. They went and sat down by a comfortable little fire that was burning in the bar, and the 'tec told 'im about a lot o' murder cases he 'ad been on himself.

'I'm down 'ere now on special work,' he ses, 'looking arter sailormen.'

'Wot ha' they been doing?' ses Sam.

'When I say looking arter, I mean protecting 'em,' ses the 'tec. 'Over and over ag'in some pore feller, arter working 'ard for months at sea, comes 'ome with a few pounds in 'is pocket and gets robbed of the lot. There's a couple o' chaps down 'ere I'm told off to look arter special, but it's no good unless I can catch 'em red-'anded.'

'Red-'anded?' ses Sam.

'With their hands in the chap's pockets, I mean,' ses the 'tec.

Sam gave a shiver. 'Somebody had their 'ands in my pockets once,' he ses. 'Four pun ten and some coppers they got.'

'Wot was they like?' ses the 'tec, starting.

Sam shook his 'ead. 'They seemed to me to be all hands, that's all I know about 'em,' he ses. 'Arter they 'ad finished they leaned me up ag'in the dock wall an' went off.'

'It sounds like 'em,' ses the 'tec thoughtfully. 'It was Long Pete and Fair Alf, for a quid; that's the two I'm arter.'

He put 'is finger in 'is weskit-pocket. 'That's who I am,' he ses, 'anding Sam a card; 'Detective-Sergeant Cubbins. If you ever get into any trouble at any time, you come to me.'

Sam said 'e would, and arter they had 'ad another drink together the 'tec shifted 'is seat alongside of 'im and talked in 'is ear.

'If I can nab them two chaps I shall get promotion,' he ses; 'and it's a fi'pun note to anybody that helps me. I wish I could persuade you to.'

''Ow's it to be done?' ses Sam, looking at 'im.

'I want a respectable-looking seafaring man,' ses the 'tec, speaking very slow; 'that's you. He goes up Tower Hill tomorrow night at nine o'clock, walking very slow and very unsteady on 'is pins, and giving my two beauties the idea that 'e is three sheets in the wind. They come up and rob 'im, and I catch 'em red-'anded. I get promotion, and you get a fiver.'

'But 'ow do you know they'll be there?' ses Sam, staring at 'im.

Mr Cubbins winked at 'im and tapped 'is nose.

'We 'ave to know a good deal in our line o' business,' he ses.

'Still,' ses Sam, 'I don't see——'

'Narks,' says the 'tec; 'coppers' narks. You've 'eard of them, cap'n? Now, look 'ere. Have you got any money?'

'I got a matter o' twelve quid or so,' ses Sam, in a off-hand way.

'The very thing,' says the 'tec. 'Well, tomorrow night you put that in your pocket, and be walking up Tower Hill just as the clock strikes nine. I promise you you'll be robbed afore two minutes past, and by two and a 'arf past I shall 'ave my 'ands on both of 'em. Have all the money in one pocket, so as they can get it neat and quick, in case they get interrupted. Better still, 'ave it in a purse; that makes it easier to bring it 'ome to 'em.'

'Wouldn't it be enough if they stole the purse?' ses Sam. 'I should feel safer that way, too.'

Mr Cubbins shook 'is 'ead, very slow and solemn. 'That wouldn't do at all,' he ses. 'The more money they steal, the longer they'll get; you know that, cap'n, without me telling you. If you could put fifty quid in it would be so much the better. And, whatever you do, don't make a noise, I don't want a lot o' clumsy policemen interfering in my business.'

'Still, s'pose you didn't catch 'em,' ses Sam, 'where should I be?'

'You needn't be afraid o' that,' ses the 'tec, with a laugh. 'Here, I'll tell you wot I'll do, and that'll show you the trust I put in you.'

He drew a big di'mond ring off of 'is finger and handed it to Sam.

'Put that on your finger,' he ses, 'and keep it there till I give you your money back and the fi'-pun note reward. It's worth seventy quid if it's worth a farthing, and was given to me by a lady of title for getting back 'er jewellery for 'er. Put it on, and wotever you do, don't lose it.'

He sat and watched while Sam forced it on 'is finger.

'You don't need to flash it about too much,' he ses, looking at 'im rather anxious. 'There's men I know as 'ud cut your finger off to get that.'

Sam shoved his 'and in his pocket, but he kept taking it out every now and then and 'olding his finger up to the light to look at the di'mond. Mr Cubbins got up to go at last, saying that he 'ad got a call to make at the police-station, and they went out together.

'Nine o'clock sharp,' he ses, as they shook hands, 'on Tower Hill.'

'I'll be there,' ses Sam.

'And, wotever you do, no noise, no calling out,' ses the 'tec, 'and don't mention a word of this to a living soul.'

Sam shook 'ands with 'im agin, and then, hiding his 'and in his pocket, went off 'ome, and, finding Ginger and Peter Russet wasn't back, went off to bed.

He 'eard 'em coming upstairs in the dark in about an hour's time, and, putting the 'and with the ring on it on the counterpane, shut 'is eyes and pretended to be fast asleep. Ginger lit the candle, and they was both beginning to undress when Peter made a noise and pointed to Sam's 'and.

'Wot's up?' ses Ginger, taking the candle and going over to Sam's bed. 'Who've you been robbing, you fat pirate?'

Sam kept 'is eyes shut and 'eard 'em whispering; then he felt 'em take 'is hand up and look at it.

'Where did you get it, Sam?' ses Peter.

'He's asleep,' ses Ginger, 'sound asleep. I b'lieve if I was to put 'is finger in the candle he wouldn't wake up.'

'You try it,' ses Sam, sitting up in bed very sharp and snatching his 'and away. 'Wot d'ye mean coming 'ome at all hours and waking me up?'

'Where did you get that ring?' ses Ginger.

'Friend o' mine,' ses Sam, very short.

'Who was it?' ses Peter.

'It's a secret,' ses Sam.

'You wouldn't 'ave a secret from your old pal Ginger, Sam, would you?' ses Ginger.

'Old wot?' ses Sam. 'Wot did you call me this arternoon?'

'I called you a lot o' things I'm sorry for,' ses Ginger, who was bursting with curiosity, 'and I beg your pardin, Sam.'

'Shake 'ands on it,' ses Peter, who was nearly as curious as Ginger.

They shook hands, but Sam said he couldn't tell 'em about the ring; and several times Ginger was on the point of calling 'im the names he 'ad called 'im in the arternoon, on'y Peter trod on 'is foot and stopped him. They wouldn't let 'im go to sleep for talking, and at last, when 'e was pretty near tired out, he told 'em all about it.

'Going—to 'ave your—pocket picked?' ses Ginger, staring at 'im, when 'e had finished.

'I shall be watched over,' ses Sam.

'He's gorn stark, staring mad,' ses Ginger. 'Wot a good job it is he's got me and you to look arter 'im, Peter.'

'Wot d'ye mean?' ses Sam.

'*Mean?*' ses Ginger. 'Why, it's a put-up job to rob you,

o' course. I should ha' thought even your fat 'ead could ha' seen that!'

'When I want your advice I'll ask you for it,' ses Sam, losing 'is temper. 'Wot about the di'mond ring—eh?'

'You stick to it,' ses Ginger, 'and keep out o' Mr Cubbins's way. That's my advice to you. 'Sides, p'r'aps it ain't a real one.'

Sam told 'im ag'in he didn't want none of 'is advice, and, as Ginger wouldn't leave off talking, he pretended to go to sleep. Ginger woke 'im up three times to tell 'im wot a fool 'e was, but 'e got so fierce that he gave it up at last and told 'im to go 'is own way.

Sam wouldn't speak to either of 'em next morning, and arter breakfast he went off on 'is own. He came back while Peter and Ginger was out, and they wasted best part o' the day trying to find 'im.

'We'll be on Tower Hill just afore nine and keep 'im out o' mischief, anyway,' ses Peter.

Ginger nodded. 'And be called names for our pains,' he ses. 'I've a good mind to let 'im be robbed.'

'It 'ud serve 'im right,' ses Peter, 'on'y then he'd want to borrer off of us. Look here! Why not—why not rob 'im ourselves?'

'*Wot?*' ses Ginger, starting.

'Walk up behind 'im and rob 'im,' ses Peter. 'He'll think it's them two chaps he spoke about, and when 'e comes 'ome complaining to us we'll tell 'im it serves 'im right. Arter we've 'ad a game with 'im for a day or two we'll give 'im his money back.'

'But he'd reckernise us,' ses Ginger.

'We must disguise ourselves,' ses Peter, in a whisper. 'There's a barber's shop in Cable Street, where I've seen beards in the winder. You hook 'em on over your ears. Get one of 'em each, pull our caps over our eyes and turn our collars up, and there you are.'

Ginger made a lot of objections, not because he didn't think it was a good idea, but because he didn't like Peter thinking of it instead of 'im; but he gave way at last, and, arter he 'ad got the beard, he stood for a long time in front o' the glass thinking wot a difference it would ha' made to his looks if he had 'ad black 'air instead o' red.

Waiting for the evening made the day seem very long to 'em; but it came at last, and, with the beards in their pockets, they slipped out and went for a walk round. They 'ad 'arf a pint each at a public-'ouse at the top of the Minories, just to steady themselves, and then they came out and hooked on their beards; and wot with them, and pulling their caps down and turning their coat-collars up, there wasn't much of their faces to be seen by anybody.

It was just five minutes to nine when they got to Tower Hill, and they walked down the middle of the road, keeping a bright look-out for old Sam. A little way down they saw a couple o' chaps leaning up ag'in a closed gate in the dock wall lighting their pipes, and Peter and Ginger both nudged each other with their elbows at the same time. They 'ad just got to the bottom of the Hill when Sam turned the corner.

Peter wouldn't believe at fust that the old man wasn't really the worse for liquor, 'e was so life-like. Many a drunken man would ha' been proud to ha' done it 'arf so well, and it made 'im pleased to think that Sam was a pal of 'is. Him and Ginger turned and crept up behind the old man on tip-toe, and then all of a sudden he tilted Sam's cap over 'is eyes and flung his arms round 'im, while Ginger felt in 'is coat-pockets and took out a leather purse chockfull o' money.

It was all done and over in a moment, and then, to Ginger's great surprise, Sam suddenly lifted 'is foot and gave 'im a fearful kick on the shin of 'is leg, and at the same time let drive with all his might in 'is face. Ginger went down as if he 'ad been shot, and as Peter went to 'elp him up he got a bang over the 'ead that put 'im alongside o' Ginger, arter which Sam turned and trotted off down the Hill like a dancing-bear.

For 'arf a minute Ginger didn't know where 'e was, and afore he found out the two men they'd seen in the gateway came up, and one of 'em put his knee in Ginger's back and 'eld him, while the other caught hold of his 'and and dragged the purse out of it. Arter which they both made off up the Hill as 'ard as they could go, while Peter Russet in a faint voice called 'Police!' arter them.

He got up presently and helped Ginger up, and they both stood there pitying themselves, and 'elping each other to think of names to call Sam.

'Well, the money's gorn, and it's 'is own silly fault,' ses Ginger. 'But wotever 'appens, he mustn't know that we had a 'and in it, mind that.'

'He can starve for all I care,' ses Peter, feeling his 'ead. 'I won't lend 'im a ha'penny—not a single, blessed ha'penny.'

'Who'd ha' thought 'e could ha' hit like that?' says Ginger. 'That's wot gets over me. I never 'ad such a bang in my life— never. I'm going to 'ave a little drop o' brandy—my 'ead is fair swimming.'

Peter 'ad one, too; but though they went into the private bar, it wasn't private enough for them; and when the land-lady asked Ginger who'd been kissing 'im, he put 'is glass down with a bang and walked straight off 'ome.

Sam 'adn't turned up by the time they got there, and pore Ginger took advantage of it to put a little warm candle-grease on 'is bad leg. Then he bathed 'is face very careful and 'elped Peter bathe his 'ead. They 'ad just finished when they heard Sam coming upstairs, and Ginger sat down on 'is bed and began to whistle, while Peter took up a bit o' newspaper and stood by the candle reading it.

'Lor' lumme, Ginger!' ses Sam, staring at 'im. 'What ha' you been a-doing to your face?'

'Me?' ses Ginger, careless-like. 'Oh, we 'ad a bit of a scrap down Limehouse way with some Scotchies. Peter got a crack over the 'ead at the same time.'

'Ah, I've 'ad a bit of a scrap, too,' ses Sam, smiling all over, 'but *I* didn't get marked.'

'Oh!' ses Peter, without looking up from 'is paper.

'Was it a little boy, then?' ses Ginger.

'No, it wasn't a little boy neither, Ginger,' ses Sam; 'it was a couple o' men twice the size of you and Peter here, and I licked 'em both. It was the two men I spoke to you about last night.'

'Oh!' ses Peter ag'in, yawning.

'I did a bit o' thinking this morning,' ses Sam, nodding at 'em, 'and I don't mind owning up that it was owing to wot you said. You was right, Ginger, arter all.'

Ginger grunted.

'Fust thing I did arter breakfast,' ses Sam, 'I took that di'mond ring to a pawnshop and found out it wasn't a di'mond ring. Then I did a bit more thinking, and I went round to a shop I know and bought a couple o' knuckle-dusters.'

'Couple o' *wot?*' ses Ginger, in a choking voice.

'Knuckle-dusters,' ses Sam, 'and I turned up tonight at Tower Hill with one on each 'and just as the clock was striking nine. I see 'em the moment I turned the corner—two enormous big chaps, a yard acrost the shoulders, coming down the middle of the road—You've got a cold, Ginger!'

'No, I ain't,' ses Ginger.

'I pretended to be drunk, same as the 'tec told me,' ses Sam, 'and then I felt 'em turn round and creep up behind me. One of 'em come up behind and put 'is knee in my back and caught me by the throat, and the other gave me a punch in the chest, and while I was gasping for breath took my purse away. Then I started on 'em.'

'Lor'!' ses Ginger, very nasty.

'I fought like a lion,' ses Sam. 'Twice they 'ad me down, and twice I got up ag'in and hammered 'em. They both of 'em 'ad knives, but my blood was up, and I didn't take no more notice of 'em than if they was made of paper. I knocked 'em both out o' their hands, and if I hit 'em in the face once I did a dozen times. I surprised myself.'

'You surprise me,' ses Ginger.

'All of a sudden,' ses Sam, 'they see they 'ad got to do with a man wot didn't know wot fear was, and they turned round and ran off as hard as they could run. You ought to ha' been there, Ginger. You'd 'ave enjoyed it.'

Ginger Dick didn't answer 'im. Having to sit still and listen to all them lies without being able to say anything nearly choked 'im. He sat there gasping for breath.

'O' course, you got your purse back in the fight, Sam?' ses Peter.

'No, mate,' ses Sam. 'I ain't going to tell you no lies—I did not.'

'And 'ow are you going to live, then, till you get a ship, Sam?' ses Ginger, in a nasty voice. 'You won't get nothing out o' me, so you needn't think it.'

'Nor me,' ses Peter. 'Not a brass farthing.'

'There's no call to be nasty about it, mates,' ses Sam. 'I 'ad the best fight I ever 'ad in my life, and I must put up with the loss. A man can't 'ave it all his own way.'

''Ow much was it?' ses Peter.

'Ten brace-buttons, three French ha'-pennies, and a bit o' tin,' ses Sam. 'Wot on earth's the matter, Ginger?'

Keeping Up Appearances

Everybody is superstitious, said the night watchman, as he gave utterance to a series of chirruping endearments to a black cat with one eye that had just been using a leg of his trousers as a serviette; if that cat 'ad stole some men's suppers they'd have acted foolish, and suffered for it all the rest of their lives.

He scratched the cat behind the ear, and despite himself his face darkened. Slung it over the side, they would, he said longingly, and chucked bits o' coke at it till it sank. As I said afore, everybody is superstitious, and those that ain't ought to be night watchmen for a time—that 'ud cure 'em. I knew one man that killed a black cat, and arter that for the rest of his life he could never get three sheets in the wind without seeing its ghost. Spoilt his life for 'im, it did.

He scratched the cat's other ear. I only left it a moment, while I went round to the Bull's Head, he said, slowly filling his pipe, and I thought I'd put it out o' reach. Some men——

His fingers twined round the animal's neck; then, with a sigh, he rose and took a turn or two on the jetty.

Superstitiousness is right and proper, to a certain extent, he said, resuming his seat; but o' course, like everything else, some people carry it too far—they'd believe anything. Weak-minded they are, and if you're in no hurry I can tell you a tale of a pal o' mine, Bill Burtenshaw by name, that'll prove my words.

His mother was superstitious afore 'im, and always knew when 'er friends died by hearing three loud taps on the wall. The on'y mistake she ever made was one night when, arter losing no less than seven friends, she found out it was the man next door hanging pictures at three o'clock in the morning. She found it out by 'im hitting 'is thumb-nail.

For the first few years arter he grew up Bill went to sea, and that on'y made 'im more superstitious than ever. Him and a pal named Silas Winch went several v'y'ges together, and their talk used to be that creepy that some o' the chaps was a'most afraid to be left on deck alone of a night. Silas was a long-faced, miserable sort o' chap, always looking on the black side o' things, and shaking his 'ead over it. He thought nothing o' seeing ghosts, and pore old Ben Huggins slept on the floor for a week by reason of a ghost with its throat cut that Silas saw in his bunk. He gave Silas arf a dollar and a neck-tie to change bunks with 'im.

When Bill Burtenshaw left the sea and got married he lost sight of Silas altogether, and the on'y thing he 'ad to remind him of 'im was a piece o' paper which they 'ad both signed with their blood, promising that the fust one that died would appear to the other. Bill agreed to it one evenin' when he didn't know what he was doing, and for years arterwards 'e used to get the cold creeps down 'is back when he thought of Silas dying fust. And the idea of dying fust 'imself gave 'im cold creeps all over.

Bill was a very good husband when he was sober, but 'is money was two pounds a week, and when a man has all that and on'y a wife to keep out of it, it's natural for 'im to drink. Mrs Burtenshaw tried all sorts o' ways and means of curing 'im, but it was no use. Bill used to think o' ways, too, knowing the 'arm the drink was doing 'im, and his fav'rite plan was for 'is missis to empty a bucket o' cold water over 'im every time he came 'ome the worse for licker. She did it once, but as she 'ad to spend the rest o' the night in the back yard it wasn't tried ag'in.

Bill got worse as he got older, and even made away with the furniture to get drink with. And then he used to tell 'is missis that he was drove to the pub because his 'ome was so uncomfortable.

Just at the time things was at their worst, Silas Winch,

who 'appened to be ashore and 'ad got Bill's address from a pal, called to see 'im. It was a Saturday arternoon when he called, and, o' course, Bill was out, but 'is missis showed him in, and, arter fetching another chair from the kitchen, asked 'im to sit down.

Silas was very perlite at fust, but arter looking round the room and seeing 'ow bare it was, he gave a little cough, and he ses, 'I thought Bill was doing well?' he ses.

'So he is,' ses Mrs Burtenshaw.

Silas Winch coughed again.

'I suppose he likes room to stretch 'imself about in?' he ses, looking round.

Mrs Burtenshaw wiped 'er eyes, and then, knowing 'ow Silas had been an old friend o' Bill's, she drew 'er chair a bit closer and told him 'ow it was. 'A better 'usband, when he's sober, you couldn't wish to see,' she ses, wiping her eyes ag'in. 'He'd give me anything—if he 'ad it.'

Silas's face got longer than ever. 'As a matter o' fact,' he ses, 'I'm a bit down on my luck, and I called round with the 'ope that Bill could lend me a bit, just till I can pull round.'

Mrs Burtenshaw shook her 'ead.

'Well, I s'pose I can stay and see 'im?' ses Silas. 'Me and 'im used to be great pals at one time, and many's the good turn I've done him. Wot time'll he be 'ome?'

'Any time after twelve,' ses Mrs Burtenshaw; 'but you'd better not be here then. You see, 'im being in that condition, he might think you was your own ghost come according to promise and be frightened out of 'is life. He's often talked about it.'

Silas Winch scratched his head and looked at 'er thoughtful-like.

'Why shouldn't he mistake me for a ghost?' he ses at last; 'the shock might do 'im good. And, if you come to that, why shouldn't I pretend to be my own ghost and warn 'im off the drink?'

Mrs Burtenshaw got so excited at the idea she couldn't 'ardly speak, but at last, arter saying over and over ag'in she

173

wouldn't do such a thing for worlds, she and Silas arranged that he should come in at about three o'clock in the morning and give Bill a solemn warning. She gave 'im her key, and Silas said he'd come in with his 'air and cap all wet and pretend he'd been drownded.

'It's very kind of you to take all this trouble for nothing,' ses Mrs Burtenshaw, as Silas got up to go.

'Don't mention it,' ses Silas. 'It ain't the fust time, and I don't suppose it'll be the last, that I've put myself out to help my feller-creeturs. We all ought to do wot we can for each other.'

'Mind, if he finds it out,' ses Mrs Burtenshaw, all of a tremble, 'I don't know nothing about it. P'r'aps to make it more life-like I'd better pretend not to see you.'

'P'r'aps it would be better,' ses Silas, stopping at the street door. 'All I ask is that you'll 'ide the poker and anything else that might be laying about handy. And you 'ad better oil the lock so as the key won't make a noise.'

Mrs Burtenshaw shut the door arter 'im, and then she went in and 'ad a quiet sit-down all by 'erself to think it over. The only thing that comforted 'er was that Bill would be in licker, and also that 'e would believe anything in the ghost line.

It was past twelve when a couple o' pals brought him 'ome, and, arter offering to fight all six of 'em, one arter the other, Bill hit the wall for getting in 'is way, and tumbled upstairs to bed. In less than ten minutes 'e was fast asleep, and pore Mrs Burtenshaw, arter trying her best to keep awake, fell asleep too.

She was woke up suddenly by a noise that froze the marrer in 'er bones—the most 'artrending groan she 'ad ever heard in 'er life; and, raising her 'ead, she saw Silas Winch standing at the foot of the bed. He 'ad done his face and hands over with wot is called loominous paint, his cap was pushed at the back of his 'ead, and wet wisps of 'air was hanging over his eyes. For a moment Mrs Burtenshaw's 'art stood still, and then Silas let off another groan that put her on edge all over. It was a groan that seemed to come from nothing a'most until it spread into a roar that made the room tremble and rattled the jug in the washstand basin. It shook everything in the room but Bill, and he went on sleeping like an infant. Silas did two more groans, and then 'e leaned over the foot o' the bed and stared at Bill, as though 'e couldn't believe his eyesight.

'Try a squeaky one,' ses Mrs Burtenshaw.

Silas tried five squeaky ones and then he 'ad a fit o' coughing that would ha' woke the dead, as they say, but it didn't wake Bill.

'Now some more deep ones,' ses Mrs Burtenshaw, in a whisper.

Silas licked his lips—forgetting the paint—and tried the deep ones ag'in.

'Now mix 'em a bit,' ses Mrs Burtenshaw.

Silas stared at her. 'Look 'ere,' he ses, very short, 'do you think I'm a fog-horn, or wot?'

He stood there sulky for a moment, and then 'e invented a noise that nothing living could miss hearing; even Bill couldn't. He moved in 'is sleep, and arter Silas 'ad done it twice more he turned and spoke to 'is missis about it. 'D'ye hear?' he ses; 'stop it. Stop it at once.'

Mrs Burtenshaw pretended to be asleep, and Bill was just going to turn over ag'in when Silas let off another groan. It was on'y a little one this time, but Bill sat up as though he 'ad been shot, and he no sooner caught sight of Silas standing there than 'e gave a dreadful 'owl and, rolling over, wrapped 'imself up in all the bed-clothes 'e could lay his 'ands on. Then Mrs Burtenshaw gave a 'owl and tried to get some of 'em back; but Bill, thinking it was the ghost, only held on tighter than ever.

'BILL,' ses Silas Winch, in an awful voice.

Bill gave a kick, and tried to bore a hole through the bed.

'Bill,' ses Silas ag'in, 'why don't you answer me? I've come all the way from the bottom of the Pacific Ocean to see you, and this is all I get for it. Haven't you got anything to say to me?'

'Good-bye,' ses Bill, in a voice all smothered with the bed-clothes.

Silas Winch groaned ag'in, and Bill, as the shock 'ad made a'most sober, trembled all over.

'The moment I died,' ses Silas, 'I thought of my promise towards you. "Bill's expecting me," I ses, and, instead of staying in comfort at the bottom of the sea, I kicked off the body of the cabin-boy wot was clinging round my leg, and 'ere I am.'

'It was very t—t—t—thoughtful—of you—Silas,' ses Bill; 'but you always w—w—was—thoughtful. Good-bye.'

Afore Silas could answer, Mrs Burtenshaw, who felt more comfortable, 'aving got a bit o' the clothes back, thought it was time to put 'er spoke in.

'Lor' bless me, Bill,' she ses. 'Wotever are you a-talking to yourself like this for? 'Ave you been dreaming?'

'Dreaming!' ses pore Bill, catching hold of her 'and and gripping it till she nearly screamed. 'I wish I was. Can't you see it?'

'See it?' ses his wife. 'See wot?'

'The ghost,' ses Bill, in a 'orrible whisper; 'the ghost of my dear, kind old pal, Silas Winch. The best and noblest pal a man ever 'ad. The kindest-'arted——'

'Rubbish,' ses Mrs Burtenshaw. 'You've been dreaming. And as for the kindest-'arted pal, why I've often heard you say——'

'*Hsh!*' ses Bill. 'I didn't. I'll swear I didn't. I never thought of such a thing.'

'You turn over and go to sleep,' ses his wife; 'hiding your 'ead under the clothes like a child that's afraid o' the dark! There's nothing there, I tell you. Wot next will you see, I wonder? Last time it was a pink rat.'

'This is fifty million times worse than pink rats,' ses Bill. 'I on'y wish it was a pink rat.'

'I tell you there is nothing there,' ses his wife. 'Look!'

Bill put his 'ead up and looked, and then 'e gave a dreadful scream and dived under the bed-clothes ag'in.

'Oh, well, 'ave it your own way, then,' ses his wife. 'If it pleases you to think there is a ghost there, and to go on talking to it, do so, and welcome.'

She turned over and pretended to go to sleep ag'in, and arter a minute or two Silas spoke ag'in in the same hollow voice.

'Bill!' he ses.

'Yes,' ses Bill, with a groan of his own.

'She can't see me,' ses Silas, 'and she can't 'ear me; but I'm 'ere all right. Look!'

'I 'ave looked,' ses Bill, with his 'ead still under the clothes.

'We was always pals, Bill, you and me,' ses Silas; 'many a v'y'ge 'ave we had together, mate, and now I'm a-laying at the bottom of the Pacific Ocean, and you are snug and 'appy in your own warm bed. I 'ad to come to see you, according to promise, and, over and above that, since I was drownded my eyes 'ave been opened. Bill, you're drinking yourself to death!'

'I—I—didn't know it,' ses Bill, shaking all over. 'I'll knock it—off a bit, and—thank you—for—w—w—warning me. G—g—good-bye.'

'You'll knock it off altogether,' ses Silas Winch, in a awful voice. 'You're not to touch another drop of beer, wine, or spirits as long as you live. D'ye hear me?'

'Not—not as medicine?' ses Bill, holding the clothes up a bit so as to be more distinct.

'Not as anything,' ses Silas; 'not even over Christmas pudding. Raise your right arm above your 'ead and swear by the ghost of pore Silas Winch, as is laying at the bottom of the Pacific Ocean, that you won't touch another drop.'

Bill Burtenshaw put 'is arm up and swore it. Then 'e took 'is arm in ag'in and lay there wondering wot was going to 'appen next.

'If you ever break your oath by on'y so much as a teaspoon-ful,' ses Silas, 'you'll see me ag'in, and the second time you see me you'll die as if struck by lightning. No man can see me twice and live.'

177

Bill broke out in a cold perspiration all over. 'You'll be careful, won't you, Silas?' he ses. 'You'll remember you 'ave seen me once, I mean?'

'And there's another thing afore I go,' ses Silas. 'I've left a widder, and if she don't get 'elp from someone she'll starve.'

'Pore thing,' ses Bill. 'Pore thing.'

'If you 'ad died afore me,' ses Silas, 'I should 'ave looked arter your good wife— wot I've now put in a sound sleep—as long as I lived.'

Bill didn't say anything.

'I should 'ave given 'er fifteen shillings a week,' ses Silas.

"Ow much?" ses Bill, nearly putting his 'ead up over the clothes, while 'is wife almost woke up with surprise and anger.

'Fifteen shillings,' ses Silas, in 'is most awful voice. 'You'll save that over the drink.'

'I—I'll go round and see her,' ses Bill. 'She might be one o' these 'ere independent——'

'I forbid you to go near the place,' ses Silas. 'Send it by post every week; 15 Shap Street will find her. Put your arm up and swear it; same as you did afore.'

Bill did as 'e was told, and then 'e lay and trembled, as Silas gave three more awful groans.

'Farewell, Bill,' he ses. 'Farewell. I am going back to my bed at the bottom o' the sea. So long as you keep both your oaths I shall stay there. If you break one of 'em or go to see my pore wife I shall appear ag'in. Farewell! Farewell! Farewell!'

Bill said 'Good-bye', and, arter a long silence, he ventured to put an eye over the edge of the clothes and discovered that the ghost 'ad gone. He lay awake for a couple o' hours, wondering and saying over the address to himself so that he shouldn't forget it, and just afore it was time to get up he fell into a peaceful slumber. His wife didn't get a wink, and she lay there trembling with passion to think 'ow she'd been done, and wondering 'ow she was to alter it.

Bill told 'er all about it in the morning; and then with tears in his eyes 'e went downstairs and emptied a little barrel o' beer down the sink. For the fust two or three days 'e went about with a thirst that he'd ha' given pounds for if 'e'd been allowed to satisfy it, but arter a time it went off, and then, like all teetotallers, 'e began to run down drink and call it p'ison.

The fust thing 'e did when 'e got his money on Friday was to send off a Post-Office order to Shap Street, and Mrs Burtenshaw cried with rage and 'ad to put it down to the headache. She 'ad the headache every Friday for a month, and Bill, wot was feeling stronger and better than he 'ad done for years, felt quite sorry for her.

By the time Bill 'ad sent off six orders she was worn to skin and bone a'most a-worrying over the way Silas Winch was spending her money. She dursn't undeceive Bill for two reasons: fust of all because she didn't want 'im to take to drink ag'in; and, secondly, for fear of wot he might do to 'er if 'e found out 'ow she'd been deceiving 'im.

She was laying awake thinking it over one night while Bill was sleeping peaceful by her side, when all of a sudden she 'ad an idea. The more she thought of it the better it seemed; but she laid awake for ever so long afore she dared to do more than think. Three or four times she turned and looked at Bill and listened to 'im breathing, and then, trembling all over with fear and excitement, she began 'er little game.

'He did send it,' she ses, with a piercing scream. 'He did send it.'

'W-w-wot's the matter?' ses Bill, beginning to wake up.

Mrs Burtenshaw didn't take any notice of 'im.

'He did send it,' she ses, screaming ag'in. 'Every Friday night reg'lar. Oh, *don't let 'im see you ag'in.*'

Bill, wot was just going to ask 'er whether she 'ad gone mad, gave a awful 'owl and disappeared right down in the middle o' the bed.

'There's some mistake,' ses Mrs Burtenshaw, in a voice that could ha' been 'eard through arf-a-dozen beds easy. 'It must ha' been lost in the post. It must ha' been.'

She was silent for a few seconds, then she ses, 'All right,' she ses, 'I'll bring it myself then by hand every week. No,

Bill shan't come; I'll promise that for 'im. Do go away; he might put his 'ead up at any moment.'

She began to gasp and sob, and Bill began to think wot a good wife he 'ad got, when he felt 'er put a couple of pillers over where she judged his 'ead to be, and hold 'em down with her arm.

'Thank you, Mr Winch,' she ses, very loud, 'thank you. Good-bye. Good-bye.'

She began to quieten down a bit, although little sobs, like wimmen use when they pretend that they want to leave off crying but can't, kept breaking out of 'er. Then, by-and-by, she quieted down altogether, and a husky voice from near the foot of the bed ses: 'Has it gorn?'

'Oh, Bill,' she ses, with another sob, 'I've seen the ghost!'

'Has it gorn?' ses Bill ag'in.

'Yes, it's gorn,' ses his wife, shivering. 'Oh, Bill, it stood at the foot of the bed looking at me, with its face and 'ands all shiny white, and damp curls on its forehead. Oh!'

Bill came up very slow and careful, but with 'is eyes still shut.

'His wife didn't get the money this week,' ses Mrs Burtenshaw; 'but as he thought there might be a mistake somewhere he appeared to me instead of to you. I've got to take the money by hand.'

'Yes, I heard,' ses Bill; 'and mind, if you should lose it or be robbed of it, let me know at once. D'ye hear? *At once!*'

'Yes, Bill,' ses 'is wife.

They lay quiet for some time, although Mrs Burtenshaw still kept trembling and shaking; and then Bill ses, 'Next time a man tells you he 'as seen a ghost, p'r'aps you'll believe in 'im.'

Mrs Burtenshaw took out the end of the sheet wot she 'ad stuffed in 'er mouth when 'e began to speak.

'Yes, Bill,' she ses.

Bill Burtenshaw gave 'er the fifteen shillings next morning and every Friday night arterwards; and that's 'ow it is that, while other wimmen 'as to be satisfied looking at new hats and clothes in the shop-winders, Mrs Burtenshaw is able to wear 'em.

Watch-Dogs

It's a'most the only enj'yment I've got left, said the oldest inhabitant, taking a long, slow draught of beer, that and a pipe o' baccy. Neither of 'em wants chewing, and that's a great thing when you ain't got anything worth speaking about left to chew with.

He put his mug on the table and, ignoring the stillness of the summer air, sheltered the flame of a match between his cupped hands and conveyed it with infinite care to the bowl of his pipe. A dull but crafty old eye squinting down the stem assured itself that the tobacco was well alight before the match was thrown away.

As I was a-saying, kindness to animals is all very well, he said to the wayfarer who sat opposite him in the shade of the 'Cauliflower' elms; but kindness to your feller-creeturs is more. The pint wot you give me is gone, but I'm just as thankful to you as if it wasn't.

He half closed his eyes and, gazing on to the fields beyond, fell into a reverie so deep that he failed to observe the landlord come for his mug and return with it filled. A little start attested his surprise, and, to his great annoyance, upset a couple of tablespoonfuls of the precious liquid.

Some people waste all their kindness on dumb animals, he remarked, after the landlord had withdrawn from his offended vision, but I was never a believer in it. I mind some time ago when a gen'leman from Lunnon wot 'ad more money than sense offered a prize for kindness to animals. I was the only one that didn't try for to win it.

Mr Bunnett 'is name was, and 'e come down and took Farmer Hall's 'ouse for the summer. Over sixty 'e was, and old enough to know better. He used to put saucers of milk all round the 'ouse for cats to drink, and, by the time pore Farmer Hall got back, every cat for three miles round 'ad got in the habit of coming round to the back-door and asking for milk as if it was their right. Farmer Hall poisoned a saucer o' milk at last, and then 'ad to pay five shillings for a thin black cat with a mangy tail and one eye that Bob Pretty said belonged to 'is children. Farmer Hall said he'd go to jail afore he'd pay, at fust, but arter five men 'ad spoke the truth and said they 'ad seen Bob's youngsters tying a empty mustard-tin to its tail on'y the day afore, he gave way.

That was Bob Pretty all over, that was; the biggest raskel Claybury 'as ever had; and it wasn't the fust bit o' money 'e made out o' Mr Bunnett coming to the place.

It all come through Mr Bunnett's love for animals. I never see a man so fond of animals as 'e was, and if he had 'ad 'is way Claybury would 'ave been overrun by 'em by this time. The day arter 'e got to the farm he couldn't eat 'is breakfuss because of a pig that was being killed in the yard, and it was no good pointing out to 'im that the pig was on'y making a fuss about it because it was its nature so to do. He lived on wegetables and such like, and the way 'e carried on one day over 'arf a biled caterpillar 'e found in his cabbage, wouldn't be believed. He wouldn't eat another mossel, but sat hunting 'igh and low for the other 'arf.

He 'adn't been in Claybury more than a week afore he said 'ow surprised 'e was to see 'ow pore dumb animals was treated. He made a little speech about it one evening up at the schoolroom, and, arter he 'ad finished, he up and offered to give a prize of a gold watch that used to belong to 'is dear sister wot loved animals, to the one wot was the kindest to 'em afore he left the place.

If he'd ha' known Claybury men better 'e wouldn't ha' done it. The very next morning Bill Chambers took 'is baby's milk for the cat, and smacked 'is wife's 'ead for talking arter he'd told 'er to stop. Henery Walker got into trouble for leaning over Charlie Stubbs's fence and feeding his chickens for 'im, and Sam Jones's wife had to run off 'ome to 'er mother 'ar.-dressed because she had 'appened to overlay a sick rabbit wot Sam 'ad taken to bed with 'im to keep warm.

People used to stop animals in the road and try and do 'em a kindness—especially when Mr Bunnett was passing—and Peter Gubbins walked past 'is house one day with ole Mrs Broad's cat in 'is arms. A bad-tempered old cat it was, and, wot with Peter kissing the top of its 'ead and calling of it Tiddleums, it nearly went out of its mind.

The fust time Mr Bunnett see Bob Pretty was about a week arter he'd offered that gold watch. Bob was stooping down very careful over something in the hedge, and Mr Bunnett, going up quiet-like behind 'im, see 'im messing about with a pore old toad he 'ad found, with a smashed leg.

'Wot's the matter with it?' ses Mr Bunnett.

Bob didn't seem to hear 'im. He was a-kneeling on the ground with 'is 'ead on one side looking at the toad; and by-and-by he pulled out 'is pocket-'an'kercher and put the toad in it, as if it was made of egg-shells, and walked away.

'Wot's the matter with it?' ses Mr Bunnett, a'most trotting to keep up with 'im.

'Got it's leg 'urt in some way, pore thing,' ses Bob. 'I want to get it 'ome as soon as I can and wash it and put it on a piece o' damp moss. But I'm afraid it's not long for this world.'

Mr Bunnett said it did 'im credit, and walked home along-side of 'im talking. He was surprised to find that Bob hadn't 'eard anything of the gold watch 'e was offering, but Bob said he was a busy, 'ard-working man and didn't 'ave no time to go to hear speeches or listen to tittle-tattle.

'When I've done my day's work,' he ses, 'I can always find a job in the garden, and arter that I go in and 'elp my missis put the children to bed. She ain't strong, pore thing, and it's better than wasting time and money up at the "Cauliflower".'

He 'ad a lot o' talk with Mr Bunnett for the next day or two, and when 'e went round with the toad on the third day as lively and well as possible the old gen'leman said it was a miracle. And so it would ha' been if it had been the same toad.

He took a great fancy to Bob Pretty, and somehow or other they was always dropping acrost each other. He met Bob with 'is dog one day—a large, ugly brute, but a'most as clever as wot Bob was 'imself. It stood there with its tongue 'anging out and looking at Bob uneasy-like out of the corner of its eye as Bob stood a-patting of it and calling it pet names.

'Wunnerful affectionate old dog, ain't you, Joseph?' ses Bob.

'He's got a kind eye,' ses Mr Bunnett.

'He's like another child to me, ain't you, my pretty?' ses Bob, smiling at 'im and feeling in 'is pocket. 'Here you are, old chap.'

He threw down a biskit so sudden that Joseph, thinking it was a stone, went off like a streak o' lightning with 'is tail between 'is legs and yelping his 'ardest. Most men would ha' looked a bit foolish, but Bob Pretty didn't turn a hair.

'Ain't it wunnerful the sense they've got,' he ses to Mr Bunnett, wot was still staring arter the dog.

'Sense?' ses the old gen'leman.

'Yes,' ses Bob, smiling. 'His food ain't been agreeing with 'im lately and he's starving hisself for a bit to get round ag'in, and 'e knew that 'e couldn't trust hisself alongside o' this biskit. Wot a pity men ain't like that with beer. I wish as 'ow Bill Chambers and Henery Walker and a few more 'ad been 'ere just now.'

Mr Bunnett agreed with 'im, and said wot a pity it was everybody 'adn't got Bob Pretty's common-sense and good feeling.

'It ain't that,' ses Bob, shaking his 'ead at him; 'it ain't to my credit. I dessay if Sam Jones and Peter Gubbins, and Charlie Stubbs and Dicky Weed 'ad been brought up the same as I was they'd 'ave been a lot better than wot I am.'

He bid Mr Bunnett good-bye becos 'e said he'd got to get back to 'is work, and Mr Bunnett had 'ardly got 'ome afore Henery Walker turned up full of anxiousness to ask his advice about five little baby kittens wot 'is old cat had found in the waste-place the night afore.

'Drownd them little innercent things, same as most would do, I can't,' he ses, shaking his 'ead; 'but wot to do with 'em I don't know.'

'Couldn't you find 'omes for 'em?' ses Mr Bunnett.

Henery Walker shook his 'ead agin. ''Tain't no use thinking 'o that,' he ses. 'There's more cats than 'omes about 'ere. Why, Bill Chambers drownded six on'y last week right afore the eyes of my pore little boy. Upset 'im dreadful it did.'

Mr Bunnett walked up and down the room thinking. 'We must try and find 'omes for 'em when they are old enough,' he says at last; 'I'll go round myself and see wot *I* can do for you.'

Henery Walker thanked 'im and went off 'ome doing a bit o' thinking; and well he 'ad reason to. Everybody wanted one o' them kittens. Peter Gubbins offered for to take two, and Mr Bunnett told Henery Walker next day that 'e could ha' found 'omes for 'em ten times over.

'You've no idea wot fine, kind-'arted people they are in this village when their 'arts are touched,' he ses, smiling at Henery. 'You ought to 'ave seen Mr Jones's smile when I asked 'im to take one. It did me good to see it. And I spoke to Mr Chambers about drowning 'is kittens, and he told me 'e hadn't slept a wink ever since. And he offered to take your old cat to make up for it, if you was tired of keeping it.'

It was very 'ard on Henery Walker, I must say that. Other people was getting the credit of bringing up 'is kittens, and more than that, they used to ask Mr Bunnett into their places to see 'ow the little dears was a-getting on.

Kindness to animals caused more unpleasantness in Claybury than anything 'ad ever done afore. There was hardly a man as 'ud speak civil to each other, and the wimmen was a'most as bad. Cats and dogs and such-like began to act as if the place belonged to 'em, and seven people stopped Mr Bunnett one day to tell 'im that Joe Parsons 'ad been putting down rat-poison and killed five little baby rats and their mother.

It was some time afore anybody knew that Bob Pretty 'ad

185

got 'is eye on that gold watch, and when they did they could 'ardly believe it. They give Bob credit for too much sense to waste time over wot they knew 'e couldn't get, but arter they 'ad heard one or two things they got alarmed, and pretty near the whole village went up to see Mr Bunnett and tell 'im about Bob's true character. Mr Bunnett couldn't believe 'em at fust, but arter they 'ad told 'im of Bob's poaching and the artful ways and tricks he 'ad of getting money as didn't belong to 'im, 'e began to think different. He spoke to parson about 'im, and arter that 'e said he never wanted for to see Bob Pretty's face again.

There was a fine to-do about it up at this 'ere 'Cauliflower' public-'ouse that night, and the quietest man o' the whole lot was Bob Pretty. He sat still all the time drinking 'is beer and smiling at 'em and giving 'em good advice 'ow to get that gold watch.

'It's no good to me,' he ses, shaking his 'ead. 'I'm a pore labourin' man, and I know my place.'

"Ow you could ever 'ave thought you 'ad a chance, Bob, *I* don't know,' ses Henery Walker.

"Ow's the toad, Bob?' ses Bill Chambers; and then they all laughed.

'Laugh away, mates,' ses Bob; 'I know you don't mean it. The on'y thing I'm sorry for is you can't all 'ave the gold watch, and I'm sure you've worked 'ard enough for it; keeping Henery Walker's kittens for 'im and hanging round Mr Bunnett's.'

'We've all got a better chance than wot you 'ave, Bob,' ses little Dicky Weed the tailor.

'Ah, that's your iggernerance, Dicky,' ses Bob. 'Come to think it over quiet like, I'm afraid I shall win it arter all. Cos why? Cos I deserves it.'

They all laughed ag'in, and Bill Chambers laughed so 'arty that 'e joggled Peter Gubbins's arm and upset 'is beer.

'Laugh away,' ses Bob, pretending to get savage. 'Them that laughs best laughs last, mind. I'll 'ave that watch now, just to spite you all.'

"Ow are you going to get it, Bob?' ses Sam Jones, jeering.

'Never you mind, mate,' ses Bob, stamping 'is foot; 'I'm going to win it fair. I'm going to 'ave it for kindness to pore dumb animals.'

"Ear! 'ear!' ses Dicky Weed, winking at the others. 'Will you 'ave a bet on it, Bob?'

'No,' ses Bob Pretty; 'I don't want to win no man's money. I like to earn my money in the sweat o' my brow.'

'But you won't win it, Bob,' ses Dicky, grinning. 'Look 'ere! I'll lay you a level bob you don't get it.'

Bob shook his 'ead, and started talking to Bill Chambers about something else.

'I'll bet you two bob to one, Bob,' ses Dicky. 'Well, three to one, then.'

Bob sat up and looked at 'im for a long time, considering, and at last he ses, 'All right,' he ses, 'if Smith the landlord will mind the money I will.'

He 'anded over his shillin', but very slow-like, and Dicky Weed 'anded over 'is money. Arter that Bob sat looking disagreeable like, especially when Dicky said wot 'e was goin' to do with the money, and by-an'-by Sam Jones dared 'im to 'ave the same bet with 'im in sixpences.

Bob Pretty 'ad a pint more beer to think it over, and arter Bill Chambers 'ad stood 'im another, he said 'e would. He seemed a bit dazed like, and by the time he went 'ome he 'ad made bets with thirteen of 'em. Being Saturday night they 'ad all got money on 'em, and, as for Bob, he always 'ad some. Smith took care of the money and wrote it all up on a slate.

'Why don't you 'ave a bit on, Mr Smith?' ses Dicky.

'Oh, I dunno,' ses Smith, wiping down the bar with a wet cloth.

'It's the chance of a lifetime,' ses Dicky.

'Looks like it,' ses Smith, coughing.

'But 'e can't win,' ses Sam Jones, looking a bit upset. 'Why, Mr Bunnett said 'e ought to be locked up.'

'He's been led away,' ses Bob Pretty, shaking his 'ead. 'He's a kind-'arted old gen'leman when 'e's left alone, and he'll soon see wot a mistake 'e's made about me. I'll show 'im. But I wish it was something more useful than a gold watch.'

'You ain't got it yet,' ses Bill Chambers.

'No, mate,' ses Bob.

'And you stand to lose a sight o' money,' ses Sam Jones. 'If you like, Bob Pretty, you can 'ave your bet back with me.'

'Never mind, Sam,' ses Bob; 'I won't take no advantage of you. If I lose you'll 'ave sixpence to buy a rabbit-hutch with. Goodnight, mates all.'

He rumpled Bill Chambers's 'air for 'im as he passed—a thing Bill never can abear—and gave Henery Walker, wot was drinking beer, a smack on the back wot nearly ruined 'im for life.

Some of 'em went and told Mr Bunnett some more things about Bob next day, but they might as well ha' saved their breath. The old gen'leman said he knew all about 'im and he never wanted to 'ear his name mentioned ag'in. Arter which they began for to 'ave a more cheerful way of looking at things; and Sam Jones said 'e was going to 'ave a hole bored through 'is sixpence and wear it round 'is neck to aggravate Bob Pretty with.

For the next three or four weeks Bob Pretty seemed to keep very quiet, and we all began to think as 'ow he 'ad made a mistake for once. Everybody else was trying their 'ardest for the watch, and all Bob done was to make a laugh of 'em and to say he believed it was on'y made of brass arter all. Then one arternoon, just a few days afore Mr Bunnett's time was up at the farm, Bob took 'is dog out for a walk, and arter watching the farm for some time met the old gen'leman by accident up at Coe's plantation.

'Good arternoon, sir,' he ses, smiling at 'im. 'Wot wunner-ful fine weather we're a-having for the time o' year. I've just brought Joseph out for a bit of a walk. He ain't been wot I might call hisself for the last day or two, and I thought a little fresh air might do 'im good.'

Mr Bunnett just looked at him, and then 'e passed 'im by without a word.

'I wanted to ask your advice about 'im,' ses Bob, turning round and follering of 'im. 'He's a delikit animal, and sometimes I wonder whether I 'aven't been a-pampering of 'im too much.'

'Go away,' ses Mr Bunnett; 'I've 'eard all about you. Go away at once.'

'Heard all about me?' ses Bob Pretty, looking puzzled. 'Well, you can't 'ave heard no 'arm, that's one comfort.'

'I've been told your true character,' ses the old gen'leman, very firm. 'And I'm ashamed that I should have let myself be deceived by you. I hope you'll try and do better while there is still time.'

'If anybody 'as got anything to say ag'in my character,' says Bob, 'I wish as they'd say it to my face. I'm a pore, hard-working man, and my character's all I've got.'

'You're poorer than you thought you was then,' says Mr Bunnett. 'I wish you good arternoon.'

'Good arternoon, sir,' ses Bob, very humble. 'I'm afraid some on 'em 'ave been telling lies about me, and I didn't think I'd got a enemy in the world. Come on, Joseph. Come on, old pal. We ain't wanted here.'

He shook 'is 'ead with sorrow, and made a little sucking noise between 'is teeth, and afore you could wink, his dog 'ad laid hold of the old gen'leman's leg and kep' quiet waiting orders.

'*Help!*' screams Mr Bunnett. 'Call 'im off! Call 'im off!'

Bob said arterwards that 'e was foolish enough to lose 'is presence o' mind for a moment, and instead o' doing anything he stood there gaping with 'is mouth open.

'Call 'im off!' screams Mr Bunnett, trying to push the dog away. 'Why don't you call him off?'

'Don't move,' ses Bob Pretty in a frightened voice. 'Don't move, wotever you do.'

'Call him off! Take 'im away!' ses Mr Bunnett.

'Why Joseph! Joseph! Wotever are you a-thinking of?' ses Bob, shaking 'is 'ead at the dog. 'I'm surprised at you! Don't you know Mr Bunnett wot is so fond of animals?'

'If you don't call 'im off,' ses Mr Bunnett, trembling all over, 'I'll have you locked up.'

'I *am* a-calling 'im off,' ses Bob, looking very puzzled. 'Didn't you 'ear me? It's you making that noise that excites 'im, I think. P'r'aps if you keep quiet he'll leave go. Come off, Joseph, old boy, there's a good doggie. That ain't a bone.'

'It's no good talking to 'im like that,' ses Mr Bunnett, keeping quiet but trembling worse than ever. 'Make him let go.'

'I don't want to 'urt his feelings,' ses Bob; 'they've got their feelings the same as wot we 'ave. Besides, p'r'aps it ain't 'is fault—p'r'aps he's gone mad.'

'Help!' ses the old gen'leman, in a voice that might ha' been heard a mile away. 'Help!'

'Why don't you keep quiet?' ses Bob. 'You're on'y frightening the pore animal and making things worse. Joseph, leave go and I'll see whether there's a biskit in my pocket. Why don't you leave go?'

'Pull him off. Hit 'im,' ses Mr Bunnett, shouting.

'*Wot?*' ses Bob Pretty, with a start. 'Hit a pore, dumb animal wot don't know no better! Why, you'd never forgive me, sir, and I should lose the gold watch besides.'

'No, you won't,' ses Mr Bunnett, speaking very fast. 'You'll 'ave as much chance of it as ever you had. Hit 'im! Quick!'

'It 'ud break my 'art,' ses Bob. 'He'd never forgive me; but if you'll take the responserbility, and then go straight 'ome and give me the gold watch now for kindness to animals, I will.'

He shook his 'ead with sorrow and made that sucking noise ag'in.

'All right, you shall 'ave it,' ses Mr Bunnett, shouting. 'You shall 'ave it.'

'For kindness to animals?' ses Bob. 'Honour bright?'

'Yes,' ses Mr Bunnett.

Bob Pretty lifted 'is foot and caught Joseph one behind that surprised 'im. Then he 'elped Mr Bunnett look at 'is leg, and arter pointing out that the skin wasn't hardly broken, and saying that Joseph 'ad got the best mouth of any dog in Clay-bury, 'e walked 'ome with the old gen'leman and got the watch. He said Mr Bunnett made a little speech when 'e gave it to 'im wot he couldn't remember, and wot he wouldn't repeat if 'e could.

He came up to this 'ere 'Cauliflower' public-'ouse the same night for the money 'e had won, and Bill Chambers made another speech, but, as Smith the landlord put 'im outside for it, it didn't do Bob Pretty the good it ought to ha' done.

The Bequest

Mr Robert Clarkson sat by his fire, smoking thoughtfully. His lifelong neighbour and successful rival in love had passed away a few days before, and Mr Clarkson, fresh from the obsequies, sat musing on the fragility of man and the inconvenience that sometimes attended his departure.

His meditations were disturbed by a low knocking on the front door, which opened on to the street. In response to his invitation it opened slowly, and a small middle-aged man of doleful aspect entered softly and closed it behind him.

'Evening, Bob,' he said, in stricken accents. 'I thought I'd just step round to see how you was bearing up. Fancy pore old Phipps! Why, I'd a'most as soon it had been me. A'most.'

Mr Clarkson nodded.

'Here today and gone tomorrow,' continued Mr Smithson, taking a seat. 'Well, well! So you'll have her at last—pore thing.'

'That was his wish,' said Mr Clarkson, in a dull voice.

'And very generous of him too,' said Mr Smithson. 'Everybody is saying so. Certainly he couldn't take her away with him. How long is it since you was both of you courting her?'

'Thirty years come June,' replied the other.

'Shows what waiting does, and patience,' commented Mr Smithson. 'If you'd been like some chaps and gone abroad, where would you have been now? Where would have been the reward of your faithful heart?'

Mr Clarkson, whose pipe had gone out, took a coal from the fire and lit it again.

'I can't understand him dying at his age,' he said, darkly. 'He ought to have lived to ninety if he'd been taken care of.'

'Well, he's gone, pore chap,' said his friend. 'What a bless-
ing it must ha' been to him in his last moments to think that
he had made provision for his wife.'

'Provision!' exclaimed Mr Clarkson. 'Why, he's left her
nothing but the furniture and fifty pounds insurance money
—nothing in the world.'

Mr Smithson fidgeted. 'I mean you,' he said, staring.

'Oh!' said the other. 'Oh, yes—yes, of course.'

'And he doesn't want you to eat your heart out in waiting,'
said Mr Smithson. ' "Never mind about me," he said to her;
"you go and make Bob happy." Wonderful pretty girl she
used to be, didn't she?'

Mr Clarkson assented.

'And I've no doubt she looks the same to you as ever she
did,' pursued the sentimental Mr Smithson. 'That's the
extraordinary part of it.'

Mr Clarkson turned and eyed him; removed the pipe
from his mouth, and, after hesitating a moment, replaced it
with a jerk.

'She says she'd rather be faithful to his memory,' continued
the persevering Mr Smithson, 'but his wishes are her law.
She said so to my missis only yesterday.'

'Still, she ought to be considered,' said Mr Clarkson, shaking his head. 'I think that somebody ought to put it to her.
She has got her feelings, poor thing, and, if she would rather
not marry again, she oughtn't to be compelled to.'

'Just what my missis did say to her,' said the other; 'but
she didn't pay much attention. She said it was Henry's wish
and she didn't care what happened to her now he's gone.
Besides, if you come to think of it, what else *is* she to do?
Don't you worry, Bob; you won't lose her again.'

Mr Clarkson, staring at the fire, mused darkly. For thirty
years he had played the congenial part of the disappointed
admirer but faithful friend. He had intended to play it for at
least fifty or sixty. He wished that he had had the strength of
mind to refuse the bequest when the late Mr Phipps first
mentioned it, or taken a firmer line over the congratulations

of his friends. As it was, Little Molton quite understood that after thirty years' waiting the faithful heart was to be rewarded at last. Public opinion seemed to be that the late Mr Phipps had behaved with extraordinary generosity.

'It's rather late in life for me to begin,' said Mr Clarkson at last.

'Better late than never,' said the cheerful Mr Smithson.

'And something seems to tell me that I ain't long for this world,' continued Mr Clarkson, eyeing him with some disfavour.

'Stuff and nonsense,' said Mr Smithson. 'You'll lose all them ideas as soon as you're married. You'll have somebody to look after you and help you spend your money.'

Mr Clarkson emitted a dismal groan, and clapping his hand over his mouth strove to make it pass muster as a yawn. It was evident that the malicious Mr Smithson was deriving considerable pleasure from his discomfiture—the pleasure natural to the father of seven over the troubles of a comfortable bachelor. Mr Clarkson, anxious to share his troubles with somebody, came to a sudden and malicious determination to share them with Mr Smithson.

'I don't want anybody to help me spend my money,' he said, slowly. 'First and last I've saved a tidy bit. I've got this house, those three cottages in Turner's Lane, and pretty near six hundred pounds in the bank.'

Mr Smithson's eyes glistened.

'I had thought—it had occurred to me,' said Mr Clarkson, trying to keep as near the truth as possible, 'to leave my property to a friend o' mine—a hard-working man with a large family. However, it's no use talking about that now. It's too late.'

'Who—who was it?' inquired his friend, trying to keep his voice steady.

Mr Clarkson shook his head. 'It's no good talking about that now, George,' he said, eyeing him with sly enjoyment. 'I shall have to leave everything to my wife now. After all, perhaps it does more harm than good to leave money to people.'

'Rubbish!' said Mr Smithson, sharply. 'Who was it?'

'You, George,' said Mr Clarkson, softly.

'Me?' said the other, with a gasp. '*Me?*' He jumped up from his chair, and, seizing the other's hand, shook it fervently.

'I oughtn't to have told you, George,' said Mr Clarkson, with great satisfaction. 'It'll only make you miserable. It's just one o' the might ha' beens.'

Mr Smithson, with his back to the fire and his hands twisted behind him, stood with his eyes fixed in thought.

'It's rather cool of Phipps,' he said, after a long silence; 'rather cool, I think, to go out of the world and just leave his wife to you to look after. Some men wouldn't stand it. You're too easy-going, Bob; that's what's the matter with you.'

Mr Clarkson sighed.

'And get took advantage of,' added his friend.

'It's all very well to talk,' said Mr Clarkson, 'but what can I do? I ought to have spoke up at the time. It's too late now.'

'If I was you,' said his friend very earnestly, 'and didn't want to marry her, I should tell her so. Say what you like it ain't fair to her, you know. It ain't fair to the pore woman. She'd never forgive you if she found it out.'

'Everybody's taking it for granted,' said the other.

'Let everybody look after their own business,' said Mr Smithson, tartly. 'Now, look here, Bob; suppose I get you out of this business, how am I to be sure you'll leave your property to me?—not that I want it. Suppose you altered your will?'

'If you get me out of it every penny I leave will go to you,' said Mr Clarkson, fervently. 'I haven't got any relations, and it don't matter in the slightest to me who has it after I'm gone.'

'As true as you stand there?' demanded the other, eyeing him fixedly.

'As true as I stand here,' said Mr Clarkson, smiting his chest, and shook hands again.

Long after his visitor had gone he sat gazing in a brooding

fashion at the fire. As a single man his wants were few, and he could live on his savings; as the husband of Mrs Phipps he would be compelled to resume the work he thought he had dropped for good three years before. Moreover, Mrs Phipps possessed a strength of character that had many times caused him to congratulate himself upon her choice of a husband.

Slowly but surely his fetters were made secure. Two days later the widow departed to spend six weeks with a sister; but any joy that he might have felt over the circumstance was marred by the fact that he had to carry her bags down to the railway station and see her off. The key of her house was left with him, with strict injunctions to go in and water her geraniums every day, while two canaries and a bullfinch had to be removed to his own house in order that they might have constant attention and company.

'She's doing it on purpose,' said Mr Smithson, fiercely; 'she's binding you hand and foot.'

Mr Clarkson assented gloomily. 'I'm trusting to you, George,' he remarked.

'How'd it be to forget to water the geraniums and let the birds die because they missed her so much?' suggested Mr Smithson, after prolonged thought.

Mr Clarkson shivered.

'It would be a hint,' said his friend.

Mr Clarkson took some letters from the mantelpiece and held them up. 'She writes about them every day,' he said, briefly, 'and I have to answer them.'

'She—she don't refer to your getting married, I suppose?' said his friend, anxiously.

Mr Clarkson said, 'No. But her sister does,' he added. 'I've had two letters from her.'

Mr Smithson got up and paced restlessly up and down the room. 'That's women all over,' he said, bitterly. 'They never ask for things straight out; but they always get 'em in round-about ways. She can't do it herself, so she gets her sister to do it.'

Mr Clarkson groaned. 'And her sister is hinting that she

can't leave the house where she spent so many happy years,' he said, 'and says what a pleasant surprise it would be for Mrs Phipps if she was to come home and find it done up.'

'That means you've got to live there when you're married,' said his friend, solemnly.

Mr Clarkson glanced round his comfortable room and groaned again. 'She asked me to get an estimate from Digson,' he said, dully. 'She knows as well as I do her sister hasn't got any money. I wrote to say that it had better be left till she comes home, as I might not know what was wanted.'

Mr Smithson nodded approval.

'And Mrs Phipps wrote herself and thanked me for being so considerate,' continued his friend, grimly, 'and says that when she comes back we must go over the house together and see what wants doing.'

Mr Smithson got up and walked round the room again.

'You never promised to marry her?' he said, stopping suddenly.

'No,' said the other. 'It's all been arranged for me. I never said a word. I couldn't tell Phipps I wouldn't have her with them all standing round, and him thinking he was doing me the greatest favour in the world.'

'Well, she can't name the day unless you ask her,' said the other. 'All you've got to do is to keep quiet and not commit yourself. Be as cool as you can, and, just before she comes home, you go off to London on business and stay there as long as possible.'

Mr Clarkson carried out his instructions to the letter, and Mrs Phipps, returning home at the end of her visit, learned that he had left for London three days before, leaving the geraniums and birds to the care of Mr Smithson. From the hands of that unjust steward she received two empty bird-cages, together with a detailed account of the manner in which the occupants had effected their escape, and a bull-finch that seemed to be suffering from torpid liver. The condition of the geraniums was ascribed to worms in the pots, frost, and premature decay.

'They go like it sometimes,' said Mr Smithson, 'and when they do nothing will save 'em.'

Mrs Phipps thanked him. 'It's very kind of you to take so much trouble,' she said, quietly; 'some people would have lost the cages too while they were about it.'

'I did my best,' said Mr Smithson, in a surly voice.

'I know you did,' said Mrs Phipps, thoughtfully, 'and I am sure I am much obliged to you. If there is anything of yours I can look after at any time I shall be only too pleased. When did you say Mr Clarkson was coming back?'

'He don't know,' said Mr Smithson, promptly. 'He might be away a month; and then, again, he might be away six. It all depends. You know what business is.'

'It's very thoughtful of him,' said Mrs Phipps. 'Very.'

'Thoughtful!' repeated Mr Smithson.

'He has gone away for a time out of consideration for me,' said the widow. 'As things are, it is a little bit awkward for us to meet much at present.'

'I don't think he's gone away for that at all,' said the other, bluntly.

Mrs Phipps shook her head. 'Ah, you don't know him as well as I do,' she said, fondly. 'He has gone away on my account, I feel sure.'

Mr Smithson screwed his lips together and remained silent.

'When he feels that it is right and proper for him to come back,' pursued Mrs Phipps, turning her eyes upwards, 'he will come. He has left his comfortable home just for my sake, and I shall not forget it.'

Mr Smithson coughed—a short, dry cough, meant to convey incredulity.

'I shall not do anything to this house till he comes back,' said Mrs Phipps. 'I expect he would like to have a voice in it. He always used to admire it and say how comfortable it was. Well, well, we never know what is before us.'

Mr Smithson repeated the substance of the interview to Mr Clarkson by letter, and in the lengthy correspondence that followed kept him posted as to the movements of Mrs Phipps. By dint of warnings and entreaties he kept the bridegroom-elect in London for three months. By that time Little Molton was beginning to talk.

'They're beginning to see how the land lays,' said Mr Smithson, on the evening of his friend's return, 'and if you keep quiet and do as I tell you she'll begin to see it too. As I said before, she can't name the day till you ask her.'

Mr Clarkson agreed, and the following morning, when he called upon Mrs Phipps at her request, his manner was so distant that she attributed it to ill-health following business worries and the atmosphere of London. In the front parlour Mr Digson, a small builder and contractor, was busy whitewashing.

'I thought we might as well get on with that,' said Mrs Phipps; 'there is only one way of doing whitewashing, and the room has got to be done. Tomorrow Mr Digson will bring up some papers, and, if you'll come round, you can help me choose.'

Mr Clarkson hesitated. 'Why not choose 'em yourself?' he said at last.

'Just what I told her,' said Mr Digson, stroking his black beard. ' "What'll please you will be sure to please him," I says; and if it don't it ought to.'

Mr Clarkson started. 'Perhaps you could help her choose,' he said, sharply.

Mr Digson came down from his perch. 'Just what I said,' he replied. 'If Mrs Phipps will let me advise her, I'll make this house so she won't know it before I've done with it.'

'Mr Digson has been very kind,' said Mrs Phipps, reproachfully.

'Not at all, ma'am,' said the builder, softly. 'Anything I can do to make you happy or comfortable will be a pleasure to me.'

Mr Clarkson started again, and an odd idea sent his blood dancing. Digson was a widower; Mrs Phipps was a widow. Could anything be more suitable or desirable?

'Better let him choose,' he said. 'After all, he ought to be a good judge.'

Mrs Phipps, after a faint protest, gave way, and Mr Digson, smiling broadly, mounted his perch again.

Mr Clarkson's first idea was to consult Mr Smithson; then he resolved to wait upon events. The idea was fantastic to begin with, but, if things did take such a satisfactory turn, he could not help reflecting that it would not be due to any efforts on the part of Mr Smithson, and he would no longer be under any testamentary obligations to that enterprising gentleman.

By the end of a week he was jubilant. A child could have told Mr Digson's intentions—and Mrs Phipps was anything but a child. Mr Clarkson admitted cheerfully that Mr Digson was a younger and better-looking man than himself—a more suitable match in every way. And, so far as he could judge, Mrs Phipps seemed to think so. At any rate, she had ceased to make the faintest allusion to any tie between them. He left her one day painting a door, while the attentive Digson guided the brush, and walked homewards smiling.

'Morning!' said a voice behind him.

'Morning, Bignell,' said Mr Clarkson.

'When—when is it to be?' inquired his friend, walking beside him.

Mr Clarkson frowned. 'When is what to be?' he demanded, disagreeably.

Mr Bignell lowered his voice. 'You'll lose her if you ain't careful,' he said. 'Mark my words. Can't you see Digson's little game?'

Mr Clarkson shrugged his shoulders.

'He's after her money,' said the other, with a cautious glance around.

'*Money?*' said the other, with an astonished laugh. 'Why, she hasn't got any.'

'Oh, all right,' said Mr Bignell. 'You know best, of course. I was just giving you the tip, but if you know better—why, there's nothing more to be said. She'll be riding in her carriage and pair in six months, anyhow; the richest woman in Little Molton.'

Mr Clarkson stopped short and eyed him in perplexity.

'Digson got a bit sprung one night and told me,' said Mr Bignell. 'She don't know it herself yet—uncle on her mother's side in America. She might know at any moment.'

'But—but how did Digson know?' inquired the astonished Mr Clarkson.

'He wouldn't tell me,' was the reply. 'But it's good enough for him. What do you *think* he's after? Her? And mind, don't let on to a soul that I told you.'

He walked on, leaving Mr Clarkson standing in a dazed condition in the centre of the footpath. Recovering himself by an effort, he walked slowly away, and, after prowling about for some time in an aimless fashion, made his way back to Mrs Phipps's house.

He emerged an hour later an engaged man, with the date of the wedding fixed. With jaunty steps he walked round and put up the banns, and then, with the air of a man who has completed a successful stroke of business, walked homewards.

Little Molton is a small town, and news travels fast, but it did not travel faster than Mr Smithson as soon as he had heard it. He burst into Mr Clarkson's room like the proverbial hurricane, and, gasping for breath, leaned against the table and pointed at him an incriminating finger.

'You—you've been running,' said Mr Clarkson, uneasily.

'What—what—what do you—mean by it?' gasped Mr Smithson. 'After all my trouble. After our—bargain.'

'I altered my mind,' said Mr Clarkson, with dignity.

'*Pah!*' said the other.

'Just in time,' said Mr Clarkson, speaking rapidly. 'Another day and I believe I should ha' been too late. It took me pretty near an hour to talk her over. Said I'd been neglecting her, and all that sort of thing; said that she was beginning to think I didn't want her. As hard a job as ever I had in my life.'

'But you didn't want her,' said the amazed Mr Smithson. 'You told me so.'

'You misunderstood me,' said Mr Clarkson, coughing. 'You jump at conclusions.'   -

Mr Smithson sat staring at him. 'I heard,' he said at last, with an effort—'I heard that Digson was paying her attentions.'

Mr Clarkson spoke without thought. 'Ha, he was only after her money,' he said, severely. 'Good heavens? *What's the matter?*'

Mr Smithson, who had sprung to his feet, made no reply, but stood for some time incapable of speech.

'What—is—the—matter?' repeated Mr Clarkson. 'Ain't you well?'

Mr Smithson swayed a little, and sank slowly back into his chair again.

'Room's too hot,' said his astonished host.

Mr Smithson, staring straight before him, nodded.

'As I was saying,' resumed Mr Clarkson, in the low tones of confidence, 'Digson was after her money. Of course her money don't make any difference to me, although, perhaps, I may be able to do something for friends like you. It's from an uncle in America on her mother's——'

Mr Smithson made a strange moaning noise, and, snatching his hat from the table, clapped it on his head and made for the door. Mr Clarkson flung his arms around him and dragged him back by main force.

'What are you carrying on like that for?' he demanded. 'What do you mean by it?'

'Fancy!' returned Mr Smithson, with intense bitterness. 'I thought Digson was the biggest fool in the place, and I find I've made a mistake. So have you. Goodnight.'

He opened the door and dashed out. Mr Clarkson, with a strange sinking at his heart, watched him up the road.

The Unknown

Handsome is as 'andsome does, said the night watchman. It's an old saying, but it's true. Give a chap good looks, and it's precious little else that is given to 'im. He's lucky when 'is good looks 'ave gorn—or partly gorn—to get a berth as night watchman or some other hard and bad-paid job.

One drawback to a good-looking man is that he generally marries young; not because 'e wants to, but because somebody else wants 'im to. And that ain't the worst of it: the handsomest chap I ever knew married five times, and got seven years for it. It wasn't his fault, pore chap; he simply couldn't say No.

One o' the best-looking men I ever knew was Cap'n Bill Smithers, wot used to come up here once a week with a schooner called the *Wild Rose*. Funny thing about 'im was he didn't seem to know about 'is good looks, and he was one o' the quietest, best-behaved men that ever came up the London river. Considering that he was mistook for me more than once, it was just as well.

He didn't marry until 'e was close on forty; and then 'e made the mistake of marrying a widder-woman. She was like all the rest of 'em—only worse. Afore she was married butter wouldn't melt in 'er mouth, but as soon as she 'ad got her 'lines' safe she began to make up for it.

For the fust month or two 'e didn't mind it, 'e rather liked being fussed arter, but when he found that he couldn't go out for 'arf an hour without having 'er with 'im he began to get tired of it. Her idea was that 'e was too handsome to be trusted out alone; and every trip he made 'e had to write up in a book, day by day, wot 'e did with himself. Even then she wasn't satisfied, and, arter saying that a wife's place was by the side of 'er husband, she took to sailing with 'im every v'y'ge.

Wot he could ha' seen in 'er I don't know. I asked 'im one evening—in a roundabout way—and he answered in such a long, roundabout way that I didn't know wot to make of it till I see that she was standing just behind me, listening. Arter that I heard 'er asking questions about me, but I didn't 'ave to listen: I could hear 'er twenty yards away, and singing to myself at the same time.

Arter that she treated me as if I was the dirt beneath 'er feet. She never spoke to me, but used to speak against me to other people. She was always talking to them about the 'sleeping-sickness' and things o' that kind. She said night watchmen always made 'er think of it somehow, but she didn't know why, and she couldn't tell you if you was to ask her. The only thing I was thankful for was that I wasn't 'er husband. She stuck to 'im like his shadow, and I began to think at last it was a pity she 'adn't got something to be jealous about and something to occupy her mind with instead o' me.

'She ought to 'ave a lesson,' I ses to the skipper one evening. 'Are you going to be follered about like this all your life? If she was made to see the foolishness of 'er ways she might get sick of it.'

My idea was to send her on a wild-goose chase, and while the *Wild Rose* was away I thought it out. I wrote a love-letter to the skipper signed with the name of 'Dorothy', and asked 'im to meet me at Cleopatra's Needle on the Embankment at eight o'clock on Wednesday. I told 'im to look out for a tall girl (Mrs Smithers was as short as they make 'em) with mischievous brown eyes, in a blue 'at with red roses on it.

I read it over careful, and arter marking it 'Private', twice in front and once on the back, I stuck it down so that it could be blown open a'most, and waited for the schooner to come back. Then I gave a van-boy twopence to 'and it to Mrs Smithers, wot was sitting on the deck alone, and tell 'er it was a letter for Captain Smithers.

I was busy with a barge wot happened to be handy at the time, but I 'eard her say that she would take it and give it to 'im. When I peeped round she 'ad got the letter open and was leaning over the side to wind'ard trying to get 'er breath. Every now and then she'd give another look at the letter and open 'er mouth and gasp; but by-and-by she got calmer, and, arter putting it back in the envelope, she gave it a lick as though she was going to bite it, and stuck it down ag'in. Then she went off the wharf, and I'm blest if, five minutes arterwards, a young fellow didn't come down to the ship with the same letter and ask for the skipper.

'Who gave it you?' ses the skipper, as soon as 'e could speak.

'A lady,' ses the young fellow.

The skipper waved 'im away, and then 'e walked up and down the deck like a man in a dream.

'Bad news?' I ses, looking up and catching 'is eye.

'No,' he ses, 'no. Only a note about a couple o' casks o' soda.'

He stuffed the letter in 'is pocket and sat on the side smoking till his wife came back in five minutes' time, smiling all over with good temper.

'It's a nice evening,' she ses, 'and I think I'll just run over to Dalston and see my Cousin Joe.'

The skipper got up like a lamb and said he'd go and clean 'imself.

'You needn't come if you feel tired,' she ses, smiling at 'im.

The skipper could 'ardly believe his ears.

'I do feel tired,' he ses. 'I've had a heavy day, and I feel more like bed than anything else.'

'You turn in, then,' she ses. 'I'll be all right by myself.'

She went down and tidied herself up—not that it made much difference to 'er—and, arter patting him on the arm and giving me a stare that would ha' made most men blink, she took herself off.

I was pretty busy that evening. Wot with shifting lighters from under the jetty and sweeping up, it was pretty near ha'-past seven afore I 'ad a minute I could call my own. I put down the broom at last, and was just thinking of stepping round to the Bull's Head for a 'arf-pint when I see Cap'n Smithers come off the ship on to the wharf and walk to the gate.

'I thought you was going to turn in?' I ses.

'I did think of it,' he ses, 'then I thought p'r'aps I'd better stroll as far as Broad Street and meet my wife.'

It was all I could do to keep a straight face. I'd a pretty good idea where she 'ad gorn; and it wasn't Dalston.

'Come in and 'ave 'arf a pint fust,' I ses.

'No; I shall be late,' he ses, hurrying off.

I went in and 'ad a glass by myself, and stood there so long thinking of Mrs Smithers walking up and down by Cleopatra's Needle that at last the landlord fust asked me wot I was laughing at, and then offered to make me laugh the other side of my face. And then he wonders why people go to the Albion.

I locked the gate rather earlier than usual that night. Sometimes if I'm up that end I leave it a bit late, but I didn't want Mrs Smithers to come along and nip in without me seeing her face.

It was ten o'clock afore I heard the bell go, and when I opened the wicket and looked out I was surprised to see that she 'ad got the skipper with 'er. And of all the miserable-looking objects I ever saw in my life he was the worst. She 'ad him tight by the arm, and there was a look on 'er face that a'most scared me.

'Did you go all the way to Dalston for her?' I ses to 'im.

Mrs Smithers made a gasping sort o' noise, but the skipper didn't answer a word. She shoved him in in front of 'er and stood over 'im while he climbed aboard. When he held out 'is hand to help 'er she struck it away.

I didn't get word with 'im till five o'clock next morning, when he came up on deck with his 'air all rough and 'is eyes red for want of sleep.

'Haven't 'ad a wink all night,' he ses, stepping on to the wharf.

I gave a little cough. 'Didn't she 'ave a pleasant time at Dalston?' I ses.

He walked a little further off from the ship. 'She didn't go there,' he ses, in a whisper.

'You've got something on your mind,' I ses. 'Wot is it?'

He wouldn't tell me at fust, but at last he told me all about the letter from Dorothy, and 'is wife reading it unbeknown to 'im and going to meet 'er.

'It was an awful meeting!' he ses. 'Awful!'

I couldn't think wot to make of it. 'Was the gal there, then?' I ses, staring at 'im.

'No,' ses the skipper; 'but I was.'

'*You?*' I ses, starting back. 'You! Wot for? I'm surprised at you! I wouldn't ha' believed it of you!'

'I felt a bit curious,' he ses, with a silly sort o' smile. 'But wot I can't understand is why the gal didn't turn up.'

'I'm ashamed of you, Bill,' I ses, very severe.

'P'r'aps she did,' he ses, 'arf to 'imself, 'and then saw my missis standing there waiting. P'r'aps that was it.'

'Or p'r'aps it was somebody 'aving a game with you,' I ses.

'You're getting old, Bill,' he ses, very short. 'You don't understand. It's some pore gal that's took a fancy to me, and it's my dooty to meet 'er and tell her 'ow things are.'

He walked off with his 'ead in the air, and if 'e took that letter out once and looked at it, he did five times.

'Chuck it away,' I ses, going up to him.

'Certainly not,' he ses, folding it up careful and stowing it away in 'is breast-pocket. 'She's took a fancy to me, and it's my dooty——'

'You said that afore,' I ses.

He stared at me nasty for a moment, and then 'e ses, 'You ain't seen any young lady hanging about 'ere, I suppose, Bill? A tall young lady with a blue hat trimmed with red roses?'

I shook my 'ead.

'If you should see 'er——' he ses.

'I'll tell your missis,' I ses. 'It 'ud be much easier for her to do her dooty properly than it would you. She'd enjoy doing it, too.'

He went off ag'in then, and I thought he 'ad done with me, but he 'adn't. He spoke to me that evening as if I was the greatest friend he 'ad in the world. I 'ad two 'arf-pints with 'im at the Albion—with his missis walking up and down outside—and arter the second 'arf-pint he said he wanted to meet Dorothy and tell 'er that 'e was married, and that he 'oped she would meet some good man that was worthy of 'er.

I had a week's peace while the ship was away, but she was hardly made fast afore I 'ad it all over ag'in and ag'in.

'Are you sure there's been no more letters?' he ses.

'Sartain,' I ses.

'That's right,' he ses; 'that's right. And you 'aven't seen her walking up and down?'

'No,' I ses.

''Ave you been on the look-out?' he ses. 'I don't suppose a nice gal like that would come and shove her 'ead in at the gate. Did you look up and down the road?'

'Yes,' I ses. 'I've fair made my eyes ache watching for her.'

'I can't understand it,' he ses. 'It's a mystery to me, unless p'r'aps she's been taken ill. She must 'ave seen me here in the fust place; and she managed to get hold of my name. Mark my words, I shall 'ear from her ag'in.'

''Ow do you know?' I ses.

'I feel it 'ere,' he ses, very solemn, laying his 'and on his chest.

I didn't know wot to do. Wot with 'is foolishness and his missis's temper, I see I 'ad made a mess of it. He told me she had 'ardly spoke a word to 'im for two days, and when I said—being a married man myself—that it might ha' been worse, 'e said I didn't know wot I was talking about.

I did a bit o' thinking arter he 'ad gorn aboard ag'in. I dursn't tell 'im that I 'ad wrote the letter, but I thought if he 'ad one or two more he'd see that someone was 'aving a game with 'im, and that it might do 'im good. Besides which it was a little amusement for me.

Arter everybody was in their beds asleep I sat on a clerk's stool in the office and wrote 'im another letter from Dorothy. I called 'im 'Dear Bill', and I said 'ow sorry I was that I 'adn't had even a sight of 'im lately, having been laid up with a sprained ankle and 'ad only just got about ag'in. I asked 'im to meet me at Cleopatra's Needle at eight o'clock, and said that I should wear the blue 'at with red roses.

It was a very good letter, but I can see now that I done wrong in writing it. I was going to post it to 'im, but, as I couldn't find an envelope without the name of the blessed wharf on it, I put it in my pocket till I got 'ome.

I got 'ome at about a quarter to seven, and slept like a child till pretty near four. Then I went downstairs to 'ave my dinner.

The moment I opened the door I see there was something wrong. Three times my missis licked 'er lips afore she could speak. Her face 'ad gone a dirty white colour, and she was leaning forward with her 'ands on her 'ips, trembling all over with temper.

'Is my dinner ready?' I ses, easy-like. ''Cos I'm ready for *it*.'

'I—I wonder I don't tear you limb from limb,' she ses, catching her breath.

'Wot's the matter?' I ses.

'And then boil you,' she ses, between her teeth. 'You in one pot and your precious Dorothy in another.'

If anybody 'ad offered me five pounds to speak then, I couldn't ha' done it. I see wot I'd done in a flash, and I couldn't say a word; but I kept my presence o' mind, and as she came round one side o' the table I went round the other.

'Wot 'ave you got to say for yourself?' she ses, with a scream.

'Nothing,' I ses, at last. 'It's all a mistake.'

'Mistake?' she ses. 'Yes, you made a mistake leaving it in your pocket; that's all the mistake you've made. That's wot you do, is it, when you're supposed to be at the wharf? Go about with a blue 'at with red roses in it! At your time o' life, and a wife at 'ome working herself to death to make both ends meet and keep you respectable!'

'It's all a mistake,' I ses. 'The letter wasn't for me.'

'Oh, no, o' course not,' she ses. 'That's why you'd got it in your pocket, I suppose. And I suppose you'll say your name ain't Bill next.'

'Don't say things you'll be sorry for,' I ses.

'I'll take care o' that,' she ses. 'I might be sorry for not saying some things, but I don't think I shall.'

I don't think she was. I don't think she forgot anything, and she raked up things that I 'ad contradicted years ago and wot I thought was all forgot. And every now and then, when she stopped for breath, she'd try and get round to the same side of the table I was.

She follered me to the street door when I went and called things up the road arter me. I 'ad a snack at a coffee-shop for my dinner, but I 'adn't got much appetite for it; I was too full of trouble and finding fault with myself, and I went off to my work with a 'art as heavy as lead.

I suppose I 'adn't been on the wharf ten minutes afore Cap'n Smithers came sidling up to me, but I got my spoke in fust.

'Look 'ere,' I ses, 'if you're going to talk about that forward hussy wot's been writing to you, I ain't. I'm sick and tired of 'er.'

'Forward hussy!' he ses. *'Forward hussy!'* And afore I could drop my broom he gave me a punch in the jaw that pretty near broke it. 'Say another word against her,' he ses, 'and I'll knock your ugly 'ead off. How dare you insult a lady?'

I thought I should 'ave gone crazy at fust, but I went off into the office without a word. Some men would ha' knocked 'im down for it, but I made allowances for 'is state o' mind, and I stayed inside until I see 'im get aboard ag'in.

He was sitting on deck when I went out, and his missis too, but neither of 'em spoke a word. I picked up my broom and went on sweeping, when suddenly I 'eard a voice at the gate I thought I knew, and in came my wife.

'Ho!' she ses, calling out. 'Ain't you gone to meet that gal at Cleopatra's Needle yet? You ain't going to keep 'er waiting, are you?'

'*H'sh!*' I ses.

'*H'sh!* yourself,' she ses, shouting. '*I've* done nothing to be ashamed of. *I* don't go to meet other people's husbands in a blue 'at with red roses. *I* don't write 'em love-letters, and say "*Hush!*" to my wife when she ventures to make a remark about it. I may work myself to skin and bone for a man wot's old enough to know better, but I'm not going to be trod on. Dorothy, indeed! I'll Dorothy 'er if I get the chance.'

Mrs Smithers, wot 'ad been listening with all her ears, jumped up, and so did the skipper, and Mrs Smithers came to the side in two steps.

'Did you say "Dorothy," ma'am?' she ses to my missis.

'I did,' ses my wife. 'She's been writing to my husband.'

'It must be the same one,' ses Mrs Smithers. 'She's been writing to mine too.'

The two of 'em stood there looking at each other for a minute, and then my wife, holding the letter between 'er finger and thumb as if it was p'ison, passed it to Mrs Smithers.

'It's the same,' ses Mrs Smithers. 'Was the envelope marked "Private"?'

'I didn't see no envelope,' ses my missis. 'This is all I found.'

Mrs Smithers stepped on to the wharf and, taking 'old of my missis by the arm, led her away whispering. At the same moment the skipper walked across the deck and whispered to me.

'Wot d'ye mean by it?' he ses. 'Wot d'ye mean by 'aving letters from Dorothy and not telling me about it?'

'I can't help 'aving letters any more than you can,' I ses. 'Now p'r'aps you'll understand wot I meant by calling 'er a forward hussy.'

'Fancy 'er writing to you!' he ses, wrinkling 'is forehead. '*Pph!* She must be crazy.'

'P'r'aps it ain't a gal at all,' I ses. 'My belief is somebody is 'aving a game with us.'

'Don't be a fool,' he ses. 'I'd like to see the party as would make a fool of me like that. Just see 'im and get my 'ands on him. He wouldn't want to play any more games.'

It was no good talking to 'im. He was 'arf crazy with temper. If I'd said the letter was meant for 'im he'd 'ave asked me wot I meant by opening it and getting 'im into more trouble with 'is missis, instead of giving it to 'im on the quiet. I just stood and suffered in silence, and thought wot a lot of 'arm eddication did for people.

'I want some money,' ses my missis, coming back at last with Mrs Smithers.

That was the way she always talked when she'd got me in 'er power. She took two-and-tenpence—all I'd got—and then she ordered me to go and get a cab.

'Me and this lady are going to meet her,' she ses, sniffing at me.

'And tell her wot we think of 'er,' ses Mrs Smithers, sniffing too.

'And wot we'll do to 'er,' ses my missis.

I left 'em standing side by side, looking at the skipper as if 'e was a waxworks, while I went to find a cab. When I came back they was in the same persition, and 'e was smoking with 'is eyes shut.

They went off side by side in the cab, both of 'em sitting bolt-upright, and only turning their 'eads at the last moment to give us looks we didn't want.

'I don't wish her no 'arm,' ses the skipper, arter thinking for a long time. 'Was that the fust letter you 'ad from 'er, Bill?'

'Fust and last,' I ses, grinding my teeth.

'I hope they won't meet 'er, pore thing,' he ses.

'I've been married longer than wot you have,' I ses, 'and I tell you one thing. It won't make no difference to us whether they do or they don't,' I ses.

And it didn't.

Shareholders

A sailorman—said the night watchman, musingly—a sailorman is like a fish, he is safest when 'e is at sea. When a fish
comes ashore it is in for trouble, and so is a sailorman. One
poor chap I knew 'ardly ever came ashore without getting
married; and when he was found out there was no less than
six wimmen in the court all taking away 'is character at once.
And when he spoke up about Solomon the magistrate pretty
near bit 'is 'ead off.

Then look at the trouble they get in with their money!
They come ashore from a long trip, smelling of it a'most, and
they go from port to port like a lord. Everybody has got their
eye on that money—everybody except the sailorman, that is
—and afore he knows wot's 'appened, and who 'as got it, he's
looking for a ship ag'in. When he ain't robbed of 'is money, he
wastes it; and when 'e don't do either, he loses it.

I knew one chap who hid 'is money. He'd been away ten
months, and, knowing 'ow easy money goes, 'e made up sixteen pounds in a nice little parcel and hid it where nobody
could find it. That's wot he said, and p'r'aps 'e was right. All
I know is, *he* never found it. I did the same thing myself once
with a couple o' quid I ran acrost unexpected, on'y, unfor-
tunately for me, I hid it the day afore my missus started 'er
spring-cleaning.

One o' the worst men I ever knew for getting into trouble
when he came ashore was old Sam Small. If he couldn't find
it by 'imself, Ginger Dick and Peter Russet would help 'im
look for it. Generally speaking they found it without straining
their eyesight.

I remember one time they was home, arter being away

pretty near a year, and when they was paid off they felt like walking gold-mines. They went about smiling all over with good-temper and 'appiness, and for the first three days they was like brothers. That didn't last, of course, and on the fourth day Sam Small, arter saying wot 'e would do to Ginger and Peter if it wasn't for the police, went off by 'imself.

His temper passed off arter a time, and 'e began to look cheerful ag'in. It was a lovely morning, and, having nothing to do and plenty in 'is pocket to do it with, he went along like a schoolboy with a 'arf holiday.

He went as far as Stratford on the top of a tram for a mouthful o' fresh air, and came back to his favourite coffee-shop with a fine appetite for dinner. There was a very nice gentlemanly chap sitting opposite 'im, and the way he begged Sam's pardon for splashing gravy over 'im made Sam take a liking to him at once. Nicely dressed he was, with a gold pin in 'is tie, and a fine gold watch-chain acrost his weskit; and Sam could see he 'ad been brought up well by the way he used 'is knife and fork. He kept looking at Sam in a thoughtful kind o' way, and at last he said wot a beautiful morning it was, and wot a fine day it must be in the country. In a little while they began to talk like a couple of old friends, and he told Sam all about 'is father, wot was a clergyman in the country, and Sam talked about a father of his as was living private on three 'undred a year.

'Ah, money's a useful thing,' ses the man.

'It ain't everything,' ses Sam. 'It won't give you 'appiness. I've run through a lot in my time, so I ought to know.'

'I expect you've got a bit left, though,' ses the man, with a wink.

Sam laughed and smacked 'is pocket. 'I've got a trifle to go on with,' he ses, winking back. 'I never feel comfortable without a pound or two in my pocket.'

'You look as though you're just back from a v'y'ge,' ses the man, looking at 'im very hard.

'I am,' ses Sam, nodding. 'Just back arter ten months, and I'm going to spend a bit o' money afore I sign on ag'in, I can tell you.'

'That's wot it was given to us for,' ses the man, nodding at him.

They both got up to go at the same time and walked out into the street together, and, when Sam asked 'im whether he might have the pleasure of standing 'im a drink, he said he might. He talked about the different kinds of drink as they walked along till Sam, wot was looking for a high-class pub, got such a raging thirst on 'im he hardly knew wot to do with 'imself. He passed several pubs, and walked on as fast as he could to the Three Widders.

'Do you want to go in there partikler?' ses the man, stopping at the door.

'No,' ses Sam, staring.

''Cos I know a place where they sell the best glass o' port wine in London,' ses the man.

He took Sam up two or three turnings, and then led him into a quiet little pub in a back street. There was a cosy little saloon-bar with nobody in it, and, arter Sam had 'ad two port wines for the look of the thing, he 'ad a pint o' six-ale because he liked it. His new pal had one too, and he 'ad just taken a pull at it and wiped his mouth, when 'e noticed a little bill pinned up at the back of the bar.

'*Lost, between—the Mint and—Tower Stairs,*' he ses, leaning forward and reading very slow, '*a gold—locket—set with —diamonds. Whoever will—return—the same to—Mr Smith— Orange Villa—Barnet—will receive—thirty pounds—reward.*'

''Ow much?' ses Sam, starting.

'Thirty pounds,' ses the man. 'Must be a good locket. Where'd you get that?' he ses, turning to the barmaid.

'Gentleman came in an hour ago,' ses the gal, 'and, arter he had 'ad two or three drinks with the guv'nor, he asks 'im to stick it up. 'Arf crying he was—said it 'ad belonged to his old woman wot died.'

She went off to serve a customer at the other end of the bar wot was making little dents in it with his pot, and the man came back and sat down by Sam ag'in, and began to talk about horse-racing. At least, he tried to, but Sam couldn't talk of nothing but that locket, and wot a nice steady sailor-man could do with thirty pounds.

'Well, p'r'aps you'll find it,' ses the man, chaffing-like. ''Ave another pint.'

Sam had one, but it only made 'im more solemn, and he got in quite a temper as 'e spoke about casuals loafing about on Tower Hill with their 'ands in their pockets, and taking gold lockets out of the mouths of hard-working sailormen.

'It mightn't be found yet,' ses the man, speaking thoughtful-like. 'It's wonderful how long a thing'll lay sometimes. Wot about going and 'aving a look for it?'

Sam shook his 'ead at fust, but arter turning the thing over in his mind, and 'aving another look at the bill, and copying down the name and address for luck, 'e said p'r'aps they might as well walk that way as anywhere else.

'Something seems to tell me we've got a chance,' ses the man, as they stepped outside. 'It's a funny feeling and I can't explain it, but it always means good luck. Last time I had it an aunt o' mine swallered 'er false teeth and left me five 'undred pounds.'

'There's aunts and aunts,' ses Sam, grunting. 'I 'ad one once, but if she had swallered *'er* teeth she'd ha' been round to me to help 'er buy some new ones. That's the sort *she* was.'

'Mind!' ses the man, patting 'im on the shoulder, 'if we do find this, I don't want any of it. I've got all I want. It's all for you.'

They went on like a couple o' brothers arter that, especially Sam, and when they got to the Mint they walked along slow down Tower Hill looking for the locket. It was awkward work, because, if people saw them looking about, they'd 'ave started looking too, and twice Sam nearly fell over owing to walking like a man with a stiff neck and squinting down both sides of his nose at once. When they got as far as the Stairs they came back on the other side of the road, and they 'ad turned to go back ag'in when a docker-looking chap stopped Sam's friend and spoke to 'im.

'I've got no change, my man,' ses Sam's pal, pushing past him.

'I ain't begging, guv'nor,' ses the chap, follering 'im up. 'I'm trying to sell something.'

'Wot is it?' ses the other, stopping.

The man looked up and down the street, and then he put his 'ead near them and whispered.

'Eh?' ses Sam's pal.

'Something I picked up,' ses the man, still a-whispering.

Sam got a pinch on the arm from 'is pal that nearly made him scream, then they both stood still, staring at the docker.

'Wot is it?' ses Sam, at last.

The docker looked over his shoulder ag'in, and then 'e put his 'and in his trouser-pocket and just showed 'em a big, fat gold locket with diamonds stuck all over it. Then he shoved it back in 'is pocket, while Sam's pal was giving 'im a pinch worse than wot the other was.

'It's the one,' he ses, in a whisper. 'Let's 'ave another look at it,' he ses to the docker.

The man fished it out of his pocket ag'in, and held on to it tight while they looked at it.

'Where did you find it?' ses Sam.

'Found it over there, just by the Mint,' ses the man, pointing.

'Wot d'ye want for it?' ses Sam's pal.

'As much as I can get,' ses the man. 'I don't quite know 'ow much it's worth, that's the worst of it. Wot d'ye say to twenty pounds, and chance it?'

Sam laughed—the sort of laugh a pal 'ad once give him a black eye for.

'Twenty pounds!' he ses; 'twenty pounds! 'Ave you gorn out of your mind, or wot? I'll give you a couple of quid for it.'

'Well, it's all right, captin,' ses the man, 'there's no 'arm done. I'll try somebody else—or p'r'aps there'll be a big reward for it. I don't believe it was bought for a *undred pounds*.'

He was just sheering off when Sam's pal caught 'im by the arm and asked nim to let 'im have another look at it. Then he came back to Sam and led 'im a little way off, whispering to 'im that it was the chance of a lifetime.

'And if you prefer to keep it for a little while and then sell it, instead of getting the reward for it, I dare say it would be worth a hundred pounds to you,' 'e ses.

'I ain't got twenty pounds,' ses Sam.

''Ow much 'ave you got?' ses his pal.

Sam felt in 'is pockets, and the docker came up and stood watching while he counted it. Altogether it was nine pounds fourteen shillings and tuppence.

'P'r'aps you've got some more at 'ome,' ses his pal.

'Not a farthing,' ses Sam, which was true as far as the farthing went.

'Or p'r'aps you could borrer some,' ses his pal, in a soft, kind voice. 'I'd lend it to you with pleasure, on'y I haven't got it with me.'

Sam shook his 'ead, and at last, arter the docker 'ad said he wouldn't let it go for less than twenty, even to save 'is life, he let it go for the nine pounds odd, a silver watch-chain, two cigars wot Sam 'ad been sitting on by mistake, and a sheath knife.

'Shove it in your pocket and don't let a soul see it,' ses the man, handing over the locket. 'I might as well give it away a'most. But it can't be 'elped.'

He went off up the 'Ill shaking his 'ead, and Sam's pal, arter watching him for a few seconds, said good-bye in a hurry and went off arter 'im to tell him to keep 'is mouth shut about it.

Sam walked back to his lodgings on air, as the saying is, and even did a little bit of a skirt dance to a pianner-organ wot was playing. Peter and Ginger was out, and so was his landlady, a respectable woman as was minding the rest of 'is money for him, and when he asked 'er little gal, a kid of eleven, to trust 'im for some tin she gave 'im a lecture on wasting his money instead wot took 'is breath away—all but a word or two.

He got some of 'is money from his landlady at eight o'clock, arter listening to 'er for 'arf an hour, and then he 'ad to pick it up off the floor, and say 'Thank you' for it.

He went to bed afore Ginger and Peter came in, but 'e was

so excited he couldn't sleep, and long arter they was in bed he laid there and thought of all the different ways of spending a 'undred pounds. He kept taking the locket from under 'is piller and feeling it; then he felt 'e must 'ave another look at it, and arter coughing 'ard two or three times and calling out to the other two not to snore—to see if they was awake—he got out o' bed and lit the candle. Ginger and Peter was both fast asleep, with their eyes screwed up and their mouths wide open, and 'e sat on the bed and looked at the locket until he was a'most dazzled.

"Ullo, Sam!' ses a voice. 'Wot 'ave you got there?'

Sam nearly fell off the bed with surprise and temper. Then 'e hid the locket in his 'and and blew out the candle.

'Who gave it to you?' ses Ginger.

'You get off to sleep, and mind your own bisness,' ses Sam, grinding 'is teeth.

He got into bed ag'in and laid there listening to Ginger waking up Peter. Peter woke up disagreeable, but when Ginger told 'im that Sam 'ad stole a gold locket as big as a saucer, covered with diamonds, he altered 'is mind.

'Let's 'ave a look at it,' he ses, sitting up.

'Ginger's dreaming,' ses Sam, in a shaky voice. 'I ain't got no locket. Wot d'you think I want a locket for?'

Ginger got out o' bed and lit the candle ag'in. 'Come on!' he ses, 'let's 'ave a look at it. I wasn't dreaming. I've been awake all the time, watching you.'

Sam shut 'is eyes and turned his back to them.

'He's gone to sleep, pore old chap,' ses Ginger. 'We'll 'ave a look at it without waking 'im. You take that side, Peter! Mind you don't disturb 'im.'

He put his 'and in under the bed-clo'es and felt all up and down Sam's back, very careful. Sam stood it for 'arf a minute, and then 'e sat up in bed and behaved more like a windmill than a man.

'Hold his 'ands,' ses Ginger.

'Hold 'em yourself,' ses Peter, dabbing 'is nose with his shirt-sleeve.

'Well, we're going to see it,' ses Ginger, 'if we have to make enough noise to rouse the 'ouse. Fust of all we're going to ask you perlite; then we shall get louder and louder. *Show us the locket wot you stole, Sam!*'

'Show—us—the—diamond locket!' ses Peter.

'It's my turn, Peter,' ses Ginger. 'One, two, three. SHOW—US—TH'——'

'Shut up,' ses Sam, trembling all over. 'I'll show it to you if you stop your noise.'

He put his 'and under his piller, but afore he showed it to 'em he sat up in bed and made 'em a little speech. He said 'e never wanted to see their faces ag'in as long as he lived, and why Ginger's mother 'adn't put 'im in a pail o' cold water when 'e was born 'e couldn't understand. He said 'e didn't believe that even a mother could love a baby that looked like a cod-fish with red 'air, and as for Peter Russet, 'e believed *his* mother died of fright.

'That'll do,' ses Ginger, as Sam stopped to get 'is breath. 'Are you going to show us the locket, or 'ave we got to shout ag'in?'

Sam swallered something that nearly choked 'im, and then he opened his 'and and showed it to them. Peter told 'im to wave it so as they could see the diamonds flash, and then Ginger waved the candle to see 'ow they looked that way, and pretty near set pore Sam's whiskers on fire.

They didn't leave 'im alone till they knew as much about it as he could tell 'em, and they both of 'em told 'im that if he took a reward of thirty pounds for it, instead of selling it for a 'undred, he was a bigger fool than he looked.

'I shall turn it over in my mind,' ses Sam, sucking 'is teeth. 'When I want your advice I'll ask you for it.'

'We wasn't thinking of you,' ses Ginger; 'we was thinking of ourselves.'

'*You!*' ses Sam, with a bit of a start. 'Wot's it got to do with you?'

'Our share'll be bigger, that's all,' ses Ginger.

'Much bigger,' ses Peter. 'I couldn't dream of letting it go at thirty. It's chucking money away. Why, we might get *two* 'undred for it. Who knows?'

Sam sat on the edge of 'is bed like a man in a dream, then 'e began to make a noise like a cat with a fish-bone in its throat, and then 'e stood up and let fly.

'Don't stop 'im, Peter,' ses Ginger. 'Let 'im go on; it'll do him good.'

'He's forgot all about that penknife you picked up and went shares in,' ses Peter. 'I wouldn't be mean for *twenty* lockets.'

'Nor me neither,' ses Ginger. 'But we won't let 'im be mean —for 'is own sake. We'll 'ave our rights.'

'Rights!' ses Sam. 'Rights! You didn't find it.'

'We always go shares if we find anything,' ses Ginger. 'Where's your memory, Sam?'

'But I didn't find it,' ses Sam.

'No, you bought it,' ses Peter, 'and if you don't go shares we'll split on you—see? Then you can't sell it anyway, and perhaps you won't even get the reward. We can be at Orange Villa as soon as wot you can.'

'Sooner,' ses Ginger, nodding. 'But there's no need to do that. If 'e don't go shares I'll slip round the police-station fust thing in the morning.'

'You know the way there all right,' ses Sam, very bitter.

'And we don't want none of your back-answers,' ses Ginger. 'Are you going shares or not?'

'Wot about the money I paid for it?' ses Sam, 'and my trouble?'

Ginger and Peter sat down on the bed to talk it over, and at last, arter calling themselves a lot o' bad names for being too kind-'earted, they offered 'im five pounds each for their share in the locket.

'And that means you've got your share for next to nothing, Sam,' ses Ginger.

'Some people wouldn't 'ave given you anything,' ses Peter.

Sam gave way at last, and then 'e stood by making nasty remarks while Ginger wrote out a paper for them all to sign, because he said he had known Sam such a long time.

It was a'most daylight afore they got to sleep, and the fust thing Ginger did when he woke was to wake Sam up, and offer to shake 'ands with him. The noise woke Peter up, and, as Sam wouldn't shake 'ands with 'im either, they both patted him on the back instead.

They made him take 'em to the little pub, arter breakfast, to read the bill about the reward. Sam didn't mind going, as it 'appened, as he 'oped to meet 'is new pal there and tell 'im his troubles, but, though they stayed there some time, 'e didn't turn up. He wasn't at the coffee-shop for dinner, neither.

Peter and Ginger was in 'igh spirits, and, though Sam told 'em plain that he would sooner walk about with a couple of real pickpockets, they wouldn't leave 'im an inch.

'Anybody could steal it off of you, Sam,' ses Ginger, patting 'im on the weskit to make sure the locket was still there. 'It's a good job you've got us to look arter you.'

'We must buy 'im a money-belt with a pocket in it,' ses Peter.

Ginger nodded at 'im. 'Yes,' he ses, 'that would be safer. And he'd better wear it next to 'is skin, with everything over it. I should feel more comfortable then.'

'And wot about me?' ses Sam, turning on 'im.

'Well, we'll take it in turns,' ses Ginger. 'You one day, and then me, and then Peter.'

Sam gave way at last, as arter all he could see it was the safest thing to do, but he 'ad so much to say about it that they got fair sick of the sound of 'is voice. They 'ad to go 'ome for 'im to put the belt on; and then at seven o'clock in the evening, arter Sam had 'ad two or three pints, they had to go 'ome ag'in, 'cos he was complaining of tight-lacing.

Ginger had it on next day and he went 'ome five times. The other two went with 'im in case he lost 'imself, and stood there making nasty remarks while he messed 'imself up with a penn'orth of cold cream. It was a cheap belt, and pore Ginger said that, when they 'ad done with it, it would come in handy for sand-paper.

Peter didn't like it any better than the other two did, and twice they 'ad to speak to 'im about stopping in the street and trying to make 'imself more comfortable by wriggling. Sam said people misunderstood it.

Arter that they agreed to wear it outside their shirt, and even then Ginger said it scratched 'im. And every day they got more and more worried about wot was the best thing to do with the locket, and whether it would be safe to try and sell it. The idea o' walking about with a fortune in their pockets that they couldn't spend a'most drove 'em crazy.

'The longer we keep it, the safer it'll be,' ses Sam, as they was walking down Houndsditch one day.

'We'll sell it when I'm sixty,' ses Ginger, nasty-like.

'Then old Sam won't be 'ere to have 'is share,' ses Peter.

Sam was just going to answer 'em back, when he stopped and began to smile instead. Straight in front of 'im was the gentleman he 'ad met in the coffee-shop, coming along with another man, and he just 'ad time to see that it was the docker who 'ad sold him the locket, when they both saw 'im. They turned like a flash, and, afore Sam could get 'is breath, bolted up a little alley and disappeared.

'Wot's the row?' ses Ginger, staring.

Sam didn't answer 'im. He stood there struck all of a heap.

'Do you know 'em?' ses Peter.

Sam couldn't answer 'im for a time. He was doing a bit of 'ard thinking.

'Chap I 'ad a row with the other night,' he ses, at last.

He walked on very thoughtful, and the more 'e thought, the less 'e liked it. He was so pale that Ginger thought 'e was ill and advised 'im to 'ave a drop o' brandy. Peter recommended rum, so to please 'em he 'ad both. It brought 'is colour back, but not 'is cheerfulness.

He gave 'em both the slip next morning; which was easy, as Ginger was wearing the locket, and, arter fust 'aving a long ride for nothing owing to getting in the wrong train, he got to Barnet.

It was a big place; big enough to 'ave a dozen Orange Villas, but pore Sam couldn't find one. It wasn't for want of trying neither. He asked at over twenty shops, and the post-office, and even went to the police-station. He must ha' walked six or seven miles looking for it, and at last, 'arf ready to drop, 'e took the train back.

He 'ad some sausages and mashed with a pint o' stout at a place in Bishopsgate, and then 'e started to walk 'ome. The only comfort he 'ad was the thought of the ten pounds Ginger and Peter 'ad paid 'im; and when he remembered that he began to cheer up and even smile. By the time he got 'ome 'e was beaming all over 'is face.

'Where've you been?' ses Ginger.

'Enjoying myself by myself,' ses Sam.

'Please yourself,' ses Peter, very severe, 'but where'd you ha' been if we 'ad sold the locket and skipped, eh?'

'You wouldn't 'ave enjoyed yourself by yourself then,' ses Ginger. 'Yes, you may laugh!'

Sam didn't answer 'im, but he sat down on 'is bed and 'is shoulders shook till Ginger lost his temper and gave him a couple o' thumps on the back that pretty near broke it.

'All right,' ses Sam, very firm. 'Now you 'ave done for yourselves. I 'ad a'most made up my mind to go shares; now you sha'n't 'ave a ha'penny.'

Ginger laughed then. 'Ho!' he ses, 'and 'ow are you going to prevent it?'

'We've got the locket, Sam,' ses Peter, smiling and shaking his 'ead at 'im.

'And we'll mind it till it's sold,' ses Ginger.

Sam laughed ag'in, short and nasty. Then he undressed 'imself very slow and got into bed. At twelve o'clock, just as Ginger was dropping off, he began to laugh ag'in, and 'e only stopped when 'e heard Ginger getting out of bed to 'im.

He stayed in bed next morning, 'cos he said 'is sides was aching, but 'e laughed ag'in as they was going out, and when they came back he 'ad gorn.

We never know 'ow much we like anything till we lose it. A week arterwards, as Ginger was being 'elped out of a pawn-shop by Peter, he said 'e would give all he 'adn't got for the locket to be near enough to Sam to hear 'im laugh ag'in.

The Interruption

I

The last of the funeral guests had gone and Spencer Goddard, in decent black, sat alone in his small, well-furnished study. There was a queer sense of freedom in the house since the coffin had left it; the coffin which was now hidden in its solitary grave beneath the yellow earth. The air, which for the last three days had seemed stale and contaminated, now smelt fresh and clean. He went to the open window and, looking into the fading light of the autumn day, took a deep breath.

He closed the window and, stooping down, put a match to the fire, and, dropping into his easy chair, sat listening to the cheery crackle of the wood. At the age of thirty-eight he had turned over a fresh page. Life, free and unencumbered, was before him. His dead wife's money was at last his, to spend as he pleased instead of being doled out in reluctant driblets.

He turned at a step at the door and his face assumed the appearance of gravity and sadness it had worn for the last four days. The cook, with the same air of decorous grief, entered the room quietly and, crossing to the mantelpiece, placed upon it a photograph.

'I thought you'd like to have it, sir,' she said, in a low voice, 'to remind you.'

Goddard thanked her, and, rising, took it in his hand and stood regarding it. He noticed with satisfaction that his hand was absolutely steady.

'It is a very good likeness—till she was taken ill,' continued the woman. 'I never saw anybody change so sudden.'

'The nature of her disease, Hannah,' said her master.

The woman nodded, and, dabbing at her eyes with her handkerchief, stood regarding him.

'Is there anything you want?' he inquired, after a time.

She shook her head. 'I can't believe she's gone,' she said, in a low voice. 'Every now and then I have a queer feeling that she's still here——'

'It's your nerves,' said her master sharply.

'——and wanting to tell me something.'

By a great effort Goddard refrained from looking at her.

'Nerves,' he said again. 'Perhaps you ought to have a little holiday. It has been a great strain upon you.'

'You, too, sir,' said the woman respectfully. 'Waiting on her hand and foot as you have done, I can't think how you stood it. If you'd only had a nurse——'

'I preferred to do it myself, Hannah,' said her master. 'If I had had a nurse it would have alarmed her.'

The woman assented. 'And they are always peeking and prying into what doesn't concern them,' she added. 'Always think they know more than the doctors do.'

Goddard turned a slow look upon her. The tall, angular figure was standing in an attitude of respectful attention; the cold slaty-brown eyes were cast down, the sullen face expressionless.

'She couldn't have had a better doctor,' he said, looking at the fire again. 'No man could have done more for her.'

'And nobody could have done more for her than you did, sir,' was the reply. 'There's few husbands that would have done what you did.'

Goddard stiffened in his chair. 'That will do, Hannah,' he said curtly.

'Or done it so well,' said the woman, with measured slowness.

With a strange, sinking sensation, her master paused to regain his control. Then he turned and eyed her steadily. 'Thank you,' he said slowly; 'you mean well, but at present I cannot discuss it.'

For some time after the door had closed behind her he sat

in deep thought. The feeling of well-being of a few minutes before had vanished, leaving in its place an apprehension which he refused to consider, but which would not be allayed. He thought over his actions of the last few weeks, carefully, and could remember no flaw. His wife's illness, the doctor's diagnosis, his own solicitous care, were all in keeping with the ordinary. He tried to remember the woman's exact words—her manner. Something had shown him Fear. What?

He could have laughed at his fears next morning. The dining-room was full of sunshine and the fragrance of coffee and bacon was in the air. Better still, a worried and commonplace Hannah. Worried over two eggs with false birth-certificates, over the vendor of which she became almost lyrical.

'The bacon is excellent,' said her smiling master, 'so is the coffee; but your coffee always is.'

Hannah smiled in return, and, taking fresh eggs from a rosy-cheeked maid, put them before him.

A pipe, followed by a brisk walk, cheered him still further. He came home glowing with exercise and again possessed with that sense of freedom and freshness. He went into the garden—now his own—and planned alterations.

After lunch he went over the house. The windows of his wife's bedroom were open and the room neat and airy. His glance wandered from the made-up bed to the brightly-polished furniture. Then he went to the dressing-table and opened the drawers, searching each in turn. With the exception of a few odds and ends they were empty. He went out on to the landing and called for Hannah.

'Do you know whether your mistress locked up any of her things?' he inquired.

'What things?' said the woman.

'Well, her jewellery mostly.'

'Oh!' Hannah smiled. 'She gave it all to me,' she said quietly.

Goddard checked an exclamation. His heart was beating nervously, but he spoke sternly.

'When?'

'Just before she died—of gastro-enteritis,' said the woman.

There was a long silence. He turned and with great care mechanically closed the drawers of the dressing-table. The tilted glass showed him the pallor of his face, and he spoke without turning round.

'That is all right, then,' he said huskily. 'I only wanted to know what had become of it. I thought, perhaps, Milly——'

Hannah shook her head. 'Milly's all right,' she said, with a strange smile. 'She's as honest as we are. Is there anything thing more you want, sir?'

She closed the door behind her with the quietness of the well-trained servant; Goddard, steadying himself with his hand on the rail of the bed, stood looking into the future.

II

The days passed monotonously, as they pass with a man in prison. Gone was the sense of freedom and the idea of a wider life. Instead of a cell, a house with ten rooms—but Hannah, the jailer, guarding each one. Respectful and attentive, the model servant, he saw in every word a threat against his liberty —his life. In the sullen face and cold eyes he saw her knowledge of power; in her solicitude for his comfort and approval, a sardonic jest. It was the master playing at being the servant. The years of unwilling servitude were over, but she felt her way carefully with infinite zest in the game. Warped and bitter, with a cleverness which had never before had scope, she had entered into her kingdom. She took it little by little, savouring every morsel.

'I hope I've done right, sir,' she said one morning. 'I have given Milly notice.'

Goddard looked up from his paper. 'Isn't she satisfactory?' he inquired.

'Not to my thinking, sir,' said the woman. 'And she says she is coming to see you about it. I told her that would be no good.'

'I had better see her and hear what she has to say,' said her master.

'Of course, if you wish to,' said Hannah; 'only, after giving her notice, if she doesn't go I shall. I should be sorry to go—I've been very comfortable here—but it's either her or me.'

'I should be sorry to lose you,' said Goddard in a hopeless voice.

'Thank you, sir,' said Hannah. 'I'm sure I've tried to do my best. I've been with you some time now—and I know all your little ways. I expect I understand you better than anybody else would. I do all I can to make you comfortable.'

'Very well, I leave it to you,' said Goddard in a voice which strove to be brisk and commanding. 'You have my permission to dismiss her.'

'There's another thing I wanted to see you about,' said Hannah; 'my wages. I was going to ask for a rise, seeing that I'm really housekeeper here now.'

'Certainly,' said her master, considering, 'that only seems fair. Let me see—what are you getting?'

'Thirty-six.'

Goddard reflected for a moment and then turned with a benevolent smile. 'Very well,' he said cordially, 'I'll make it forty-two. That's ten shillings a month more.'

'I was thinking of a hundred,' said Hannah dryly.

The significance of the demand appalled him. 'Rather a big jump,' he said at last. 'I really don't know that I——'

'It doesn't matter,' said Hannah. 'I thought I was worth it —to you—that's all. You know best. Some people might think I was worth *two* hundred. That's a bigger jump, but after all a big jump is better than——'

She broke off and tittered. Goddard eyed her.

'——than a big drop,' she concluded.

Her master's face set. The lips almost disappeared and something came into the pale eyes that was revolting. Still eyeing her, he rose and approached her. She stood her ground and met him eye to eye.

'You are jocular,' he said at last.

'Short life and a merry one,' said the woman.

'Mine or yours?'

'Both, perhaps,' was the reply.

'If—if I give you a hundred,' said Goddard, moistening his lips, 'that ought to make your life merrier, at any rate.'

Hannah nodded. 'Merry and long, perhaps,' she said slowly. 'I'm careful, you know—very careful.'

'I am sure you are,' said Goddard, his face relaxing.

'Careful what I eat and drink, I mean,' said the woman, eyeing him steadily.

'That is wise,' he said slowly. 'I am myself—that is why I am paying a good cook a large salary. But don't overdo things, Hannah; don't kill the goose that lays the golden eggs.'

'I am not likely to do that,' she said coldly. 'Live and let live; that is my motto. Some people have different ones. But I'm careful; nobody won't catch me napping. I've left a letter with my sister, in case.'

Goddard turned slowly and in a casual fashion put the flowers straight in a bowl on the table, and, wandering to the window, looked out. His face was white again and his hands trembled.

'To be opened after my death,' continued Hannah. 'I don't believe in doctors—not after what I've seen of them—I don't think they know enough; so if I die I shall be examined. I've given good reasons.'

'And suppose,' said Goddard, coming from the window, 'suppose she is curious, and opens it before you die?'

'We must chance that,' said Hannah, shrugging her shoulders; 'but I don't think she will. I sealed it up with sealing-wax, with a mark on it.'

'She might open it and say nothing about it,' persisted her master.

An unwholesome grin spread slowly over Hannah's features. 'I should know it soon enough,' she declared boisterously, 'and so would other people. Lord! there would be an upset! Chidham would have something to talk about for once. We should be in the paper—both of us.'

Goddard forced a smile. 'Dear me!' he said gently. 'Your pen seems to be a dangerous weapon, Hannah, but I hope that the need to open it will not happen for another fifty years. You look well and strong.'

The woman nodded. 'I don't take up my troubles before they come,' she said, with a satisfied air; 'but there's no harm in trying to prevent them coming. Prevention is better than cure.'

'Exactly,' said her master; 'and, by the way, there's no need for this little financial arrangement to be known by anybody else. I might become unpopular with my neighbours for setting a bad example. Of course, I am giving you this sum because I really think you are worth it.'

'I'm sure you do,' said Hannah. 'I'm not sure I ain't worth more, but this'll do to go on with. I shall get a girl for less than we are paying Milly, and that'll be another little bit extra for me.'

'Certainly,' said Goddard, and smiled again.

'Come to think of it,' said Hannah, pausing at the door, 'I ain't sure I shall get anybody else; then there'll be more than ever for me. If I do the work I might as well have the money.'

Her master nodded, and, left to himself, sat down to think out a position which was as intolerable as it was dangerous. At a great risk he had escaped from the dominion of one woman only to fall, bound and helpless, into the hands of another. However vague and unconvincing the suspicions of Hannah might be, they would be sufficient. Evidence could be unearthed. Cold with fear one moment, and hot with fury the next, he sought in vain for some avenue of escape. It was his brain against that of a cunning, illiterate fool; a fool whose malicious stupidity only added to his danger. And she drank. With largely increased wages she would drink more and his very life might depend upon a hiccupped boast. It was clear that she was enjoying her supremacy; later on her vanity would urge her to display it before others. He might have to obey the crack of her whip before witnesses, and that would cut off all possibility of escape.

He sat with his head in his hands. There must be a way out and he must find it. Soon. He must find it before gossip began; before the changed position of master and servant lent colour to her story when that story became known. Shaking with fury, he thought of her lean, ugly throat and the joy of choking her life out with his fingers. He started suddenly, and took a quick breath. No, not fingers—a rope.

III

Bright and cheerful outside and with his friends, in the house he was quiet and submissive. Milly had gone, and, if the service was poorer and the rooms neglected, he gave no sign. If a bell remained unanswered he made no complaint, and to studied insolence turned the other cheek of politeness. When at this tribute to her power the woman smiled, he smiled in return. A smile which, for all its disarming softness, left her vaguely uneasy.

'I'm not afraid of you,' she said once, with a menacing air.

'I hope not,' said Goddard in a slightly surprised voice.

'Some people might be, but I'm not,' she declared. 'If anything happened to me——'

'Nothing could happen to such a careful woman as you are,' he said, smiling again. 'You ought to live to ninety—with luck.'

It was clear to him that the situation was getting on his nerves. Unremembered but terrible dreams haunted his sleep. Dreams in which some great, inevitable disaster was always pressing upon him, although he could never discover what it was. Each morning he awoke unrefreshed to face another day of torment. He could not meet the woman's eyes for fear of revealing the threat that was in his own.

Delay was dangerous and foolish. He had thought out every move in that contest of wits which was to remove the shadow of the rope from his own neck and place it about that of the woman. There was a little risk, but the stake was a big one.

He had but to set the ball rolling and others would keep it on its course. It was time to act.

He came in a little jaded from his afternoon walk, and left his tea untouched. He ate but little dinner, and, sitting hunched up over the fire, told the woman that he had taken a slight chill. Her concern, he felt grimly, might have been greater if she had known the cause.

He was no better next day, and after lunch called in to consult his doctor. He left with a clean bill of health except for a slight digestive derangement, the remedy for which he took away with him in a bottle. For two days he swallowed one tablespoonful three times a day in water, without result, then he took to his bed.

'A day or two in bed won't hurt you,' said the doctor. 'Show me that tongue of yours again.'

'But what is the matter with me, Roberts?' inquired the patient.

The doctor pondered. 'Nothing to trouble about—nerves a bit wrong—digestion a little bit impaired. You'll be all right in a day or two.'

Goddard nodded. So far, so good; Roberts had not outlived his usefulness. He smiled grimly after the doctor had left at the surprise he was preparing for him. A little rough on Roberts and his professional reputation, perhaps, but these things could not be avoided.

He lay back and visualised the programme. A day or two longer, getting gradually worse, then a little sickness. After that a nervous, somewhat shamefaced patient hinting at things. His food had a queer taste—he felt worse after taking it; he knew it was ridiculous, still—there was some of his beef-tea he had put aside, perhaps the doctor would like to examine it? and the medicine? Secretions, too; perhaps he would like to see those?

Propped on his elbow, he stared fixedly at the wall. There would be a trace—a faint trace—of arsenic in the secretions. There would be more than a trace in the other things. An attempt to poison him would be clearly indicated, and—his wife's symptoms had resembled his own—let Hannah get out of the web he was spinning if she could. As for the letter she had threatened him with, let her produce it; it could only recoil upon herself. Fifty letters could not save her from the doom he was preparing for her. It was her life or his, and he would show no mercy. For three days he doctored himself with sedulous care, watching himself anxiously the while. His nerve was going and he knew it. Before him was the strain of the discovery, the arrest, and the trial. The gruesome business of his wife's death. A long business. He would wait no longer, and he would open the proceedings with dramatic suddenness.

It was between nine and ten o'clock at night when he rang his bell, and it was not until he had rung four times that he heard the heavy steps of Hannah mounting the stairs.

'What d'you want?' she demanded standing in the door-way.

'I'm very ill,' he said, gasping. 'Run for the doctor. Quick!'

The woman stared at him in genuine amazement. 'What, at this time o' night?' she exclaimed. 'Not likely.'

'I'm dying!' said Goddard in a broken voice.

'Not you,' she said roughly. 'You'll be better in the morning.'

'I'm dying,' he repeated. 'Go—for—the—doctor.'

The woman hesitated. The rain beat in heavy squalls against the window, and the doctor's house was a mile distant on the lonely road. She glanced at the figure on the bed.

'I should catch my death o' cold,' she grumbled.

She stood sullenly regarding him. He certainly looked very ill, and his death would by no means benefit her. She listened, scowling, to the wind and the rain.

'All right,' she said at last, and went noisily from the room.

His face set in a mirthless smile, he heard her bustling about below. The front-door slammed violently and he was alone.

He waited for a few minutes and then, getting out of bed,

234

put on his dressing-gown and set about his preparations. With a steady hand he added a little white powder to the remains of his beef-tea and to the contents of his bottle of medicine. He stood listening a moment at some faint sound from below, and, having satisfied himself, lit a candle and made his way to Hannah's room. For a space he stood irresolute, looking about him. Then he opened one of the drawers and, placing the broken packet of powder under a pile of clothing at the back, made his way back to bed.

He was disturbed to find that he was trembling with excitement and nervousness. He longed for tobacco, but that was impossible. To reassure himself he began to rehearse his conversation with the doctor, and again he thought over every possible complication. The scene with the woman would be terrible; he would have to be too ill to take any part in it. The less he said the better. Others would do all that was necessary.

He lay for a long time listening to the sound of the wind and the rain. Inside, the house seemed unusually quiet, and with an odd sensation he suddenly realised that it was the first time he had been alone in it since his wife's death. He remembered that she would have to be disturbed. The thought was unwelcome. He did not want her to be disturbed. Let the dead sleep.

He sat up in bed and drew his watch from beneath the pillow. Hannah ought to have been back before; in any case she could not be long now. At any moment he might hear her key in the lock. He lay down again and reminded himself that things were shaping well. He had shaped them, and some of the satisfaction of the artist was his.

The silence was oppressive. The house seemed to be listening, waiting. He looked at his watch again and wondered, with a curse, what had happened to the woman. It was clear that the doctor must be out, but that was no reason for her delay. It was close on midnight, and the atmosphere of the house seemed in some strange fashion to be brooding and hostile.

In a lull in the wind he thought he heard footsteps outside, and his face cleared as he sat up listening for the sound of the key in the door below. In another moment the woman would be in the house and the fears engendered by a disordered fancy would have flown. The sound of the steps had ceased, but he could hear no sound of entrance. Until all hope had gone, he sat listening. He was certain he had heard footsteps. Whose?

Trembling and haggard he sat waiting, assailed by a crowd of murmuring fears. One whispered that he had failed and would have to pay the penalty of failing; that he had gambled with Death and lost.

By a strong effort he fought down these fancies and, closing his eyes, tried to compose himself to rest. It was evident now that the doctor was out and that Hannah was waiting to return with him in his car. He was frightening himself for nothing. At any moment he might hear the sound of their arrival.

He heard something else, and, sitting up suddenly, tried to think what it was and what had caused it. It was a very faint sound—stealthy. Holding his breath, he waited for it to be repeated. He heard it again, the mere ghost of a sound— the whisper of a sound, but significant as most whispers are.

He wiped his brow with his sleeve and told himself firmly that it was nerves, and nothing but nerves; but, against his will, he still listened. He fancied now that the sound came from his wife's room, the other side of the landing. It increased in loudness and became more insistent, but with his eyes fixed on the door of his room he still kept himself in hand and tried to listen instead to the wind and the rain.

For a time he heard nothing but that. Then there came a scraping, scurrying noise from his wife's room, and a sudden, terrific crash.

With a loud scream his nerve broke, and springing from the bed he sped downstairs and, flinging open the front-door, dashed into the night. The door, caught by the wind, slammed behind him.

With his hand holding the garden gate open, ready for

further flight, he stood sobbing for breath. His bare feet were bruised and the rain was very cold, but he took no heed. Then he ran a little way along the road and stood for some time, hoping and listening.

He came back slowly. The wind was bitter and he was soaked to the skin. The garden was black and forbidding, and unspeakable horror might be lurking in the bushes. He went up the road again, trembling with cold. Then, in desperation, he passed through the terrors of the garden to the house, only to find the door closed. The porch gave a little protection from the icy rain, but none from the wind, and, shaking in every limb, he leaned in abject misery against the door. He pulled himself together after a time and stumbled round to the back-door. Locked! And all the lower windows were shuttered. He made his way back to the porch, and, crouching there in hopeless misery, waited for the woman to return.

IV

He had a dim memory when he awoke of somebody questioning him, and then of being half pushed, half carried upstairs to bed. There was something wrong with his head and his chest and he was trembling violently, and very cold. Somebody was speaking.

'You must have taken leave of your senses,' said the voice of Hannah. 'I thought you were dead.'

He forced his eyes to open. 'Doctor,' he muttered, 'doctor.'

'Out on a bad case,' said Hannah. 'I waited till I was tired of waiting, and then came along. Good thing for you I did. He'll be round first thing this morning. He ought to be here now.'

She bustled about, tidying up the room, his leaden eyes following her as she collected the beef-tea and other things on a tray and carried them out.

'Nice thing I did yesterday,' she remarked, as she came back. 'Left the missus's bedroom window open. When I opened the door this morning I found that beautiful Chippendale glass of hers had blown off the table and smashed to pieces. Did you hear it?'

Goddard made no reply. In a confused fashion he was trying to think. Accident or not, the fall of the glass had served its purpose. Were there such things as accidents? Or was Life a puzzle—a puzzle into which every piece was made to fit? Fear and the wind . . . no: conscience and the wind . . . had saved the woman. He must get the powder back from her drawer . . . before she discovered it and denounced him. The medicine . . . he must remember not to take it . . .

He was very ill, seriously ill. He must have taken a chill owing to that panic flight into the garden. Why didn't the doctor come? He had come . . . at last . . . he was doing something to his chest . . . it was cold.

Again . . . the doctor . . . there was something he wanted to tell him . . . Hannah and a powder . . . what was it?

Later on he remembered, together with other things that he had hoped to forget. He lay watching an endless procession of memories, broken at times by a glance at the doctor, the nurse, and Hannah, who were all standing near the bed regarding him. They had been there a long time, and they were all very quiet. The last time he looked at Hannah was the first time for months that he had looked at her without loathing and hatred. Then he knew that he was dying.

SUPER **DC** HEROES

BATMAN

THE FOG OF FEAR

WRITTEN BY
MARTIN POWELL

ILLUSTRATED BY
ERIK DOESCHER,
MIKE DeCARLO, AND
LEE LOUGHRIDGE

BATMAN CREATED BY
BOB KANE

STONE ARCH BOOKS
MINNEAPOLIS   SAN DIEGO

Published by Stone Arch Books in 2009
151 Good Counsel Drive, P.O. Box 669
Mankato, Minnesota 56002
www.stonearchbooks.com

Library of Congress Cataloging-in-Publication Data
Powell, Martin.
    The Fog of Fear / by Martin Powell; illustrated by Erik Doescher.
    p. cm. — (DC Super Heroes. Batman)
    ISBN 978-1-4342-1154-5 (library binding)
    ISBN 978-1-4342-1365-5 (pbk.)
    [1. Superheroes—Fiction.] I. Doescher, Erik, ill. II. Title.
PZ7.P87758Fe 2009
[Fic]—dc22   2008032401

Summary: On a bright spring morning, a dark cloud of smoke engulfs
Gotham City. The fearsome Scarecrow has turned day into night.
Surprisingly, the crook doesn't resist Batman's attempt to arrest him. From
behind the bars of his cell, the Scarecrow reveals that his evil experiment
has already been set in motion. When the black smoke mixes with water, it
produces a gas that fills people with fear. A thunderstorm is approaching
the city. Can Batman save the citizens of Gotham from their worst
nightmares?

Art Director: Bob Lentz
Designer: Brann Garvey

1 2 3 4 5 6 14 13 12 11 10 09

Printed in the United States of America

TABLE OF CONTENTS

CHAPTER 1

THE FOG OF FEAR

Darkness crawled across the morning sky like a giant bat from a nightmare. The residents of Gotham City stared up from the streets, or peeked out of windows, for a sign of the vanished sun. Somehow, mysteriously, it had become twilight before noon. A sudden fear of the dark gripped the entire city.

Then, a bright light sliced through the shadows. The Bat-Signal shined against the darkened clouds. It was a welcome sight for their frightened eyes.

"Never dreamed I'd have to shine the Bat-Signal in the daytime," Commissioner Gordon said. He stood on the police department rooftop. "I hope Batman sees it . . . wherever he is."

The towering smokestacks of the Gotham City power plant spit a thick cloud of black fog high above the skyline. Creating its own eclipse, the darkness draped over the panicked streets. It grew like a great uncoiling snake. Before long, the bright morning spring air was as dark as midnight.

The citizens of Gotham would have been even more afraid, if they'd seen the figure atop the highest smokestack. Dressed in tatters and thin as a skeleton, the weird being shed small scraps of straw with every footstep.

He pulled a glowing jack-o'-lantern from a bag in his hand. He had already tossed several others down into the smoldering smokestack. The ragged man cackled a laugh like the sound of breaking glass.

"Trick or treat, Gotham City," the Scarecrow cried, ready to drop a pumpkin into the next chimney. "Today is Halloween — six months early!"

Schingggg!

Suddenly, a Batarang flew through the air and knocked the pumpkin out of the Scarecrow's grasp. A black-cloaked creature appeared out of nowhere, his eyes burning white-hot through the slits of his cowl.

"Not in my city," the Batman said.

Now it was the Scarecrow's turn to be afraid.

"Too late, Batman!" the Scarecrow shrieked. "You've lost already!"

Flinging his sleeves, the Scarecrow threw a clump of stinging straw into Batman's face. Like a bundle of living rags, the villain dashed around the narrow rim of the smokestack. Escape was the only thing on his evil mind.

Gripping a hooked rope, the Scarecrow prepared for his descent. Twice, he rapidly glanced behind. His eyes grew wide with surprise through the holes of his mask. Where was Batman? Among the drifting ribbons of the thick fog the Scarecrow's enemy was nowhere to be seen.

The Scarecrow quickly hurried down the long rope. An evil smile crossed his lips. Had Batman fallen to his doom? Perhaps he was finally rid of his enemy forever.

Fast as lightning, a Batarang struck the Scarecrow's glove. His fingers released the rope. The villain waved his arms helplessly and fell toward the earth below.

Batman appeared through the curtain of darkness, swinging on his Batrope. His cape flapped in the wind. In a single motion, the Caped Crusader snatched the Scarecrow from his fall.

"Don't be afraid, Scarecrow," Batman said. He gripped a small device on the rope that lowered them both gently to the ground. "I'll make sure you're safe," he said, "inside a strong jail cell."

CHAPTER 2

SINISTER SECRETS

Commissioner Gordon paced anxiously. His shoes scraped the tarred rooftop of Police Headquarters. The creeping darkness of the Scarecrow's black fog still covered the streets in shadows. Gordon was beginning to fear for his city.

"You're sure this stuff isn't poisonous, Batman?" the Commissioner asked.

The Dark Knight was standing near him on the edge of the rooftop. His fluttering cape blended with the black fog.

"My lab tests confirm that this fog is not poisonous," Batman replied. "Because it's heavier than air, it will linger in Gotham City until the wind carries it out to sea. The weather will change in our favor in a few days. Until then, everyone has to get used to living in the shadows."

Commissioner Gordon frowned at the dark fog.

"That's easy for you to say, Batman," he said. "Still, I feel sorry for anyone scared of the dark."

Batman's eyes narrowed. "That's just it," he said. "The Scarecrow works through fear. Even after I captured him at the power plant, he seemed strangely sure of himself. It's as if he still has some fearful secret that I haven't solved yet."

"Gotham City is safe because of you," said Commissioner Gordon. "At least the threat of the Scarecrow is over, and he is safely locked up."

The Dark Knight shook his head thoughtfully. "It's not over yet, old friend," he said quietly.

"That's just what I'm afraid of," said the commissioner.

• • •

It was always dark in the Batcave, secretly located beneath Wayne Manor. Later that afternoon, inside the hidden cavern, Batman removed his cape and cowl, revealing the face of billionaire Bruce Wayne. Wayne peered into a high-powered microscope. He fought a yawn, rubbed his tired eyes, and got back to work.

Behind Bruce rose a tall, dark set of stairs. Alfred the butler was coming down the stairs into the underground laboratory. "Miss Kyle called, Master Bruce. She's waiting to meet you for lunch at the restaurant," said Alfred.

Bruce prepared a thin orange-colored slice upon a glass slide. He added a drop of a glowing chemical.

"Call her back with my apologies, Alfred," he said. "It's going to be dark as night in Gotham City for the next few days. Commissioner Gordon's policemen are working 24-hour shifts. Batman can do no less."

Alfred peeked over Bruce's shoulder. He stared at a strange orange vegetable sitting on the table.

"Isn't it a bit early for carving pumpkins, sir?" Alfred asked.

Bruce smiled. "This belonged to the Scarecrow," he explained. "He filled these pumpkins with a secret chemical before tossing them into the power plant smokestacks. The result was the black fog that is still plaguing the city."

"Well, sir," offered Alfred, "I'll admit this fog is troubling. However, it's hardly the same kind of trick the Scarecrow has used against you in the past."

Bruce rose quickly, grabbing his black cowl and cloak. "Exactly," he said. Bruce filled the compartments of his Utility Belt. "There's more to this black fog than meets the eye. And, one way or the other, the Scarecrow is going to tell me its secret."

Arkham Asylum was like a madhouse from another world. Locked within its electrified iron gates lived the deadliest criminals ever known. Even in the daylight, the building looked like a bad dream. The black fog added even more to its eeriness.

The headlights of the Batmobile sliced through the inky clouds of fog. The front guards saluted as Batman stepped out of the vehicle. He passed into the dreadful place without a word. Caged doors opened before him with a motorized hum. The Dark Knight knew his way through the twisted corridors all too well.

"If I'd known you were coming, I'd have baked a Bat-cake!" a voice giggled from behind a cell door.

Batman stopped and glared at the white face pressed against the bars.

"Joker," he said through gritted teeth.

The Joker's blood-red lips continued to curl upward toward his yellow eyes. Batman's face remained like stone, unsmiling. Upon reflex, his gloved fists tightly clenched.

"Hey, Bats! When are you gonna bring back the sunshine?" the Joker said. A chuckle hissed between his teeth.

"What's the matter, Joker?" asked Batman. "Afraid of the dark?"

"You gotta be kidding, Bat-brain!" the killer clown gleefully cried. "I just want to know when you're gonna ruin the Scarecrow's party! He's been raving about his 'Crime of the Century' for hours. Such a bore. Frankly, just between us boys, I think he's nutty as a filbert!"

Batman whirled from the cell. He had to focus on the problem at hand. The mystery of the Scarecrow was waiting to be solved.

Jonathan Crane had once been a brilliant professor of psychology. He specialized in the study of fear. That was before his mind snapped and he turned to crime. As the Scarecrow, Crane had always been defeated by Batman, no matter how ingenious his crimes. This time Crane was certain things were going to be different.

Crane looked almost harmless without his fearsome costume. Tall and thin with an evil smirk on his face, he sat in his cell quietly reading. Batman studied him silently for several minutes.

"I'm only going to ask you this once, Crane," the Dark Knight warned. "What's the secret of the black fog?"

Crane continued reading, as if he'd heard nothing. Then he smugly smiled.

"You'll know soon enough, Batman," the evil genius replied. "Now, if you'll excuse me, I'm trying to broaden my mind."

Batman's brain worked at top speed. He read the titles of the volumes on Crane's crammed bookshelves. Many of the books were old. Some were ancient. Most of them seemed to be about the so-called "four elements": fire, water, earth, and air. Hundreds of years ago, men called alchemists believed that the world was made of just these four ingredients.

Could Crane's formula be related to the four elements? wondered Batman.

Immediately, the Dark Knight had the answer.

'Earth' would equal the jack-o'-lanterns. 'Fire' was added from the power plant smokestacks. 'Air' joined the mix, forming the black fog. One element was missing: A single ingredient that would turn the black fog deadly.

"Water!" Batman exclaimed.

RUMMMMMMBLE! Batman's blood ran cold. His sharp ears caught the rumble of an approaching thunderstorm.

From out of Crane's thin lips came the Scarecrow's awful laugh.

CHAPTER 3

CLOUDED BY FEAR

Commission Gordon leaned against his office desk to steady himself. The news Batman had brought was shocking. Gordon knew that the Dark Knight was almost never wrong.

"If what you're saying is true, Batman," he said, "then all of Gotham is about to be scared to death!"

"There's no doubt about it," Batman assured him. "When I visited Scarecrow's cell, I solved the mystery of his plan. I detected the poison in his formula."

"Once this black fog is mixed with water," Batman continued, "all who breathe it will experience their most dreadful fears. Unless we act quickly, the city is doomed to be trapped forever inside their worst nightmares."

Gordon went to the window and glanced outside. It was just past three o'clock in the afternoon, yet the sky was still dark as midnight. The Bat-Signal was still burning against the black clouds, just as the Commissioner had ordered. Its presence gave looters and other criminals second thoughts. The Bat-Signal also gave hope to Gotham City's honest citizens.

BRRROOMMM! The approaching thunderstorm growled in the distance. Jagged shards of lightning flashed on the horizon.

"This coming storm will drench the city in terror," Gordon said. He thumped his fist hard against the sill. "Is there anything that can be done?"

Batman nodded. "We can clean the air of the black fog before the rain begins," he said. He sounded confident, in spite of the odds against him.

Commissioner Gordon spun on his heels. He greatly respected his friend, but this idea sounded impossible.

"But how, Batman?" he asked. "You said that there won't be enough wind in Gotham for days. How can we possibly speed up Mother Nature?"

The Caped Crusader moved to the window and opened it. He fired a grapple and rope to a neighboring building.

"With our courage and our wits," Batman remarked.

 He swung away, disappearing into the murky air.

Batman swooped high above the streets of Gotham City. People down below saw the shadow of a huge bat flying through the strange fog. None of them knew it was really the Caped Crusader.

Batman used his rope and grappling device to swing from building to building. His goal was a tall, white skyscraper near the edge of the city. Inside the building was a high-tech laboratory owned by one of the world's greatest scientists, Dr. Kirk Langstrom. Batman hoped that Langstrom's science would be strong enough to defeat the Scarecrow's evil formula.

As the Dark Knight swooped through the fog, tiny water droplets collected on his armored suit. The mist pressed cold and damp against his cowl.

Without warning, Batman's rope changed shape. Instead of a thin silken cord, he was holding onto a deadly boa constrictor.

"What —?" yelled Batman. He released his grip on the snake and began to fall.

Batman shot a grappling hook toward another nearby building. *ZING!* Just in time, the new rope pulled him upward. He barely missed hitting a statue coming out from the side of an office building.

That was close, thought Batman. *But what is going on?*

Again, his rope transformed. This time it turned into a super sticky web. A monstrous spider snapped its drooling jaws. Its giant head thrust toward the startled hero.

"You can't be real," said Batman, shaking his head. He shot out his feet and swung quickly around his rope, building up speed. Then he aimed his boots at the fearsome mouth of the spider. Instead of feeling the impact, Batman's feet met nothing but air.

It's an illusion, he thought. *It must be the mist. There's just enough water in the air to combine with the black smoke and make me see things.*

Batman frowned. *If this is how the Scarecrow's fog can affect the brain with just a little water, then the rainstorm will create a total panic.*

Batman increased his speed and swung toward the white skyscraper. Things were worse than he imagined.

CHAPTER 4

THE LIVING NIGHTMARE

"I knew I could count on you, Kirk," Batman said. He shook the scientist's hand.

Kirk Langstrom stood in his white lab coat, a deep contrast to Batman's black and grey Batsuit. Still, the two men shared at least two traits. Both were brilliant. Both wanted to save their city.

"You cured me, Batman. I owe you everything," Langstrom replied. "When I experimented with the bat-serum, I turned into the monster, Man-Bat."

"You were the only one who helped me," said Langstrom. "I'll never forget that."

The Dark Knight remembered those frightening nights when his friend had changed into a powerful creature. Although not truly evil, the Man-Bat was wild and uncontrollable. Those memories were like a nightmare to both men.

"This is Gotham's only hope," Batman stated. "You are the world's greatest living expert on bats."

"Takes one to know one, I guess," Langstrom said. He smiled, almost sadly, as he unveiled his experimental machine.

The device on Langstrom's laboratory workbench looked like something from a science-fiction movie. It was made of blinking lights and coiling wires.

Batman noticed that Langstrom himself stared at the machine with dread. As much as the scientist wanted to help, he was still hiding something.

"I haven't tested it yet," Langstrom said quietly. "But if it works, the machine should send out a high-pitch sound. The sound can only be heard by the sensitive ears of bats. Bats are the most common mammal in North America. Millions of them will be awakened by this sound, flying to wherever it leads them."

Batman was impressed. The machine was exactly what he needed.

"That's all I need to know," he said, reaching for the device.

The Dark Knight slowly flipped a small switch.

The machine glowed, then started to hum. Although Batman could feel only a slight vibration in the air, Langstrom's ears immediately began to ache.

Within minutes, hundreds of bats swooped and fluttered against the window of the lab.

"It works!" cried Langstrom.

Batman turned off the machine, well satisfied.

"It's perfect, Kirk," he said. "I have just enough time to get this machine back to the Batcave before the thunderstorm starts."

There was an eerie silence in the room. Langstrom had retreated into a far corner, away from the harsh light in the lab.

Batman was alarmed by the sounds of the scientist's heavy breaths. He took a step toward his friend.

"Kirk? Are you all right?" he asked.

No answer came from the dark corner. Then Batman heard the sounds of more rapid breathing. He heard a slow ripping of cloth. Then he saw a sudden spreading of monstrous wings.

The Man-Bat had returned. Langstrom had been transformed by the effect of his sound machine!

The Dark Knight braced himself as he saw the burning red eyes glare at him. The creature sprang forward. Batman was driven back by the muscular weight of the monster. He crashed backwards through tables of shattering glass.

There was no more expert fighter in the world than the Batman. But for a moment, even his fists were useless against the strength and speed of the Man-Bat.

The beast's claws gripped Batman's throat with a blur of motion. Sharp teeth gleamed behind the gruesome growl. Batman's brain was spinning, close to blacking out. His gloved fingers groped for his Utility Belt, his only chance.

FLASH! A bright flare shined in Batman's hand. The Man-Bat howled in rage. It flung itself through the window.

The Dark Knight caught his breath. He watched the Man-Bat escape into the gloomy sky, carried by its giant wings.

"You feared this would happen, didn't you?" Batman said to himself. "Kirk, why didn't you tell me?"

CHAPTER 5

BATMAN VS MAN-BAT

Less than an hour later, the Batplane screamed out of the Gotham sky. The storm was almost upon the city. There wasn't a moment to lose.

Kirk Langstrom's amazing invention was wired into an amplifier within the plane's cockpit. All Batman needed to do was press the switch . . . and hope.

The sound was much too high for the Dark Knight's human ears. Several minutes passed before he knew for sure that it was operating. Then, suddenly, there they were.

"Bats!"

The bats obeyed the sound machine, following close behind the Batplane. They came in an endless stream, thousands and thousands of them. Countless tiny wings flapped through the air. Soon, the black fog softened to a grey. The sky was alive with the swarm of fluttering wings.

The Batplane streaked through the clouds. It rocketed above rooftops and sliced between buildings. The bats followed, sweeping away the fog with every beat of their leathery wings. In a few minutes the Scarecrow's black fog was no more.

Batman turned off the sound machine. The swarm of bats cleared the skies and returned to their hidden lairs. The Dark Knight was about to breathe a sigh of relief when another threat struck from the sky.

WHAM! Something hard collided against the hull of the Batplane. Batman saw the jagged wings and glowing eyes of his attacker.

The Man-Bat had also answered the call of the machine. In a mindless rage, the Man-Bat struck the Batplane. Batman fought hard to regain control. He had to take this battle down to the ground, out of the Man-Bat's element. His sharp eyes found a safe place to land — an old cemetery outside of the city.

The Batplane glided down among the twisted trees and tombstones. It came to a stop just as the rain started to fall.

Leaping from the cockpit, Batman peered skyward. The rain poured down, making it hard to see.

The Man-Bat was fast and strong. The Dark Knight knew he would only get one chance to defeat the beast.

A furious flash of lightning revealed the Man-Bat, swooping out of the sky like a prehistoric monster. Batman dropped and rolled away as the creature's deadly talons grabbed only mud. Again the flying fiend shot toward Batman like a demon, but its claws found only open air. A spinning kick to the creature's chest finally brought the Man-Bat to earth.

The monster rose up from the mud, towering above Batman. Pain and hatred grew in Man-Bat's mind. It let out a terrible snarl. Batman's right hand went to his Utility Belt, retrieving an item, which he hid behind his glove.

"Kirk!" Batman said. He tried to calm the beast. "I want to help you. Kirk, don't you know me?"

The Man-Bat's wild eyes softened a moment. The creature tilted its head in confusion. Batman approached the creature slowly. Deadly as Man-Bat might be, Batman had to get close enough to touch.

A sudden clap of thunder startled the beast. ROOAAARRR!!

Its clawed wings wrapped tightly around Batman's throat. Nothing could break the monstrous grip. It was too strong. But the Dark Knight's right hand was free, and that was all he needed. He made a quick move, pressing a sharp object against the creature's hide.

The Man-Bat released its stranglehold in a snap. It appeared to grow dizzy and staggered. Finally, it dropped to its shaggy knees.

The Batman returned the object to his Utility Belt. It was a needle that had contained the antidote to the Man-Bat formula.

Before Batman's eyes, the giant beast seemed to shrink. Its fur slowly melted away. The huge wings grew smaller and disappeared. In a few moments, scientist Kirk Langstrom crouched in the creature's place. Batman carefully helped his friend stand.

"Batman?" Langstrom asked. "What have I done?" He remembered nothing from the past few hours.

Batman placed a grateful hand on Langstrom's shoulder. "You saved the city, Kirk," he said softly. "The black fog is gone, blown away by the wings of bats. Your machine worked just as you said. You're a hero."

The storm was over. The rain had ended, and the Scarecrow's evil nightmares vanished with the coming sunshine.

"I had a terrible dream about Man-Bat," said Langstrom, confused. "I was afraid he had come back. Afraid he'd try to hurt you."

Batman smiled. "Nothing to be afraid of now," he said.

It was going to be a beautiful day in Gotham City.

Scarecrow, The

REAL NAME: Professor Jonathan Crane

OCCUPATION: Professional Criminal

BASE: Gotham City

HEIGHT:
6 feet

WEIGHT:
140 pounds

EYES:
Blue

HAIR:
Brown

Jonathan Crane's obsession with fear took hold at an early age. Terrorized by bullies, Crane sought to free himself of his own worst fears. As he researched the subject of dread, Crane developed a strong understanding of fear. Using this knowledge, Crane overcame his tormentors by using their worst fears against them. This victory led to his transformation into the ultra-creepy super-villain, the Scarecrow.

G.C.P.D. GOTHAM CITY POLICE DEPARTMENT

- Crane became a professor at Gotham University to further his terrifying research. But when his colleagues took notice of his twisted experiments, they had him fired. To get revenge, Crane became the Scarecrow to try to frighten his enemies to death.

- Crane doesn't use conventional weaponry. Instead, he invented a Fear Toxin that causes his victims to hallucinate, bringing their worst fears and phobias to life. The gas makes the weak and gangly Crane look like a fearsome predator in the eyes of his prey.

- Even though he preys on the fears of others, the Scarecrow has a fear of his own — bats! Crane has been chiropteraphobic, or afraid of bats, since his first encounter with the Dark Knight.

- Crane's mastery of fear has come in handy. While locked up in Arkham Asylum, Crane escaped from his cell by scaring two guards into releasing him!

CONFIDENTIAL

BIOGRAPHIES

Martin Powell has been a freelance writer since 1986. He has written hundreds of stories. In 1989, Powell received an Eisner Award nomination for his graphic novel *Scarlet in Gaslight*.

Erik Doescher is an illustrator and video game designer based in Dallas, Texas. He attended the School of Visual Arts in New York City. Erik illustrated for a number of comic studios, and then moved to Texas to pursue videogame development and design. However, he has not given up on illustrating his favorite comic book characters.

Mike DeCarlo is a longtime contributor of comic art whose range extends from Batman and Iron Man to Bugs Bunny and Scooby-Doo. He resides in Connecticut with his wife and four children.

Lee Loughridge has been working in comics for over 14 years. He currently lives in sunny California in a tent on the beach.

GLOSSARY

antidote (AN-ti-dote)—something that stops a poison, or negative effect, from working

descent (di-SENT)—a climb down or to go down to a lower level

flare (FLAIR)—to burn with a sudden, bright light

illusion (i-LOO-zhuhn)—something that appears real but does not actually exist

plaguing (PLAYG-ing)—troubling or afflicting

shattering (SHAT-ur-ing)—breaking into tiny pieces

transformed (trans-FORMD)—changed into something else

DISCUSSION QUESTIONS

1. The Scarecrow preys on his victim's worst fears. Do you have a fear? What are some things that lots of people are afraid of?

2. Why do you think people feel fear? Can fear ever be a good thing? Why or why not?

3. Batman and Kirk Langstrom work together to protect the city of Gotham. What makes a good team? Can you think of other ways the duo could have stopped Scarecrow's plan?

WRITING PROMPTS

1. Batman is a super hero. If you were Batman, how would you fight crime? Who would you ask for help? Write a story about your adventures as Batman.

2. Batman's friend, Kirk, turns into Man-Bat. If you could turn into any animal, which would you choose? Why? Draw a picture of yourself as a half-animal, half-human.

3. Graphic novels are often written and illustrated by two different artists. Write a story, and then give it to a friend to illustrate.

MORE NEW
BATMAN
ADVENTURES!

EMPEROR OF THE AIRWAVES

POISON IVY'S DEADLY GARDEN

THE REVENGE OF CLAYFACE

FUN HOUSE OF EVIL

FIVE RIDDLES FOR ROBIN